BELOVED DECEIVER

"I must apologize, Mr. Banning. I shouldn't have turned our meeting into a race."

"It was a damned fool thing to do, Miss Adair."

"You don't like me, Mr. Banning, and I certainly don't like you."

Her bluntness caught Cain off guard but only for an instant. He replied easily, "You're wrong about my not liking you. I do, you know. And my men said you sailed like an angel—even though you did give us one hell of a scare."

He watched enthralled, as her disbelief turned to astonishment and then delight. The storm was over. He saw her rosy lips part, saw a flash of soft white throat as she threw back her head and emitted low, musical laughter.

"It was rude of me to say I didn't like you," she murmured. "I'm sorry. I was angry. Maybe we could start over . . . "

Cain sank deep into her flame gold eyes. "I'd like that . . . " he said huskily.

Beloved Deceiver

Joan Van Nuys

AVON BOOKS ◆ NEW YORK

BELOVED DECEIVER is an original publication of Avon Books. This work has never before appeared in book form. This work is a novel. Any similarity to actual persons or events is purely coincidental.

AVON BOOKS
A division of
The Hearst Corporation
1350 Avenue of the Americas
New York, New York 10019

Copyright © 1994 by Joan Van Nuys
Published by arrangement with the author
Library of Congress Catalog Card Number: 94-94316
ISBN: 0-380-77208-6

First Avon Books Printing: November 1994

AVON TRADEMARK REG. U.S. PAT. OFF. AND IN OTHER COUNTRIES, MARCA REGISTRADA, HECHO EN U.S.A.

Printed in the U.S.A.

RA   10   9   8   7   6   5   4   3   2   1

To my sister, Betty Lambert,
the idol of my girlhood, my best friend always,
and still my inspiration.
I love you, Bebe.

Prologue

1745, The Sea of Marmara

Pain awakened Ben from his long sleep. Pain in his back and shoulders, pain in his entire body, and his head ached damnably. He screwed his eyes shut, willing himself to go back to sleep again, but it was not to be. Memories swarmed through his head as if it were a lighted stage: the fat little Turkish merchant ship, *Safira,* wallowing badly as she attempted to flee his and Tom's two sleek marauding sloops ... shots fired over her bow ... grappling hooks clawing her stem and stern as the hooded howling men boarded her to a wild cacophony of drums and pipes ... and the treasure—two hundred and sixty thousand pieces of eight, countless barrels of jewels and gold plate, bags of diamonds, and bolts of silk and linen. And the one treasure that stood out above all the others: the maid. The princess Ana, daughter of Sultan Mehmed Kemal, ruler of Izmir.

Ben smiled, savoring in his mind's eye the image of her beautiful face, tawny eyes, and her cascade of glossy, red-brown hair before a flood of harsher memories hit him broadside: his and Tom's fight over her, a battle that finally dissolved their shaky partnership, although they were forced to sail side by side for protection through the pirate-infested waters. And then the storm, a whirling dervish that had come roaring at them straight out of hell.

For hours, his *Bluebird* had weathered the nightmare only to be struck fatally by a stray lightning bolt at the very end. Injured, and with his ship going down, Ben accepted Tom's offer to bring his men and booty aboard the *Hawk*. It was the last thing he wanted, but he had no choice. He'd managed to get Ana over safely before he passed out and—he froze. Good God, did the bastard have Ana locked in his cabin? He tore off the covers, sat up, croaked:

"Ana?"

"I am here, Benscott."

Ben went weak hearing her soft voice and the rustle of her silken garments—and then she was there beside him, the faint scent of roses that clung to her skin filling his nostrils. She knelt, wrapped her arms about his legs, and lay her head on his lap. He was so touched, and his relief was so great, he began to shake. Seeing tears in her eyes, he smoothed back her hair and worried that she was so pale.

"There now, my lady, you mustn't weep." In all of his thirty-two winters, he had never seen such a little beauty. He muttered, "I just got a wee crack on the head when a spar fell. That's all, I'm fine now. I'm just fine. Come, lady, sit up here on the bunk beside me." When she obeyed, he nodded and gave her hand an awkward pat.

"I have been so afraid, Benscott," Ana whispered. "I thought you were going to die . . ."

"I don't aim to die, lass."

Ben frowned. He had not seen her this frightened since that day two weeks ago when they'd hoisted their black flags and boarded the *Safira*. His skin still crawled as he remembered the men's howls and hoots at their first sight of her slender, heavily veiled figure, and remembered their awed silence when her veils had been removed to reveal her white luminous skin and delicious curves and beautiful face. They had begun pawing and squeezing her on the spot, every man of them eager to be the first to have his turn with her. And then Tom had ordered them to stand back—he would sample her first.

Ben's anger flared, and his compassion. Knowing full well Tom would give her to the others when he finished with her, Ben challenged him. Tom grinned, accepted, and promptly tried to knee him. It made Ben murderous. He downed him in a brutal battle, but he knew the lass was still not safe. It had always been share and share alike aboard the two ships, and now the men were muttering. Then and there, Ben relinquished his claim to the *Safira*'s other booty. He yielded it all for the maid and had then carried her weeping aboard the *Bluebird*. But he had not touched her. He gave her his cabin and had not laid so much as one finger on her. He still had not, nor would he. Poor fool that he was, he had fallen head over heels in love with the lass.

"Benscott—"

"Aye, your highness?" He thought for the hundredth time what a miracle it was that she spoke English.

"If we do not live to see the dawn," Ana kept her voice low, "know that I am glad I was stolen from the *Safira* and that I am with you." When he stared at her in disbelief, she nodded. "It is so. I was on my way to a man I do not know. A sultan. He lives in Topkapi Palace in Istanbul and he has hundreds of wives already. My father gave me to him, and I feared I would be naught but an odalisque or a concubine in his harem. . . ." She added shyly, her eyes downcast, "But you I care for, Benscott, and I think you even care for me a bit. If I die this day, I will die in peace."

Ben's heart soared. It was another miracle. "My God, lass, I more than care for you! I've loved you since I first clapped eyes on you!" When he saw her tremble, he went on gruffly, "And I promise you this, no one is going to put you in any harem, ever, and no one's going to die today. There's naught to worry about, I swear it. And now, as much as I'd like to stay here with you and talk, I'd best get out on deck and see if my mates need any help."

He felt a fierce stab of pain in his temple as he rose, and for the first time was aware of the bandage on his head. He whistled. "I guess I got more of a crack than I thought. How long have I been pegged out?"

"You have slept three days and two nights," Ana whispered, "and please, you must not try to leave or make any noise. The door is locked anyway."

Ben stared at her blankly. Three days and two nights? It was an eternity. And what did she mean, the door was locked? What in hell was this? He muttered, "My crew . . . ?"

Unlike Tom Gregg and his rowdies, his crew were good men, all of them. There was not a mean man among them. He'd recruited them when he and Tom first began hauling cargo, and then when hard times came, he had hit on the idea of piracy to augment their incomes. Many respectable men were doing it, and he'd just meant to do it for a year or two until their fortunes turned around. Tom and his men had jumped at it, but Ben's own lads had balked; they wanted no part of violence. Ben had agreed with them. Only when he promised there would be no bloodshed was he able to coax them into it.

He'd never admitted to them—hell, he'd been ashamed to admit to himself even—how much he enjoyed the thrill of the chase and claiming booty. But by then Tom's cruelty had begun to surface. Ben didn't rebuke him before the others, it would not have been seemly, but he confronted him in private. If it continued, he warned, their partnership was over. That day finally came. He told Tom he'd help take one more ship, and that would end it. The ship had been the *Safira*.

"My crew?" he asked Ana again, sensing now that something unthinkable had happened to them while he slept.

"They are gone," Ana murmured. "After they brought their chests aboard, Thomas Gregg forced them into the longboats. He said they would be all right because we were close to land."

Ben felt his heart shaking his body. Close to land? God Almighty, they'd been nowhere near land when the storm struck. He said gruffly, "You're mistaken." She had to be mistaken. Tom had a cruel streak, aye, but abandoning men in a stormy sea . . . Surely not. It was a death sentence.

Ana shook her head and pointed to a porthole. "I am not mistaken. I saw it all through that window, and it is all I have thought of since." She had written it down in her journal. The shouts and screams and curses ... Jonathan, the tall man with the sand-colored beard, stabbed before her very eyes and thrown overboard to feed the fish ... his brave young son forced to go along with the others into that desolate gray bank of mist and rain. Her dreams had been filled with it.

"My lads ..." Ben's gorge rose along with his fury. "My poor lads ..." He wanted to tear the cabin to pieces and tear Tom Gregg limb from limb. He got blindly to his feet, but Ana pulled him back down to the bunk.

"Please!" It was a soft hiss in his ear. "You must be silent and listen to me, Benscott. It is worth our lives."

"Young Seth?" Terror struck Ben anew. "Is he here aboard the *Hawk?*" The lad, the son of Jon Darby, his best friend and his quartermaster, had come aboard the *Bluebird* as cabin boy several years ago and surely, surely Tom had not abandoned a child of ten along with the men. He was a family man with a wife and a young son of his own back in England. Ben gripped Ana's arms so tightly she winced. "Tell me," he rasped. "What of Seth?"

Knowing she must not keep any of the terrible truth from him, Ana said quietly, "He was made to row off with the others. His father is—dead, Benscott." Seeing how white his face had become, she wanted to hold and comfort him, but she dared not. His rage must be loosed first. "I am so sorry ..."

"What happened?" Ben's voice broke.

"The father demanded his son remain aboard." Ana's voice was tremulous. "Thomas said he was in no position to demand anything. The father lunged at him"—Ana lowered her head, unable to bear the terrible look in those flame-blue eyes—"and Thomas stabbed him. His men—threw him overboard."

Ben said through clenched jaws, "Was he still alive?"

"Aye. He—cried out."

Ben's senses reeled. God, God, God. Jon had more good

in his little finger than Tom Gregg had in his entire body, and he'd be alive this day if he himself had not talked him into this hellish venture. "Did Seth see this?"

Ana said quietly, "Aye." It was a thing she had wept over a hundred times, and her heart trembled as she gazed upon her companion's agony. He was a handsome man, this Benscott—tall, with a strong, comely face that was framed by his unruly brown hair and beard. He was also a man more gentle with a woman than she had ever known, but now the look in his burning eyes frightened her. Even so, she must tell him everything while she still had the courage, and before the guard came. She said, "There is more, Benscott."

"How could there be?" Ben growled.

Ana drew a deep breath. "Thomas told your men that you were unconscious with your injuries, but he was acting under your earlier orders and dared not disobey you. He said you—would beat him again. He said you had planned all along to keep your share of the *Safira*'s treasure and rob them of theirs and maroon them . . ." She stared at the deadly light in those suddenly narrowed eyes and lay a warning finger across his lips. "Benscott, before your God and mine, I know he lied. You are a good man. But if you would have us live, make no sound. We can escape this night, but the guard must not know you have awakened." She handed him a small, pearl-handled dagger. "I have kept this hidden . . ."

Everything within Ben cried out for Tom Gregg's blood in return for his treachery. And his loyalty to his men cried out for him to return to that place where they had been abandoned—in the middle of the Sea of Marmara. But common sense told him that even if he had a ship, it was too late to save them. Vengeance must wait. The most important thing now was to get Ana away from Tom Gregg and his devil crew before it was too late. He quaked thinking that perhaps it was too late already. He asked thickly, "Has anyone touched you?"

"Nay." Ana shook her head and her long dark-red hair swung with the movement. She said simply, "I told them

I was bleeding." She pointed to the corner where a heap of bloody rags lay. She gave him a wry smile. "They are your dressings, Benscott . . ."

Ben nodded, thankful that she was as brave and clever as she was beautiful. And if she had some plan of escape, he had damned well better listen to it. He said low, "Tell me your thoughts, my lady. Why do you think we can escape tonight?"

"We are in the same port as last night," Ana whispered, "and last night they were gone drinking until dawn. They left but one guard."

Ben's gaze slitted. "How do you know?"

"He—came to me last night. He said we were alone. I heard no other sound on deck, nor have I heard any this eve." She knew better than to tell him that the man had been insulting and had told her that none would come if she screamed. In addition, he had stolen one of her earrings and a favorite pendant she had worn about her neck. But in the end, he had gone off, disgusted by the blood, and had not harmed her. "He said he would come again this eve."

"Did he now?" Ben fingered the dagger's stiletto point and contemplated the sweetness of cutting the devil's throat.

Ana took one of his big hands in hers. "I see well what you are planning, Benscott, but you must not do it. You are not a killer as are these others. We must think only of escape, and this night might be our only chance. Promise me you will do naught but render him unconscious and bind him. Please . . ." Hearing the key turning in the lock, she whispered, "He is here! Quickly, beloved, lie down on the bunk again and close your eyes."

Ben's gaze widened in astonishment, but he obeyed. Beloved. She had called him beloved. In that instant, he knew that he would give her anything in this life and do anything in this world that she might ask of him. Anything.

1746, Boston Harbor

Ben stood on the ship's deck at the rail, his arm wrapped tightly about his young wife's slender body. Thinking of the year of hardship and arduous travel that lay behind them, he gave thanks. With Ana disguised as a lad, they had sailed across the Aegean, Ionian, and Mediterranean seas and passed through the Straits of Gibraltar. After an interminable wait for good weather, they had booked passage to cross the North Atlantic, and with Ana in feminine garb at last, they were finally approaching their destination. Boston.

As they sailed into the setting sun, it looked like paradise to Ben—the restless waters of a deep, sheltered harbor, the long breakings of the surf against craggy headlands, the curving beaches with reedy marshes and inlets poking wet fingers into the green, parklike land beyond. It was a land he knew was suitable for grazing and farming, and he had heard there was plenty of fresh water and abundant timber for shipbuilding. What more could a man want?

"We're home, my lady," he said.

"I love it already." Ana's softly accented voice was breathless with excitement. She removed the gauzy scarf from her head and let the wind lift her long hair. She pointed. "Will you build me a little house on one of those hills, beloved?"

Ben laughed. "A little house? Darlin', I'll build you a mansion. A palace. I can see it now, a grand stone place with towers and a hundred rooms and stables and a carriage house . . ."

Ana smiled at the love she saw in his eyes. "A cottage is all I require, Benadair."

"Fine. We'll live in a cottage—but only while the house is being built, I promise you."

To pay their passage, he had sold three pieces of the priceless jewelry—rings, earrings, bracelets, and necklaces—she had managed to keep hidden in a pouch in her skirts along with her dagger. The sale of several more pieces would set him up in business, he knew, but the remainder he would not touch. They would bring her a fortune if ever she chose to sell them, but such a decision was hers alone to make. He had taken from her all that he intended to take, and he would return it in good measure. He had a good business head, and he was not afraid of hard work.

What was even more important, there were thousands of miles between her and the sultan to whom she had been given. She would be safe here in Boston, and so would he. He had changed his name from Scott to Adair, and there was naught to connect him with the past. Only his memories, and those he would never forget. Like terrible sores, they bled constantly within him. Hastily pushing the thought of them away, he said low to his darling, "I'm going to give you the world, my lady. Just wait and see."

Ana smiled up at her tall husband. "What would I do with the world, Benadair, when I already have all I want?"

"So you have all you want, do you?" Ben drew her hard against him. "And just what might that be?"

She gave him a mysterious smile. "I have you, and then there is . . ." She hesitated.

Ben pretended a frown. "I'm waiting." When she stood on tiptoe and whispered in his ear, he swore he heard bells ringing. "You're sure?"

"I am sure." Laughing at the look of joy spreading over his face, she declared, "If it is a boy, we will call him Benjamin, but I think it is a girl, and her name is Ayisha."

Ben grinned down at her beautiful flushed face. "I-eesha? Well, now, uh, that's mighty pretty, your highness, but have you thought of Priscilla or Anna? Actually, I'm partial to Pandora myself. Or Amy . . ." Anything but I-eesha. God Almighty, it sounded like a sneeze.

Ana patted her small flat belly. "She is Ayisha Adair, my husband, and that is that."

Ben threw back his head and his laughter startled the gulls sailing over their heads. "Then I-ee-sha it is, your highness." He placed his hands on her abdomen, gently cradled it, and bent to press his lips to it. "Our babe will live the life of the princess she is, and so will you. Neither of you will ever want for anything, I promise you." He felt as if his heart would fly out of his chest and take wing with the happiness he felt just then. God's breath, life couldn't be better . . .

Chapter 1

May 1765, England

Cain Banning entered his father's darkened bedchamber and moved quietly to the bed where the old man lay. His questioning eyes met those of the woman tending him. She shook her head and whispered, " 'e's been out o' 'is 'ead most o' th' day, sir. Scared me terrible 'e did as 'e's not bin this bad afore, but 'e's quieted now. 'E's even took a sup o' broth fer me an' took 'is medicine."

Cain nodded. "Thanks, Mary, that's good to hear." He shed his coat and tossed it onto the sea chest that stood in one corner. "I'll stay with him while you have some supper and take a rest."

The woman dipped him a curtsy. "I'll do that, sir. I'll be i' th' kitchen wi' Mrs. Parfrey when ye wants me agin." She studied him with frankly admiring eyes and thought what a handsome man he was with those deep blue eyes of his against his dark skin and that lovely full head of chestnut hair. She did like a man with hair and height and muscles. She sighed, said hopefully, "Sh'll ye be wantin' a tray brought up?"

"Maybe later," Cain replied. "I'll let you know."

He watched as she hurried out, a big kindly maid with a shining red face and strong, capable hands. He was lucky to have found her to ease his father's last days, for he had no doubt that Thomas Gregg was dying. Returning a worried gaze to the frail figure lying on the bed, Cain saw that his blue eyes were open. They were sunken and too bright, but they were lucid now and fastened on him hungrily.

"Hello, Father."

"Thee's a good son, Cain Gregg." Tom's voice was like the scraping of dry leaves across a stone path.

Cain marveled at how his feelings for the old boy had changed. Most of his life he'd hated him, but shortly after he'd gotten him home, Tom had muttered that he never should have taken a wife. Anna was a good lass who deserved far better than he'd given her, and he'd been no father to Cain at all—and he was damned sorry. It had touched Cain. Now Cain smiled down at him.

"A good son, eh? What have I done recently?"

"I've told thee a dozen times, lad. Thee hasn't wandered like th' other Greggs."

The smile left Cain's face. He lay a hand on the fragile shoulder. "And I've told you a dozen times, man—I've wanted to. I still do." Sometimes he doubted that he himself should take a wife.

"But thee hasn't gone off. That's what counts."

Tom was too weak to continue, and his head ached. It was filled to bursting with thoughts jabbing and tormenting him and giving him no peace. Where had the years gone, and why had he wasted them as well as his fortune—his lovely shining fortune of gold and gems and pieces of eight? And how had he become so old and shrunken and sick? He had to get well, for he had things to do still. He had more seas to sail and women to bed and treasures to steal. And he had to find and kill Ben Scott before the bastard found and killed him, although much of the time now he was not always sure who Ben Scott was or why he needed killing. He knew only that he so hated the devil it was an eternal flame scorching him. Feeling its sickening heat washing over him once more, he sat up, eyes staring.

Like lightning striking, he remembered. Ben Scott had been his partner, first in business and then in piracy. He was the bastard, by God, who'd talked him into being a damned sea rover in the first place. And then he'd gone and abandoned his own crew at sea, claimed for his own bloody self the woman they should have shared, and stolen her away from him in the middle of the night. Nor could he forget the bloody beating he'd given him in front of his men. Tom tossed his head wildly, thinking how unfair it was the devil had escaped the punishment he'd planned for him.

Cain watched his father with troubled eyes. "What is it, Father? What can I get you?"

He had Gregg eyes, Tom thought. Not pale washed-out Banning eyes, but eyes as deep blue as midnight in the tropics. Like his own. Gregg eyes under good, strong Gregg brows. Like his own. But then his son was not his anymore. He was gone from his house and was a high-and-mighty Banning now, a force to be reckoned with at the Banning yards, he'd heard tell. Doubtless the company would be his some day.

As for himself, everything he'd ever had was gone—son, wife, treasure, the princess, the *Hawk*, his men, his health. Everything. And all because of that damned viper, Ben Scott. Tom had intended to sell him into slavery in one of the port towns. He'd savored the thought, savored telling him and taking the woman before his very eyes. But Ben had escaped and carried her off into the night. Her necklace and an earring, stolen by one of his men, were all that he had to remind him of what might have been. These many years they had kept the fires of his revenge burning. Tom groaned. Ah, God, he could stand it no longer. Rage was eating him alive.

"Kill 'im!" he cried, and shook his fist at the shadows dancing on the low-raftered ceiling. "Kill th' friggin' bastard. Promise me ye will!"

Cain stroked back the wisps of hair clinging to his father's damp face and held a cup of water to his lips. He asked calmly, "Who is it I should kill?" He'd heard this wild talk from Tom before but could never get a lucid answer from him.

"Ben Scott," Tom gasped, the breath wheezing in his lungs. "Promise . . ."

Cain did not show his surprise. He had never seen the
man but knew he had been his father's partner in the pros-
perous cargo-hauling business they'd had. Now he asked
gently, "Why is it I'm to kill him, Father? I thought he
was your mate."

"Wrong was done me," Tom muttered. "He—beat me
bloody, an' he deserted me. Afore that, he abandoned 'is
own men at sea. In truth, it was me who did it b'cause he
made me. He made me send them off. Holy Jesus . . ."
Why had he not told Cain of this earlier? Cain would have
avenged him. Ah, God, now he remembered why. It was
a secret. A secret about the *Bluebird* that no one must
know. No one. Not even God. He trembled at the thought
and then laughed just as suddenly as he felt the roll of his
vessel beneath his feet and smelled the tang of the salt
breeze.

God's bones, why was he worrying so? He was young
and strong and healthy and he was rich beyond his wildest
dreams. He threw back his head and laughed, recalling
how easy it had been to take that sloppy little Turkish merchant ship on her way to Istanbul. And he was going to
have the soft golden woman Ben Scott had claimed for
himself or his name was not Tom Gregg—and he'd share
her with no one. The bitch was his.

He frowned, realizing suddenly that they were in the
midst of a fierce squall. As he looked on, clinging hard to
the rail, the *Bluebird*, off to his starboard, seemed to explode before his very eyes.

"She's struck!" he shouted.

"Father, wake up!" Cain gripped Tom's thin shoulders
and gave him a shake.

"She'll go down!"

Cain said gruffly, "You're dreaming. You're safe on
land with me and naught's going to harm you." He looked
on in amazement as Tom Gregg leapt from the bed to the
middle of the room where he stood waving his arms.

"Holy God, the *Bluebird*'s goin' t' go down wi' all that
booty! God's holy hooks!" Tom raised his hands to his
mouth and bawled across the expanse of gray frothing

waves, "Bring it aboard, Ben! We'll clap on t' ye till ye git th' princess and yer chests an' crew moved over here t' th' *Hawk!*"

"Come, man, it's all right." Cain took him firmly by the hand and drew him back to his bed. "Ben's booty and the princess and his crew are all safe aboard the *Hawk.*"

Tom blinked glassy eyes. "Ye're certain?"

"Aye, you can go back to sleep."

Tom allowed himself to be lowered to his bed and gently tucked in, but he knew he would not sleep. He'd not had a decent night's sleep since the *Bluebird* went down. At the thought, he began to shake again. He hated it when he saw things so clearly, for he saw now that Ben Scott had done no real wrong, but he had. He himself had sinned. And when he died, he was going to burn forever in the devil's hellfire. He looked up at his son, the whites of his eyes showing, and he clutched Cain's strong hand. "God mustn't know, lad. Promise ye'll nay tell 'im ..."

Cain shook his head, his heart full of pity. "You're not to worry, man. I'll not tell Him." He bent, touched his lips to the dry, fevered forehead. "Sleep now, and we'll talk again later. I'll be here."

For a long, long time, Cain sat brooding, gazing at his father and remembering how deeply he had once loved him. Cold and secretive as the man was, gone to sea for months, aye, sometimes years at a time, he had nonetheless been Cain's god, and Cain had worshipped him. In the few brief interludes they were together, he had tried desperately to please him but never succeeded. Nor had his mother. Cain had been furious with her, blaming her unjoyous welcomes and shrill voice for driving his father away again so quickly. But his eyes were opened during his father's last homecoming.

Finding his wife in the ground and his young son with the Bannings, Tom Gregg had agreed without protest to their adopting him. He stayed only two days before he went off whistling. Cain's heart hardened as he finally came to grips with what he had always refused to believe: his father neither loved nor wanted him. Nor had he loved his wife. No wonder she had wept so much of the time and screamed at him when he returned for those fleeting periods of time. As he'd said, he never should have taken a wife, never had a child. He was a wandering man like his father and his father's father and all the Gregg men before him . . .

Cain had not seen him again until six months ago when the skipper of a Banning vessel had heard of his whereabouts and told him. Cain had gone immediately to the thatched hut on the windswept southern coast of England. Seeing that Tom Gregg's wandering days were finally over, he invited him to share his home. When Tom refused, Cain had taken matters into his own hands. The old boy was gravely ill, and he was damned if he'd have him dying in some cold shabby cottage alone.

He leaned forward now, watched sadly the labored breathing through those thin, pale lips and wondered, Who is this man whose blood runs in my veins? In truth, he had no idea. He knew only that once more he felt a certain love for him, and he wished things had been different between them. And he was sorry for him. He was damnably sorry, for it was clear that his father was terrified of dying. Cain hoped somehow to ease his mind before the end came, but it was not to be. Within the hour, Thomas Gregg was dead.

Heart galloping, the tall seaman used the knocker on the gleaming black door of the townhouse pointed out to him, and then he stood back and waited. It was hard to believe that after all of these years and thousands of miles, his search was ended, that a casual conversation with a stranger in a pub in Torbay had finally led him to one of his prey. Of course Tom Gregg would not recognize him, but so much the better. The shock would be the greater for it. He smiled grimly and played over in his head once more the words he had said so often in his dreams. "Captain Gregg, I'm Seth Darby. I was cabin boy on the *Bluebird* and I have a message for you from her crew . . ." God, but he was going to enjoy this, seeing the old devil shake in his boots as he realized he was about to pay for his crimes.

Seth straightened his shoulders as the door opened. He frowned, seeing it was only a thin, middle-aged housekeeper rather than a butler who stood there. It surprised him. A lot of things surprised him. With all the loot the bastard had stolen, he'd expected him to be living in a mansion in the best part of town with a slew of liveried servants to wait on him hand and foot. And he'd expected him to have changed his name.

Nellie Parfrey scowled up at the man standing on her master's stoop. He was a ship's man, and as he snatched his cap off his roughly cut, sand-colored hair, she said sharply, "If it's work ye want, mister, apply at th' yards. The master don't take apple-cations here t' home."

"I'm not applying for work," Seth's voice was deep and resonant, and loud enough to reach the interior of the house. "I'm here to see Thomas Gregg. Fetch him, please."

Nellie blinked at the command in his tone. "Well, now, it so happents that ain't possible."

Seth took a step forward. "I've traveled thousands of miles to see your master and I don't aim to be turned away, m'am. You fetch him quick, or I'll fetch him myself."

At that, Nellie called shrilly, "Master Banning, ye'd best come. It's someone t' see poor Mr. Gregg."

Poor Mr. Gregg? Seth felt an icy premonition as footsteps approached from the back of the house. Suddenly he was looking into Thomas Gregg's blue eyes, but they belonged to a man his own age. He cleared his tight throat. "Sir, I've come to see Thomas Gregg. We—have unfinished business between us."

Cain studied the seaman with interest. In the six months his father had dwelt in his house, he had mentioned little of his past. Not until the end. He said, "I fear you're too late. Thomas Gregg died last week." Seeing the stranger's face turn pale, he spoke low to Nellie Parfrey and she hurried away.

"Died?" Seth whispered, and felt his knees go weak. In the daze that came over him, he allowed himself to be drawn inside the house, led quickly to a study that smelled of leather and burning pine wood, and lowered into a chair before a hot fire. "Died . . ." He shook his head, unable to believe this could have happened. Not when he'd been about to collect a measure of justice, a scant measure to be sure, for all of those poor devils who had perished because of two men's greed. Thinking of the unfairness of it, he began to shake.

When Cain's housekeeper brought the mug of hot rum he had requested, he put it between the stranger's cold hands and cupped his own about them. "Drink this," he ordered. When the seaman had swallowed half of the mug's contents and color returned to his cheeks, Cain said quietly, "This seems to be a matter of great importance to you. My name is Cain Banning, and Tom Gregg was my father. Can I help you in some way?"

Seth threw back his head, loosed a wild burst of laughter, and took another deep swallow. "Nay, man, you can't help. Not unless you can tell me where to find Ben Scott."

Cain's eyes shuttered. Ever since his father's passing, he had been pondering his last hours and the things he'd talked and raged about—Ben Scott, a ship called the *Bluebird*, some kind of booty and a princess. He had thought at the time that Tom Gregg was delirious, but then he'd found, among the meager belongings in his father's sea chest, an exquisitely wrought gold pendant and a matching earring fashioned of seed pearls, tiny diamonds, and emeralds. Studying the fragile things, Cain had been thunderstruck. It was the sort of jewelry that might well belong to a princess. And now here was another man talking about Ben Scott. He asked carefully, "What exactly was your business with my father?"

Seth rose and extended a hand. "I'm sorry, I should have introduced myself. I'm Seth Darby. Twenty years ago I was cabin boy on the *Bluebird*, commanded by Ben Scott. As for the business between your father and me"—he shook his head—"I guess there's naught to be done about it now."

Cain felt a stirring of excitement. First Ben Scott, now the *Bluebird*. What in hell was this all about? He had been studying Seth Darby as he spoke and he liked what he saw. The man had an open pleasant face, wide-spaced gray eyes, and a neatly trimmed beard. His hair and nails and clothes were clean. All in all, there was a look of honesty and responsibility about him. He said, "Why don't you let me decide if there's naught to be done."

Seth shrugged. "It's a thing that involved only your father—and Ben Scott." And the families of sixty dead men.

His thoughts raced. Did he dare tell this Cain Banning what he was about? He had always been a man of instinct and intuition, and both were telling him that this son of Thomas Gregg was not the bastard his father was. Tom, damn his wicked soul to everlasting hellfire, would have kicked the three plump cats sleeping contentedly before the fire and then skinned them for the fun of it. This man had touched each of them with a reassuring hand when they had been startled by the arrival of a stranger in the study. And old Tom never would have been content to live in such a simple dwelling as this with his new-found glut of riches.

Looking about him, Seth saw simplicity and quiet well-being. The window curtains were spotless but patched, and the desk and chairs and tables were old but they were good—and they were polished to such a rich patina they gleamed in the firelight. The housekeeper's doing, of course, but Seth hadn't a doubt she would have gotten away with less if her master allowed it. But naught would slip past this man. He saw it in the way Cain Banning carried himself and in the directness of his eyes and his speech.

As for Tom Gregg's vast treasure, either the devil had spent it all, or his son refused to touch it, or he knew naught of it. Seth's instinct told him it was the latter. His instinct also told him that only a fool would be lulled into unwariness by Cain Banning's gentle treatment of his cats. He'd seen murderers who could not harm a butterfly. Nay, caution was still the word.

"My father mentioned Ben Scott before he died," Cain said, "but I know naught of the man. Only that Ben was once his business partner. I'd like very much to hear what you have to say."

Meeting those direct, dark blue eyes under their strong, straight brows, Seth made an instant decision. He answered grimly, "Then I'll tell you, but I doubt very much you'll like hearing it. Some of my information I got from my father. He was quartermaster of the *Bluebird* and Ben Scott's best friend—or so he thought. The rest is from my own experience."

The logs turned to embers and the room grew dim as Cain listened in silence. He heard how the two business partners, at Ben's urging, had gone from cargo hauling to piracy. For nearly two years they sailed and looted side by side, but when Tom grew increasingly cruel, Ben objected and gave him an ultimatum: Stop the violence or he'd pull out. His men doubted he would. They had seen the glow in his eyes when they were on the hunt. He loved the life of a sea wolf too much. But the day finally came when Ben said they were going back to cargo hauling—but first they'd take one more ship. That ship was the *Safira.*

"—the longboats never reached land, of course," Seth muttered. "The seas were still running high from the storm, and it wasn't long before we were swamped. We clung to our craft for what seemed forever, and then some of my mates started slipping into the deep, too tired to hang on. It turned out they were the lucky ones, for by then the sharks had found us."

Seth shivered, remembering. He stared defiantly at those wintry eyes, so like Tom Gregg's, gazing at him from Cain Banning's dark face, and told himself he should hate the man. For damned sure he would not trust him. The clock ticked and the cats purred in their sleep as the silence stretched between them.

Cain said quietly, "It would seem you were the luckiest of all."

"Aye. I was the only one left when a Turk merchant ship came by. I had a chunk chewed out of my right leg before they got me aboard ..." He still had nightmares, saw the water roiling and turning red, saw the monsters feasting on his screaming mates and knew they would soon be coming for him.

"How old were you?"

"Ten winters." Seth finished his rum and set the mug on the floor. "That's enough of that," he said gruffly, certain Cain Banning had not believed a word he said. "Except I'll say God was with me. My rescuers were good men. They patched me up, and I sailed with them for years and learned their tongue." And ever since he'd been on the lookout for the *Hawk* and his two blood enemies.

Everything in Cain warred against what he had heard. His father had been an uncaring man and a selfish one, aye, but cruel? To the point of abandoning men at sea? He thrust the thought away, yet Thomas Gregg's last tortured hours would seem to prove he had done the black deed. But it was on the orders of another, he reasoned angrily. He'd had to do it. But the thought did not console him. His father would have foreseen the swamping of the craft, foreseen the men slipping into the deep and the approach of those black fins ...

He said stiffly, "I'm sorry. My mates and I were once swept overboard in the South China Sea and there were sharks ..." It was one of the worst memories he had.

Seth looked up at him sharply. "I never thought you'd believe me. I thought you'd come out swinging."

Cain went to his desk, unlocked a drawer, and retrieved the necklace and earring he had found in his father's sea chest. He handed them to Seth Darby and watched his gray eyes widen. "My father died in terror," he said low. "He raved about the *Safira*, the *Bluebird*, a storm, a princess, and he wanted me to kill Ben Scott. He said Ben had wronged him and had made him abandon his men at sea. I thought he was delirious until I found these, and now you tell me this story."

"Sweet Jesus . . ." Seth carried the pieces reverently to the window where the afternoon sun struck from them a million glittering splinters of ice and fire. "They're hers, the princess Ana's. She was wearing the necklace when we brought her aboard the *Bluebird.* I remember because I'd never seen such a beautiful thing before—nor had I seen such a beautiful woman . . ."

Cain had not responded to his father's cry to avenge him, but he knew now that he would. No matter how long it took or what it cost, he would avenge him. For there at the end, he'd seen a side of the man he had never known. Tom Gregg regretted the mistakes he had made. He was a weak man and a wandering man, but not until he joined up with Ben Scott did he become an evil man who lived in fear of eternal damnation. Cain said quietly, "I want the bastard as much as you do. You can count on me for help, Darby."

Seth studied Cain Banning's dark, inscrutable face and warned himself that it could be a trick. "Why should I?"

"Because I mean to avenge my father. He was no angel, but neither was he the devil incarnate. Scott must have had some powerful hold over him or he'd never have abandoned men at sea. And if he told you land was nearby, it was."

Seth's lip curled. "I'd expect you to defend him."

Cain shook his head, nigh sickened. "Naught can excuse what he did, but I promise you, he regretted it. He died in torment."

Seth studied the other's grim face for long moments before he nodded, then said gruffly, "Welcome aboard." He held out his hand.

Cain clasped it. "I regret I can't join you now. I have company business to attend to these next few months, but after that, you can count on me. Where do you propose to look next?"

"I'm headed for Boston. My father said once it was Ben's destination when he was through pirating. Every two years when I hit town, I haunt the docks and pubs and shops, but it's been fruitless without knowing what he calls himself or what kind of work he does."

Cain grinned. "I'll be damned, Boston's where I'm going. I'm leaving tomorrow. My uncle and I are in shipbuilding and we're thinking of opening a yard there."

Now Seth grinned. "I'll be damned."

"Can I offer you a berth on the *Sea Eagle?*"

"That, or you can bunk on my ship. But we ought to be together. We have planning to do."

"That we do," Cain said. "Sail with me aboard the *Eagle* then. We weigh anchor tomorrow at sunrise."

Chapter 2

June 1765, Boston

Ayisha was passing her sister's bedchamber when she spied Aimee struggling to pull a brush through her curls. "Do you need help, honey?"

"I need new hair!" Aimee protested. "I absolutely hate this mop. Colette was fixing it but she's gone off to iron my ribbon. And this gown," she made a face and plucked at it nervously, "—is it all right, do you think?"

"It's beautiful," Ayisha answered truthfully. "I've always loved it." It was a layered confection of peach silk and lace which made Aimee's cheeks and lips appear pinker than ever.

"But—does it look good on me?"

"It looks perfect on you." Seeing the uncertainty in Aimee's brown eyes, she smiled. "In truth, you look gorgeous, and now here's Colette to finish your hair."

Ayisha perched on the bed to watch as Colette assumed command of her mistress's silver-backed hairbrush. Within minutes she had brought order to Aimee's cape of brown, silky curls, gathered them within the ribbon, and tied a fat satin bow at her nape. She then gave Aimee a hand mirror and stepped back to admire her work.

"*C'est magnifique,* Mees Aimee. You are very beautiful. *Vraiment!*"

"It's true," Ayisha said firmly. "Go to the looking glass and see for yourself." But as she watched her sister revolve slowly, looking through both mirrors, she knew

24

Aimee was seeing only what she believed herself to be: a maid who was not clever, not beautiful, not interesting, and not exciting compared to her older sister.

"But will Jeremy like it?"

Ayisha wanted to shake her. "Of course he'll like it—and he'll love the way you look in it."

Aimee's troubled gaze met Ayisha's. "I know it's going to be a wonderful party, but I feel guilty. I still think of him as your man."

Ayisha held her head. "What am I going to do with you? He's not my man. How can I convince you?"

Now Aimee laughed, hugged herself, and began to dance about her bedchamber. "I just needed to hear you say it one more time. Oh, Pan, he's the handsomest thing I've ever seen in my life! He's glorious!"

Ayisha grinned. "I'm sure he'd agree with you." She had debated for several days whether or not to deliver a gentle warning to Aimee about Jeremy. She had just made her decision.

"You really don't like him much, do you?" Aimee murmured.

"It's not that I don't like him. I just think you should be a bit careful. Don't be too swayed by his good looks."

Aimee stared at her. "Did he hurt you?"

"Oh, Aimee, nay! I'd certainly have warned you."

"He got fresh with you?"

"Nay, he was a perfect gentleman always."

"Then what? You were seeing him almost every day and then you said you got tired of each other. But did you really? I need to know."

Ayisha saw that she was right. What had been a private matter between herself and Jeremy Greydon should no longer be private now that Aimee was involved. She said simply, "He wanted to wed me."

Aimee blinked. "He knew after three weeks that he wanted to spend the rest of his life with you?"

"So he said . . ." Actually, he had proposed at the end of the first week, but Ayisha had laughed and told him to stop teasing her. By the end of the third week, he was so insistent she'd had to explain, not too gently, that she was not ready to marry anyone. He thereupon replied sharply that it was just as well. He wouldn't have a woman who stank of horses and brine.

Aimee sighed. "He must have loved you madly."

"He never said so." He had said all sorts of unbelievable things—that she was ravishing, and his thoughts of her tormented him day and night, that she was the first woman he had ever wanted to wed . . . all of that, but not once had he ever said he loved her. And she had not even realized it until this instant.

"Was he crushed when you refused?" Aimee was feeling quite sorry for the poor man.

Ayisha's lips curved, remembering. "He was furious. I don't think it ever occurred to him that I might say nay."

"Why did you?" Aimee asked softly. Studying her sister's beautiful, pensive face, she felt a familiar pang of admiration. Her own eyes had no golden lights in them and her hair was just plain brown and held no glints of fire.

"I had several reasons. The biggest one was that I sensed he was interested in—something more than just me."

Aimee looked at her in disbelief. "You can't mean Papa's money."

"I'm afraid I do." She had found it very hard to swallow that anything about herself could make a man as eager and as persistent to wed her as Jeremy Greydon had been.

Aimee's silvery laughter ran out. "Pan, you can't be serious! His papa has all of those exotic import shops—actually Jeremy says they're his already. And you," she shook her head, "—just look at yourself in the mirror and then tell me he was after Papa's money!" She yearned to ask if Jeremy had kissed her, but of course he had if he'd wanted to wed her. She added softly, "I doubt I'd turn him away if he ever proposed to me."

Ayisha felt a rush of concern. It was exactly what she feared, but perhaps Aimee was right. Jeremy's father was a vastly wealthy man and so would Jeremy be one day. Maybe he was the perfect mate for her younger sister. He wanted a woman he could command and Aimee was young, only seventeen, and docile and obedient. She needed a strong hand to hold on to. Since their mother's death, Ayisha's had been that hand, both for her and their father. She still had tears of her own that had not been shed. She put the thought from her mind and perfected the drape of the pink bow in Aimee's hair.

"There. You look perfectly beautiful. But just remember," she added softly, "he's a charmer. When are you expecting him?"

"Any minute." As Aimee caught up a straw hat and a small embroidered handbag, the first-floor maid knocked softly on the open door.

"Mr. Greydon is here, Miss Aimee."

"Thanks, Henny." Aimee laid a hand on her heart and turned to Ayisha. "Oh, Panny, do wish me luck." Filled with fright and excitement, she swept through the wide center hallway, down the graceful curving staircase and there he was waiting for her—tall, blond as a Norse god, and exquisitely dressed in skintight satin breeches, a ruffled silk shirt, and a dark, sublimely tailored waistcoat. The sight of him left her without breath or words.

"Good afternoon, my lady." Jeremy raised her hand to his lips.

"G . . . good afternoon." Seeing the way his blue eyes gleamed over her, she felt weak with relief. He did like the way she looked. He did indeed.

Ayisha, following behind, said cheerily, "Hello, Jere."

"Good afternoon, Ayisha."

"What a lovely day for a garden party."

"Isn't it? I see you're back from a sail."

"Actually, I'm just about to leave. The tide should be just perfect." She saw his eyes flicker over her man's shirt and cut-off cotton trews, saw the faint twitch of his mouth. She smiled. "Well, I'll be on my way." She kissed Aimee's flushed cheek. "Do have a wonderful time, Hon, and remember what I said."

"I will, and please be careful. I always worry about you in that tiny boat in the open sea. Is Mac going, too?"

"Aye. He'd skin me if I went out on such a grand day as this without him."

Ayisha fairly flew as she left behind her the great stone-and-timbered ivy-covered dwelling with its two guard towers and its mullioned windows and its two wings stretching out as if it would embrace the sea. As she reached the stable, MacKenzie Fitzgerald was just bringing their bridled bareback mounts out into the sunshine.

"I figured it was a sailing day. Was I right?"

"You're right." Ayisha laughed as the wind lifted her hair like a pennant and whipped it about her flushed face. "It's perfect for it."

Mac's grin was white in his dark face. "I couldn't agree more."

It did his heart good to see her so happy. After the death of the mistress of Seacliff, he had wondered if she would ever again be the fearless, laughing lass he had known since the day she was born. The lady's passing had fair taken the heart out of her, as it had them all. But now with summer settling in and the passage of almost two gray years behind them, the gloom was finally disbursing.

In silent camaraderie, the two rode down the trail carved in the thickly wooded hillside to the white sand cove at its base. Leaving their mounts in the paddock Mac had fenced for the purpose, they walked to the boathouse where Ayisha's minnow-sleek sailboat was kept. After carefully checking it over, they faced into the wind and the tide and then the *Dolphin*'s sails billowed with the freshening breeze.

As Ayisha's capable hands worked the tiller, Mac gazed on her contentedly. She was barefoot, her skin pale gold from the summer sun, and to keep her long mahogany-colored hair from her eyes, she had knotted it at the nape. What a honey she was in the old clothes he had worn as a lad—the trews cut off and one of his ancient blue workshirts not hiding the lovely swells of her breasts. She was a real beauty, within and without, and lucky would be the lad who won her.

Looking at Mac's dark Irish face, Ayisha felt a surge of

warmth and love for him. His smile told her that there was no place he'd rather be than right there, right now. Nor was there anyplace else she would rather be. She reached out, caught his hand. "Thanks, Mac."

"For what, lady?"

"You know well for what." Her friends and her sister were terrified of the sea and horses, and her father, who loved both, was gone most of the time. "Without you I'd have no one to ride and sail with."

Her folks and his had become fast friends during an Atlantic crossing when he was five and she was but a speck in her mother's womb. His father had overseen the building of Seacliff and managed the estate until his death. His mother, Pegeen, at first the cook and nursemaid, now ruled the household staff. Mac himself was stablemaster and maintained the Seacliff smallcraft—two sailboats and a rowboat. He was also her brother, her teacher, her best friend, and her confidant.

"You have my own thanks, lass," Mac said. "A man couldn't ask for better company." He returned the pressure on her small, competent hand and grinned at her. "Do you remember your first time aboard a ship?"

Ayisha made a face. "I got sick as a dog."

"Aye, but you recovered in short order and found your sea legs." An apprentice seaman himself in those days, he'd been amazed by the way the wee lass of seven winters had taken to the sea like a bird took to the sky. He chuckled at the memory and said, "You climbed a boarding ladder and ratlines like a little monkey—and cussed! God's breath, but you could cuss. Your poor mum nigh swooned away when she heard you."

Ayisha laughed. "And your mum washed my mouth out with soap." She turned serious then and pulled the tiller toward her. "Let out the sheets a little, Mac, we're getting too close to the wind."

Mac saluted. "Aye, skipper."

On their four-week journey from Southampton to Boston, Cain and Seth had talked and plotted daily at the round oak table in Cain's cabin. Now as they neared the end of their voyage, Cain continued to fill sheets of foolscap with notes. Seth studied him with narrowed eyes. After making an almost instantaneous decision to trust the fellow, he'd since been beset by worries. Not that Cain had done anything to shake his trust, it was just that once they were aboard ship, his appearance had changed.

Gone was the clean-shaven, respectable-looking co-owner of Banning Limited; in his place was a man captaining his own armed brig, dark, lean, hungry looking, naked to the waist, and with a blood-red sash keeping his long hair from his eyes. He was a man completely at home with the scream of the wind, the roll of the sea, and a pitching deck. Never in his life had Seth seen a man who so resembled a marauding sea wolf. Begod, but the damned fellow did. It fair sent the shivers up his spine to think that his partner in this venture had Tom Gregg's blood running in his veins. He constantly had to push the ugly thought away and tell himself he was becoming a regular old woman with his worries.

"You haven't a clue as to what he might call himself now?" Cain asked.

"Only what he'll not call himself. For certain it'll not be Ben Scottman nor Scott Benson."

"Do you think he kept his first name?"

"Chances are he did. It's harder to change the first than the last."

"And unless he's a master of disguise, we're looking for a man roughly six feet tall with light blue eyes who walks like a sailor."

"Maybe. But for sure, he'll be lean and fit. He'd never let himself go. And he was distinguished looking. He always minded me more of a churchman than a man of the sea. Since he's nearing sixty, I suppose his hair's gray or white—or he might be bald. Or wear a wig." Seth stroked his beard. "I think I'd recognize him, but I can't be sure. But the lady I'll never forget, and she can't be anything but beautiful still. She was sixteen or seventeen winters at the time which would put her in her mid-thirties now. A relatively young woman."

Cain grinned. "Aye, with dark red locks and amber eyes and creamy skin and an exotic look to her." He suspected the lad, Seth, had been in love with her.

Seth sighed. "Aye. I'd not seen her like before, nor have I since. She was a dream. And she looked royal—the way she walked and talked and held her head."

He muttered a string of oaths thinking of his lost love in the power of a man like Ben Scott. For he had loved the maid. Child though he was, he had loved her deeply. And to think, he'd once admired Ben and thought he was kind. What in hell could have happened to the man to turn him into the devil himself? But then he knew. It was Ana's beauty and the vastness of the *Safira*'s treasure. He'd seen the change in Ben when he'd fought Tom for her. They all had.

"You know, man, there's a chance they're both gone," Cain said gently.

Seth waved it off. "I'll not let myself think that way. We're going to find the bastard, and we'll start the search this very day. It's still early. We'll find lodgings, probably at the Red Horse on King Street, grab a bite and a pint, and then we can rent horses and start."

"I'll buy a newspaper. It should list concerts and plays if there are any. If he's come up in the world, maybe he'll have acquired a taste for culture."

"And let's not forget gaming houses. There are three close to the Red Horse. And let's learn when the town meetings are held—and there's church on Sundays."

"Ladies like assemblies and carriage rides in the parks." Cain was writing it all down. "And I'll be all over the area scouting property to build on or a yard to buy."

"I'll keep my eyes peeled at the docks."

"What about your name?" Cain asked.

Seth looked at him. "What about my name?"

"If the man's been hiding all this while, caution is a part of his life. If he hears the name Seth Darby—"

"After all this while, he's probably overconfident and thinks he's safe."

"I say call yourself something else."

Seth saw the wisdom of it. "How about Duncan? Seth Duncan. It was my mother's maiden name."

"Seth Duncan. Aye, it'll do."

Seth rose and, feeling the heat of the chase, began to pace the cabin. "The bastard's going to pay compensation in full for every one of my dead mates." He himself would carry it directly to the families. He knew exactly who the surviving kin were and where they lived, for he had kept in close touch with them. Seeing Cain's eyes narrow, he said sharply, "What's the look for? Do you think I mean to make off with the loot myself? Because if you do, we'll bloody well do it together."

Surprised by his sudden vehemence, Cain said easily, "Nay, man, I trust you, but I'm not keen on the plan as it stands."

It was the same fate that would have befallen his father had he not died first and it left him with a bad feeling. They would promise Scott immunity in exchange for the money and then betray him as he had betrayed his own men. He would be hauled back to England in irons and handed over to the Crown for piracy, abduction, and abandonment at sea.

"It's not even an eye for an eye," Seth said through tight lips. "I'll not throw the bastard to the sharks, much as I'd like to." But Cain had hit a nerve. Treachery, even toward an enemy, was not his way and it fair sickened him to think of it. So don't think of it, he told himself. If he found the devil, he'd just do it.

"He could involve you," Cain reminded him. "You sailed with him, you could well go to the gallows with him."

"So be it. It's a price I'll gladly pay if my mates can finally rest in peace."

Hearing six bells, Cain corked the inkpot, rose, and clasped his hands behind his back. "We should be nearing the outer islands."

"I'll get my gear collected."

After he departed, Cain gathered his own gear and went out on deck where he watched with satisfaction his men preparing for their eventual entry into the crowded harbor. Walking to the side, he studied the distant curving shoreline with its bulking headlands and the greenery of the forested commons. He was always grateful to make port with all hands safe and his vessel intact after an arduous sea voyage, but his arrival here had a different feel to it—a sense of well-being and contentment. It was strange. If he believed in omens, he might well think he would soon be calling Boston home, that Banning Limited was going to buy or build a successful yard here. But then he did not believe in omens.

He was reflecting on it when, out of the corner of his eye, he detected movement where no movement should have been. His heart lurched as he saw a sliver of a sailboat slicing through the whitecaps and saw that it and the Sea Eagle were on a collision course. Within seconds, they would reach the same spot in the shipping corridor at the exact same time. God's blood. The small craft was moving too fast to reef the mainsail, but if they hove to now they might be saved. He cupped his hands to his mouth and bellowed to his helmsman, "Bear to port! Now!"

As the order was relayed he shouted to the two figures in the sailboat, "Bear to starboard and heave to. Now! Bear your craft to starboard!" God, were there imbeciles manning it?

He continued to shout and wave his arms to warn them away, but on they came. He could already imagine the carnage: the broken bodies, the slender gleaming craft broken in half, its white sails blood spattered and spread upon the water where they would eventually sink. The two would have to be retrieved, and there would be an inquiry. God, nay! Don't let it happen! He heard Seth's voice in his ear.

"What's happening? I heard a commotion."

Cain pointed, shouted to the two again, and saw that the Sea Eagle's starboard rail was lined now with men whose warning shouts joined his own.

"The helmsman's jist a lad!"

"Nay, lookut that long hair. It's a maid! Gawd, she's a beaut!"

"She's racin' us! Don't she know she could be kilt? What's the feller mean, lettin' 'er do sich a thing?"

"B'Gawd, lookut 'er fly. She's not goin' t' turn nor stop, she's goin' for it! She's on a run. The little wench is goin' t' cut right in front o' us wi' room to spare!"

"She's in luck."

"Luck, nothin', man, that's sailin', that is. Lookut 'er! Jesus, I never seen a sailboat go so fast! Whew!"

"She sails like a angel! Hoo, lookut, she's wavin'!"

There was a mass movement to the *Sea Eagle*'s other rail as the sleek minnow and her beautiful helmsman shot in front of their bow and disappeared on the other side. The men were laughing and shouting after her, "Bye-bye, darlin' . . ."

"G'bye, sweet thing, come back again, do."

"An' leave yer boyfriend at home . . ."

"Come aboard next time, girlie, an' let me gi' ye a good time . . ."

Cain did not follow them but remained rooted to the starboard rail, his guts churning. He had been so sure he was about to witness a tragedy, his mind and body could not adjust to reality—the reality that the little witch had actually outrun them and been playing a game with them, playing a damned game with his two-hundred-ton fourteen-gun brig. It was clear she'd had no idea of the danger she'd been in, not the way she was laughing and waving at them. God's life, he could still see her beautiful upturned face and laughing lips, the sun striking her amber eyes so that they looked pure gold under the exotic slant of her dark winged brows. Her hair had been the same color. Like dark fire.

Cain stood very still, remembering the way she had looked and remembering what Seth had told him about the stolen princess. A shiver tingled over his bare skin even before Seth returned to his side, a dazed look on his face.

"What is it, man?" Cain asked gruffly, but he already knew.

"That—was her," Seth muttered. "The princess. She had the same hair, the same face and eyes. Cain, it was her!"

"Listen to yourself," Cain said sharply. He was still shaking. "That was no woman in her middle years. That was a maid ..." a young soft, smooth, lithe, laughing maid who was so beautiful and so daring she had fair stolen his heart away even as he had wanted to put her over his knee and thrash her.

"I swear to God, Cain. It was Ana."

"Nay, man, it wasn't. If anything, it was her daughter." Suddenly he hadn't a doubt of it. Nor did he doubt now that they would find Ben Scott in Boston.

Chapter 3

"**G**ood morning, my darlin's." Ben Adair's blue eyes lit with pleasure as his girls entered the dining chamber to breakfast with him. They did not always arise this early.

"Good morning, Da." Ayisha brushed a kiss over her father's silver temple and went to the sideboard where an array of tempting food awaited her in chafing dishes. She lifted the lids and sniffed. "Hmmmm. I think I'll have some of everything this morn. It all looks wonderful."

"Good morning, Papa darling." Aimee kissed her father's weathered cheek and sat down at his left.

"You're not eating, lass?"

"Certainly I'm eating. Fruit and some tea."

Noting her glowing face and eyes, Ben chuckled. "You look like a kitten with cream. Either you've just snatched some poor creature from death's door or you've found a new beau." To see her blush and hear her silvery laughter warmed his heart.

"Actually, it's a party . . ."

"Ah. A party that's coming, or a party that's over?" What treasures they were, and how blessed he was to have them. He had lost his beloved, aye, but she still lived in Aimee's gentle heart and in Ayisha's daring. And both maids had her lovely form and strikingly beautiful features. He was twice-blessed.

"Both, actually. There was the most wonderful garden affair yesterday afternoon, and somehow it just stretched on and on till evening—and this afternoon we're invited to another."

"Are you now? You and Pan, I suppose?" He was teasing, and she knew it.

"Nay, Papa. Jeremy Greydon and I."

"Well, well, Jeremy Greydon . . ."

He tried to keep the smile on his face. Failing that, he took a bite of steak and kidney pie and washed it down with ale. He had already been through a siege of worrying about Ayisha when the fellow had swept her off her feet. She had soon come to her senses, thank God, but Aimee was another matter.

Of the two, she was the little mother, the nurturer and healer and keeper of the home fires. She yearned for a man to love and please as a moth yearned for a flame, but Ben's every instinct warned him that Greydon was not the one for either of his daughters. He had a dislike for any man who was too smooth and smiling and with no consistency to speak of. And that was Greydon. The fellow wore ten different faces with ten different people, and he could only pray that Aimee would see it. He turned to Ayisha on his right.

"How about you, Pandora? What surprises have you to spring on your old man this beautiful day?" There was a light in her eyes, too, but more than likely it was a horse or sailing that had put it there. As always, she was dressed for either.

"No surprises, Da. I'm going to take Omar and Satan out for extra long rides this morn because they missed out yesterday. Mac and I went for a wonderful sail."

Seeing the pink that swept across her face, Ben's eyes narrowed. What was this now? Ayisha and Mac Fitzgerald? He looked down at his plate, pretending not to notice, and wished with all his heart that Ana had not left him to sail these uncharted waters alone. He loved Mac like a son, aye, but he'd always thought the lad was more brother than beau to the maid. He took a last bite of pie, chewed, swallowed it, and nodded.

"It was a grand day to be on the water. I wish I'd been

with you. It seems I've been letting business take up far
too much of my time."

"But it's important . . ."

"I'll tell you what, my beauty. How about if we go for
a sail after dinner? I'll not make any appointments and
we'll have the whole eve to enjoy ourselves." He basked
in the smile that spread across her face and lit the whole
room.

"It sounds wonderful."

"That's my girl." He wiped his mouth on a napkin and
got to his feet as Pegeen Fitzgerald sailed into the room,
her white, starched apron crackling like sails in the wind.

"Was breakfast satisfactory?"

"It was grand, Mrs. Fitzgerald. My compliments to the
cook, as always." Out of the corner of his eye, Ben saw
her lifting lids, peering into the steaming depths of the silver containers and snapping them back on.

"Cook will want to know if it was as grand as all that,
why you ate so little. 'Twasn't enough to keep a bird
alive." She flashed a look of approval at Ayisha's heaped
plate and the gusto with which she was eating.

Ben patted his flat belly. "Now, Peg, any more and I'd
be putting on a pauch. We can't have that." The truth was,
his digestive juices were not what they'd been when he
was a young man.

"And you?" Pegeen asked Aimee. She'd been second
mother to these maids ever since they were bairns, and she
was not about to see either of them starve to death when
there was good food on the table. She was taken aback by
the vacant look on the child's face. "Lass, are you ill?"

Aimee sighed. "It's just that—food seems unimportant
now."

Pegeen folded her arms over her ample front and fixed
Aimee with her sharp brown eyes. "Unimportant in comparison to what, pray?" The girl had never been much of
an eater, but this was pitiful—a few swallows of tea and
a bit of apple.

"I'll be leaving," Ben interrupted, wanting to be away
from the woman talk he knew was sure to follow. He gave

Ayisha a wink and a tap on the arm. "We'll have ourselves a good sail, lass. I'll look forward to it."

"I, too, Da." Ayisha blew him a kiss, her tall, strong, silver-haired father, and returned her attention to Pegeen and Aimee. Her sister's dreamy gaze was now directed out the window toward the blue-green expanse of sea where a continuous parade of ships was visible.

"Answer me, lass," Pegeen said crisply. "In comparison to what is your food unimportant?"

Aimee pouted. "Must we talk about it now?"

"Your mama would want to know," Pegeen said more gently, seeing tears sparkling in her young mistress's eyes. Sweet Mary, it still was not safe to talk of Herself. Maybe it never would be. She stared after Aimee helplessly as the maid rose and drifted listlessly from the room. Pegeen turned to Ayisha. "What ails the lass?"

Ayisha finished the last of her rashers and eggs and touched a napkin to her mouth. "She's in love."

"God's me! In love?" Pegeen blinked as the truth dawned. "You don't dare to tell me it's with that pompous fop of a popinjay who took her out yesterday!"

Ayisha grinned. "That's the one." It described Jeremy well.

As she cantered through Adair pine forests overlooking the sea, Ayisha wondered what Pegeen would think of her pirate. For certain, not a pompous fop of a popinjay. Nay, this one was a man. She laughed, remembering the look on his face when he'd spied her, and she marveled that she had thought of naught but him ever since their encounter. She had even dreamt about him last night, and in her dream as well as her memories of him, he was always a pirate. Not that she had ever, in her many sea journeys with her father, seen a pirate. It was just that he looked as she imagined a pirate might look—tall, whipcord lean, sun darkened, naked to the waist, a scarlet band taming his coppery, wind-whipped hair, a dangerous light in his dark eyes . . .

She shivered, a delicious sort of shiver, and wondered

who he was. The question pounded through her with every thud of Satan's hooves. His vessel had been called the *Sea Eagle*, and she had assumed, from his air of command, that he was the captain. But then perhaps he was not. Perhaps he was the cook or the helmsman or a foremastman. It mattered naught. All that mattered, quite simply, was that he was the most gorgeous thing she had ever seen.

It had been a long day, and Ben was tired. He reflected wistfully how eager he had been in earlier days to serve his new land and his new city in any way he could. He had encouraged one and all to come to him—tradesmen, churchmen, neighbors, his fellow businessmen. He had been so grateful for his own new life, there was naught he wouldn't do to help his fellow man get ahead. It had helped soften his guilt over the *Bluebird*, but only a bit. Not a day went by that he did not mourn his lost crew and think how different things would have been had he not taken to piracy and not been so damned greedy for one last chance at booty. But then he would not have met Ana nor had his two precious jewels. Nay, it was to be. It was his kismet that things had gone as they had. It was written in his forehead.

Now twenty years had passed. He was old and he was weary, yet folks still needed him for one thing or another. He had made himself indispensable, it seemed, and he would be on call for the people of Boston until he closed his eyes for the last time. But for the rest of the day, he told himself firmly, they could damned well do without him. Today he was going to leave early, go home, go for that sail with Ayisha, and then have a hearty dinner to please Pegeen. Aye. He was looking forward to both and naught was going to prevent it. Not even God himself. As he began clearing his desk, a tall stranger appeared suddenly in the office door that always stood open. Ben looked up scowling.

"Mr. Adair?"

"Aye?"

Cain had been ready to conclude his business activities

for the day when he spied the office for Adair Enterprises and stayed his step. Ben Adair was a man several others had advised him to see, so why not now? But he quickly sensed that the man behind the desk was about to do what he himself yearned to do—quit early and head for a pub. He smiled and held out his hand. "Sir, I'm Cain Banning of Banning Limited, Southampton. We're shipbuilders, and we're thinking of opening a new yard in Boston. I'd like to discuss it with you. Could we set up a time for tomorrow?"

Ben rose, met the stranger's penetrating blue eyes and returned his hard handshake. God above. Even in his very proper business attire, this young Banning minded him of open seas and billowing sails and spray stinging his face. Now why in blue blazes couldn't his girls bring home someone like this instead of a damned dawcock like Greydon? In fact, why didn't he just take the lad home himself? For a fact, they'd swoon dead away, both of them, if they clapped eyes on him. He cleared his throat, offered a silent prayer that the fellow was not wed or affianced and said, "I'd like very much to talk to you about your business, young man, but I'm ready to close shop for the day. Why not come to dinner and we can talk afterwards?" As the man's brows met over his deep blue eyes, Ben gazed at him in puzzlement. Now where had he seen such eyes before? They looked familiar—but then his own eyes were not as sharp as they used to be. He was probably mistaken.

"That's kind of you," Cain said. "Are you sure it won't be any trouble?"

"No trouble. Always plenty of food in the house. Plenty."

"Then I'd be pleased to accept. If you'll give me directions . . ."

Ben sensed a slight hesitancy. "Is there a problem?"

Seeing the candor in the older man's eyes, Cain was forthright. "I'd be grateful if you could include my mate, Seth Duncan. We've been at sea for a month and he'd appreciate home cooking as much as I would."

"It's done," Ben said. "Where are you lodging? I'll send a carriage for you. Eight o'clock."

"Sir, there's no need . . ."

"It's best. The streets are not safe at night and the way is strange to you. I'm on a bluff overlooking the sea and it'll be pitch black when you leave."

Cain grinned. "You've talked me into it. We're at the Red Horse on King Street. And thank you, sir. I'll look forward to it."

Seth gazed at the fragrant pine woods without seeing them as their carriage rocked and creaked its way up the narrow road to the summit. He muttered, "I've thought of naught but her all day."

"I've thought of her, too," Cain admitted. In truth, his head had been filled with the memory of their glorious sea sprite. "I guess you still think she's Ana's daughter."

"Aye. Now if only her devil father is still alive and if only we see her again—and we're in a position to follow her. I haunted the docks but there wasn't a sign of her."

"Did you ask anyone about her?"

"Everyone. No one's ever seen such a person."

"Strange. I'd've guessed she was on water more than land."

"Maybe they know her and are protecting her."

"It wouldn't surprise me."

Seth gave a long, low whistle as their destination came into sight. "Sweet Jesus, look at this, will you? Your Mr. Adair knows how to live."

Looking out the carriage window, Cain was surprised to see a vast stone dwelling with ivied turrets, parapets, diamond-paned windows, and sheep grazing on the greensward. It was an honest-to-God medieval castle. He, too, gave a low whistle. "He didn't strike me as the castle type. I guess I was wrong."

As the carriage rolled to a stop, a footman appeared, opened the door, and helped them out. Several large dogs, smiling, tails wagging, came to greet them. A great oaken door swung open to reveal a butler of great dignity in full livery. "Good evening, gentlemen, please follow me. Mr. Adair will be with you shortly."

Ben appeared just then, coming from the back of the house. "I'm here, Soames." He smiled, shook hands with the two graciously. "Glad to have you, son—and you, Mr. Duncan. I just got back from a sail and I'd like to change. It won't take a minute. Seat them on the terrace, Soames, and get them something to drink. White wine for me. Excuse me, gentlemen?"

"Of course." Seeing that Seth was staring after their host as he mounted the curving staircase, Cain said, "Are you coming, man?"

"Aye."

When they were alone on the stone terrace sipping their drinks, Cain looked about and said quietly, "What do you think—is this as close as we'll get to royalty in the colonies?"

He reckoned that the old boy was worth millions and decided it would be nice, it would be very nice indeed, to watch the sun rise over the sea every morn from this terrace. The sea. He took another swallow of his drink and thought, brooding, that it was the one way, the only way he was like his father. The sea was in his blood, and he knew well that if he ever yielded to its call to far places, he was lost. He would be another wandering Gregg man.

Aware suddenly of Seth's taut face and continuing silence, Cain walked over to him, lowered his voice, and said "Man, what is it? Have we found him?"

"I'm—not sure," Seth muttered. "I thought so at first but now I'm not sure . . ."

"He's got blue eyes, he's six feet, and he could pass for a bishop," Cain kept his voice hushed. "And he has money. Tons of money."

"It's too easy. He can't have fallen into our laps our second day here. Things don't work that way. At least not for me, they don't."

"Maybe your luck's due to change—and don't forget, you've put in twenty years already." But he hoped Seth was mistaken. He'd taken a liking to Ben Adair. Any man who would invite two complete strangers into his home and feed them was damned decent.

Seth emptied his wineglass and said under his breath, "He's coming. Let's find out if he has a daughter."

Ben came toward them smiling and dressed now in elegant formal attire. "Sit down, gentlemen. Make yourselves comfortable. More wine?" He watched as Soames came bearing cut crystal decanters on a teak tray and filled their glasses. He sat, took a sip of his wine, and said, "So, when did you two arrive in Boston?"

"Late yesterday afternoon." Cain was remembering a pair of tawny eyes, hair like dark flame, a teasing smile, a wave . . .

"Are you in shipbuilding also, Mr. Duncan?"

"Nay, Mr. Adair, I haul cargo." Seth was experiencing a rare headiness as Ben Adair's blue eyes and voice grew more and more familiar.

It was some moments before Ben said quietly, "I used to do a bit of hauling myself in my youth. It's a good way to see the world."

"It is that," Seth said gravely, his gaze drawn suddenly to the French doors which opened onto the terrace. A maid stood there with a tall, fair-haired man behind her. When she made a small sound of exclamation, their host rose, went to her, and caught her hand.

"Darlin', join us."

"I—didn't mean to interrupt, Papa."

"Interrupt? God bless my soul, I've been hoping you'd get home from your party in time for dinner with our guests. Come and meet them. This is Mr. Banning and Mr. Duncan. They arrived in Boston yesterday from Southampton. Gentlemen, my daughter Aimee and her friend, Jeremy Greydon."

Cain bowed and mouthed the appropriate words, but he was stunned. It was his sea nymph. Which meant, God help her, God help all of them, that they had found their prey. Ben Adair, with his churchman's face and his kind blue eyes and generous hospitality was the pirate, Ben Scott. But as Aimee drew near, smiled shyly, and gave him her hand, Cain saw that she was not at all the maid he had met at sea. She looked like her, aye, but the fire was not there. Not in her eyes, not in her hair, not in her spirit. Aimee Adair was but a pale shadow of the girl who had so electrified him yesterday. Knowing that no two maids could so resemble each other without being sisters, Cain felt a sense of mounting anticipation.

Ben had not missed the widening of his daughter's eyes as she smiled and gave both tall Englishmen her hand and curtsied. Relief swam through his veins as he realized it was happening just as he'd hoped. She had seen the difference between these two and the dandy she had in tow. Feeling munificent, he said: "Greydon, you're welcome to stay to dinner if you like." He half hoped the fellow would accept, if only to be found lacking in comparison.

"Thank you, sir, I will. It's kind of you."

"Fix yourself a drink. Wine, ale, gin, rum . . ."

"Thank you, sir."

Cain saw immediately that Ben Adair did not like the man. His voice and his manner were polite, but he didn't like him. And Cain himself did not like the stunned look in Seth's eyes as he stared at Aimee. He was pondering it when Ben turned toward the terrace doors and again held out a welcoming hand.

"So, darlin', here you are . . ."

Cain's heart lurched as he saw who stood there. It was as he'd suspected—Ben Adair had a second daughter. And as he'd suspected, it was she who was his sea nymph. Slender and wand straight, she carried herself as if aware of her sovereignty. Her mass of mahogany hair, cascading down her back and over her breasts, was a striking contrast to the bottle green silk gown she wore. And her eyes . . . in God's name, what color were they? He decided they were gold—amber gold, as if the afterglow of the sun were imprisoned inside their depths. Meeting them, he was enchanted by the vivacity he saw there, the boldness and hidden laughter. She was just the sort of maid who would ignore danger—or go out of her way to seek it.

"My love, this is Mr. Duncan. Seth, my daughter, Ayisha. Ayisha, meet Mr. Banning. Cain, my daughter, Ayisha."

Ayisha. The name was as beautiful as its bearer. "Miss Adair, it's my great pleasure." Lifting her small soft hand to his lips, Cain caught an elusive but tantalizing scent of jasmine.

"Mr. Banning, how lovely, actually meeting you . . ." Ayisha's lips curved as she marked the dazed look in Cain Banning's eyes. "I hope you're not still angry with me."

Walking onto the terrace and seeing him there, she had blinked in disbelief. Da had said they were having guests to dinner but for it to be him—her pirate. He was dressed now in very conservative evening attire and his thick chestnut hair was caught back by a narrow black ribbon instead of a scarlet sash. Her head felt so light suddenly she feared for a moment she would faint, but she clenched her teeth, lifted her chin, and walked firmly across the terrace. She was surprised to see that his eyes were blue, so deep a blue they were almost purple, and he was taller than she had imagined. The top of her head came only to his chin.

Ben scowled at his older daughter's pink face and at the small flickering muscle in their guest's jaw. "What's this? You've already met?"

When Cain Banning remained silent, his eyes locked on hers, Ayisha said, "No, we haven't really *met*, Da. We— passed at sea."

"Did you now?" For many years, he had allowed this headstrong daughter of his to sail when and where she chose, for her ability was the equal of any man he knew— but she knew he did not like her in the shipping lanes. And there was nowhere else they could have passed each other.

Cain crossed his arms and continued to gaze at the maid, his mouth tilted. She had begun it, let her finish it. And if she left out any of the pertinent details, he would damned well supply them. But he would do it later. He had no wish to embarrass her before this small gathering.

"When Mac and I were out yesterday," Ayisha began,

"we sailed around Lovell Island—it's so beautiful there."
In the silence that had fallen, she smiled up into that
steady blue gaze and said easily, "There was never any
danger, Mr. Banning."

"Wasn't there, Miss Adair?"

"I promise you there wasn't." Ayisha could still see him
at the rail—broad shoulders, lean, sun-darkened torso, the
red band about his hair. "I know what I can do and what
my craft can do." Seeing the bewilderment on her father's
face, she said lightly, "We were bound for the same spot,
Da. I—got there before he did."

Seeing that she considered the incident a lark, Cain
could not remain silent. He said low, for her father's ears,
"Sir, she cut across my bow."

"With room to spare!"

"You came dangerously close to being rammed, Miss
Adair. In case you don't know, the wind is capricious."

Ayisha felt her blood running hotter. "I know about
wind, Mr. Banning."

Ben muttered, "Now, girl, you know I don't like you in
the sea lanes."

"I've sailed in the sea lanes for years, Da." She gave
Cain Banning a frigid look. "I've just never—raced anyone there before."

Cain's smile was wintry. What she meant was, she had
never been caught before.

For her father's sake, Ayisha struggled to contain her
temper. She returned their guest's cool smile and said
meekly, "I'm terribly sorry if I caused you concern."

Cain felt his knees turning to water. She enchanted and
intrigued him, but he could not be soft with her. He and
Seth were about to tear her world apart and destroy the
only life she and her sister had ever known. He dared not
be soft with her nor allow himself to be drawn to her. He
said crisply: "My concern is that you'll do it again, Miss
Adair. With grave consequences."

Ayisha's smile froze on her lips. "I've been sailing since
I was seven winters, Mr. Banning. Please don't waste any
sleep over me."

Cain bent to her ear and caught an intoxicating whiff of jasmine. "If you've been sailing since you were seven winters, lady, there's less excuse than ever for your recklessness. My vessel had the right of way. You should know that. If you don't, you'd better learn it. And your father should clip your wings until you learn proper respect for the sea."

His rudeness left Ayisha speechless. Before she could recover her wits and her tongue, Soames had appeared.

"Dinner is served."

"Good." Ben quickly took his daughter's arm. "Come along now, everyone. I'm sure we're all hungry."

Chapter 4

Ayisha was amazed to see the dining chamber ablaze with candles and their very finest linen draping the table. In addition, the places were set with the best of her mother's crystal, china, and silver, and the sideboard, lit by two bronze candelabra, was heaped with food seen only on special occasions—roast poultry and beef, meat and cheese tarts, vegetables, soup, salads, and such an array of sweets she could scarcely take them all in. But then it was a special occasion. These were the first guests to dine at Seacliff since her mother's death. She pursed her lips. What a pity that one of them should be a boor like Cain Banning.

She was still simmering. So he thought she should have her wings clipped, did he? And to think, she had actually been attracted to the man. Watching Peronelle and Nicole serve, and noting their stolen glances at him and their pink cheeks and bright eyes, she was hugely annoyed. Doubtless he was used to women falling at his feet, but she certainly was not going to be one of them. In fact, she was not even going to speak to him or look at him the rest of the evening.

She gazed coolly about the table, at Aimee—rosy, glowing, so beautiful in her gown of daffodil yellow. Jeremy—his aristocratic nose pinched at the nostrils. Ayisha smiled. She knew the look well. He was jealous. Jealous of Seth Duncan sitting to her left, and jealous of the pirate in the seat of honor to her right at the end of the table. Her eyes moved on to her father, resplendent in satin and ruffles and beaming benevolently on them all. Her heart warmed. She had not seen him so happy or contented in months.

She knew then that she could not spoil his evening by continuing her silent battle with Cain Banning. The man was a guest in her home, after all, and she would not be petty. She would be pleasant to him if it killed her. Turning to him, she saw that his dark gaze was fastened determinedly on the row of candles down the center of the table. It was clear he was as bent on ignoring her as she was him. She leaned toward him and said softly, "Once again, Mr. Banning, I must apologize. I shouldn't have turned our meeting into a race."

Cain had willed her to disregard him for the remainder of the evening. With that having failed, he answered crisply, "I hope you mean that, Miss Adair. It was a damned fool thing to do."

She could scarce believe his continuing rudeness. It infuriated her. Why even bother to be civil to such a boor, she fumed, when it was obvious he hated her? She bit her tongue against a sharp retort and told herself to let it lie. For Da's sake, let it lie. She said naught. She gave Cain Banning her sweetest smile and returned her attention to the food on her plate.

Cain cursed himself. He had not missed her shock nor the battle she had fought to allow his oafishness to pass. Damnation, what an impossible evening this was turning out to be. It was not in him to be rude to anyone, especially a woman, yet he continued to batter her feelings as if she were his worst enemy instead of a soft young maid who was his hostess. It could not go on. He had to make amends. He took a sip of burgundy and said quietly, "My men greatly admired your sailing, Miss Adair." He watched her raise disbelieving eyes that glowed gold in the candlelight. He stared. She was incredible. Those eyes, the beauty of her face, the flame-streaked auburn mane tumbling about her shoulders . . .

Ayisha said softly, "You don't like me, Mr. Banning, and I certainly don't like you, so please don't patronize me."

Her bluntness caught Cain off guard but only for an instant. He replied easily, "I understand well why you don't like me. I don't blame you, but you're wrong about my not liking you. I do, you know, and God forbid I should patronize you. I thought it fitting you knew my men said you sailed like an angel—even though you did give us one hell of a scare." He watched, enthralled, as her disbelief turned to astonishment and then delight. The storm was over. He saw her rosy lips part, saw a flash of soft white throat as she threw back her head and emitted low, musical laughter.

Ayisha could not resist asking, "And what did the captain think?" She shook her head then. "Nay, I take it back. Don't tell me. I'll stop while I'm ahead."

Cain said drily, "The captain had never seen an angel sail—'till yesterday. He agrees with them."

She looked down at her plate, face flaming. He needn't have said a word of this, but he had—and he'd said he liked her. And she believed him. It made up for everything. She murmured, "It was rude of me to say I didn't like you. I'm sorry. I was angry."

"I'll not accept any apology."

She met his eyes. They were the deep blue of twilight just before night fell and they held a surprising gentleness. Confused, she murmured, "It was a terrible thing to say to a—a guest."

"I doubt you've ever had such a rude guest."

Ayisha blinked. "Maybe we should start over . . ."

Cain felt his doom closing in on him as he sank deeper into those flame gold eyes. He said huskily, "I'd like that."

She gave him her hand and clasped his firmly. "I'm Ayisha Adair. How lovely actually meeting you."

Cain said gravely, "It's my great pleasure, Miss Adair. I'm Cain Banning and I apologize for being a brute."

"I apologize for nearly running you down yesterday. I promise I'll be more careful in the future." At least with him she would.

"And I promise you, I'll sleep more easily." Holding her

hand, he wondered how anything so small and soft could be so strong and competent.

Ayisha's eyes danced over his somber dark face and thick chestnut hair. She remembered it without the ribbon. "I have to confess, when I saw you at the rail of the *Sea Eagle* without a shirt and with that red band around your head, I thought you'd make a grand pirate."

"Did you now?" Cain bared his teeth in a smile, but her words chilled him. He wondered how much she knew about her father's past. "So what do you think now that I'm on land with more clothes on?"

She studied his heavy lidded night blue eyes. "I'd have to say you look like one still. You have quite a dangerous look about you, you know." She grinned. "Quite intriguing."

Cain's teeth grated. If this wasn't the damndest conversation he'd ever had. And the damndest two days he'd ever spent. He said carefully, "You seem to have firsthand information about pirates."

Ayisha shook her head. "Not really. I've never even seen one though I sail with Da frequently. I guess it's because our vessels are so heavily armed."

"It sounds as if your father is a wise man." Unless she was an exceptional actress, she was as unaware of Ben Adair's past and the horror it held as he himself had been of his father's past. And he wondered, Was there no way she and her sister could be spared what was to come? But he knew there was not, not if he and Seth followed the course they had planned. Now the very thought of it stole his appetite. "You say you sail with your father?"

"Aye. I go with him frequently on buying trips."

Cain could not imagine such a thing until he remembered she was his sea sprite. "Do you enjoy being on a large vessel as much as your sailboat?"

Ayisha smiled. "I love anything to do with the sea. I'm far happier on water than on land—except for when I'm on a horse."

Gazing on her shining eyes and beautiful, animated face, Cain felt a sudden closeness toward her. She had just named the two things he loved most in this world. But never had he admitted to anyone, hardly even to himself, his intense yearning for the sea. He said gravely, "You're a very unusual woman, Miss Adair."

"Please, Ayisha."

He nodded. "Cain."

"My family calls me Pan, too, short for Pandora." She wrinkled her nose. "That's Da's doing."

Cain grinned. "Ayisha's the perfect name for you." He liked the sound of it and the way it felt on his lips.

"What is your work, Mr. Banning?" Aimee asked suddenly.

Cain was glad to be drawn from his bewitchment. He replied almost gruffly, "I'm a shipbuilder, Miss Adair."

He suspected she was holding hands beneath the table with Greydon. Her every glance toward him was worshipful. He devoutly hoped it meant she was spoken for since Seth could not tear his eyes from her. Hell, for the old boy to fall head over heels in love with Ben Scott's daughter would wreak all kinds of havoc with their plans. That he himself was intrigued by Ayisha was misfortune enough.

"How very interesting," Aimee bubbled. "Jeremy has a very successful import-export company. He always has ships coming and going from all over the world." She looked at Seth Duncan shyly. "What is your work, Mr. Duncan?"

"I haul cargo," Seth said. "Worldwide." He added hoarsely, "Call me Seth."

"Do call me Aimee, Seth."

"I'd like that. It's a beautiful name—Aimee . . ."

"My goodness, how sweet of you."

Ayisha was thrilled. Her sister's face was flooded with color of a sudden and her eyes said that she was fascinated by their tall, sandy-haired dinner guest. Ayisha herself had immediately liked the openness and honesty of Seth Duncan's face and his gray eyes. He looked safe—solid and strong and comfortable and safe. Like a fortress. Cain Banning, on the other hand . . .

She stole a sidelong look at him as he talked to her father. He, too, was solid and strong, aye, but there was more. He had that tantalizing aura of danger about him— danger and power and mystery and excitement. He was the open welcoming sea under a shining sun, but with a storm and an unknown adventure on the horizon. How strange that he should remind her of the very things she was drawn to. Her heart beat harder, and she was gladder than glad that they had started over.

"Are you in Boston on business, Banning?" Jeremy Greydon spoke for the first time.

"Aye," Cain replied shortly. Ben Scott was not the only one who did not like this dandy. Cain did not like him either.

"Is this your first visit?" Aimee asked.

"I was in port many years ago as an apprentice seaman. I never got to see the city."

"This time you must. Boston is beautiful."

"What I've seen, I like." He marveled at how very much she resembled her sister, yet he sensed they were as different as day and night. As beautiful as Aimee was, he did not feel for her the hot current of excitement that Ayisha's nearness sent crackling through him.

"What of you, Seth?" Aimee fixed her melting brown eyes on him. "Have you been to Boston before?"

Seth smiled. "At least ten times. It's grown huge since my first visit. Were you born here?"

"Aye, both my sister and I are born and bred Bostonians, Papa's from England, and Mama was—from Turkey. He met her there when he was hauling cargo."

In the silence that fell, Ben said thickly, "My wife passed on two years ago."

Seth muttered, "I'm sorry. Truly."

"My sympathy," Cain said and meant it. Seth, he knew, was deeply shaken.

As the conversation resumed and moved to politics and the weather and business, Ayisha listened politely, but her entire awareness was focused on the man beside her. Her every sense was electrified by him and filled with him. It was more than his exciting appearance—his dangerously handsome face and wide shoulders and intelligent, dark eyes, more than the sound of his deep, articulate voice and the remembered touch of his big, warm hand holding hers. It was as if she had found, for the first time in her life, someone like herself, as if they were two of a kind. She felt comfortable with him. At ease with him. Safe. How very odd, she thought, raising her glass to her lips. Her hand shook.

Seeing it, and sensing she was thinking of her mother, Cain yearned to comfort her. It had been many years since his own mother had died, but he still remembered the void her passing had left inside of him. He lowered his voice, "I wish I could wave a wand and take away the hurt."

"Thank you." She bit her lip. She would not blurt out the truth, that it was he who was making her tremble, not thoughts of her mother. She would not, dared not tell him that. She would hate herself if she did. But why not tell him part of the truth? Just part. Why not tell him he was kind and she liked him. Why not? The words grew more and more irresistible, playing over her tongue, tempting, taunting, teasing, daring her. Damn, she couldn't *not* say them. She swallowed, plunged, "It was good of you to say that—about my mother. It was kind. I—like you, Cain Banning. I like you very much." Oh, heavens, she had done it. She'd gone and blabbed it and now he was probably scared away forever.

"You honor me."

Cain was floored. He knew full well what courage it had taken her to admit such a thing, and he was overwhelmed by guilt. Here they were, she and Aimee, still grieving over their mother, and now he and Seth were about to rob them of their father—and probably everything they owned, including Seacliff. The Crown would seize everything, and with good reason, he had to remind himself sharply. The luxury in which they lived had been bought with the loot plundered from the *Safira*'s helpless passengers, and it had been safeguarded by the deaths of an entire shipload of men. He must never forget that, nor forget the sharks—nor the frightful death his own father had died.

"I do miss my mother terribly," Ayisha said, tracing the gold rim of her goblet with a finger. "I have to remind myself constantly that she had a wonderful life. She loved us deeply and we loved her, and she adored this house and this town—and the town loved her. Few are so fortunate in life."

"That's so," Cain said. And because of him, she would not be one of those few. It cut through him like a knife.

Jeremy Greydon did not like either Englishman. Cain Banning had that calm, easy air of power and authority about him that raised his hackles, and Seth Duncan minded him of a lovesick ox. But then the fellow was a nobody who needn't concern him. Besides, he had Aimee well under his thumb. Nay, it was this wolf, Banning, who made him uneasy. He did not like the hungry way he looked at Ayisha.

As he listened vaguely to the conversation, his thoughts drifted to Ben Adair and his fortune. And it was a fortune. The old boy was a shrewd businessman who owned part or all of more companies than any other man in Boston. A bank, trading and fishing fleets, a shipyard and several of its affiliated industries—he was into everything. And Jeremy had seen that the way to the pot of gold was to wed one of Ben's daughters. And none too soon. His own creaky old devil of a father was too mean to die. He would outlast them all and keep him on the same tight rein forever. At least none knew of his humiliation. All in Boston thought it was he himself who was running the business. Begod, it was a crime. He was tired of waiting to claim what should have been his years ago. The stingy old bastard.

But these maids—Jeremy's pale eyes slid over them—were both beauties, thank God, for he would have pursued them in any event. Ayisha had been his first choice, but that was water over the dam. Aimee was far better suited to his purpose. She was docile, pliable, and eager to please him—all the things Ayisha was not. And she was hungry for him. Pressing his leg against her soft thigh, he felt her tremble and seek his hand. The wench wanted him, there was no doubt. And after they were wed, he would see to it that Ayisha paid in full for leading him on and making a fool of him. It still infuriated him to think how she had jilted him. Perhaps a boating or a riding accident . . .

In the meantime, this Banning was a man to watch. He saw in him the first threat to his carefully laid plan since he had first conceived it. He damned well did not intend to share his future wealth with a second son-in-law. He lay down his knife and fork, wiped his mouth on his napkin and said, "I had a vessel repaired last summer at your yards in Southampton, Banning. You have a very successful operation going there. How many ships do you turn out a year?"

"Fourteen."

"Admirable." Jeremy felt a trifle ill, for it was a large number. Ben Adair would be impressed. "Are you the sole owner?"

"My uncle and I own it jointly."

"I see." He felt a quickening of anger seeing how Ayisha was looking at him. The little bitch had never looked at him that way. Keeping his voice level, he asked, "Were you thinking of locating in Boston?"

"We hope to."

Jeremy yearned to tell him to keep his damned shipyard in England, he wasn't wanted here, but he could not do such a thing. In fact, his throat was so tight, he could not make any reply at all and signaled Peronelle to bring him more wine. As he drank it, he brooded that this day which had begun with such promise was ending with a threat he never could have imagined—a threat he must deal with immediately. He would send a man back to England on the very next sailing to look into Banning's background. There was not a man alive who did not have something to hide—and if worse came to worst, there was always Cuba. He made a monthly run to the island and traded more than goods when he was there. If he meant to possess the entire Adair fortune, he'd have no qualms whatsoever about pressing the bastard and selling him into indenture. No qualms whatsoever.

It was past midnight when Ben Adair's carriage deposited his dinner guests at their lodgings in the Red Horse. They had made the journey in stunned silence, and upon reaching their chamber and mending the fire they sank into two chairs before the hearth and stared at each other numbly.

Seth muttered, "God Almighty, can you believe it?"

Cain let out a long, ragged breath, shook his head, and gazed at the flames. He was unwilling to talk or even think about the evening that had just ended. It seemed like a dream now, filled as it was with soft eyes, soft lips, soft skin, a soft body, flame-kissed hair ... He pushed the heady thought of her away. The dream was ended and this was reality. He was awake and back in the world.

Seth was destroyed. He leaned forward, elbows on his knees and his sandy head bowed in his big hands. "Man, man, man, now what?"

"We have to rethink."

Cain yearned to dump the whole mess into Seth's hands, for without him, it never would have come about. But that was not true. It had been there all along, rotting and festering, a continuing nightmare for the families of the men who had gone to sea and never come home because of Ben Scott and Tom Gregg, families who had lost the strong right arms of husbands, sons, and brothers.

"After all these years of wanting revenge," Seth muttered, "feeling it, smelling it, tasting it, I actually have the black-hearted bastard in my hands, and what does he do? He betrays me again." He shook his shaggy head and ran a big hand over his beard. "Daughters, by God. Two of the fairest, sweetest maids a man could ever hope to see. Caesar's ghost, what are we to do? Did you ever see anything so beautiful? And did you see the way she looked at me?"

Cain was sinking deeper into his own gloom. "Aye, and I saw the way you looked at her." He saw, too, in the dark reaches of his mind, his father's last terrified hours. He said gruffly, "He's got to pay."

Seth gave him a distraught look. "I know it, but everything has changed. Those blessed maids . . ."

"Aye." His mate was so affected by Aimee that he'd not noticed Cain's own dilemma—or that Ayisha was by far the fairer of the two maids. "I'd say now that we shouldn't rush into anything."

Seth nodded. "Aye. We should go slow. We have more to consider now than we did before." It was a far cry from clapping Ben Scott into the hold and dragging him before the Crown in leg irons.

Cain said glumly, "If we destroy him, we destroy them." And that he would not have.

Seth gazed mournfully into the fire and cracked his knuckles. "How about if we demand compensation for the crew and naught else?" His innards quaked when Cain gave him a hard look with eyes that reminded him of Tom Gregg.

"That's it? You don't even want to plot some way to ruin him financially?"

"That's it. I'd get no pleasure from the bastard's being destitute if it means those two will suffer." Seth knew it was not fair, weighing the happiness of two maids against the tragedy faced by the dead men's kin. Those folk had been waiting these many years to hear that Ben Scott and Tom Gregg had departed this life at the end of a rope. But damn it, he didn't care. He would not hurt those maids for the world. Seeing Cain's somber face, he asked anxiously, "What do you think?"

Imagining the two women disgraced and homeless and

at the mercy of the brutes who prowled the streets of every city, Cain felt a profound sense of relief. He said, "Fair compensation is enough."

Remembering his earlier worries about his new mate, Seth breathed more easily. "Good. And how about if we say naught to Ben for awhile yet? I'd—like to get to know Aimee better first." He was hoping—hell, he didn't know what he was hoping. He knew only that he did not want to begin the assault on her father immediately.

Cain shrugged. "Take your time. My visit here will probably be a lengthy one with all the people and places and things I have to see. I've told my men to take any odd jobs that suit them."

Seth rose and began to prowl the room. "I might as well tell you, man—when I saw Aimee, it fair knocked the pins out from under me. I could love her." Ignoring Cain's wintry gaze, he added, "And the way she looked at me, I think she could love me. It's a thing I want to explore. She asked me back tomorrow eve and I accepted."

Cain had heard. She wanted him to see three robins she had been caring for. He said, "Ayisha wants to show me their horses."

"Come along with me tomorrow then."

"Nay," Cain said quickly. "I accepted without thinking, but I'm not going back."

Marking the flush on his friend's dark face, Seth said softly, "She'll be hurt if you don't."

And hurt if he did, Cain thought angrily, remembering her confession. She liked him, and God knows, he liked her. There was something special between them, they both had felt it. He shook his head. "It wouldn't be wise."

Seth sat down again in front of the fire. "Suit yourself. I guess I have faith that things will work out." He gave the log a thoughtful poke. "What do you think of Greydon?"

"I wouldn't turn my back on him."

Seth nodded. "Nor I. He bears watching." He sighed,

thinking of the fellow in his fancy clothes looking like the angel Gabriel himself, all beautiful and shining. And here he was, about to blackmail his new love's father. It wasn't fair . . .

Chapter 5

Ayisha was finishing her breakfast when her sister wandered out onto the terrace in her nightdress and robe. "Good morning, honey." She gave her a smile.

Aimee yawned. "G'morning." She gazed blearily at the green Atlantic glittering under the morning sun, sank into a cushioned chair and murmured, "How long have you been up?"

"Not long." Ayisha poured a cup of tea and took it to her. "Didn't you sleep well?"

"Not too well." Aimee closed her eyes against the dazzle and took a grateful sip. "Thanks. It tastes good."

Ayisha poured a cup for herself and returned to her chair. She mused that her own sleep had been fitful. She had dreamt the night long of a pirate with midnight blue eyes and coppery hair. "I never heard about your party yesterday with Jeremy. Was it fun?"

"Oh, aye. Great fun."

Aimee kept her eyes closed. Her head had been whirling when she went to bed last night and it was still spinning. She had thought, when she came home from the party with Jeremy Greydon, that he was the answer to every dream she'd ever had. Not once had he left her side, and he'd told her over and over how beautiful she was. And she had felt beautiful. For the first time in her life, she had felt beautiful. And then, then, in her very own house, she had met a tall, sandy-haired stranger with gray eyes who had made her feel as if she were the only woman on this earth.

She was so confused at this point that she could scarcely think straight.

"Last night was great fun, too, wasn't it?" Ayisha asked quietly. She was hoping for a miracle, something that would take Jeremy out of Aimee's life and put Seth into it.

"Aye." It sighed out as Aimee remembered those gray eyes burning through her. "Our guests were—quite something."

Ayisha grinned. "Weren't they though . . ."

"When Cain Banning turned into an iceberg and your eyes started to shoot sparks, I thought the whole evening was ruined."

"So did I. But we started over and everything got smoothed out." She asked casually, "Did you like Seth?"

"He's—different from Jeremy."

"Very different." Ayisha took another swallow of tea. "He seemed much taken with you."

"I know." Aimee had tried to tell herself the lovely warmth she'd felt bubbling through her during dinner was from Jeremy's hand slipping unexpectedly over her thigh, but she knew it was not. It was the heat from Seth Duncan's eyes. She sipped her tea and said finally in a small voice, "I'm afraid I like him too much, Pan."

Ayisha was thrilled. "How could you possibly like him too much?"

"I fear he's like a ship passing in the night. He'll be gone soon and I'll never see him again."

A ship passing in the night. It was a thing Ayisha had never even considered in her eagerness for Jeremy to be banished from Aimee's life and for Seth Duncan to take his place. She said gently, "Maybe he's looking for a safe harbor."

"Oh, aye, and maybe a pig could fly."

Pegeen Fitzgerald appeared bearing two small crystal fruit bowls on a napkin-covered tray. "Here's some lovely fresh compote from Cook, my chickies,"—she looked from one lovely face to the other—"and I want every bite eaten. And while I'm thinking of it, those were two grand gentlemen who came last night. Handsome and polite and respectful, unlike some I could name, and I do like to see a man who dresses sensibly."

Ayisha swallowed her laughter, but Pegeen had mirrored her own thoughts exactly. She said gravely, "Then you'll be happy to know Cain's coming this eve to see the horses."

"God's me!"

"And Seth's coming to see my robins . . ."

Pegeen glowed. "Well, there!"

Aimee added loyally, "But I still think Jeremy dresses divinely."

"And I say a man should look like a man. Now eat your fruit. It will put roses in your cheeks."

Ayisha took a taste. "It's wonderful, but Mac's waiting for me. Save it for me for later, please?"

"I'll eat mine later, too," Aimee said. "I have to feed my babies. They're hungry all the time now."

The sun was still high in the west when Aimee looked in on Ayisha and saw that she still wore trews, an old faded blue shirt, and boots. "Pan! For goodness' sake, have you forgotten? Seth and Cain will be here any minute! Aren't you going to dress?" She had never known a maid to think less about her clothing and hair and nails than Ayisha.

Ayisha blinked. "I hadn't planned to. Cain's coming to see the horses, and we'll probably ride."

"Ride? After sitting on a horse for half an hour to get here? I thought he was going to look at them. If he wants to see their paces, can't Mac show him?"

Ayisha saw instantly the reasonableness of her words. "You're right. I should change."

"I'll be on the terrace." Aimee blew her a kiss and was gone.

As she tugged off her old clothes, Ayisha decided she was being ridiculous. She was nervous enough about seeing Cain Banning again without the awkwardness of being in a gown. Voluminous skirts that swished did not go well with horses—she would frighten them. But studying herself in the looking glass, she knew Aimee was right. She looked like a ragamuffin. She had to change. She quickly pulled off her shirt, trews, and boots, performed a hasty toilette with cold water, and quickly slipped into her undergarments and a silk tangerine-colored gown. After hurriedly tugging a brush through her hair, she ran down to the terrace.

Aimee smiled. "That's much much better, and I do love that gown." Hearing the approach of horses, she felt a shiver of anticipation. "You're just in time! They're coming! Oh, Panny, my heart's going so fast, I'm going to die of excitement! I can't bear it! Shall we go out front and meet them or will we seem too eager?"

"It's perfectly all right to greet them. It's good manners. Come on."

But Ayisha was uneasy suddenly. What if Aimee were right about liking Seth too much? Perhaps he was a ship in the night. But at this point, it was too late to turn back. They had seen each other, and tonight Seth was going to learn that Aimee was as intrigued by him as he was by her. He would see it in her glowing face and starry eyes. Ayisha feared that she, too, was glowing. Her face felt warm and her heart was thumping. But when she and Aimee got to the front of the house, she saw that her eager anticipation was for naught. Seth Duncan was quite alone.

Ayisha watched as he handed his mount over to a stableboy and turned toward Aimee. Feeling like an interloper, she quickly stepped out of sight. She would not have him seeing her all decked out to greet a man who had not bothered to come. It would be embarrassing for both of them. Hastening to the rear of the house, she stole up to her bedchamber and donned her riding clothes again. But she did not want to ride, nor did she want to sail or read or do much of anything. She just wanted to sit quietly and feel the hurt.

As Seth handed his mount to the groom, he saw Aimee coming toward him, Aimee in a swirling, sea green gown with her brown hair lifting in the wind and a glow in her brown eyes. He took off his hat and clutched it tightly between his hands.

"Good evening, my lady." He wished to heaven his voice would behave and that he would know how to act with her. Did he dare show how much he cared or would it frighten her away? Not knowing the answer, he patted the heads of several dogs who had appeared.

"Mr. Duncan—Seth! H—hello . . ."

Aimee raised her hand in a small, uncertain greeting. She wished to goodness she knew how to act with him. Last night seemed like a dream, the way he had looked at her—like a prince looking at his princess at the end of a fairy tale. Surely she had imagined it all. Nothing that romantic could ever happen to her. She swallowed, cleared her throat. "Thanks for coming."

"Thanks for asking me to come."

His voice was deep and rumbly and made her shiver. "Thanks for wanting to see my robins. No other man would care . . ."

Seth grinned. "I've been looking forward to it." The truth was, he'd given them no thought at all beyond telling Cain about them. His thoughts had been of Aimee alone.

"Well, then, come along." She watched as he stripped off his coat, lay it with his hat on the step, and then rolled up the sleeves of his blue shirt. His forearms were hard and brown and a shadow of fine golden hair lay upon them. She was keenly aware of them and his height as she walked beside him.

"You must be quite an animal lover," Seth said as they entered the stable.

"Oh, aye, I love them all, except I'm afraid to ride the horses, I've fallen so often. But I love them just the same." She pointed to one of the stalls and opened the door a slit. "The babies are in here."

Seth saw that the stall door had netting stretched across its open upper half, and the window to the outside was netted also. He nodded. "The netting's clever. Is it your work?" Her face was a perfect oval and her brown eyes were soft and lustrous. He was shocked by the realization that the maid was more beautiful than her mother had been.

Aimee smiled. "It was my idea, but Mac did it. It's to keep the birds in and the cats out." She dropped to a sitting position in the straw, gathered her skirts close, and patted the spot beside her. "If you'll sit down, they'll come. They're over there." She pointed to a corner. "Don't laugh, but—I chirp to them. They think I'm their mother."

Seth lowered himself to the straw and watched in silent amazement as Aimee, her pink lips puckered, chirped, and the three half-grown robins fluttered over, chirping back and hopping onto her lap, into her hands, allowing her to stroke them. He said gravely, "Is it permissible to smile?"

Aimee giggled. "It's all right—laugh with me, do. They're such silly little things, aren't they? I know they've just eaten, but they're already hungry again."

Seth chuckled, held out his hand. One of the chirping youngsters immediately hopped onto it, followed by the other two. He said carefully, "I guess if they were on their own, they'd be eating all the time."

"Aye. From dawn to dusk."

"Will you free them soon?"

Aimee's face turned solemn. "As soon as I find the heart. I know they're big enough and I do want them to be on their own and happy, but—" She cupped one between her hands and kissed its downy head. "It's so hard . . ."

Seth felt a stab of envy that a bird should be held by her soft hands and be the recipient of a kiss from those rosy lips. He asked low, "Would you like me to help?"

Looking up, Aimee saw in his intense gray eyes a look that had naught to do with birds. She blushed. "It—would be kind of you."

"It would be my pleasure. Would you like to do it now?" He warned himself not to touch her hair nor stroke her soft skin with his fingers.

Aimee drew a deep breath. It was the moment she had been dreading, but with him beside her, perhaps she could face it. She pointed to a brass birdcage in one corner of the stall and murmured, "Aye, please. I'd be grateful. The cage has been sitting there waiting for this day."

"It should do the job just fine." He retrieved it, opened its door, and held it while Aimee, her eyes brimming, collected the robins one by one and slipped them in.

Walking in silence toward a nearby meadow, Seth was nigh overcome by emotion. He had never seen a more beautiful maid, nor one more gentle and tenderhearted. He had told Cain he wanted more time to get to know her, that he could love her, but God's breath, he loved her already. And the way she looked at him had fair lit a fire under him. He was not going to let the lass slip through his fingers because of the circumstances. She could love him, he knew she could. He would make her love him. And by the time she learned his real reason for being there, their love would have overcome every obstacle.

Marking that they were in the center of the meadow and that her soft lips were tightly compressed, he said gently, "This looks a good spot, but are you sure you want to do it? We could wait if you're not ready."

Aimee looked up at him, eyes swimming. "I'm ready."

Seth smiled. "I think you are, lass."

Studying him, she liked everything she saw. She liked the twinkle in his gray eyes and she liked his face. It was not handsome like Jeremy's but it was strong and rugged and kind and his smile warmed her through and through. And she liked his sand-colored hair and neat beard and his big hands and his hard brown arms. Oh, she did like him.

Seth knelt, set the cage in the grass, and opened the door. The birds did not move nor did they make a sound. They huddled together, their eyes bright and watchful of this new thing. When he tilted the cage so they could slide out, they flapped their wings fiercely to stay where they were.

"They don't want to go," Aimee said hopefully. "They're afraid."

Seth chuckled. "Not for long."

He reached in, grasped one in each hand, and felt their hearts pounding furiously against his curved fingers as

Aimee captured the third. He watched as she touched her lips to their heads, and then they tossed them up, surrendering them to the sky. Watching as the three swept together into the blue with powerfully beating wings, Aimee cried, "Oh, Seth, look at them! Look how beautiful and strong and confident they are. They're not babies anymore! They know just what to do!" She clapped her hands.

"I figured they would." Seth was laughing, delighted for the robins and delighted by her delight. Dear God, what an adorable child she was. It had just come home to him that she could not be more than sixteen or seventeen winters.

"I couldn't have done it without you," Aimee murmured.

Seizing the moment, Seth put an arm around her shoulders and pulled her close. "Of course you could." When she melted against him, just as if she belonged there, he was tempted to kiss her fresh parted lips long and hard. He bent to them, but feeling her trembling, held back. Nay, man, he told himself. It was too soon, far too soon. She was a babe, for God's sake, and he was a man of thirty winters. He gave her a reassuring hug instead. "If you couldn't have done it today, why then you'd have done it tomorrow or the next day."

"I would have helped you," a voice said sharply from behind them.

Aimee spun. "Jeremy! M—my goodness!" She had not known he was coming nor had she noticed his approach on foot, and it was clear that he was angry. His face was dark red and he was breathing heavily—and Seth's gray eyes looked like the sea in winter, icy and threatening. She felt a small thrill of disbelief and pleasure. They were actually jealous of each other. Because of her. My goodness.

Ayisha was in bed reading when Aimee tapped on her door and entered. Seeing that she looked distraught, Ayisha put her book down and sat up. "What is it? Wasn't it a good evening?"

Aimee sank onto the bed. "It was glorious—but Pan, I didn't remember 'till I was passing your door that Cain was supposed to have come! It was out of my mind so completely, I didn't even ask where he was. How stupid can I be! Oh, Pan!"

"Honey, really—"

Aimee shook her head. "Stupid, stupid, stupid. There I was, having the most marvelous time and—"

Ayisha lay a finger over her sister's lips. "Believe me, I'm glad you didn't ask. Just think if Seth had told Cain I was all dressed up and waiting for him. Think how I'd have felt."

Aimee looked more hopeful. "I guess it would've been ghastly."

"It would've, aye. What you did was just right."

"I wonder what happened? He said he'd come, didn't he?"

"Aye, but he's a busy man. He'll probably come another night this week." It was what she had been telling herself over and over all evening. "Forget him and tell me about you and Seth. I want to hear everything."

Aimee plumped a pillow, leaned it against the head-board, and got herself settled. Her eyes shone. "He was wonderful. He helped me say good-bye to my robins and helped me see it was best for them. Panny, you should have seen them fly! They were splendiferous."

Ayisha laughed. "I wish I could have seen it." If nothing had come of the evening but that, it was well spent. "It sounds as if you really like him."

"I do. He's sweet and gentle and strong and funny . . ."

Ayisha saw her hesitation. "But?"

Aimee shook her head. "Jeremy came this eve, too—unexpectedly."

"And they're different."

"Like day and night. Jeremy's so handsome and dresses so elegantly and he's sophisticated and polite and attentive a—and smooth. He's almost too good to be true. People turn and look at him and it makes me feel important to be with him." She stared at her fingernails. "It's stupid of me to care, but I do. It matters. And I hate myself because it does."

Ayisha said gently, "I was as swept away by him as you are."

Aimee pulled off the ribbon confining her curls and wound it around one finger. "I know you told me to be careful, that he was a charmer—but Pan, what's wrong with being a charmer?"

Ayisha smiled. "You already said it. He's too good to be true." She studied her sister's pensive face for some moments before she asked, "Did Seth leave when he came?"

"Nay. They both left a few minutes ago, and they both asked if they could come back tomorrow eve." She giggled, thinking of it. "I can't believe it, two men glaring at each other over me. Me!"

Ayisha laughed at her bright eyes and her excitement. "Why not you?" It was the best thing that could have happened. For too long Aimee had walked in her shadow, and maybe now she would see it had never been necessary. That night as she blew out her candle and closed her eyes, she told herself that Seth was going to win Aimee's heart, and when he came tomorrow eve, Cain Banning was going to come with him. She willed him to come.

As he rode down State Street, Cain felt his anger with himself mounting. He was thinking of Ayisha far too much and feeling more and more guilty for having avoided her for two weeks. But if he saw her even one more time, he knew it could not end there. He would want to see her again and again and again. He saw it happening to Seth. The old boy had been to Seacliff every night since he'd met the maid, and he'd sent his ship and his men off to do their contracted work without him. All he could think about was Aimee and love and marriage.

To Cain's way of thinking, it was a betrayal of the worst sort. Aimee would not know until it was too late that loving Seth meant choosing between him and her father, for there could never be peace between the two men. He drew a deep, angry breath, released it, and told himself he would never do that to Ayisha, even if his thoughts about her were of love and marriage—which they were not.

They were thoughts of the lustiest sort ... bed ... long, slender, rounded limbs ... white breasts ... soft scented skin ... moist pink lips ... slumberous golden eyes ... husky whispers ...

Hell, he had to see her again. He had to. Just one more time. It was fair. She had said she liked him, and her eyes had said more than that. Go back to her, man, go—a few kisses, some embraces, running his hands over her softness, inhaling the sweetness of her. That was all, he would never harm her and it wouldn't be binding. He shook his head then, tightened his lips, signaled his mount to canter. Nay. A maid lost her heart and soul much easier than a man, and considering his and Seth's plans for Ben Scott, he would not risk it.

Nor had he forgotten for one instant the damnable sword that hung over his head. Every day it was there, the sword of his wanderlust, and especially when he went to sea it was there—the yearning to go and not look back, not to care whether or not he ever returned home again: When his father had gone off whistling for the last time, Cain had vowed he would never break any woman's heart as Tom Gregg had broken his mother's. He would never wed. But when he became a man and saw it was a vow he might not be able to keep, he swore instead that the curse would never rule him. But it tried, daily it tried. And the only sure way to protect Ayisha was to do what he had already done—hurt her now so that her heart would not be broken later.

Cain's thoughts were jerked back to the present as he marked a smartly trotting bay and a familiar carriage coming toward him. He watched tensely as it halted at the curb and a footman opened the door. A maid alighted—Aimee. He held his breath, seeing that she was followed by Ayisha. He slowed his mount, reined, his heart in his throat.

Ayisha spied him instantly, a tall, dark-clad figure on a large, black gelding. She had known that seeing him in town was a possibility and had even considered what she might do if they met by chance. Ignore him? Look at him blankly as if trying to recall who he was? Act as if it mattered naught whether she ever saw him again? She had not decided then nor could she now. At the last possible moment, she gave him a polite smile. "Hello. You're still in town . . ."

"Aye, I'm still in town." As Aimee greeted him cordially and continued on into a dressmaker's shop, Cain castigated himself. Why had he not foreseen this and had an excuse ready for not having returned to see the horses? But then she would have seen it exactly for what it was—an excuse. And Ayisha Adair was not a woman to whom one made lame excuses. He said gruffly, "I'm glad to see you again, Ayisha."

It was the truth. He had been starving for the sight of her these past two weeks and he couldn't help but feast his eyes on her. She wore a silky tangerine-colored gown, so simply cut that he could see the outline of her body beneath it—the beautiful rounds of her breasts, the curve of her hips swelling out from her small waist, the long, slim lines of her legs. Realizing that he was staring, he said crisply, "You—look very nice . . ." Nice? God's blood, she was a goddess. A miracle of perfection. Skin like cream, a soft berry-kissed mouth, hair like a sunset, and those exotic amber eyes of hers. Panther eyes. . . . His breeches suddenly felt too tight.

"How kind of you to say so," Ayisha replied without warmth, but her heart turned over. There it was again, the same spark, the same heat in his eyes that she had seen before. And now it was gone, just as before, hidden so quickly she could almost believe it had never happened. But why? Why hide such a thing? What was so awful about letting her know he liked her and found her attractive? She had never known such a man before. She kept her mouth smiling and her eyes neutral. She made a small gesture of farewell. "I must go. Aimee's waiting for me . . ."

"Of course." Cain saw well that he had hurt her, and she was still hurting. And she was angry. He was disgusted, totally disgusted with his handling of the entire matter. There

was a right way and a wrong way to do everything, and he
had gone about this completely the wrong way. He heard
himself saying, "I've not forgotten your horses, Ayisha. I'll
get out to see them yet. These two weeks have been busy
ones for me."

Ayisha's eyes glinted. So busy, she thought bitterly, that
he could not even send a message with Seth saying he was
busy? Hah. It was hardly likely. She refused to spend another day, another week, another instant even wondering if
he were coming and wondering if she had only imagined
there was something special between them. She said
coolly, "I wouldn't dream of taking up your time when
you're so busy. Please don't give it another thought." She
gave him no chance to reply but turned and marched into
the dressmaker's. She felt his eyes upon her.

Chapter 6

Before Ben left for work, he sought out Mrs. Fitzgerald and found her in the pantry. He asked quietly, "Have you a minute, Peg?"

"Certainly." Seeing his seriousness, she closed the door behind them. "Is aught wrong, sir?"

"Nay, Peg, it's just that I'm not home enough to know what's happening with my lasses. I was hoping you could tell me."

Pegeen frowned. "I'm not sure what it is you want to know."

Ben patted her hand. "Of course you don't. To start, is there something going on between Ayisha and Mac? Understand, I'd be delighted. I'd just like to know."

Pegeen stared at the worry lines on his comely face. "My Mac?"

"Your Mac. MacKenzie Fitzgerald."

Peg laughed. "God's me, sir, there's naught that I know of betwixt them. They're like brother and sister, those two. Why would you even ask such a thing?"

Ben waved it off. "It's unimportant. Now tell me about Cain Banning. The night he was here, I heard him tell Ayisha he'd be back to look at the horses. Has he done that, do you know?"

"Nay, sir." Pegeen shook her head. "It's been two weeks and we've seen neither hide nor hair of him."

Ben felt a sinking sensation in his gut. He had seen Cain only once since then. The lad had come to his office the next day and Ben had steered him toward several yards that were under shaky management and might be on the market. They had talked of naught but business, yet he'd pegged him for a prospective son-in-law. What a damned presumptuous old fool he'd been, getting his hopes up like that.

"What of Ayisha?" he asked Pegeen. "Is she disappointed?"

"Aye, but she's not letting on. You know how she hides her feelings."

Ben's smile was tender. "Well I know." Even when she was a little thing, she'd grit her teeth and get right back up on her horse after a tumble—or climb back into the boat after a dunking. She was a tough little thing, his little Pandora. "What of the other fellow?" he asked. "Seth Duncan. I saw him leaving one eve as I was coming home."

"He's been back every night to visit Aimee."

"You don't say." That at least was good news.

Pegeen said low, "I call it a blessing. He's nice looking, he's neat and clean, and he's respectful, unlike some I could name."

Ben nodded, narrow eyed. "The one you could name, Peg—has he been about?"

"Regular as clockwork."

"I see." He had used to dream, with considerable pleasure, of the day when he would retire and leave his many businesses in the competent hands of the men his daughters would wed. It never once had occurred to him he would not approve of them. Not until Greydon had begun hanging about. He drummed his fingers on a sideboard and said to Pegeen, "What's your opinion of the fellow? I need a woman's feelings on this."

Pegeen sniffed. "He's a charmer."

"And the other two?"

"The other two are charming."

Ben scowled. "What's the difference? It sounds one and the same to me."

"Indeed it isn't. His high-and-mightiness works at it, the other two don't have to."

It made Ben chuckle. "That's damned well put."

Pegeen folded her hands over her middle. "The way I see it, the man wants to wed an Adair maid and doesn't care a fig which one."

Ben nodded, gave her hand another pat. "You've got good sense and some to spare, my friend. I'll continue to rely on it."

As his carriage transported him toward the city, he thought darkly of how Greydon had chased Ayisha and how he'd held his breath with worry, knowing if he forbade her to see him, it would make the fellow more irresistible than ever. But the thing had had a happy ending. Now it was Aimee he was after. Once again, if he forbade her to see the devil, he would be an even greater temptation. It was damnable, but it was the way of it.

Cain accompanied Seth to Seacliff the day after he had seen Ayisha in town. His conscience would allow naught else, and besides, he was starving for the sight of her. At the house, the castle, he was told by Soames that Miss Ayisha was at the stable. But he did not find her there. No one was there. Putting his mount in the paddock, he strode about looking for her and thinking, hugely annoyed, that she could be anywhere if she had gone riding—in the woods, on the beach . . . He stopped in his tracks, spying her finally. She was in the meadow up ahead, and she was aboard one of the biggest stallions he had ever laid eyes on. And she was riding bareback. Bareback. God's blood.

He kept his distance, watching enthralled as the horse moved from a trot into an even-gaited, glass-smooth canter that floated him on invisible wings through the tall grass. Gazing on the sight, Cain was unashamedly thrilled by the maid's easy mastery of the great animal and by her beauty. She looked fragile and almost like a child—slender as a young sapling, slim shoulders, her back arrow-straight, hands unmoving, long hair lifting in the wind like a dark flame—but unlike a child, she was in complete control. And the horse . . .

The hair rose on Cain's arms seeing that the stallion was an Andalusian—roman nose, crested neck, full shoulders, gleaming gray coat, the tail well carried. He could have been an *haute école* stallion—except that was absurd. What would such an animal be doing in Boston? In addition, he lacked the spirit and the showy action of a high-school horse. Even as Cain watched, the beast grew more tired and dispirited and old looking, so much so that Cain felt sorry for him. He drew a deep breath, folded his arms, and continued to watch quietly, although his thoughts were far from quiet. This old boy could have been his own old stallion from the Becker Stud. Seeing him had given him quite a turn there for a moment.

After walking and trotting Willi in a steady but easy half-hour's workout, Ayisha slow-walked him around the meadow several times before halting. She leaned forward and stroked his glossy neck. "I think that's enough, old darling. I don't want to tire you."

Her heart never stopped aching when she considered that he could not see the glory around them, the deep grass and blue sky and the sun. She could only hope that he received as much pleasure from their rides as . . . She froze, seeing Cain Banning at the edge of the meadow. Good grief, how long had he been standing there watching her? She sat taller, felt her cheeks sting as she met his eyes, saw the admiration in them. She yearned to greet him warmly, show her pleasure at his taking time from his busy schedule to come, but she caught herself. She said coolly, "Hello, I didn't see you." She turned Willi's head toward the barn, gave him a gentle nudge.

"I hope it's all right," Cain said. "I came with Seth, and Soames told me where to find you." As he walked beside them, he ran his hand over the stallion's well-muscled shoulder and gave him several affectionate pats. "He's quite a horse. I haven't seen an Andalusian in a long while."

Ayisha had intended to be courteous to him, but nothing beyond courtesy. Now her eyes widened. "You say he's an Andalusian? I didn't know. No one around here has ever seen this breed before."

Cain felt sick, noting for the first time the milky cast to the animal's large, gentle eyes. Hell, the old boy was blind. He stroked the sleek, muscular neck again and asked gently, "How did you get him?"

"Da and I were at a farm sale and saw him being auctioned off as a plow horse. Can you imagine such a thing?"

"I can't conceive of it. Was he blind then?"

"Aye."

Cain shook his head. It was unbelievable that no one had recognized his stud value. "He's very special."

"I know he is." Ayisha rubbed Willi's neck. "I had to have him, and while my father would never admit it, his heart's as tender with animals as mine and Aimee's. We couldn't let Willi—his real name is Prince Wilhelm—pull a plow." She grinned down at Cain. "You might as well know, most of our horses were rescued. None of them are fancy, and it's just as well because I never learned to ride properly. I just hang on."

Cain grinned. "I doubt anyone could teach you a thing." It made her even more amazing, for she rode as she sailed, with extraordinary grace and ease.

Dismounting inside the stable, Ayisha felt it happening again—she was warming to him, feeling close and comfortable with him because they both cared about the horse. She told herself firmly she was not going to be caught in the same turmoil and worry that had trapped her before. It simply was not worth the unhappiness. She said, "I'll show you the other horses, but I haven't time for anything else. This is a busy day."

"Don't trouble yourself. I can look around on my own."

She put Willi in his stall. "It's all right. It won't take but five minutes to show them to you." She went to the stall next to Willi's where a big bay had stuck his head over the stall door and was looking at them curiously. "This is King." She stroked his cheek and hand-fed him a bit of hay. "He was a carriage horse and half-starved when we got him. And Omar, our Arab"—she moved to the next stall and stroked the white gelding's coat lovingly—"was foundered. He belonged to a business colleague of Da's who was going to put him down." She crossed to the other side of the stable and gently rubbed the nose of the black giant gazing down at them. "This is Satan. He gets a breathing problem if the hay is dusty. His owner was going to put him down, too."

Cain chuckled. "You meant it when you said they were rescued."

"All except Darby." She moved to the next stall where a beautiful chestnut gelding was snorting and pawing the straw underfoot. "Da bought him as a yearling, and he's his pride and joy."

Darby. Cain kept his face masked. It was Seth's name. More to the point, it was the name of Seth's father, Jonathan Darby, Ben Scott's best friend. Cain's narrowed eyes measured the splendid animal, all seventeen hands of him. He was a saddle horse and undoubtedly a jumper. He said low, "He's very handsome."

"Isn't he though?" Ayisha gave the horse a bit of hay. "Actually, he's very gentle despite the way he's plunging around now. He knows we're going for a ride. I was about to exercise him. My father hardly has the time anymore."

"Is it something I could do for you?" Cain asked. He was puzzled that no stable lads were about.

"Nay. I couldn't ask you to do that. I know how valuable your time is."

"I've taken the afternoon off. Come, let me help."

Studying his face, Ayisha sensed that he would never say anything he did not mean. She said quietly, "I'd appreciate it." Involuntarily, her gaze swept the rest of him—his height, the breadth of those hard shoulders and the narrowness of his waist and hips, his long, thick hair glinting red and brown and gold all at the same time. She forced her mind back to the issue at hand. "I suppose you'd like a saddle."

Cain chuckled. "You mean you ride this one bareback, too?" Darby was still rearing and plunging.

"Aye." Once again she saw the admiration in his dark

eyes, but she absolutely refused to be charmed by him. "He is gentle, I promise."

Cain shook his head. "You're way out of my class, lady. I'll use a saddle." She was growing more remarkable by the moment.

She pointed. "There's the tackroom—and we put them in the crossties to tack up. My father's saddle is the big one, it should fit you." She handed him a leather strap. "Here's a leadshank to bring him out, and I'll get you the hoof pick. We always make sure their hooves are clean before we ride."

"A fine practice." As he attached the crossties to Darby's bridle, Cain was astonished to see the maid entering his vacated stall with a wheelbarrow and shovel.

Seeing his face, Ayisha frowned. "Is something wrong? Do you need help with his hooves?"

Cain's laughter—amusement, approval, admiration all in one—made Darby's ears prick. "I've never seen the mistress of a manor mucking out stalls before."

Ayisha dug in swiftly, easily, and heaved the muck into the barrow. "I do it when I'm needed and I'm needed today. Everyone's sick and our stablemaster's away."

"I'm here and I'm available," Cain said.

"What about your ride on Darby?"

"First I'll muck out." It was suddenly a matter of honor. She was but a maid and far too fragile, too beautiful to do such dirty, tiring work.

Ayisha saw again that he meant what he said. She replied softly, "We'll do it together."

Cain's voice, too, was soft. "And then we'll ride together." God knows, he wanted to be with her, and what could be safer than being on horseback . . .

"Agreed." She did not allow herself to smile.

With the two of them busy, the work went so swiftly they were soon cantering through the pine woods, Ayisha on Omar and Cain on Darby. But the play of sun and shadows, the sound of birdsong, and the peace of the woodlands did not ease his growing confusion. It made no sense that this beautiful lass at his side, one of the wealthiest

women in the land and one with royal blood flowing
through her veins, should muck out stalls, ride other people's cast-off horses, and be sublimely unconcerned that
she was dressed like a vagabond lad and had straw in her
hair. It made no sense. And it made less sense that Ben
Scott, the devil who had somehow forced his father to
abandon the men of the *Bluebird* at sea, should have raised
two such gentle daughters and should himself have such a
tender heart for animals. Nay, it made no sense at all.

Cain kept his eyes straight ahead, but he was hotly
aware of Ayisha on the spirited white Arab. He marveled
that she rode with her whole being—heart, mind, body and
soul—and that she seemed part of the wind and the sun
and the animal itself. He was tempted to tell her of his admiration, but her cool reserve held him at bay. She had
talked with him politely enough, but it was clear she
had not forgiven him and such an observation would not
be appreciated. He remembered suddenly the sun on her
hair as her small craft had plunged through the green sea
toward the *Sea Eagle,* remembered the dinner by candlelight and the fine current of fire tingling between them.

His thoughts shifted from memories to dreaming;
dreaming he had brought his mount to a halt, imagining
her amber eyes widening and her lips parting as he whispered that she was the most glorious thing he had ever
seen and he wanted to make love to her. He clenched his
jaws, resisted the enchantment. But then why not let his
imagination run wild? It was the only way he would ever
have her.

One question was pounding through Ayisha's head over
and over. Why had he stayed away? The admiration in his
eyes when he watched her, the warmth in his voice when
he spoke to her—everything about him said he liked her,
so why, why, why had he not returned sooner? She sensed
that he had forced himself to come today. She ordered herself not to think of it, not now when all was so perfect.
She switched her thoughts eagerly to the fact that his love
for horses was as great as her own and that he was a fine

rider. He was completely and effortlessly in control of his mount and his hands were wonderful, light and elastic and sensitive. She grew weak thinking that they were also big and warm and strong. And they were sun darkened and work hardened.

But he had not come back, her inner voice nagged again. The only reason he was here now was because he was ashamed of himself. He felt guilty. She chewed her lip. Damn, she could not stand this impasse. It was ridiculous, playing this game of silence with him. Why not just ask him point-blank what was wrong? Heart thudding, she brought Omar to a halt. On either side of the path was deep grass, and through the trees was a clear view of the Atlantic, green and glistening.

She said, "This is my favorite spot on the trail." As they gazed on it, she tried to compose what to say and how to say it, but her thoughts were jumbled. She ordered herself to make it simple, don't complicate it, just do it. Do it. Keeping a white-knuckled grip on the reins, she swallowed and asked in a small voice, "Why did you stay away so long?"

Taken unawares, Cain hesitated, then said finally, "I—hadn't planned to see you again, Ayisha." Hearing the words that had just left his lips and seeing the angry flush suffusing her face, he muttered, "I thought it best." God's breath. He'd never meant to tell her the truth except he'd been so taken aback by the question he couldn't think quickly enough to lie. Hell and damnation. He added gruffly, "I've put that badly."

"Not at all." Ayisha's cheeks were burning. She had been overbold and she deserved to be embarrassed. His meaning was perfectly clear: He knew she was crazy for him and he was telling her bluntly that he already had someone back in England. She shrugged. "I wanted to know, and you told me. I appreciate your honesty."

Cain's unsmiling eyes met and held hers. To make any kind of explanation would only make matters worse. He muttered, "I'm sorry."

She waved it off. "Don't be." But she was crushed, and

she felt such resentment and jealousy toward the unknown woman that she could have wept. She said only, "I'm going back."

Pegeen kept an especially watchful eye on Aimee and Seth Duncan that afternoon. She had kept close tabs on them all along, of course—and while she'd said naught of it to Himself, there wasn't a doubt in her mind, none whatsoever, that the fellow was in love with the lass. Head over heels. But for love to work, it took two, and she was not so sure about the maid. When Aimee greeted the man, Peg swore she saw the lovelight in her eyes, but when she greeted that dandy, Greydon, she looked the same way. In love. It made Pegeen want to shake her. How could the maid not see the difference between the two?

Seth had known within two days of meeting Aimee that she was the woman for him; he was going to wed her. Now two weeks had passed, and he was surer than sure of his own feelings for the lass. There was no reason on this earth for him to put off the question any longer. Except for his fear. What if she said nay? Then what would he do? The thought terrified him, for he knew he could not live without her.

"You're so quiet," Aimee murmured. It was late afternoon and they were nestled on a settee on the terrace, Seth's arm wrapped around her and their heads together. She was enjoying hugely the exciting sensation of his hard, warm body pressing against hers full-length, from her head down to her toes.

"I'm thinking," Seth muttered.

"What about?"

Taking her small hands in his, Seth ordered himself to say it and get it over with. Even if he waited another week, another month or year, he would still be terrified of what she would say. He drew a deep breath. "I'm thinking about us, cosset." He gazed down at her trusting brown eyes and sweetly curved mouth. She was so beautiful, it made him ache with wanting to look at her.

Aimee blinked, seeing his stern face and tight mouth. "You look so worried. Oh, Seth, what is it? Have you learned you have to leave?" It made her weak to think of it, for it had been so lovely being with him every day— taking long drives, walking along the beach and feeding the gulls, having picnics, talking, kissing. She had begun to hope, aye, to believe that he would stay in Boston forever.

Seth lifted her hands to his lips, kissed one and then the other, and said huskily, "Wed me, Aimee."

Aimee was so astonished, she could not speak. She could only gape up at him with wide eyes as he nibbled her fingers. She breathed finally, "Wed you?"

"Aye, little one."

"My goodness. We—scarcely know each other. It's only been two weeks."

"I've known you forever," Seth murmured, taking heart from the glow in her eyes. He touched his lips to her hair and her smooth, pale cheek. "I met you in my dreams long ago and knew you were the only woman in the world for me. Aimee, I love you."

"My goodness . . ." His words thrilled her, and he was gazing at her as he had that first night, like a prince who had found his princess. She had not quite believed it then and she could hardly believe it now. Except she wanted to. Oh, she wanted to . . . "I—don't know what to say."

"Say aye."

Her heart was fluttering like a bird caged within her ribs. "I do like you, Seth, I do. I've liked you dreadfully from the first moment I saw you, but—"

Seth's mouth was dry suddenly. "But what?"

"I've been afraid t—to like you too much."

Seth scowled. "Afraid? Of what? Tell me you're not afraid of *me.*"

Aimee gave her head a violent shake. "Never! I was afraid of losing you. I was afraid you'd be going away soon."

Seth stared. She was afraid of losing him? God's breath, this was better than he'd ever hoped for. He said eagerly,

"Darlin' lass, I'd take you with me. We'd have a grand adventure, and we could live anywhere in the world you chose."

Aimee's heart sank, for it was exactly what she had feared. She whispered, "No matter how much I might want to, I couldn't. I'm not like my sister. The sea frightens me—and I could never leave Papa or Panny. I love them too much." She tried to smile through the tears gathered in her eyes. "I'm sorry. I've disappointed you."

"Nay, sweeting, nay." Seth's arm tightened around her small, soft body. "I'll do whatever's needed to make you happy. I'll not leave. I'll stay right here with you at Seacliff if it's what you want."

In God's name, what was he letting himself in for? He had hoped, after confronting Ben and getting the money, to put as many miles between himself and the old man as possible. In truth, he never wanted to see him again—and now, now to be promising to live here. God's bod . . . He suppressed a shudder and looked up scowling as Mrs. Fitzgerald hurried toward them.

"Mr. Greydon is here to see you, lass. I told him you had another caller, but he—"

"Oh!" Aimee jumped to her feet.

Seth growled, "Tell him again, Mrs. Fitzgerald."

"Nay, Peg, I can't be rude," Aimee murmured. "I forgot completely that he was taking me to the Masons for an early dinner this eve. I must see him. Oh, dear . . ."

"Do you want to go?" Seth asked softly.

"Aye. A—and nay."

"Do you want to wed me?"

"I—need time," Aimee whispered. As Jeremy, graceful and impossibly sleek in velvet and ruffles, strode onto the terrace, she murmured, "H—hello, Jeremy, I'm not quite ready yet."

Jeremy smiled and said smoothly, "Take your time, my sweet. I'm early." He acknowledged Seth Duncan's presence with the stiffest of nods and said sharply to the housekeeper, "Have Soames bring me white wine."

Aimee was in a daze as she stood between the two men

in her life: the one who had just said he loved her and wanted to wed her, the other, the Norse god with whom she had been infatuated since she'd first set eyes on him. Not knowing which way to turn or what to say, she gave Seth a beseeching look.

Seth responded instantly to her silent call for help. He said crisply, "She'll not be going with you, Greydon."

Jeremy's eyes narrowed. "The lady has not said so."

"I'm speaking for the lady." Seth put his long arm around Aimee's shoulders. "I've just asked her to be my wife."

Jeremy looked at Aimee in disbelief. How could she even consider such a clod? His jaw worked for some moments before he muttered, "Aimee, for God's sake . . ."

It was as if Aimee were seeing him for the first time. There was no question his face was wonderfully handsome and without a flaw, but the look on it just then quite made her shiver. His perfect mouth was twisted in an ugly way she had never seen before and rage glittered in his pale eyes. She could not meet them. She looked away, felt Seth's protecting arm holding her more closely.

"It's all right, darlin'," Seth said low. "You needn't go with him, and you needn't answer me till you're ready."

Looking up into his face, Aimee saw kindness. He was so strong and so gentle, and he'd been so darling and tender with her robins. And he had said he loved her. Loved her! He'd said he had met her in his dreams and she was the only woman in the world for him. She felt so warm and loved and protected of a sudden it fair left her weak with the thrill of it. But marriage. She wanted to be with him and do things with him, aye, but marriage was forever and she'd known him such a short time . . .

"This is madness," Jeremy growled. "You don't know the first thing about this fellow." Thank God that when he'd sent a man off to England to investigate Banning, he had the good sense to include this dolt in his inquiries also. Thank God.

"It's so," Aimee murmured, "I know naught about him

so I'll not say aye or nay to his proposal until I do. But I really shouldn't see you again, Jeremy. Not until I've decided." When his face turned dark red, she whispered, "That's the way it's going to be. I'm sorry . . ."

Chapter 7

On the way back to Seacliff, Ayisha rode in stony silence, as did Cain. In silence they rubbed down their steaming mounts and returned them to the stalls. Ayisha then went to the pump, washed her hands, and cooled her flushed face. Cain followed suit. She handed him a clean towel from the tack room and said quietly, "Pegeen will have something cool for us to drink." The thought gave her no pleasure. She felt empty. She had not felt so empty since her mother died.

"I should leave . . ."

Ayisha shrugged. "Do what you want."

Hell, he'd just remembered— "I'll need to see Seth just for a minute." And then he would leave, he brooded, as they walked toward the house.

He was in a terrible mood which was growing blacker by the instant. He could do naught right where this maid was concerned. After coming here for the sole purpose of easing the hurt he had caused her, he'd succeeded only in wounding her further. Humiliating her. The only good that could come of it was that she would never want to see him again—which was exactly as it should be. She would already hate him if Ben ever revealed his secret to his daughters. He frowned, seeing the expensive carriage that stood in the driveway.

"You have visitors."

"It's only Jeremy."

As they walked back to the terrace, Ayisha recalled

89

vaguely that he was taking her sister to an early dinner or some such thing. She felt a flare of annoyance. If Aimee liked Seth Duncan so much, why on earth didn't she just say nay to Jeremy and be done with it? There could be trouble otherwise. Reaching the terrace, she saw that it had already arrived. There was a crackle of tension among the three standing there—Aimee, Seth, and Jeremy. Jeremy's handsome face was stained dark red, Aimee's was pale, and Seth looked as if he had just slain a dragon. Ayisha looked from one to the other of them.

"Hello. Are we—interrupting something . . . ?"

Aimee's voice was tremulous. "Seth asked me to wed him."

"Honey, how wonderful!" It was exactly what she had hoped for. No wonder Seth looked like a dragon slayer.

"I haven't given him an answer yet."

Ayisha's gaze went to Jeremy. She was surprised to see that the anger had left his face and he was once more his usual smooth self. He gave Aimee a small, courtly bow.

"I shall await your decision with great confidence, my dear."

Aimee gave a nervous little laugh. "Yes, well . . ."

Jeremy held up a hand and said firmly, "It's all right. Take whatever time you need to decide." His eyes, placid now, flickered briefly over Ayisha and Cain Banning standing behind her and returned to Aimee with a touch of sadness. "I guess I'd best be getting along home."

"Oh, Jeremy, nay!" Aimee protested. "Do go on to Masons. Do! I know you were so looking forward to it."

"My dear, our hostess would not appreciate a single man's upsetting her carefully made seating arrangements."

Ayisha was warring with herself. She would never forget Jeremy's telling her she smelled of brine and horses, but she was still smarting from Cain Banning's saying he had not intended to see her again. As Jeremy bade them good evening and turned to leave, she made a hasty decision.

"Jere, wait!" she called. "I think I'm in the mood for a dinner party." She felt Cain's dark eyes suddenly burning through her. He had been talking low to Seth, but now she had all of his attention. "I'll go with you. If you'll have me, that is . . ."

Jeremy's eyes lighted. "It would be a pleasure." He turned to Aimee, "But only if you approve, cosset."

Aimee gave a nervous giggle. "You're embarrassing me! Of course you must go, both of you."

He was too clever by far, Ayisha thought angrily, but she had begun this game and now she would play it. She said cheerily, "Good. It's settled. I'll run up and change."

"I'll wait for you in my carriage."

"I'll not take long, I promise." Knowing exactly what she was about, Ayisha hastened into the house, counted to five, and went back out. Going to Cain, she gave him a contrite smile. "I can't believe I almost went off without saying good-bye. But then it's really farewell. I did appreciate your help this afternoon. It was kind of you." She returned to the dim quiet of the house, and as she ran up the stairs to her bedchamber, her heart was pounding. Something strange had just happened. Strange and unexpected. She had hurt him. She could not imagine why, she knew only that she had. The grim lines of his face and mouth showed that he was angry, aye, but his eyes said he had been wounded. It should have made her feel quite triumphant, but it did not. It unsettled her completely. She had hurt him.

On his solitary ride back to town, Cain told himself not to be a damned fool. He had no right to be jealous of Ayisha, and he certainly had no cause to worry about her. Any maid who could ride and sail like a man was an even match for a man. But his heart knew it was not so. Skilled and brave as she was, she was as soft and slim and fragile as any other maid and no match for a cunning predatory wolf like Greydon. He feared for her. And his hurt gnawed

at him. It pained him to the core to think of her going off
with that bastard when he wanted to be with her himself.
And she had wanted to be with him. Over and over he
heard her voice asking why he had not returned sooner—
and over and over he heard his damned impertinent answer. Where had his brains been?

Brooding, he prowled the streets of Boston after dinner,
visited pubs, gaming houses, and docks, and looked in on
his own vessel. He tortured himself relentlessly, recalling
how he had hurt her. He had been careless and thoughtless,
saying he would return to see the horses when he knew he
would not, and then telling her—God's breath, how had he
gotten the words out?—telling her it was best he not see
her again. He tried to drown his guilt in the pubs but succeeded only in getting drunk. The guilt remained. When he
returned finally to the Red Horse, Seth was there and
eager for talk.

"Man, I haven't a doubt my maid's going to say aye!"
His gray eyes were snapping with jubilation. "She confessed she was afraid of liking me too much and of losing
me. Hallelujah!" He was beaming, prowling their small
chamber, unable to sit still. "The sweet darlin'—I love her
so much, I'm about to explode!"

Cain watched him in envious silence. If only he could
show Ayisha his own feelings as easily, but it was not in
him. His fear of harming her was too powerful. He said
low, "Does she know she'll be losing you for months on
end?"

"She'll not, man. I've told her I'll not leave her. It's
time I settled down."

Cain kept his face still. "Her father might have something to say about that when he knows who you are and
why you're here."

Seth's smile was serene. "Where's your faith, man?
When she says aye, as I know she will, and when Ben sees
how happy she is, he'll agree. I know he will. It'll all work
itself out. It'll be all right." It had to be all right.

Cain gloomed into the fire and gripped his hands together so tightly his knuckles cracked. He would never understand the man. Seth Darby was as decent a fellow as he'd ever known which made what he was doing even more of a mystery. If he loved the maid as much as he said, how could he bring down on her all the heartache which would follow his wedding her? What did he expect Aimee to do when she learned the truth—abandon her father and cleave unto him alone? Or did he think Ben would never tell his girls, meekly pay his debt and forgive the two of them for forcing it from him?

Cain sighed deeply and shook his head. Nay. Ben Scott was not such a soft, weak man as all that. He'd been a pirate, for God's sake. If he didn't skewer Seth first he was going to hate him, forbid Aimee to see him, and possibly turn his back on her for loving him. Their family could be shattered by it.

Studying Cain's closed face, Seth thought what a pity that he was such a grim kind of fellow who took life so seriously. It was plain to see that he had an eye for Ayisha, and what harm was there in a little innocent flirtation and fun? Seth did not mean bedding the maid, nay. That he would not look on at all kindly. But a bit of easy talking and laughing and companionship would hurt no one. He rose, poked the fire, and sat back down.

"How did it go with the horses?" He was careful not to mention Ayisha's name for he had seen the chill between them.

"All the stablehands were ill so I helped her muck out, and then we rode." Cain kept his voice even. "She has a fine old Andalusian stallion she's smothering with worry. She's so afraid to ride him, the old boy's lost heart. I felt damned sorry for him."

Seth chuckled. "It sounds like Aimee and her robins. I figure she'd've smothered the little blighters to death if I hadn't stepped in." He stole a glance at Cain's dour face in the flickering half light and thought how very much he looked like Tom Gregg just then. It was uncanny. But in no way were the two alike. In no way. He said quietly, "Maybe you need to take a hand with the horse."

Cain growled, "I'll not go again."

Seth shrugged. "Suit yourself."

The thought of her with Greydon consumed Cain suddenly: Ayisha in his arms, Ayisha kissing him, being kissed, being caressed, squeezed, pawed . . . He rose, strode to the window, and glared out at the small, high moon sailing over the city.

Seth watched him for some moments before saying, "Aimee mentioned something odd this eve." When Cain made no reply, he continued. "She says Pan doesn't like Greydon. She stepped out with him earlier in the year, but ended the thing. Aimee thought it was strange she went with him today, considering."

Cain looked at him sharply. "Did she say why Ayisha didn't like him?"

"Aye. He wanted badly to wed her and she decided he was after the old boy's money. She told Aimee to be careful and not get swept away."

Cain stared at him. "I'll be damned."

Seth grinned. "My words exactly. Interesting, isn't it, a maid seeing such a thing? He's a smooth, pretty sort of bloke, after all, and filled with flattery. I liked it that Aimee saw fit to tell me." He socked a fist into his left hand. "She's going to be mine, man! I feel it in my bones. She's going to be Mrs. Seth Darby before the month's out . . ."

Seth's elation was lost on Cain. He was remembering the murderous look on Greydon's face that afternoon, and it chilled him. The man was being thwarted, first by Ayisha and now Aimee, and that sort of fellow did not take such things lying down. Cain wondered gloomily if he meant to pursue Ayisha again. She'd certainly been encouraging enough. Drumming his fingers on the sill, he reminded himself irritably that he was not her keeper. If she wanted to step out with Greydon, she'd jolly well have to accept the risks.

But as he tossed on his narrow bed that night, he knew it was not that simple. She had gone off with Greydon only because he himself had hurt her. She had wanted to show him she didn't care. And now, God's breath, what if the devil took advantage of her vulnerability with false kindness and a smooth tongue? What if Greydon took up where he had left off and began courting her again?

Cain stared at the window and the moonlight streaming through and tried to still his churning worries, but he could not. Ayisha was wary, but Greydon was smooth and clever. He would be devious. Cain had seen his counterparts in every port he'd visited, men who seized the moment and followed their advantage swiftly—overpowering and seducing a maid to force her to accept marriage rather than dishonor. The thought struck him with terror. Nay, by God, he would not let it happen. Not to Ayisha.

The need to guard her was a flame scorching him for he was responsible for her turning to Greydon. Yet to protect her, he needed to be near her, but he had burned that bridge behind him. He got out of bed and prowled the small room as Seth slept, sifting through every excuse he could think of that might allow him to return to Seacliff. He pondered it the night long, and when the sun sent its pale rays streaming through the window finally, Cain had fastened onto the best one—an idea Seth had given him.

He would offer to take a hand with the Andalusian. He found himself hoping fiercely that Ayisha would accept, not only so he could watch over her—that was his primary purpose, aye—but for his own peace of mind, he had to discover if Prince Wilhelm were *haute école*. If he was not, Cain hoped still to find a way to add some light to the darkness of the old boy's days, to give him something to live for. He vowed he would.

Ayisha was glad that Mac was not back from his trip, for his absence gave her something to do besides brood. Unlike yesterday, she could pick and choose her chores this day. The stableboys, while not completely recovered from their brief illnesses, had returned to work and were able to feed, water, and muck out. It left Ayisha the things she liked best, grooming and exercising their five mounts.

As she picked Satan's hooves, she reflected that the stable had been a source of comfort to her ever since she could remember. She had never been one to run to her mother or Pegeen with her cuts and bruises as Aimee had. If she had any kind of hurt, she had always wanted to be alone with the animals. The deeper the pain, the more she craved their companionship and the dim quiet of the stable. She loved its soft light and peacefulness, the smell of clean straw and fresh hay, the twitterings and flutterings of the sparrows that lived in the rafters, and she especially loved the horses.

Finishing Satan's hooves, she applied the curry comb and a stiff brush to his black coat and worked on his right side, from his ears back to his rump. As she did, the same thoughts haunted her over and over—a pirate shouting an angry warning to her from the deck of his vessel . . . a magnificent-looking pirate. And then there were thoughts of the dinner that night—candles flickering . . . a thin wire of fire sizzling between them . . . her hand in his . . . his eyes, almost black in their intensity, making her melt. He had said she sailed like an angel and he wished he could wave a wand to make her feel better. But then yesterday, yesterday he had said coldly that he had not intended to see her again. It was best he didn't . . .

Simmering, she worked on Satan's other side and wondered if he had seen that his words had crushed her. She had tried to hide it, but he had knocked the wind right out of her. She had felt so close to him so quickly—God's truth, she had never felt that way about a man before. And she had thought, she really had, that he'd felt it, too. But she knew now it was wishful thinking.

She angrily knocked the dirt out of the brush on the sole of her boot, attacked Satan's mane with it next, and told herself he had not felt a bit of what she felt. He was completely without feeling and it was good to know. A man like that she didn't need, and she was glad she had learned it before she'd made a complete fool of herself.

As for being a fool, she had taken the dunce's cap, going to that dinner party with Jeremy. Despite his seeming devotion to Aimee, it seemed he was as avid for her as ever and wanted to see her again. Well, she was not going to see him, rude or not. There was no way on this earth she would ever go out with him again. Thinking of how Seth had snatched Aimee away from him, she felt resentment that Cain was not like Seth. Sensing suddenly that she was being watched, she turned and saw a tall, silent figure at the far end of the barn. Oh, nay, please—not Jeremy . . .

Seeing her start like a spooked filly, Cain called, "I'm sorry, I didn't mean to frighten you."

Ayisha's cheeks burned. "I was startled, not frightened." She could not imagine why he was there, but she clamped down on her tongue rather than ask. Let him do the talking.

Cain walked toward her and said genially, "Are you without your stable lads again today?"

"They're here," she said shortly.

"I can help with the grooming, if you'd like."

"There's no need." She bit her tongue again so she would not lash out at him, but the temptation was too great. "You'd have to look at me. But then I suppose you could close your eyes." How childish, but how lovely to let her wrath flood out.

Cain gave a low laugh. "Actually, I like to look at you. You're quite beautiful, you know." His amused gaze moved over her soft lips, so tightly compressed, and the frown drawing her brows together. She was pink and furious and so completely enchanting he yearned to pull her into his arms and give her a thorough kissing. He put the thought away. He was here to guard her from Greydon, not from himself. He said gently, "I came to apologize, Ayisha. What I said yesterday was—poorly put."

She wished she could make light of it, say he was making much ado out of nothing, but she could not. He would know. She made no reply, thumped the brush against her boot again, and brushed Satan's knees and hocks.

Cain sighed and raked his fingers uneasily through his hair. "It sounded as if I had a wife or a fiancée and that I thought—"

Ayisha's eyes blazed. "—that I would seduce you and lure you away from her!" She blinked, shocked by her own words. Ladies did not say such things, and she had been raised very carefully to be a lady. Mama would be turning in her grave . . .

Cain threw back his head and laughed at her wonderful forthrightness. He said quietly then, "If there were such a person, Ayisha, which there isn't, my worry would be that you would make me forget her."

Feeling her fury ebbing, washing out to sea, she tried to hold it close. She said stiffly, "Indeed."

"It's so. But the truth is, I have no woman in my life. No wife, no fiancée, not even a mother or a sister. My reason, my only reason, for saying the cruel thing I did is a very strong one. I hope you believe me."

Ayisha tried not to smile. "But you don't intend to tell me what it is."

"Nay."

Now her eyes were dancing. "Do you rob banks? Trip old ladies?" His mouth curved. "Maybe you cheat at cards."

"You're not even close."

"Then it's probably what I suspected in the beginning. You're a sea wolf. A pirate." She saw a flicker in his dark eyes that was quickly hidden.

"Nay, Ayisha. I'm not a pirate."

A wonderful calm was settling over her. She handed him a sponge, pointed to a bucket of water, and said quietly, "You can wipe his face if you'd like." Picking up a towel, she began to burnish Satan's coat with it. "I suppose you realize how strange and mysterious this all sounds."

"I do." He saw with relief that he had won the battle. They were on friendly terms again.

"And I suppose you still can't see me anymore—because of this one thing . . ."

"Not the way I'd like to see you." Every day, every hour, learning more and more about her. "Know, Ayisha, if it were in my power, it wouldn't be this way."

He looked so grim, she was moved to reach across Satan's back and give his hand a light, friendly pat. She smiled. "It's all right. I trust you. If you say this is the way it has to be, why then this is the way it will be."

Chapter 8

Watching Satan submitting so docilely to having his face cleaned, Ayisha murmured, "I don't believe it. He always fusses when I do that."

Cain's smile shone white in the half light. "Maybe it's because I'm almost as tall as he is." He ran a practiced hand over the gelding's shoulders and withers and said casually, "I've been thinking about your Andalusian. Would you let me try him before I leave?"

Ayisha hesitated. "You know he can't see . . ."

"I haven't forgotten."

"I baby him. I've never ridden him hard."

"I'll be very careful."

She sighed. She didn't like it, but she didn't want to seem like an overprotective mother. She nodded. "Of course, it's fine. If you'll take Satan out to the paddock, I'll put Willi in the cross ties and we can do him next." She had another currycomb and brush waiting for him when he returned. As they worked in unison, she on Willi's left and Cain on his right, she found it impossible to keep her eyes on the Andalusian's sleek coat and off Cain's dark, bare arms. How long and powerful they were . . .

"I had a horse like this when I was a lad," Cain said quietly.

"Really?" She was surprised and more than pleased that he had mentioned it.

"Aye. He was a big, beautiful gray Andalusian stallion . . ." Memories flowed over him, not just of the horse,

100

but of the wretched lad he had been. His mother in the ground, the Bannings, so stiff and polite and unsmiling, coming for him and taking him from the small, grim cottage where he had been born to their great, grim estate on Cockburn Moor. Cain had hated the place and lived for the day when his father would return from sea and take him away from Banning Hall. But when Tom Gregg finally came, he'd left within two days, and he left alone. Cain had shut himself in his room and raged and wept, hating everything and everyone. He had not wanted to live, for what was left to live for? And then one day his uncle had come home with Juan Fandango.

Seeing the distance in Cain's eyes and the tenderness about his mouth, Ayisha said gently, "I think you loved your horse very much."

"Aye." Cain's throat ached remembering the time he had come home from sea, he'd been seventeen, to find that Dango had died.

"Will you tell me about him?" She tried not to stare at the sudden glitter in his eyes and wondered, Were those tears? She looked away. Of course they weren't. Men did not cry. Certainly dangerous-looking pirate types like Cain Banning did not cry. She said softly, "I'd love to hear . . ."

Cain shrugged. "There's not much to tell. I was ten winters and cocky and rebellious and resentful as hell. I lived with my aunt and uncle and I'll never know why he didn't ship me off to sea, but he didn't. He gave me Juan Fandango instead."

A giggle slipped past her lips. "Juan Fandango?"

"Aye. I called him Dango."

"I love it! Dango. Was he a colt? Did you train him yourself?"

Her warmth and interest and the glow in her eyes seemed to Cain like sun shining on his memories, lifting the darkness that had always smothered them. He replied, "Nay, he was old, and already well trained. His owner had put him out to pasture."

"But—you did ride him?"

He grinned. "After a fashion. Before I moved to Banning Hall, I lived on the coast and went to sea every day on a fishing boat." Seeing the widening of her eyes, he added, "I'd never been on a horse before."

"I see."

"So I was sent to horse school."

She could not suppress another giggle. "Horse school?" It was wonderful, having him talk to her this way, and she was filled with questions.

"Aye." Cain allowed his dancing dark eyes to rest on her across the safety of Willi's broad back. "Horse high school. *Haute école.* I had to learn to maneuver the old boy." Her hair was glorious, long and lustrous and heavy, and she had knotted it at her nape to keep it out of her face. He remembered that when the sun shone on it, glints of flame and gold leapt from its brown depths. He tore his thoughts from her and put them firmly to the matter at hand. "Dango's owner, Anton Becker, raised and trained *haute école* Andalusians, and since his place wasn't far from ours, I rode over every day for a lesson."

Ayisha's eyes shone thinking of it. "I envy you."

Cain laughed. "I hated it. All I wanted was to go galloping across the moors in my own sloppy way, but old Becker wouldn't hear of it. He wouldn't allow any of his horses to go to untutored hands, even if their glory days were over."

"What do you mean, glory days?"

"Becker trained stallions for royalty—for palace guards and pulling carriages and reviewing troops. Some found their way into the circus and the bullring because of their fancy footwork, but primarily they went to royalty. Of course, they were all in their prime—young and strong and vigorous."

Ayisha thought wistfully that he was strong and vigorous and in his prime. Like a young stallion. She quickly pushed the dangerous thought away. "That's fascinating. I've never seen any of those things, a parade or a circus or a palace guard. I can't imagine what sort of footwork a horse might learn that would be so different."

Cain grinned. "If you ever saw an *haute école* stallion, you'd know, lady. You'd know."

"Ever since you told me Willi is an Andalusian, I've wondered where Andalusia is."

"It's a region in Spain. When the Moors came ages ago, they bred their own horses to the Spaniards'. The result was the Andalusian." Cain took care not to look at her as he worked. Her bare arms were so slim and smooth and sun kissed he wanted to reach across Willi's back, catch one, and press kisses up and down its silky length. He dragged in a deep, shaky breath and felt frustration nigh swamp him. He was being torn in two—fearing for her if he stayed away, and fearing for her if he didn't. It was an impossible situation he had locked himself into.

Ayisha watched as he put the saddle on Willi and carefully cinched the girth. She smiled. "You learned well in your horse school."

"Why do you say that?"

"You're gentle with Willi, and you rode Darby as if you were part of him. And you have wonderful hands . . ." She imagined what they would feel like, holding her, moving over her, caressing her. She sighed, told herself to stop it, not even to think it when he had made it quite clear that such a thing was never going to happen. She handed him the bit and watched tensely as he slid it into Willi's mouth. She murmured, "No man has ridden him for ages. Not since we got him. His mouth's very tender . . ." When Willi made no complaint and Cain moved next to adjust the stirrup length, she said, "I—hope you're not too heavy." He was ever so tall and probably weighed twice as much as she did. Oh, dear . . .

Seeing her very real fear, Cain took her hands in his and pressed them reassuringly. "I'm not too heavy, trust me. I'll not harm him. I'll be very careful." He adjusted the other stirrup, but the warmth and softness and smallness of her hands had jolted him.

Ayisha was electrified. His hands were so big and warm and strong and he had held hers so gently—but it was the look in his eyes that was making her pulses pound. They had been kind and full of reassurance, aye, but there was hunger in them, too. She was not a complete innocent. He wanted her. He wanted her very badly. Bewildered, she followed him as he led Willi out into the hot July sun. She watched in further puzzlement as he carefully examined the stallion's left croup.

"Is anything wrong?"

"Not at all." Cain's heart pounded as he ran his fingers over the brand. God's hooks, this was crazy. Prince Wilhelm was not only an *haute école* stallion, he was one of Anton Becker's Andalusians. God alone knew why and when the poor old boy had been brought across the sea, but it hardly mattered any more. At least he was not pulling any damned plow, and he had a loving, caring mistress—but what an amazing thing. He gave Willi's rump a pat and collected the reins.

"Were you looking at his brand? I could never quite make it out. It seems to be a little crown or something."

"You're right," Cain muttered. "It's a crown."

A crown over an elaborate AB designating the stud that supplied the horses for half of the royal houses of Europe. But he did not want to tell Ayisha that just yet. He wanted to see what Willi had retained, if anything. Talking to the stallion low and easily, Cain put his foot into the stirrup and lifted himself lightly aboard Willi's strong back. Willi never moved. Cain stroked his neck again and continued his low talk.

"So, old man, let's see what we can do. We're both a bit rusty, but that doesn't mean we can't have ourselves a good time. Easy now, Willi. Easy, old lad . . ."

Ayisha held her breath as Cain Banning held Willi to a slow walk around and around the outside of the paddock. When no catastrophe occurred, the stallion's back did not cave in nor did his legs collapse under him, she called, "I guess you're not too heavy after all. He looks good."

Cain called back, "Do you ride him in the meadow?"

"All the time."

"Is there any unevenness there? Any gopher holes?"

"Nay, it's level and he's familiar with it." She almost

laughed aloud seeing that Cain looked every bit as dangerous on Willi as he had at the rail of the *Sea Eagle*. She
guessed he would make even Pegeen's herb garden a place
of mystery and intrigue were he to set foot in it.

"I'm taking him there," Cain said.

Following after them, Ayisha recalled Aimee's saying
that no man ever rode for pleasure. She had even agreed—
but Cain Banning was proving them both wrong. He was
enjoying himself thoroughly. His face was smoothly impassive, but there was no mistaking the excitement in his
eyes—just as there was no mistaking the hunger she had
seen in them. She felt a thrill thinking of it. He had wanted
to kiss her, and she had wanted him to. But it was over.
Over before it had even begun. After today, she would not
be seeing him anymore.

She wanted to weep suddenly. On this beautiful blue
and gold July day, birds singing, the fragrance of wildflowers and meadow grasses heavy in the air, and Cain,
his eyes filled with the strangest light, sitting straight and
grave on a suddenly young-looking Willi, Ayisha yearned
to weep. Her eyes blurred as she lowered herself to the
deep grass and sat crosslegged, watching.

If only she could shake off the feeling of closeness she
had for this man, as if they were two halves of the same
whole. She didn't want to feel it, she wanted to hate him,
to not care about the ridiculous mystery that was keeping
them apart. But she could not hate him or laugh about it
because she did care. She did. . . . Seeing him there on her
most favorite of all the horses, she could not ignore the
emotions sweeping through her. Sadness, longing, resentment, regret, hurt—and joy, delight in his delight with
Willi and in Willi's very evident pleasure. Darling
Willi. . . . She frowned and focused her attention on him.
Her mind had been drifting so, she was not at all sure
when the change in him had come about.

She stared at his proudly arched neck and pricked ears
and at the slow, skimming walk he was performing. It was
a walk so different from his usual heavy-footed plodding
that she sat straighter in astonishment. What was Cain

doing to cause such a transformation in him? She stared harder but she could not detect a thing. He seemed just to be sitting there in the saddle doing naught except she knew it wasn't so. He must be doing those things he had learned in horse school, and they were turning Willi into a changed animal. The stallion's whole bearing had become dignified and regal, and he seemed totally absorbed, turned inward, as if his sightless eyes were seeing again those things the young Willi used to see and do—a young Willi in his prime . . .

Eyes brimming, Ayisha sat spellbound in the grass as Cain put the stallion through an array of paces—a dazzling, skimming walk, a dancing, fire-filled trot, a graceful canter, in which he seemed to float above the ground, and then once more the skimming walk, which brought them to where she was sitting. She arose, stunned.

Cain smiled, seeing her wet eyes and transfigured face. "So, what do you think?"

She was laughing, trying hard not to weep. "You said I'd know if th—the steps were different—and I do. Oh, Cain, I do! He's an *haute école* stallion, isn't he?"

"He is, aye."

Tears were streaming down her face now. "I'm sorry, it's stupid to bawl when I feel so happy, but it was just so beautiful and touching—and so thrilling what you did together. And what you've done for him! Cain, he looked so young and so alive. Thank you! Thank you so much for doing this for him!"

Cain dismounted and stroked the stallion's neck with deep affection, smiled at the joy suffusing her face. "Are you ready for another surprise?"

She stared up at him. "I can't imagine what . . ."

"His brand says he's from the Becker Stud."

Ayisha's breath caught. "What? Where your Dango came from?"

"Aye. The fancy swirls under the crown are an AB. There will be another mark under the saddle indicating his sire and dam."

"I've seen it!" She was breathless—from his news and from his standing so close to her. "I'm dreaming!"

"It's unreal, I agree."

It was she who was like a dream, Cain thought. He dared look at her only a moment before forcing his hungry eyes back to the stallion. He could not suppress the heat pounding through him or ignore the heady effect she had on his senses. How in God's name could he go through with this scheme with Willi? In truth, he didn't know, and if he had any human kindness in him at all, he would leave her now and never come back.

"What you did with him was amazing," Ayisha murmured, her thoughts still filled with the sight. "I couldn't see that you were doing a thing. You just seemed to be sitting there."

Cain laughed. "Four years of schooling helped." His uncle had been a wise old bird. He had known that learning to ride and care for a horse would so fill the days of an unhappy young lad that he would have no time for anything else. The old horse had turned Cain's thoughts away from himself and his bitterness. Dango had saved him from himself.

"Willi loved it. Thanks again. Really, I—can't thank you enough."

"It was my pleasure."

"He looked so spirited and happy." Not old and tired and blind . . .

"That he did." The time was drawing nigh when she would ask him to return for Willi's sake—or he would offer. Or would the moment pass without either of them saying anything? And damned if he was not sure but what it was best.

Ayisha could not meet his eyes, nor could she bear to stand so close to him without touching him, yet she had to talk to him. She moved to Willi's other side and neatened the unruly strands of his mane. She said low, still not looking at Cain, "Do you—think you could come back again?" Before he could reply, she added quickly, "To ride Willi, I mean. I'd not come anywhere near, I promise."

She felt a surge of anger toward him that he should make things so complicated. Her stolen glances at his face now showed that he would not even look at her. Neither of them could look at the other. It was ridiculous. It took all of her discipline not to demand more of an explanation for his behavior than the mysterious one he had given her.

But she was not in any position to demand anything. She was asking a very great favor of him, one that only he could give. She was asking him to bring back into Willi's dark days a thing that had been lost to him these many years—a reliving of his youth, of his glory days. She did not know when anything had mattered to her quite so much—except her mother's recovery.

Cain did not reply immediately. This was exactly what he had hoped for when he had conceived his plan, but now he was growing more and more uncertain of the rightness of it. It would be a good thing for the horse, aye, and he saw well that he could accomplish what he had intended. It would be easy to watch over Ayisha and warn her of danger, should it appear. But he saw more clearly than ever that grief could come of it. She was infatuated with him—he did not flatter himself that it was anything more—and he was equally infatuated with her. But it could easily and quickly grow into something much deeper. She was beautiful, and he yearned to bed her. But he could not do that to her. A woman such as Ayisha would give herself only to the man she loved, and love must not enter into this. Not ever. Even were he not about to hurt her deeply, he would not risk it, given who he was—a Gregg man.

"Please . . ." Ayisha murmured. He was silent for so long, she wondered if he had even heard her. "Will you come back and ride Willi while you're in Boston? I know I'm asking a lot, but—"

"You're not," Cain replied gruffly. "Willi's superb. I meant it when I said it was a pleasure to ride him."

Ayisha was ashamed that her reasons for wanting him to return were not entirely for Willi, but she didn't care. She wanted Cain Banning and she was willing to do anything to spend more time with him. She murmured, "Does that mean you'll come?"

"Aye." Cain damned himself to hell and back, but he could no more have stayed away from her than he could have hoisted Willi onto his back and trotted off with him.

"Thank you. Thank you so much. It means a great deal to me, and as I said, I'll stay away. You won't have to see me."

Cain did not reply. Guilt had him by the throat.

Chapter 9

Ben Adair's temper had always been fiery and as easily doused as it was kindled. But it had mellowed since the death of his wife. His daughters rarely saw him angry anymore. He had decided life was too short to waste it foolishly. It was why, as he breakfasted with them on that Saturday morn in July, he masked his huge annoyance over Jeremy Greydon's hanging about the place once again. Reminding himself that Aimee at least was pleasing him, he patted her hand and gave her a warm smile.

"So, darlin', have you decided yet? Will you be wedding the young man?"

Aimee blushed. "Aye, Papa. And to think, it all came about because you invited him to dinner. I think I fell in love with him that very first night."

Ben leaned over and kissed her cheek. "I couldn't be happier. There's something about the fellow that I liked from the first instant I saw him." He turned, studied his elder daughter. She was so like his Ana, brave and high spirited, and with the same amber eyes and reddish-brown hair—it sometimes stabbed him in the heart to look at her. He covered one of her hands, too, and said low, "And how is it with you, child?"

"Fine, Da." Ayisha wondered at the sudden gravity of his face.

Ben patted her hand and tried to collect his thoughts. He was not at all sure how to begin. He had never been a heavy-handed father, and now he feared his laxness had been a mistake. He should have planned his maids' lives

110

for them as other fathers did. God knows, Aimee's path had taken this happy twist through no doing of his own. It had been pure luck. He squeezed both their hands and said abruptly, "I haven't done well by you girls as a father . . ."

Ayisha stared at him in bewilderment. "Not done well by us? Da, how can you say such a strange thing? We want for naught."

"Except a father. I'm gone far too much of the time, I always have been, and I've not forgotten I left your up-bringing to your mother and Pegeen."

Aimee cried, "Papa, we're fine! Please don't say such a thing. We know you have to work."

"I've not guided you."

"Of course you've guided us," Ayisha said. She would have laughed had he not looked so grim. Instead she kept her voice easy. "What's this about, Da?"

Ben sat straighter. There was naught to do but spit it out. He looked at Aimee, his gentle lamb, and patted her hair. "My darlin', I'll say it again—I couldn't be more pleased that you've chosen Seth Duncan to wed. My mind will be completely at ease when you're in his hands." He looked at Ayisha then, shook his head, took both her hands in his. "But you, my honey, you worry me."

Now Ayisha did laugh. "Me? Worry you? Why?" She was astounded.

"It shames me that Aimee has found a good man to take care of her with no help from me. I know—I brought him home, but that's not the point. The point is, I didn't ar-range the match and I mean to do better by you, my little Pandora."

Understanding finally what was happening, Ayisha asked quietly, "Are you saying—you're going to choose a husband for me?"

"I'm saying," Ben's voice was rough, "that when the time comes, I can't face your mother if I don't give you some guidance."

Ayisha was aware of two things in the hush that had fallen over the dining chamber. Aimee was softly weeping, and her father had spoken of his own death. It was a thing he had never done before. She felt her heart quiver. "Are you ill, Da?"

"Only when I think of Jeremy Greydon," Ben muttered, and clasped his hands tightly on the table before him. "Now hear this, lass, and hear it well. I don't like him. I didn't like him when he was sniffing around you the first time. I didn't like him when he was courting Aimee, and I like him even less now that he's chasing you again. I can't for the life of me understand why you're encouraging him with the likes of Cain Banning around. Now there's a man—and he's a man with a heart, working with old Willi the way he is." He shook his silver head, felt his own heart making his whole body shudder with its heavy pounding. "I've never told you girls what to do. I always assumed you had good heads on your shoulders, but now I wonder about you, Ayisha."

She blinked. When he called her that, it did not bode well. She asked quietly, "Do you want me to wed Cain Banning then?"

Ben turned dusky red. It went against his grain, telling the child who to wed, but it was his duty as a father. It was his right. He asked sharply, "Would you rather have Greydon?"

She smiled. "Nay, Da, I'd rather have Cain."

It shocked him for he'd been primed to give her a lecture. He shook his head. "By all that's holy, I'll never understand women." But then he didn't understand how the sun and the moon and the stars swung in their courses either. "If that's the case, why in tarnation do you have Greydon hanging around?"

Aimee giggled. "She wants to make Cain jealous."

Ben felt a weight lift from his shoulders, but he scowled at Ayisha nonetheless. "Is that so, girl?"

Ayisha turned pink. "Aye." She would far rather he hadn't known as she was not proud of herself, but quite simply, she didn't know what else to do. And it would not be for much longer.

Ben's eyes bored through her. "Why would you need to make the man jealous?"

"He—gives Willi all of his attention."

"He hasn't shown any interest in you at all?"

"He has little time when he comes and Willi takes it all." She could not tell him the truth. She hadn't even told Aimee the truth.

Ben felt his blood simmering from his scalp to his toes. What ailed the confounded fellow? Was his daughter, one of the two most exquisite jewels in Boston, aye, in the world, not beautiful enough for him? Or did he like men? God above. But some of her news at least was heartening. He muttered, "Then you're not starting up again with Greydon?"

"Nay! Believe me, Da. I just want for Cain to see the two of us together."

Ben drummed his long fingers on the table. "I don't like it. Toying with a man like that is dangerous. He'd be furious if he learned what you were about and I'd not blame him." He shook his head. "Nay, Ayisha, I can't allow it."

"I need just a little more time. Hardly any."

"Nay, lass."

"Da . . ." Her eyes were melting. "Just another week, please? A week to ten days? Pretty please, Da, and if naught's come of it by then, I'll stop it gladly. I don't want Jeremy around any more than you do."

Ben felt hot and his pulses were pounding in his temples. It was a damned outrage that his daughter, his pearl, need go to such lengths to make a man notice her. Men far more important than Cain Banning had been asking for her hand and Aimee's since both of them were husband high. The girls did not know, of course. He'd never told them of the stir they had caused at their first assembly, but begod, Banning should know. And now she wanted a week to woo him, the poor cosset. Ten days. He sighed, knowing well he could deny her naught.

"Very well," he said heavily. "Ten days. But you're not to go off with him, do you hear? No parties, no rides in the country or walks in the woods or on the beach. I want you here at the house in plain sight. Do you understand?"

She knew very well what he was saying. He feared

Jeremy would try and take advantage of her. "I understand. And thanks, Daddy. A million thanks." She leaned
forward and kissed his cheek.

Mac did not like it. Ayisha seemed a different girl from
the laughing maid he had sailed with last. Now, despite
perfect weather and water conditions, she was quiet and
withdrawn, her pensive gaze on some inner sight he
wished he could share with her. Was it because that
damned hound, Greydon, was courting her again? he wondered grimly. Was that what she was brooding about? He
watched her swift, sure handling of the *Dolphin*'s sails for
some moments and then said, "Where are you, lass? For
certain, you're not with me." He watched her incredible
long-lashed eyes widen as if she were surprised to see him
there and saw a smile transform her face.

"I was thinking of Willi and the change that's come
over him."

"Ah. Willi." If she was thinking of the horse, she was
thinking of Banning, too. He was curious about the fellow,
and about his friend. He'd been so busy catching up with
his work since returning to Seacliff, he got only a quick
account of the amazing goings-on in his absence—
Aimee's unexpected engagement and Banning's daily riding of the old stallion. It was a bewildering change of pace
that he was not yet accustomed to.

"Tell me about this Banning," he said.

"Am I as obvious as all that?"

"I know you, lass."

Ayisha said quietly, "Then maybe you can tell me if I'm
in love with him."

"In love?" Mac's laughter soared out across the green
water. "If you have to ask, lassie, the answer's nay. You're
not in love."

"I tingle when I look at him."

Mac grinned. "I tingle all the time. A storm coming, a
sail billowing, a beautiful horse, a beautiful woman, a sunset, a pint on a hot day, a pint on a cold day. Love's more
than tingling and goosebumps, cosset."

"Mac, be serious. It's more than tingling. I've never felt this way about anyone before. I can't think about anything but him, and I don't like it! I feel trapped."

Seeing that her eyes were wet, he asked gravely, "Does he tingle when he looks at you?"

"He doesn't look at me."

Mac studied her in disbelief—the glorious color of her hair and eyes and skin, the sweet perfection of her face and body. He said gruffly, "What do you mean, he doesn't look at you?"

She could tell Mac. He was the only one she could tell. Keeping her hands and eyes on the tiller, she said, "He only comes for Willi."

"Maybe the man has a lass."

"He says nay. He says it's just best that we—not see each other."

Mac felt his temper stirring. "Did he explain this mystery, or don't you see it as a mystery?"

"I do. When I asked him about it, he said he had a—a very strong reason."

"Did he, by God?" Here was the poor lass pining away, letting the fellow ride her favorite horse, and getting naught in return.

Seeing the anger crackling in Mac's brown eyes, Ayisha shook her head. "Mac, nay. You'll not talk to him about it."

"Why not?"

"Because you're not my keeper, and it's not why I told you. I told you because I had to tell someone—and because you said once that there was a big difference between love and infatuation and I need to know what it is."

Mac gave a silent groan. "Wouldn't your sister be a better one to ask?"

Ayisha shook her head and pushed a wind-tossed strand of hair out of her eyes. "She wants me to be in love with him."

"How about my mother?"

Ayisha laughed. "She already has us wed."

God. Mac sighed, reached across, and gave her hand a

hard squeeze. "I'd say it sounds like a crush, girl." He willed it to be so. Cain Banning did not deserve her.

"Are you sure? Because if you are, I'll tell Jere today not to come any more."

Mac stared at her. "Is that why the devil's been hanging around? You're trying to make Banning jealous?"

"Aye. It's shabby of me, I know. I'm even starting to feel a bit sorry for him." As they sailed, she had been thinking of her father's words—that toying with Jeremy's affections could be dangerous. She knew it was so. She had already seen it. He was becoming possessive again and wanting to kiss her all of the time and it simply wasn't worth the struggle. Not if what she felt for Cain was an infatuation that would be gone tomorrow or next week.

Mac studied her and tugged at his dark beard. "This isn't like you, lass. Greydon's sure to sense it, and it could be damned nasty."

"I know—but back to the other—" Ayisha looked at him hopefully. "Do you really think what I feel is only a crush?"

Mac ran a hand through his hair. "You're putting me on the spot. I'm not the Almighty, I've only got my own experience to go on, but aye, I think it's a crush."

Ayisha nodded, almost glad. Mac had never steered her wrong, and it helped her to make a decision. "This eve will be the last then. I'll tell him I can't see him again." She doubted it had done any good anyway. Cain was as remote as ever. Sensing a shifting of wind and current, she said, "Let's turn back. It's going to take us a while to tack in."

As they beat their way back to the bay, there was an unnatural silence between them. Mac said abruptly, "I see Banning's just come down to the dock. I wonder what he wants." Watching him dismount and put his horse in the paddock, Mac's fingers itched. He wanted to deck him, hurting Ayisha as he had with his aloofness, but then he'd best keep out of it. She'd not thank him for interfering.

As he waited for the *Dolphin*'s return, Cain strode through the hard-packed sand angrily and told himself to keep a clear head. Think about Willi. Think about the beauty of this place, the vast expanse of pine woods and green sea and blue sky. Think about the land and the yards he'd looked at. But all were swept from his mind when he thought of Ayisha.

Ayisha sailing her small craft through the choppy sea, laughing, waving at him ... Ayisha by candlelight in her bottle-green gown, her skin silken and scented with jasmine ... Ayisha weeping in quiet joy as he'd put the old stallion through his high school paces ...

He saw her with Greydon then ... a vision in tangerine silk ... husky laughter ... intimate talk as they strolled side by side in the sunset ... his arm snaked around her waist and pressing her body close to him ... bending low to speak in her ear ... kissing her soft, white throat, her lips ...

His muscles tightened, hardened as he reflected that the devil would probably be coming this eve again. It was enough. He'd had enough of his hanging about. He had plotted this entire scheme to protect her if it seemed necessary, and now it was necessary. How could the little witch allow him to court her that way when she neither liked nor trusted him? What a fool she was—or else she was a complete innocent. Seeing the *Dolphin* tacking into the bay finally, he strode to the dock, reminding himself to stay calm, composed, unruffled.

"Is anything wrong with Willi?" Ayisha called as they neared the dock.

"Willi's fine." Cain caught the rope she threw and helped tie up. "I need to talk with you, Ayisha. Now." Sensing Mac's hostility, he offered no greeting, nor did he receive one.

Mac said tautly, "I'll stow her, lass. You go on."

Seeing Mac's tightly compressed lips and icy eyes, Ayisha was sorry she had confided in him. She said to Cain, "Shall we walk along the shore?"

"If you'd like." Lowering himself to the beach, he quickly removed his boots and stockings, and with Ayisha by his side, scuffed through the hot sand. He felt his tense muscles relaxing even before the cool water lapped at his feet.

Ayisha kept her eyes lowered to the blue-green wavelets creaming about her ankles and wondered why he was there. He shouldn't have been. But since he was, she would put it to good use. "This gives me another chance to thank you. Willi looks wonderful."

"He's responding well."

All of Cain's senses were aroused by her nearness. For days, his memories of her had taunted him, but they were as naught compared to the reality of having her there with him as they walked through the shallow surf. His stolen glances devoured her, the graceful curves of her shoulders and breasts and long, slim legs, her small, white feet and long auburn hair. She was a vision, a dream, and her low, soft voice was the voice of the stars and the wind and the murmur of the sea.

He caught himself, appalled by the thoughts he was thinking. If he hoped to keep this maid from more heart-break than what she already faced because of him, he could not think such things. He must not. His bewitchment by her would show in his every word and gesture. He had to be crisp with her. Impersonal.

Ayisha felt the glow within her expanding, stealing into her arms and legs and flooding her heart with its golden warmth. Cain was doing naught but walking by her side, but his nearness was making her tingle from head to toe. She had asked Mac if she were in love, but she saw now that she did not need anyone to answer that question for her or tell her the difference between love and infatuation. She was in love.

Love was filling her, brimming over inside of her with such lavish abundance that she saw everything around her through a golden mist—the sand, the sun, the sea and the creatures in it, the careening gulls, the ship in the distance and all aboard it. She loved them all. If only she could tell Cain how she felt, it might change everything. But she could not. She dared not. She murmured, "Willi always used to stand with his head down and his tail drooping. Now it seems he knows you're coming and he's waiting for you ..." And someday soon, Cain would be returning to England, and what would Willi do without him? In truth, what would she do? She was frightened suddenly, wondering if that was why he wanted to see her. To tell her he was leaving. She looked up at his grim profile, dark etched against the blue-green sea and the whitecaps. "Why did you want to talk with me? It sounds serious."

"Seth and I think it is."

Seth and he? Was it to do with Aimee then? Or her father? Or had Seth, darling Seth, actually made Cain see that walking and talking with her would not result in some unspeakable calamity. She asked carefully, "What is it?"

"It's about your friend, Greydon."

"Jeremy?" She was almost afraid to breathe. "What about him?"

"I notice he's around a bit." Cain cursed the strangled sound of his voice.

"That's so. We're friends. We enjoy each other's company." He had noticed! He'd notice and he was angry! Her heart began to beat harder.

"I thought he was your sister's friend."

"He used to call on me. I knew him first."

Cain kept his eyes fastened on the beach stretching out before them. "So, he courted you, decided he preferred your sister, and now that she's taken, you've taken him back." He knew that wasn't at all the way of it, but he wanted to hear it from her.

Ayisha studied his angry, down-turned mouth and the small muscle working in his jaw and wanted to shout with the jubilation flooding through her. She shrugged instead and lengthened her stride to keep up with his. "If it doesn't bother me," she asked calmly, "why should it bother you?"

"What bothers me," Cain growled, "is that you rejected the man, you warned your sister about him, yet you—" He clamped his jaws shut. He had been about to say she'd allowed him to slobber over her. He was sounding like an interfering old woman.

Ayisha emitted a soft chuckle. "How do you know all that? But then I guess Aimee told Seth . . ." She was delighted, seeing that he was choked with fury. Her plan was working far better than she had ever dreamed it would. He was furiously, wonderfully, magnificently jealous, and it made her wonder if she should continue having Jeremy come for just awhile longer. "It's true, I did stop seeing him. It was quite generous of him to let me tag along to the dinner the other day. I warned Aimee about him because he's such a charmer."

Cain said curtly, "He's a man you shouldn't play games with, Ayisha. It could be dangerous."

She gave him her most placid gaze and said sweetly, "It's very nice of you to be concerned. I appreciate it. And I'll certainly be careful not to play games with him." She picked up a small shell, examined it, and tossed it into the outgoing tide. "Was that all you wanted to say? I really should be getting back to change. He'll be coming soon."

Cain's eyes narrowed. "You don't believe me."

"I believe that you believe what you're saying,"—she was enjoying herself—"but rest assured, Jeremy's always been a perfect gentleman. He'd never harm me. Besides, I can take care of myself." Her eyes danced. "I have muscles."

Muscles? In those slender white arms of hers? Cain held his tongue and held back his cynical laughter. He wanted to tell her he had known too many men like Greydon for whom women were naught but prey. The devil was dangerous and not to be trusted, but he could not say such a thing without proof. He said only, "Promise me you'll be careful."

"Oh, I will, and I do thank you, and I thank you a million times for Willi."

Cain was stunned to feel her soft breasts pressed suddenly against his chest and her soft mouth brushing a kiss over his cheek. It was done swiftly and in all innocence, but it set him afire. He was burning to pull her into his arms, kiss her rosy mouth, bury his face between her breasts, inhale her elusive jasmine scent. As his hunger for her grew, so did his fear for her.

Ayisha gave him a teasing smile. "Come on, I'll race you back to the horses."

Watching her splash off through the shallows, Cain knew he could not allow the moment to pass. He had to show her the danger she was in. Reaching her side in two long strides, he slid his arm around her waist.

"Maids who play with fire get burned, Ayisha. I'll say it again, Greydon is dangerous. You'll not escape him if he doesn't wish it." For days, his thoughts of her had tortured him, and now here she was, warm and soft in the circle of his arms.

Ayisha gazed up at him in astonishment. She whispered, "I could, you know. Believe me I could." Fear and anger always gave her strength, whereas in this man's arms, she was powerless.

"Nay, Ayisha. You could no more escape him than you can escape me." Turning her toward him roughly, Cain pinned her arms behind her and captured her mouth with his. She was so small and slim and silky and honey-sweet, every yearning he had suppressed since the first moment he'd seen her swelled into one great headlong rush, heating and hardening him and deepening his kiss.

Ayisha was stunned at finding herself in Cain Banning's arms and being kissed. And he was right. Maids who played with fire got burned. His fire was scorching her.

Cain warned himself to stop. He had made his point. She surely saw now that if Greydon wanted his way with her, she had no hope of escaping. His own hands refused to release her and his mouth sought hers more hungrily. He was as trapped by her beauty as she was by his strength, and only when he heard her soft moan did he release her.

"I'm sorry"—his voice was husky—"I didn't mean to hurt you."

"You didn't," she said faintly. He had opened a door and shown her paradise, and now it had closed again.

"I wanted only to show you what could happen between a maid and a man bent on having her. You could be in great danger, Ayisha."

Ayisha gave a small, uncertain laugh. "You've shown me well. I've—been burned, Cain."

And so had he, Cain thought numbly. So had he. He saw now that this was no mere infatuation. He had never planned on losing his heart and his soul—but he had. The imprint of her body still seared him, and the taste and the scent and the feel of her still clung to him like a web of gossamer. He would never be free of her, yet naught had changed. She was as forbidden to him now as she ever was.

Ayisha was dazed, her body fire-filled as they walked toward the paddock. What had happened between them—and how had it happened? It had been hard enough to keep away from him before, how could she ever do it now? He was starved for her, as starved as she was for him—and she wanted more of him. She wanted more, and more and more and more. She had to tell him. She could not keep such a thing locked away in her heart. It would show on her face and in her eyes and her voice. He would know.

"Cain, I—" She jumped as Jeremy's voice rang out from the top of the bluff. She heard the annoyance in it.

"Ayisha, are you down there?"

Cain was tempted to bellow back that she was with him but restrained himself. He said gruffly, "Remember what can happen . . ."

She smiled. "I'll remember. Actually, I was going to tell him this eve that I couldn't see him anymore."

"Is that so?"

"You don't believe me."

"You're right, I don't believe you."

"I'm sorry, but it happens to be so." She watched as he retrieved his boots and stuck them into his saddlebag.

"Ayisha!" It was another bellow from the top of the cliff. "Answer me!"

"I'm coming, Jere, for heaven's sake." She turned back to Cain. "Could we talk some more? Maybe after he leaves?" She was certain he would say nay, but he nodded.

"Come to the meadow," Cain said. "I'll be with Willi."

Chapter 10

J eremy was waiting for her at the stable, tall and stiff and with his mouth drawn into a false, tight-lipped smile. "Did you forget I was coming?"

"Not at all." Ayisha handed Omar to a groom. "The wind shifted, and we had to tack all the way back." Her skin crawled as his eyes lingered on her breasts after sliding over the rest of her. "Jere, there's something we should talk about right away. Let's walk."

Seeing Cain Banning placing his mount in the paddock, murder stirred in Jeremy's heart. "Was he out with you—Banning?"

"I've never sailed with him. I was out with Mac. Cain is here to work Willi."

Jeremy studied her beautiful, flushed face with hard eyes. The fellow was about to work the stallion, aye, and perhaps they had not been sailing, but they had been together on the beach. He felt it in his bones and it enraged him so, he wanted to throttle her. He had lost her once and he was damned if he'd lose her again. Grasping her upper arm, he began to march her toward the house. "I'll wait on the terrace while you change."

Ayisha bristled and shook off his hand. They were both angry, and it was the worst time in the world to tell him what she had to tell him, but she was not going to put it off. She had to end this madness here and now. "I don't intend to change, Jere. As I said, I want to talk to you."

"Indeed." The way she was blushing, he knew already what it was, and he cursed himself for his incredible stu-

124

pidity. The damned witch had been using him as bait to snare the Englishman and now she was ready to kiss him good-bye. Kiss? He gave a silent laugh at the thought of the few kisses he had managed to steal from her. Nay, he would not even get a kiss out of it. At the thought, he wanted to force her down, spread her legs, thrust himself into her, and if she screamed and fought him, so much the better. She deserved to be punished. They all did—Ayisha, her stupid bird-loving sister—he had never wanted Aimee in the first place—the two Englishmen, the old man. He yearned to slay them all. They had all thwarted him, and no one thwarted Jeremy Greydon or got in his way without paying for it. No one.

As they strolled past a profusion of flower beds, Ayisha scarcely saw the brightly colored blossoms. She was on the shore in Cain Banning's arms and he was kissing her. He was actually kissing her. Had it really happened? She smiled. Aye, it had happened. But now was not the time to think of it. Not when she had somehow to disentangle herself from Jeremy without hurting him too much. But then knowing him, he would be more furious than hurt. He was used to getting his own way.

"Jere . . ."

"I'm waiting." His face was impassive. When she still did not speak but plucked a long blade of grass and wound it about one finger, he said gruffly, "I think you are about to say good-bye to me, Ayisha. Again."

Her eyes flew to his face. Seeing that he was not angry, she was relieved. She said gently, "I'm sorry, but in all fairness, you should be seeing a woman who can think about a future with you. I can't, Jere. We're too different."

His smile went unseen. Little did she know that her future was with him, whether she liked it or not. She was going to be his wife. He had thought of little else since that glorious night when he had taken her to the dinner instead of her sister. And if his man in London found no shady doings in Cain Banning's past that could be used against him, it mattered naught. There were other ways to be rid of him, and other ways to have this bitch for his own.

The sight of her never ceased to heat his blood, and dressed in her boy's garb, she excited him more than ever this eve. It outlined every curve of her body. In God's name, how could a man not want to squeeze those luscious breasts and her soft thighs and arms. Dragging in a deep breath to calm himself, Jeremy led her toward the far edge of the green where the pine woods began.

"Differences between a man and a woman can be overcome, sweeting," he said smoothly, "and changes made." But it was she who was going to change. The woman who bore his name and his children was not going to ride and sail like a man. She would stay in his home and manage it and dress and behave as a woman should.

Ayisha laughed. "We can't overcome our differences, Jere. They're too vast."

"You surprise me, Ayisha. You had me thinking you'd changed when you went out with me again—and when you invited me here again and again and again. And when you allowed me to kiss you."

Hearing the sharp edge to his voice, Ayisha realized he had been hiding his anger. She should have known. She said firmly, "I enjoyed talking with you, Jere, I always have. You're an interesting man, but I hope you don't make too much of a kiss or two."

"*Au contraire.* You're so damned stingy with them, I make very much of it when you see fit to bestow one. In fact, I wonder now, was I permitted those several small rewards because you hoped Banning was watching from afar?" He gave a sharp laugh seeing pink suffuse her face. "Well, well, I hit the bloody mark right on, didn't I?" He looked at her in disgust. "What an ass I've been. You were using me to make the bastard jealous."

Ayisha quickened her step. She had seen him angry, aye, but this was more than anger. This was rage, red-faced white-lipped rage, the veins pulsing at his temples, his eyes rolling and wild looking. Even so, she managed to say quite calmly, "I'm going back ..."

"I'm right, am I not?"

"You're being ridiculous."

"Nay, my love. I'm right. It's written all over your face." He caught her abruptly, spun her about, and spooned her against him, her back to his chest. He crossed his arms roughly over her breasts, crushing the soft flesh.

"Let me go, Jere." She kept her voice low, but he was hurting her and she was growing uneasy.

Jeremy ignored her plea. "You cared naught about making a fool of me, did you? Naught mattered but making that dog notice my attentions to you."

Ayisha tried to writhe free, but he tightened his grip, rendering her helpless. She trembled, more with rage than with fear. After assuring Cain that she could take care of herself, it seemed she could not, and she felt ten different kinds of fool. She snapped, "I'm not impressed by your strength, Jeremy."

He gave an ugly laugh. "You will be impressed by my lovemaking, sweeting."

She grew very still and fought the panic that nigh overwhelmed her. Lovemaking. Dear God. Her flesh crept. His breathing had grown shallow and fast, and it was disgustingly hot and wet on her neck. What an idiot she was to have come so far from the house with him. Da had warned her, and she herself knew better. Now they were far beyond earshot of the barn and the meadow where Cain was working Willi. What a fool . . .

"There's a lovely spot in the woods where the grass is deep, cosset." He began walking, forcing her to move along ahead of him.

She dug her heels into the ground. "If you rape me, Jeremy," her voice shook, "I'll kill you. I swear it."

Rape. That she even knew such a word excited him further. "Come along, little wench." He marched her forward. "Don't balk, or I'll carry you."

"I'll kill you if you touch me that w—way, you disgusting, turnip-headed swab!"

He chuckled. "I'm trembling in my boots." He slid his

wet tongue along the skin beneath her ear and licked her
as he took a breast in each hand and squeezed.

The pain turned Ayisha's fury to fear. She struggled
against him wildly, opening her mouth to scream, but it
was smothered as he forced her head to one side and took
her mouth in a deep kiss.

The silly bitch. He had no intention of raping her and
becoming a fugitive from her damned father—but what
man could blame him for claiming a few of the kisses she
should have given him all along? As he plunged his
tongue into her mouth again and again and his hands
roamed, cruel and grasping, over her body and between
her legs, he saw well that she was terrified. Good. It was
overdue, and it gave him as much pleasure as did her
sweetness and softness beneath his hands and his mouth.

Cain could not keep his mind on Willi. All he could
think of was Ayisha. Ayisha with Greydon, laughing and
walking and talking with him, being kissed by him ...
Ayisha and himself on the beach, his losing all control,
kissing her, wanting to make love to her. Hell. The little
wench was too damned delectable. His head was filled
with the memories of how sweet and fresh she had tasted
and how soft she had felt in his arms. But it would not
happen again. He wouldn't allow it. And now he had to
put her from his thoughts and concentrate on Willi. This
was Willi's time.

He closed his eyes and forced everything from his head
but the work at hand: communicating with the stallion.
The pressure of his legs against the animal's sides, the
careful distribution of his weight on its back, the guidance
of his hands on its jaw through the reins. "So, Willi," he
spoke low, easily, "let's get busy. I've been wasting your
time, old fellow." The stallion did not respond.

Only when Cain found himself losing all patience did he
realize it was not the horse who was at fault. It was himself. His mind still was not on what he was doing. It still
was on Ayisha. He brought Willi to a halt, absently rubbed
his neck and wondered if she had done what she said she

would: tell Greydon that tonight was the last time she would be seeing him. If she had, how was he responding? Amicably, angrily, disbelieving?

Scowling in the direction of the house and beyond to where the woods met the green, he wondered where they had disappeared to. Spying them finally, just as they drifted from sight, he felt a vague uneasiness. What was taking her so long? Was Greydon trying to talk her out of it? His uneasiness growing, he returned Willi to the stable, bridled his own horse, mounted, and stood in the stirrups. Eyes narrowed, he searched the distant field, but the two were nowhere in sight. He sensed it then. Danger. He smelled it, tasted it, heard it, felt it deep inside of him. Ayisha was in danger. His precious little love was in danger . . .

His little love.

As he urged his mount to a gallop, the thought of it electrified Cain. His little love. He loved her. From the first moment he had seen her, he'd been fighting his deep feelings for her, but he was not going to fight them any longer. He loved her. Beyond all else in this world, he loved her. But she must not know it yet, not yet, because naught else had changed. The important thing was that he knew. It so exhilarated him that he felt ten feet tall and as strong as ten men—and God help Greydon if he had harmed her in any way.

Spying them at the far edge of the field, a red rage swam over Cain. The bastard. Even at this distance, he saw that Greydon was holding Ayisha fast despite her struggles and was kissing her, his damned greedy paws all over her.

"Ho!" Cain shouted. "Release her, man!" He watched Greydon turn, startled, and after a brief hesitation, obey. "Move away from him, Ayisha," he added tersely. "Far away." He dismounted, approached the man slowly, his dark eyes marking him for annihilation. "So, Greydon . . ." It was a growl.

Jeremy straightened and licked his lips. "This is no business of yours, Banning."

Cain bared his teeth in a smile that was not a smile. He
turned to Ayisha. "Shall I make it my business, Ayisha?"
He saw in her eyes that she was terrified and that the skin
about her mouth was reddened from Greydon's rough
beard. Only then did he see that her shirt gaped open, re-
vealing the deep, velvety shadow between her breasts.
Damn the devil.

"Please—aye," she answered. "I don't want him to
come near me again."

Seeing where his eyes were drawn, Ayisha buttoned her
shirt with trembling fingers. Her body felt raw, her
thoughts screaming with what had just happened. Jeremy
would have taken her if Cain had not come—or would he?
She could not be sure. Perhaps he had just wanted to hurt
and terrify and humiliate her. Punish her. He had used his
hands and mouth brutally, and when she had tried to bite
and knee him, he'd nigh choked the breath out of her. Her
throat still burned. She covered her eyes, felt herself on
the verge of hysteria, but caught herself. Cain was here
now, her furious angel, and everything was all right.

"You heard her," Cain rasped, continuing his slow men-
acing walk toward his enemy. "It's my business now, and
after I've concluded it, you're leaving and you're not coming back."

Jeremy gave a harsh bark of laughter. "I'll go when I
decide to go, not because you order it." He drew a con-
cealed dagger, waved it grandly, and lowered himself into
a crouch.

"Cain, please—come away." The sight of Jeremy's
deadly blade struck Ayisha with horror, for Cain was un-
armed. "Please . . ."

Cain glowered at her and pointed to the field. "Stand
over there and be quiet."

She obeyed. He was the pirate now, and the predatory
look on his face chilled her.

All of Cain's attention was fastened on Greydon—the
wild look in his eyes, the tic in his right cheek, the slight
trembling of his hands, his grandiose flourishes with the
blade. Having fought many battles in his early seafaring

days he had learned many things. Now he recognized the telltale signs of a man who was all show and no substance. He waited calmly, eyes watchful, for his enemy to make the first move, the wrong move. Greydon did. He feinted, made a clumsy attempt to trip Cain, and feinted again. Within moments, Cain had knocked the dagger from his hands and begun thoroughly and methodically to trounce him. He showed no mercy. Any man who would force his will on a helpless maid did not deserve mercy. And this was not just any maid—this was Ayisha. Out of the corner of his eyes, he saw her draw near.

"He's hurt, Cain."

"I'm not hurt," Jeremy growled. He climbed to his feet, and wiped the sweat, blood, and dirt from his face.

Cain studied him for some moments. "I trust you're ready to leave. Of your own accord." Receiving a murderous look in reply, he nodded. "Good. You can wait at the bottom of the hill for your mount."

Jeremy's face turned a darker shade of red. "You expect me to walk to the bottom of the hill?"

Cain's mouth curved. "If you need help, I'll accompany you. A groom will bring your horse."

"This is an outrage."

"Go. Leave your weapon where it is."

Jeremy's eyes burned. "You'll pay for this, Banning. Never doubt it. You'll pay."

The ugly words and the wild look he hurled at Cain frightened Ayisha. After he was gone, she murmured, "He hates you and it's all because of me."

"Nay, Ayisha. He and I would have been enemies in any event." Cain tilted up her chin so he could look at her face. Seeing how white it was, he asked softly, "Did he— harm you?" He forbade himself to lift her up in his arms, cradle her against his heart, and comfort her.

"I'm fine." She stood straight and very still as he touched her cheek and the raw skin about her mouth. He had saved her and he was her love, but she could not tell him. At the thought, she struggled anew not to weep. "He—frightened me, that's all." Her lips quivered as she remembered Jeremy's sinking his teeth into one of her breasts, forcing his hand between her thighs, squeezing her. She had tried to scream but his mouth sealed hers. She had been disgustingly weak and helpless, she who was always so strong and quick. She was so very ashamed. It was a thing she could not tell anyone, not even Aimee. And if she told Cain or her father or Mac, she feared what they might do.

"It's all right to cry," Cain said gently. "You'll feel better if you do."

She said faintly, "I—I'm fine, really . . ."

The words were no sooner out than she was weeping. A far numb part of her noted that she was crying as a child cried, great gasping sobs torn from the very depths of her, her hot tears scalding her cheeks. She had not cried this way even when Mama had died, for she had needed to be strong. At the thought of Ana Adair lying in the ground, she wept harder. She was unable to stop.

Oh, Mama, Mama, I miss you so. You would have held me and known what to do and told me how to handle this ugly thing. I could have told you what happened. Oh, Mama . . .

Cain had never seen a woman weep so. All that mattered suddenly was that he comfort her. Naught else was of any importance. He wrapped his arms about her tenderly, tucked her head against his chest and cradled it with his hand. He stroked her hair, felt her tears soaking his shirt, and wondered what to say. What could he say? He murmured finally, "It's all right. Everything's all right, I promise." For certain, Greydon would never touch her again.

Ayisha nodded, but she could not stop weeping. Her grief, her fright, her love for him which would never be returned, all of it was pouring out of her like a waterfall. She gasped, "I—I'm sorry. I'm making a s-scene . . ."

"Nay . . ." But he was concerned. He had encouraged her to weep, but this was not normal weeping. This held such despair and desperation that he feared for her. Now he did lift her into his arms and cradled her against him.

"Hush, now, little one. Shhhhh. It's all right. It's all right. You're safe with me."

He marveled that she could be so beautiful, even in grief, tears webbing her long, dark lashes, drowning her eyes—and her mouth, it was so soft, so very soft and trembling. Sweet God, he wanted to kiss her again, this time to kiss the pain and hurt away. He bent his head, gently brushed her lips. When he heard her small sigh, he brushed them again, returned once more to taste them, and finally to kiss them gently but firmly.

When she wound her arms around his neck and offered him her mouth hungrily, he gave a low growl of pleasure. Her kiss stirred him as no kiss had ever stirred him before, and he returned it deeply. As he slid his hands over her arms and shoulders and felt her soft body pressed against him, he thought how easily she had caught fire. How easy to take her, to yield to the hunger and the wildness trembling inside of him and sink into the ecstasy that was waiting for both of them.

Cain curbed himself sharply, told himself this had to stop and it was up to him to stop it. If he held her one more instant, gave her one more kiss, all of his tightly held control would be lost. There would be no turning back. He would carry her into those fast-darkening woods, lay her down, and make her his. At the thought, his heart beat faster. But nay, dammit, he was not going to do it. He lowered her gently to her feet and put her from him, his hands still on her shoulders.

Finding herself suddenly at arm's length from him, Ayisha looked up into his night blue eyes. In them, she saw that he wanted her, but his mouth had a stubborn set to it. What had happened? Everything, his kiss, his holding her, had been wonderful beyond her wildest imaginings, and had he not comforted her and told her everything was all right? She touched his face. "What is it?"

Cain caught her hand. He wanted to raise it to his lips, to kiss it, but instead he freed it. "Know, Ayisha, that what just happened between us changes naught."

She stared up at him, disbelieving, but saw that, as al-

ways, he meant what he said. She whispered, "Why? I
don't understand." She felt cold without his kisses and his
warm arms around her. It was as if half of her had vanished when he said those words, as if her own sun were
sinking as the earth's sun was disappearing behind the
trees.

"It's not what I want, know that," Cain muttered.

She crossed her arms. "I think it's exactly what you
want. I think it gives you some perverse sort of pleasure
to hurt me."

"Ayisha . . ."

Her eyes glittered. She had had enough. "You set out to
hurt me from the very beginning, God knows why, and
you're going to keep right on. I wish I could hate you, I
really do. In truth, I have at times. But then I see you on
Willi, or you gallop up like a knight in armor and rescue
me—and kiss me . . . Damn you, Cain Banning!" She
started blindly across the field.

Cain caught up with her and walked beside her in silent
torment. He could not bear for her to hate him, nor could
he bear to give her up. There was no way on this earth he
could give her up. Hell, why couldn't he be like Seth? Not
for one instant had Seth doubted Aimee would be his although he had as much or more reason than himself to
hate Ben and extract revenge against him. Yet Seth knew
absolutely that everything would work out in the end. He
had faith.

Cain's heart thundered as he glimpsed a faint light at the
end of his long, dark tunnel of misery. Faith. He felt it stirring within him suddenly as he reflected that Ayisha cared
for him deeply, that much was clear. And when she
learned the truth—nay, if she learned it, for Ben might
never tell her—if she learned the truth, she would never
turn him away, because by then she would love him as
deeply as he loved her. He would make her love him. It
was a promise. For now, all he needed was for her to trust
him.

"You needn't walk with me," Ayisha snapped. She began to stride rapidly through the tall grass, arms swinging. "I'm sure it's against your principles."

"I want to walk with you."

"Well, don't! This is one of those times when I hate you completely." She stopped and faced him like a young warrior maid, chin high, feet apart, hands on hips. "I never want to see you again. In fact, I wish you'd never come here and never ridden Willi." But thinking of the old stallion without him fair took the heart out of her. It would be less painful to lose him herself than for Willi to lose him. She picked up her stride again.

Cain fell into step beside her and said quietly, "If I hadn't come for Willi, I'd have found another reason to return."

Ayisha kept her eyes straight ahead, but she was surprised. She said crisply, "I don't believe you."

"Believe it. I was worried about you. With Greydon hanging around so much, I wanted to make sure you were safe." Hell, he'd forgotten Greydon completely. But then let him stew at the foot of the hill awhile longer. This was far more important.

She stopped, facing him again. "You don't dare to tell me the only reason you've been riding Willi was to spy on me and Jeremy!" Her eyes sparked fire.

"You know it's not." He continued, "I'd've wanted to work with Willi even if I hadn't been concerned about you." His eyes danced. "Admit it, my concern was justified."

"Don't be smug." She was miffed by his cheerfulness when her own heart was breaking. "I hate smug men."

"I hope I'm not smug. The truth is, I'd never have forgiven myself if anything had happened to you." When she didn't answer, he said, "I have something else to tell you."

"I don't want to hear it." She started off.

"You're going to anyway." He caught her hand and kissed it.

Ayisha looked up at him in bewilderment. What had happened? What on earth had happened when just moments ago he'd said that the passion they'd shared had

changed naught. Now his eyes, his mood, his whole bearing were so different, it could mean only one thing.
"You've found a way we can be together?"

"I've found a way, aye."

"Can we walk and talk and laugh and sail and ride together?"

"Aye." Cain lifted her high into his arms and held her
close. "And we can do this." He kissed her.

"Oh, Cain ..." She clung to him, her own arms
wrapped tightly about his neck. "How can this be? I don't
understand."

"Trust me. It's all I need—for you to trust me."

"You know I do. I trust you with my life." As she lifted
her mouth for another kiss, she heard hoofbeats, heard
Cain swearing under his breath. She saw Jeremy then,
crop flailing, eyes glittering as he bore down on them.
Cain spun them both out of his path to go sprawling on the
ground. She sat up and gasped, "Cain, are you all right?"
She had forgotten all about Jeremy waiting for his mount.

"Aye. More important, are you? That was a hard fall."

"You took the brunt of it," she whispered.

Staring at the devil's dust, Cain decided that Greydon
was crazy. He could have killed or maimed both of them.
He helped Ayisha to her feet and muttered, "It's my fault.
If I'd sent his mount down right away it wouldn't have
happened."

Ayisha saw that the color had left his face. "That's no
excuse for his doing such a thing!"

"What did he say? He was mouthing something."

She looked away. "I didn't hear."

"I think you did. What was it?"

"He said—we'd both pay." She tried to laugh. "I don't
want you worrying. It was naught but his anger talking."
But she could still see the big, black gelding coming at
them, frothing, and see the hatred glittering in Jeremy's
pale eyes.

Chapter 11

When Ayisha and Cain returned to the house, they found Aimee and Seth in the front. Aimee's face was white, Seth's was dark as a thunderhead.

"Pan! What happened? We thought you were with Jeremy, but he just galloped by in a rage—"

"—and nearly ran us down," Seth growled.

"I'm sorry, it's my fault," Ayisha said. "I told him I wasn't going to see him anymore and he—took it badly."

"That's putting it mildly," Cain snapped. "And I don't want you blaming yourself."

Aimee stared at Ayisha's disheveled hair and the dark marks on her bare arms. "Did he do that to you?"

Looking down, Ayisha was shocked to see the ugly, dark bruises that stood out so vividly against her white skin. "I—guess so . . ."

"Begod, man, what are we waiting for?" Seth asked.

"Oh, Panny, did he—"

Ayisha shook her head. "I'm all right. Really."

"I still say let's go after the scum," Seth growled.

"Cain already did." Ayisha gave him a grateful glance. "I don't know how he knew I was in trouble, but he came after me. Jeremy pulled a knife on him and—"

Aimee cried, "A knife!"

"Aye, but Cain disarmed him and trounced him."

"Good old lad." Seth clapped him on the shoulder. "I wish I'd seen it."

"But a knife! And those awful bruises. Pan, Papa has to know!"

"Nay, Aimee."

"I agree with your sister." Cain was wishing he'd
thrashed him more soundly. "Your father has to know."

"Nay! Aimee, you know how Da feels about us. Tell
them. He'd go into a rage, and if he should happen to in-
jure or slay Jeremy . . ." She shook her head. "I'll not have
him in prison or hanged over the likes of Jeremy Greydon,
and that's the end of it. He's not to know. Not ever. Promise me, all of you, that you'll not say anything. Aimee? Do
tell them."

Aimee clung to Seth's hand and looked worried. "I
don't like it, but she's right. Papa would go after him. The
main thing is that you're unharmed, Panny, and Jeremy
was punished. Cain, thank you. Thanks so much!"

She saw clearly that more had taken place than just a
battle between the two men. Ayisha's face was glowing,
and Cain's eyes, when he looked at her, held an adoring
light she had not seen before. Her hand stole to her heart.
They had found each other, and it was the most marvelous
thing that could have happened. It meant a double wedding in May with Ayisha by her side marrying the man she
loved.

Cain and Seth returned to the Red Horse in silence. After giving their mounts over to a stable lad, Seth muttered,
"I'm going to get soused."

Cain's smile shone white in his dark face in the lantern
light. "I'll join you." But not to get soused. Tonight called
for a celebration.

When the two were seated in a shadowy corner of the
pub with three tankards before each of them, Seth tilted
his head and drank long. He said finally, "I never knew I
was a coward, but I am, man. I am."

Cain put down his tankard and wiped his mouth.
"What's this about?"

"The wedding. Things are getting out of control.
Aimee's making plans for the biggest damned wedding
Boston has ever seen."

"When's it to be?"

"Early next year sometime, but she's already having the gown designed and thinking about who to invite and what to feed them." Seth rubbed his tired eyes and ran nervous fingers through his hair. "I can't bring myself to tell her she shouldn't be making all of these plans just yet." He took another long drink and made a doleful face. "Man, you don't know how lucky you are not to have fallen for Ben's other daughter."

Cain said quietly, "But I have, old man." He could not tear his thoughts from what had happened between them this eve. He was filled with her—the way she looked and talked and laughed, the taste and the feel of her, the imps dancing in her golden eyes, the way the sun made her hair glitter with a hundred different lights.

Gaping at the half smile on Cain's handsome face, Seth saw that he was not teasing. "You're in love with Ayisha?"

"Aye. I haven't told her yet, but it's there. It's been there from the beginning."

Seth gave a soft groan. "I should've known, seeing the way you looked at her this eve." What surprised him was that Cain had stayed noble as long as he had. He did not know one other man who would have done it or could have. "What made you change your mind? You feared my love for Aimee would harm her."

Cain grinned and clapped his shoulder. "Your shining example changed me, mate."

Seth blinked. He'd been glad that one of them was spared the madness—a stabilizing force, so to speak—but now Cain was as lost as he was. He muttered, "God help us all." As he finished off the first tankard and raised the second to his lips, Cain frowned and stayed his hand. "Wait just a damned minute. What do you mean, God help us all? You were the one who had the faith that this would all work out."

Seth reddened. "It will, man, it will. I just don't know how or when."

Cain tilted his chair back, crossed his arms, and studied his companion with angry eyes. "I thought that's what having faith was all about—believing something would happen without knowing the how or the when or the why of it."

"That's so," Seth lifted the second tankard and took a grateful swallow. "That's very so."

"Well then?" Cain was not a religious man, but he wanted desperately to believe in that mysterious power that would give him Ayisha. Seth had been so strong and confident and rocklike, so sure of himself, that it had all seemed possible. Now he saw the rock crumbling.

"In truth," Seth took another long swallow, "I haven't had a lot of experience at this sort of thing. Faith, I mean." He stared long at the fire before adding, "In fact, I'm as new at it as you are. It comes and it goes, an' right now it's gone. Maybe I'll hop onto your coattails, old man." The ale was reaching his brain so that the angry glitter in Cain's eyes did not faze him. He grinned. "In fact, maybe I meant to get us started on the love thing an' you were meant to get us through it."

Cain lowered his chair with a thud. It was foolishness, total foolishness. "Nay, my friend. Against Ben Scott, we're together, but where the maids are concerned, we'll be on our own." It was clear now that he could not count on Seth or on some unknown thing called faith to strengthen him. The only thing he could count on was himself and his deep desire to have Ayisha for his wife. And make no mistake, he was going to have her. He added firmly, "I'm going to need more time before we talk to Ben."

Seth shrugged, drained the second tankard. "Take it."

"I will." Immediately he felt guilty. It had been days since he had given any thought to Ben Scott's abandoned crew or the families who had been robbed of their men. He sank his head in his hands.

Seth frowned. "What's wrong?"

"We've forgotten why we're here. There are people waiting." He marked that Seth's eyes were glazed and he knew he was drinking too fast.

Seth nodded. "So there are. An' since they've been

waiting twenty years, what's another month or two or three?"

Cain kept his temper. "If you weren't so stewed, you'd not ask the question."

Seth laughed. He hadn't felt so good in a blue moon. "It's not as serious as you think, old man, so why not drink up an' take your time with the little wench? Hell, take half a year an' so'll I. That way we'll make sure their love's strong enough to stand the storm when it comes. If they love us as much as we love them, why then old Ben won't do a thing when we tell him. He'll not utter a peep, man. He'd never hurt his girls. They mean the world to him." He snapped his fingers. "Barmaid, bring me another."

Cain held up a warning hand when the maid approached. "No more."

"I've only had three, man, an' you're not my keeper."

"Tonight I am. You've had it." He drew Seth's arm across his shoulders and with an effort, got him hauled to his feet and lugged up the narrow stairway to their lodgings. He dumped him into bed, pulled his boots off, and after opening the one small window, fell into bed himself. Lying in the stifling room, hearing the revelry going on below in the street, Cain brooded that they could have had the money by now, and Seth could have been on his way back to England with it.

But nay, they'd had to go and fall in love. And he was glad. He was gladder than glad, and if it was selfish of him, so be it. Nothing so wonderful had ever happened to him before. But he did need time, and he needed to move with caution even though he was certain that Seth was right—Ben would do naught to hurt his daughters. But this was the man whose orders had doomed his own crew, including his best friend, to death. He could well imagine the old boy being so enraged when he learned the truth of who they were and why they were there that he might even order the two of them slain—or he might hide the maids away so they'd never see them again. And that Cain could not bear.

* * *

The next day as Ayisha watched Cain riding Willi, she wondered when she had ever been so happy. The answer was never. Never in her life had she been so happy. And she knew that Willi had not been so content in a long, long time. Probably not since those days when he'd had eyes that could see. Nor had he looked so magnificent—his tail arched and his ears pricked and his feet performing steps that filled her with wonder.

Cain had tried to explain them to her, patiently telling her the names for what he was doing and what they meant—the shoulder in, *la croupe au mur,* the *passade,* the *pirouette*—but it was too much to absorb. How did a horse ever learn such intricate maneuvers, she wondered, and how did a person ever learn to give the complicated commands to elicit them—the slight pressure of leg muscles, the smallest movement of a finger or the shifting of one's weight in the saddle . . .

Ayisha sighed, stretched out on her stomach in the grass, chin in hands, and watched Cain, entranced—his hard thighs gripping Willi's barrel, his natural erect posture, hips pressed slightly forward, arms relaxed, his big hands curved over the reins. He was doing naught yet doing everything, his handsome face grave with concentration. She smiled suddenly, wanting to laugh outright. He was her pirate again, his long chestnut hair flying in the wind, a look of danger about him. And then the bubble burst as he halted and looked over at her with a boyish grin.

"He's one of the best," Cain said.

"I can tell. It's like heaven, the way you two look together." She walked beside them toward the stable, her hand on Willi's neck. "What was the gait you just did?"

"It's called the *Paso de Andadura.* It's between a walk and a trot." Inside the stable, Cain removed the saddle, Ayisha the bridle, and they began to towel the stallion's steaming coat.

"Were all the horses at the Becker Stud as good as Willi?" she asked. The sleeves of his white shirt were rolled up showing his arms, and she loved the look of them, the muscles rippling as they moved. Her heart pounded as she remembered how they had felt wrapped around her and imagined their being around her again. To think, from now on they would be talking, laughing, sailing, kissing . . .

"The stallions were in various stages of development," Cain replied. "Some were very advanced and some were beginners being worked on the longe."

"I see." She wanted to touch the dark stubble that shadowed his jaw and crept halfway down his throat, touch the clean lines of his mouth, play with his long hair . . . hold his hard body in her arms . . . kiss him . . . again and again and again. She swallowed and forced her eyes back to the stallion's wet coat. "Is Willi advanced?"

"Aye, but we might never know how far."

"Why not?"

Cain was well aware of her hungry scrutiny before she had looked away, pink cheeked. Now he studied her—the sweep and length of those long, dark lashes; the luscious curve of her neck and shoulders; her soft mouth pursed so seriously; the warm cream texture of her skin . . . and those ugly dark marks on her white arms. His anger was like lightning striking when he thought of Greydon's manhandling her, but he turned it away. The thing was done. She was safe, and this moment was for jubilation. For the first time, he felt no fear nor remorse nor guilt at being with her. He felt only joy and excitement. But he had to keep himself in check for there was no way he could hold and kiss her as much as he wanted to. There was no way.

He answered her last question, "The difficulty and the strain, the rigors of advanced *haute école* movements are tremendous on a horse. We'll have to build up to them slowly, Willi and I, and as he attains each new level, I'll decide whether or not he has the stamina to go to the next one." Seeing that her eyes had turned dreamy, he smiled. "What are you thinking of?"

She grinned and continued her careful circular toweling of Willi. "You and Juan Fandango. I was imagining what

you must have been like when you were a boy. Tell me
about it. I want to hear everything."

Cain was amazed that she would care. "There was
naught of interest in my life before Dango came into it,
believe me."

"I want to hear it anyway." Her brows pulled together
then. "But only if it's—something you can talk about. If
you can't, I understand. I don't want to pry."

Cain smiled. "My boyhood's an open book—one that
will put you to sleep."

"Never. You say you lived on the coast and went out on
a fishing boat every day?"

"Aye."

"Was your father a fisherman then?" Seeing the sudden
veiling of his eyes, she bit her tongue. She had done it
again.

"Nay."

When he made no further reply, she added quickly, "Did
you enjoy the work?"

"I enjoyed the sea and the sky and dreaming of far-off
places."

Her face lit. "Really? I'm the same way. Ever since I
first set foot on a ship, I've loved the feel of the sea and
the sky, and I've dreamed of going to far-off places."

"I thought you traveled with your father."

"Only up and down this coast. Never anywhere interesting or exciting."

Cain asked softly, "And where would that be?"

"Almost anywhere but the eastern seaboard. I'd love to
sail the Mediterranean ... the South China Sea ... the
South Pacific. And I'd love to see my mother's
homeland—I especially want to go there, but Da says nay.
He says there are pirates."

"There are."

She sighed. "I guess you've been everywhere."

"I've been many places, aye, but not everywhere. I went
to sea when I was fifteen, and for the next ten years I
sailed in one capacity or another."

"And now you're the captain of your own ship."

"Aye."

"And you can go wherever you want."

"That's not quite true."

He was a Gregg. He would always hear the call to go to those far mysterious reaches of the earth—and he would always fight it. Ayisha's words had reminded him of the sword hanging over his head. He'd actually forgotten it for a bit.

Seeing the shutters lower over Cain's eyes again, Ayisha marked that there were two things that made him go all wintry—talk of his father and of sailing to distant lands. She said softly, "If it's all right to ask—how old are you?"

"Twenty-nine." He chuckled, seeing her eyes widen. "I know, it's ancient. How old are you?"

"Nineteen. And don't you dare say you're ancient!" But she was shocked. She had imagined he was twenty-three or twenty-four, but to be almost thirty . . . Why, he would think she was an infant. She ran her hands over Willi's coat. "He's dry now. We can put him away and walk if you'd like."

"It sounds good."

As Cain led Willi into his stall, Ayisha went outside, pumped a bucket of water, filled a dipper, and drank deeply. She splashed the rest over her face and arms and offered Cain a fresh dipper. She watched enchanted as he drank from it and then poured the remainder over his head, drenching himself. He grinned then squeezed the glittering droplets out of his hair.

"That feels better."

She laughed, loving his boyishness. "We can get wetter than this if you'd like. There's always the ocean. Why don't we go for a swim?"

Cain blinked. "Swim? You?"

Her laughter sang out. "Swim. Me."

"Ouch. I should have known you'd not be content to wade in ponds and puddles."

"I do that, too, but not when there's an ocean handy. Actually, Da wouldn't let me board the Ayisha for my first sea voyage until I'd proven I wouldn't sink. Mac taught me."

The ever-present Mac, thought Cain with considerable annoyance. "To answer your question, aye, I'd like to swim."

"Me, too! Mac and I usually ride down." She called to a stable lad working nearby. "Jonah, please bridle Omar and King for us. Don't bother with saddles."

"Aye, Miss."

Within minutes she and Cain were mounted and traversing the steep, mossy trail down to the beach. Ayisha called back over her shoulder. "The surf or the bay?"

"You choose." His hungry eyes were devouring her straight back and slim shoulders, her small waist and the flare of her gently curving hips—and her little round rump. He was seized with an overwhelming desire to cup his hands under it and snug her hard against him. Hell, his trews were already too hot and tight to be thinking such thoughts. The water was going to feel good . . .

"The surf then," she called. "Just for a little, and then we can swim and paddle in the bay. But I warn you, it'll be freezing."

"It won't bother me a bit." God knows, it was just what he needed.

After leaving the horses in the paddock, they tugged off their boots, Cain removed his shirt, and they walked into the creaming water as it rushed to meet them.

"Brrrr. It's frigid, but I love it!" Ayisha cried. "Look, the tide's coming in and it's high."

"There's been a storm at sea." Cain's eyes were blue slits of concern as he measured her slight form against the six-foot waves breaking offshore. "Are you sure you want to go in here?"

"I'm sure. It's glorious!" She frowned up at him. "Unless you're worried . . ."

"Only for you."

She laughed. "Don't be. I turn into a fish when I hit the water." She knotted her heavy hair at her nape, tucked her shirt into her trews, and looked up at him, eyes dancing. "Let's go!"

"I'm with you." He watched her jump, laughing, over the smaller waves rolling in, watched her point to where the larger ones were breaking. Already his teeth were chattering.

"Mac and I dive through those to get to where the swells are." Seeing his concern, she hesitated. "Is anything wrong?"

Cain was frowning. "You're sure you've done this before?"

"A thousand times."

He could not imagine it. One good hard wave would knock her senseless. The last thing he saw was her waving, eyes teasing, a smile on her lips, and then she dived into a foaming six-footer and was gone.

The thundering of Cain's heart equaled the roar of the surf. He ordered himself not to stand there gaping and worrying but to find her. Find her. Go, man. Plunging into a wave as she had, he churned through the water, surfaced, and tried to spot her. She was nowhere.

"Ayisha?" Sent tumbling by a cresting giant, he gained his feet and sliced through another wall of icy gray-green water, his fear for her propelling him rapidly beyond the crashing breakers. Surfacing, he found himself in a glass-smooth sea being lifted off his feet and lowered again by the gentle swells. He cupped his hands to his mouth and bellowed, "Ayisha! Where are you? Ayisha?"

Panic mounting, he wondered why he had ever allowed her to do such a dangerous, damned-fool thing. She was just a small frail maid and this was the sea. It was a killer. God's death, he had been out of his mind to let her go. He had just found her and already he had lost her.

"Ayisha!" he cried again, his voice breaking. As he stared about him at the emptiness, shivering, certain that his world had just ended, he was grasped suddenly from beneath the water and his legs pulled out from under him. Even as he went down his laughter rang out. She was safe. She had been safe all along. Opening his eyes underwater, seeing her impish smile, he caught her fast and brought her to the surface with him.

"You little devil!" His voice did not sound like his own.

Ayisha sank, popped up laughing, and gasped, "My feet don't touch bottom here!"

"Good," he said thickly, and pulled her close.

She was laughing still, but he could not laugh with her. He was shaking, so great had been his fear and now his relief that she still lived. He wrapped his arms about her tightly as a swell lifted them and gazed, mesmerized, at the water's green reflection on her beautiful face. Her skin was white and cool and gleaming and the sea's crystalline drops webbed her lashes and glistened on her pink lips. She was a mermaid, a water sprite, a Siren. He had never seen anything so beautiful in his life.

The laughter died on Ayisha's lips. "Cain, wh—what's wrong?" His face was blanched beneath its sun-darkness—and what was that odd look in his eyes? She stared, scarcely daring to believe what she saw in them, for it looked as if—as if he cared for her deeply. She slid her arms about his neck, whispered, "Cain, talk to me."

Cain could not take his eyes off her. He feared she would disappear if he did. He muttered, "I thought I'd lost you."

"But you didn't. Here I am, right here in your arms."

He tried to smile but his lips were numb. He stroked back a long, wet tendril of flame-dark hair that had escaped from the knot and said again low, "God help me, I—thought I'd lost you . . ." He sought her mouth, kissed it hungrily, kissed her eyelids, her throat, her temples, and thought how delicious she felt pressed against him in the water, so soft and small and smooth and wet and cool. He felt his throat stinging with unshed tears, felt his love for her overwhelming him, his love and his yearning to care for her and protect her from harm for the rest of his days. "I thought I'd lost you," he murmured yet again. It was all he could say, all he could think of.

"It's all right," Ayisha replied gently. "I'm here." Her joy, like dawn rising, was illuminating and warming her in the icy water. He had not said it, but she knew—he loved her. She saw it in his eyes, heard it in his voice, felt it in his kiss and in the tender yet desperate way he was holding her. Cain Banning loved her. Wordlessly she drew his face down to hers, offered him her parted lips and, buoyed by the water, slipped her legs about his waist and pressed her hungry body to his.

Chapter 12

⌒◯◯⌒

Cain took Ayisha's mouth in a long, deep kiss and then did what he had been yearning to do for the past hour. He cupped his hands under her small, firm buttocks and pulled her close. Despite the chilliness of the Atlantic, the heat of it filled and swelled him.

Ayisha's breath caught, feeling her body pressed so tightly to his and his hardness thrusting against her. This could not be happening ... it couldn't be real ... but it was. He was holding her so closely, so hungrily and desperately—and she was so hungry for him, and so excited and happy and thrilled, she laughed to cover her confusion.

"No man has ever held my bottom before." She pushed his thick, wet hair behind his ears and slid her arms around his neck again. "What I mean to say is—if any had tried, I'd have slapped him."

Cain laughed. "I'm glad to hear it."

She smoothed her hands over his glistening dark shoulders, down over his bare chest, being careful not to touch his nipples and the crisp dark curls surrounding them. She whispered, "I've been waiting for you to do this."

Cain felt her tremble and felt a tremble beginning within his own body. Of the many pale hands that had given him pleasure, none had stirred him as hers did. He murmured into the curve of her neck and shoulder, "Let's go ashore."

"Aye ..." She had been thinking, how lovely if they could lie in the sand together ... how lovely to feel his body touching hers from head to toe and in every secret, fiery place in between.

"But I'll not have you darting off again like a little minnow," Cain said gruffly. "We'll go together. I don't want you out of my sight." He began bearing her shoreward.

Ayisha's eyes twinkled. "It's not that I don't enjoy this—but if we start swimming in one of those swells, we'll be ashore a lot faster. If you'll just put me down."

Thinking of the ocean's claiming her, Cain's arms tightened about her. He said huskily, "I'm—not sure I can."

But Ayisha had seen the perfect swell looming behind them. "Cain, this is a good one. Do let me go. I'll not disappear again, I promise!"

Seeing the green shining mountain towering suddenly behind them, he knew she was right. He was making an ass of himself. He released her. With her swimming by his side like a sleek young seal, he began stroking powerfully through the water. Seconds later, the two of them were spewed from the foaming breaker into the shallows. Hand in hand they waded to shore, onto the hard-packed sand, and then to where the sand was dry and hot and clung to their wet feet.

Ayisha's heart was flying, her blood running hot and fast. She yearned to be in his arms again, held so closely she could scarcely breathe. And she wanted him to kiss her again—kiss her all over. And she wanted to tell him that she loved him and tell him of her strange and wonderful feeling that he was her other half and that she was not whole without him. Her lips quivered in her eagerness to tell him.

But within her a wiser, quieter self was shaking her head, holding a finger to her lips, calming her quickened breathing. A wiser quieter self who told her that ladies did not go first, not at times like this. Men went first. They deplored females who gushed and were too forward. Nay, as much as she wished it, she would not speak of it. She looked up and tried to keep in step with Cain's long strides.

"It seems I've made a habit of frightening you. I'm sorry. I don't mean to."

Cain remained silent. He was remembering his first glimpse of her rising out of the sea and laughing, her blue cotton shirt dripping water, clinging tightly to her gleaming body and showing its every beautiful curve and valley and her hard, pearl-like little nipples. He had decided, at that glorious instant when he had known she was safe, that he would tell her how he felt. He must. He could not put it off any longer. He stopped and took her by the shoulders. "Do you know why I was frightened, Ayisha?"

"Aye." His gaze, like a blue flame, was burning through her as she twisted her dark hair into a rope and wrung the water out of it. She smiled up at him. "I—think you rather like me, Cain Banning."

"I more than like you, Ayisha Adair."

Her heart took wing with the gulls and somewhere, maybe in her head, she heard a lark singing. She said faintly, "I'm not quite sure what that means, that you 'more than like me.' " But she knew, she knew. She just wanted to hear him say it.

"It means, little wench," Cain said low, "that I love you." He saw her eyes widen, felt within himself the shock of what he had said. He had never spoken those words to any woman before—except his mother. He had been a small lad and she had been weeping and he had tried in the only way he knew to comfort her. Now he gave Ayisha a gentle shake and said again softly, "I love you, Ayisha."

I love you.

Ayisha caught and held the unbelievable words and the moment to her heart, a heart so filled with joy she could not speak. This was the man who had not wanted to see her again, the man who had hurt her so many times. And now he had said he loved her. She heard a whole chorus of larks singing.

Cain tilted up her chin and frowned seeing that her eyes were wet. "God, I've made you unhappy."

"Unhappy?" She laughed. "Oh, Cain, nay! I'm not unhappy. I've loved you since the very first night. Nay, even before that. I loved you from my very first sight of you shouting at me from the *Sea Eagle!* And to think—you love me! Oh, Cain!"

Cain's own laughter joined hers as relief swept over him. He drew her down to the sand with him, gathered her into his arms, and they lay in joyous silence, the only noise the sounds of the surf and the gulls crying and wheeling across the blue. He murmured finally, "The surprise isn't that I love you, sprite—it's that you love me after the way I've treated you."

Ayisha raised herself on an elbow and studied his frowning brows and the remorse on his face. "Let's see now, how have you treated me . . ." She tapped her mouth with a finger. "You tried to save me from being run over by your ship . . . you rescued me from Jeremy and a fate worse than death . . . you helped me muck out stalls, also a fate worse than death . . . you've worked long hours with Willi . . ."

"I've been rude, critical, sharp-tongued, and insulting. I've hurt you over and over."

"And I've hurt you. But no more—it's all in the past. We've kissed and made peace. In fact"—she sat up, her eyes golden pools of mischief—"I think we need to do it again, just for good measure . . ." She slid a leg over his abdomen and once astride him, bent and kissed his mouth.

Cain's breath came out in a rush as her breasts grazed his bare skin and he tasted the warmth and sweetness of her lips. He wanted to strip off her wet clothing and take her right there. He said huskily, "You like to live dangerously, Ayisha."

She whispered, "Maybe I like being in danger from you." She stroked his chest, loved its hardness and the heavy thudding of his heart beneath her hands. Her mouth curved in a smile. "I wonder why your heart is pounding so?"

Cain pulled her down against him and covered her mouth with his. Rolling over, he caged her swiftly and neatly beneath him. Her hands, moving slowly, sensuously across his back, down over his buttocks and up his spine sent fresh desire pulsing through him. "Little vixen ..."

Feeling his very core aching with his need for her, he kissed her mouth again and again, each time more roughly and deeply than the last. He knew he was hurting her, squeezing the breath out of her as he was, yet she was yielding, returning his kisses and caresses as hungrily as he was giving them. He trembled at the thought of having her there in the hot sand and giving her the same pleasure she would give him. It brought him to the very edge of rapture before he saw that it could not be. He could not make love to her until they were safely wed and she knew all there was to know about him. It was aeons in the future, but it was the way it had to be and that was that.

Holding tightly to the thought, he rolled onto his side, loosed his fierce hold on her, and told himself just to enjoy her—the silkiness of her skin and those long, sweeping sable lashes, the sweet taste of her mouth, the wonderful scent of her—of sea and hot sun and jasmine. Aye, he would hold her just a little while longer. He was no animal that he could not control his hunger for her.

"Cain ..."

"Aye, cosset?"

She had been thinking and thinking, and the more she thought, the more she wondered why the man was always the first to say "I love you" and "Will you marry me?" Certainly it was how things were and the way she had been taught, but why? It was stupid and she was tired of it. And since he had been the one to say "I love you," she would say the other. Now. Before she lost her courage. She swallowed, drew a quick breath, and said in a voice she could scarce hear, "Will you—wed me, Cain Banning?"

Gazing down at her beautiful upturned face, Cain was struck silent by her openness and innocence and bravery. And he was filled to overflowing with his fierce love for her. He laughed softly and kissed the tip of her nose.

"Well?" Her voice had a quaver in it.

He shook his head. "God's life, Ayisha, there's none other in the world like you."

"You think I'm too bold," she said faintly.

"Not at all. You caught me off guard. I've been remiss. I should have asked you."

"Why? What's wrong with my asking you?"

"Because it's"—he knew his eyes were laughing—"it's just not the way of it."

She saw well that he was teasing her. She smiled sweetly. "Did you ever intend to ask me?"

He tilted up her chin. "Isn't that what it's all about when a man and a woman love each other? To wed? It is where I come from."

She pressed onward. She was so close, so very close. "Is this a proposal?"

Cain's muscles hardened as his arms tightened about her. "Aye. From a man who can't live without you." He cocked a dark eyebrow. "Do you want me on bended knee? You have but to say it." His hand stole to her breast and explored it gently.

"No bended knee," Ayisha whispered. She lay her hand atop his, thrilling to its size and strength and marveling at its tenderness as he caressed her. "I want you here beside me. Close."

"Then that's where I'll be. Here beside you. Close." He tasted her mouth again and began unbuttoning her shirt. "Will you wed me, Ayisha?" She made no answer, but clung to him and buried her face in his neck. "Ayisha . . . ?"

Overcome, she murmured finally, "I'll wed you, aye. A thousand times aye."

As he opened her shirt and cupped her naked breasts in his hands, it was like flame caressing her, and when he touched his tongue to her nipples, the fierce sweet heat of it shot through her and into parts of her body she had never felt before, never known existed. She gasped and arched against him.

Gazing on her, Cain's breath caught in his throat. She was beautiful beyond all imagining—skin like cream, her nipples small, perfect red berries tipping her plump, white breasts. And then he saw the marks on them. They were fading but still visible, ugly reddish-purple bruises about the right nipple and several darker ones covering both breasts. He touched them tenderly, felt his rage rising and nigh smothering him so that he could scarcely mutter, "Did Greydon do this to you?"

"Aye." Her voice was small for she had seen his fury and feared what he would do.

He had bitten her, Cain thought. The damned bloody bastard has used his teeth on her in addition to mauling and pawing her. God Almighty. "I should have come to you sooner." It was a growl. "I'm sorry . . ."

Ayisha stroked his cheek. "You were wonderful to have come at all. To have known to come."

"I should have half killed him, that's what I should've done. In fact, if I'd known about this"—he touched gentle fingers to her again. His fury left him speechless.

"It's all right. I'm all right."

Cain shook his head and kept his protecting hands over her breasts for long moments. "No man will ever hurt you like this again," he said.

She was warmed, touched deeply. Never had she felt so small and cherished and protected—like a maiden of old with a knight to guard her. She raised one of his hands to her lips, gently bit and tasted his knuckles and smiled up at him, her eyes tear-bright. "I feel as safe as if I were in God's pocket. That's what Peg would say."

Cain brushed her sleek, damp head with his lips. "Aye, as if you were in God's pocket."

The words, like the stroke of a great sword, brought him down. She trusted him completely, and he, who could not bear the thought of her being hurt, might soon inflict upon her a hurt a hundredfold worse than the bruises Greydon had given her. As her small hand crept over his chest and arm and throat, loving him, caressing him, he held her closer and thought angrily of God, of all the God words he used unthinkingly—God Almighty and God's hooks and breath and death and bones. . . . Why in hell did he do it when there was no God? He had decided it, finally and irrevocably, on the day Tom Gregg had said good-bye to him for the last time and gone off whistling.

"Maybe we could all be wed together," Ayisha exclaimed suddenly. "Aimee and Seth and you and me. We could have a double wedding! Oh, Cain, she'd just love that!"

Her sudden gay laughter was a burst of sunshine on his dark thoughts. "Aye. Why not?"

"I can't believe this! We're going to wed! And just a short time ago you didn't want to see me anymore. I still don't understand how everything could have—" She ceased in mid-sentence, looked up at him, smiled. "Nay, love, I haven't forgotten. I'll have no explanations. Trust me for that as I trust you."

"Someday soon we're going to have a long talk, you and I." But how much he told her, he brooded, would depend upon her father. "Know, Ayisha," he said gruffly, "that people are sometimes forced to do things they'd never normally do."

"I know." He looked so tormented of a sudden. She knelt by his side and took his hand. "But there's naught that we can't handle between us. Our love will conquer everything. It's what Mama always said to Da when he was low."

Cain almost laughed. Ben Scott low? His resentment tasted bitter in his mouth. What had the old man to worry about in the halcyon days before his wife had died? He had gotten clean away with his horrendous crime and was awash in gold and luxury and the respect of a whole city. And now it was his innocent daughters who were going to suffer if this damned thing went badly.

He dragged in a sharp breath and was tempted to tell her the whole ugly story then and there and trust her to understand. He was sick to death of lying. The words burned his lips in his eagerness to confess, but caution kept him silent. Nay. He could not. Their love was too new, too fragile to take on such a heavy burden so soon. He could not risk losing her. But it was time he began to open the window on his past. Just a crack. He said, "You asked

earlier if my father was a fisherman . . ." His mind and
tongue, his whole body balked at continuing the conversation so that he had to force the words from his mouth. "He
wasn't. He hauled cargo, and he—was a wanderer, my
father."

Ayisha sat very still, seeing the change that was trans-
forming his face—lips folded, dark brows bunched together, blue eyes iced over. She had never seen him look
so gaunt. Even so, she said brightly, "That's interesting.
My father hauled cargo too. I'm not sure what you mean,
though, when you say he was a wanderer."

Cain said shortly, "He didn't have blood in his veins.
He had seawater. Seawater and roving."

She hid her uneasiness. "I'd have understood him, I
think. Whenever I go out in the *Dolphin*, I wonder what it
would be like to go sailing off beyond the horizon—"

"—and keep going till you reach the ends of the earth."
Cain raised himself to sit beside her, let the sand sift
through his fingers.

"Aye. You've felt it too then?"

"Every day of my life. It's a powerful pull."

"Aye, but I've been tethered to a powerful anchor.
Aimee and my father and Seacliff"—she flashed a grin at
him—"and the *Dolphin*'s not exactly the *Sea Eagle*." She
took his hand again, studied his long tapering fingers and
smooth oval nails, and held it to her cheek. "Tell me about
it. Wandering, I mean. Is it as exciting as it seems?"

Cain stroked her hair with his other hand. "I've never
done it."

"Never done it! Why? If I were an unfettered man, I'd
have been all over the world a hundred times by now."

Cain said quietly, "I'll not be like my father."

Without thinking, she asked, "Didn't you like him?" Oh,
nay! She held her breath. What a stupid, prying question.
But he surprised her. He answered.

"He was my god," Cain replied. "Only after my mother
died did I see the kind of man he was and what he'd done
to her with his roaming."

Ayisha said carefully, "I'll listen if you want to talk about it."

"I don't. Suffice it to say he'd be gone for months and come home for two days and go off again whistling. He cared naught that her life was empty without him or that we both needed him. His father was the same, and his father's father before him. I refused to be another link in the chain."

She felt cold despite the hot sun. "Maybe there was naught to hold them at home, those others."

"There was everything to hold them. Wives and children who loved them and depended on them, business responsibilities—but when the damned call came, they went."

When the call came . . . Ayisha had never heard of such a thing before. A call. It frightened her. The sun still shone, the sky was so bright it hurt her eyes, and the gulls still wheeled across its blue dome screaming. Naught had changed, yet everything had changed. "Are you saying this might happen to you? To us? That someday you might just go off and—not come back?" When he remained silent, she whispered, "Cain . . . ?"

Just talking of it, thinking of it had sent Cain's thoughts winging as they always did to places he yearned to see again and places he had never been. He steeled himself against them, the beckoning of distant green waters and glittering golden domes, of noisy bazaars and trackless deserts and the mysteries of dark, steaming jungles. But this time, this time it was different. He sensed it, knew in his grateful heart that his yearning now was not for those far shining mysterious places. This time he was being drawn to stay right where he was, close by Ayisha's side.

"Cain, answer me!" He was frightening her with his strange silence and shining eyes—and then suddenly he was laughing and laughing. She was indignant. "Why are you laughing?" When he said naught, but lifted her high in his arms and spun her about, covering her face and her breasts with hungry kisses, she said sharply, "Know, Cain Banning, if you go wandering off, I'm going with you!

You'll not sail off to the ends of the earth without me! Know that!" She struggled against him but could not break free of his long arms wrapped around her. "Let go, damn you, so I can wallop you!"

Cain continued kissing her, her beautiful flushed face and pink mouth, her hair and arms and throat and breasts. A miracle had just touched him and she was at the very heart of it.

"Kisses will get you nowhere!"

Still laughing, he drank in the sight of her and the wondrous feel of his love for her—and he drank in his new-found freedom from a thing that had deviled him his entire life. The sword was gone. It was gone absolutely. He felt as if he could fly.

Ayisha stared at him. He looked so happy and there was such a joy, such an ease about him that she saw there was a new mystery here. She was almost afraid to speak or even to breathe for fear of breaking the spell but her curiosity got the better of her. She whispered, "What happened just now? If it's something you can tell me . . ."

"It's something I can tell you, aye." For the first time in his life, he was exactly where he wanted to be. With her. He wanted to be with her and have her in his arms and in his life forever. He said, "What happened, my dearest sprite, was you."

Chapter 13

The grandfather clock on the landing had just chimed ten when Aimee tapped on the open door of her sister's bedchamber and looked in. "Hello! You're still awake . . ."

"Aye." Ayisha lowered the book she had taken to bed with her. She had read two chapters and could not remember a word of them. All she could think of was Cain. She smiled at Aimee. "Come on in. I was hoping I'd see you before I fell asleep." Actually, there was no chance of her sleeping a wink this night. She had been dying to tell Aimee her glorious news as soon as Cain left, but she had been off with Seth the livelong day. And when they came home, they had sat on the terrace talking low and kissing for hours.

As Aimee sat on the bed and stared at her sister's pink face, a happy suspicion was dawning. "What's going on?"

Ayisha hugged her knees and beamed. "Guess."

"Cain?"

"Aye. Oh, Aimee, he loves me, and wants to wed me!" When Aimee shrieked and hugged her, Ayisha giggled and hugged her back. "I'm almost afraid to believe it for fear he'll change his mind—or for fear it's only a dream."

"It's not a dream, and he'll not change his mind—don't even think it! Oh, Pan! Oh, my goodness. Do you realize what this means? We can be wed together! It's the very thing I was hoping for. Have you told Peg yet?"

"I wanted you and Da to know first."

Ben said from the doorway, "What's this? What am I supposed to know first?"

Pegeen appeared behind him clutching a broom. "I heard someone shriek. Did you find the mouse that was in my kitchen this morn?"

Ben chuckled. "Now, Peg, when did either of these lasses ever screech at the sight of a mouse? More likely they'd put out bread and cheese for it." Seeing Ayisha flying toward him in her nightdress, he held out his arms. "By the saints, what is it, girl?"

"It's Cain, Da. He wants to wed me!"

"Wed you?" Ben closed his eyes and offered up a prayer. "Well, well, well, does he now?" He pulled her into his arms and held her close, his little girl. "I'll have to admit, I'm pleased. I thought the lad would never get around to it."

Ayisha kissed his cheek and went next into Pegeen's open arms. "He loves me, Peg," she whispered. "He says he hasn't the words to tell me how much."

"Well, there!" Pegeen gave her a kiss and felt her eyes misting. "It's happened just like I hoped it would. From the first instant I saw those two, I knew they were made in heaven for you lasses."

Aimee gasped, "Jeremy will have apoplexy!"

Ayisha shot her a warning look. "Nay, he will not. I think he's forgotten the Adair girls completely." But in truth, he had been on her mind almost as much as Cain. She could not forget his hateful threats to them. Not that she thought he would actually harm them, but it was an ugly memory hanging over her head. And Aimee was right, he would have apoplexy when he heard the news.

"Well, my darlin's,"—Ben put an arm around each of them—"I can see that you're bursting with wedding plans, but this old man's weary. I've had a long day. But when I put my head on my pillow tonight, know that I'll be thinking of you and that I'm very happy for both of you. You've chosen good men. Tell them when they ask me for your hands formally, my answer will be aye." He kissed the tops of their shining heads and thanked God and his darling Ana for them. He said huskily, "Your mama would be pleased."

She could rest easy now, he thought, walking down the hall to their bedchamber. He was always glad when the day was ended and he had a reason for going there. It was the one room in the house she had decorated in the style of her homeland, and he felt closer to her there than anywhere else. Within its cool confines, he was in another world. Her world. Whitewashed walls, latticed windows, a tiled floor and upon it, a scattering of richly hued Oriental rugs. Sitting himself on a low divan heaped with plump satin pillows, he tugged off his boots, removed the constricting clothing he wore into the city, and slipped into a silken caftan.

He went out onto the balcony then, stretched out on another divan, and lay staring into the darkness and listening to the soothing rhythm of the sea far into the night. He and Ana used to lie there together, his left arm holding her close and her head on his shoulder. He could still imagine her small hand on his chest or tangled in his hair while his own hand moved over her lashes and lips and the perfect planes of her face. Sometimes they would talk, comfortable end-of-the-day talk—or they would make love.

He sighed and wondered how so many years had slipped by so quickly. Where had they gone when it seemed only yesterday that he had been a young man possessed of the most beautiful woman in the world. He saw in his mind's eye, as if it were just happening, their escape from the *Hawk* . . . their arrival in this wonderful land . . . the birthing of their precious babes . . . the building of Seacliff . . . the expansion of his businesses . . . the growth of his wealth.

And then had come the blossoming of his maids into flowers as rare and exquisite as their mother herself had been. Now they had found good men and his heart nigh overflowed with his joy and relief. Ana would have been pleased. Suddenly feeling her close, he smiled. Aye, she was well-pleased, his darling. He knew. Death had not cut the close bonds that had bound them together.

He sighed, climbed heavily to his feet, and returned to their bedchamber finally. A lamp, burning low, cast dancing shadows over the things she had loved—the polished teak tables and brass candlesticks, the gilt-framed mirror before which she had combed out her long, dark red hair, the curtained alcove holding their sleeping couch. Going to it, Ben removed his caftan and lay down and inhaled her rose scent which still hung faintly in the air. Pressing her pillow to his lips, he thought how very much he missed her still. God's life, how he missed her . . .

After nearly a month of looking at properties and shipyards and debating whether to buy one or to build, Cain had reached a decision. It would be more profitable in the long run for Banning Limited to buy an existing yard than to build one. He had found three, one in Boston and two in Philadelphia, and while he favored the Boston location, he had to inspect thoroughly the other two and look into their suppliers before a final decision was made. As he and Seth rode to Seacliff that eve, he told him his plans and that the *Sea Eagle* would sail at dawn for Philadelphia. He added, "Will you keep an eye on Ayisha for me?"

Hearing the undertone of worry in his voice, Seth looked at him sharply. "It goes without saying I'll watch over her. Greydon's not hanging about again, is he?"

"It's just an uneasy feeling I have. I wish she'd tell her father what happened, or Fitzgerald."

"Nay, man. Aimee swears we did the right thing, keeping it quiet. Both men are hotheaded where the maids are concerned, and she fears what Ben would do if he knew." At the thought of what still lay ahead for the two of them, Seth breathed a string of oaths. "Probably the same thing he'll do to us."

"Put it away, man. I don't want to think about it tonight. I have too much else on my mind."

"You're right. Besides, it's a different thing entirely with us. We love them. We're going to wed them and—" At a blazing look from Cain, he broke off in mid-sentence. Seeing the girls, he threw them a wave. "There they are, the darlin's, coming to meet us." Within seconds, Aimee was in his arms being smothered by his kisses.

Cain dismounted and slid an arm around Ayisha. "Hello, sprite."

"Hello."

She was so quiet, he said in her ear, "Are you all right?"

In truth, she was not all right. She had not been able to dispel the strange feeling that yesterday had not happened, that she had dreamed they'd gone into the sea together and kissed and lain in the sand telling each other of their love. She whispered, "Was yesterday real?"

Cain smiled and brushed a light kiss across her lips. "It was real." What he still could not believe was the miracle of her—the perfect pale oval of her face, her luminous skin—and those eyes. All of the heat and passion and mystery of the East lay in their amber depths. He kissed her again, deep and lingering, and felt her small tongue touching, dancing with his, felt the fast beating of her heart against his. He freed her mouth then and just held her, savored having her in his arms. He heard her murmur against his chest, "Do you—love me still?"

His chuckle was a low rumble. What a child she was in her uncertainty and insecurity. A woman would have seen well the power she had over him. "If I say aye, would you believe me?"

"I'd believe you."

"Then listen well: Aye, Ayisha, I love you." He kissed her again and warned himself not to devour her. She was so soft in his arms, soft as a whisper, and the scent of her was the fragrance of an exotic blossom on a sultry day. He stroked back her hair, saw glints of flame winking in the sun's lengthening rays, and added huskily, "I love you a hundred, a thousand times aye. Now are you happy?"

She laughed and slid her arms around his neck. "Now I'm happy."

"Good." How young she was, he thought, and how shining and innocent and precious. And how very vulnerable. As they took his mount to the paddock, he said, "I'm going to be away for awhile. I'll be leaving in the morn."

"On business?"

"Aye. There are two places in Philadelphia I want to see and I'm not sure how long I'll be gone."

She did not show her disappointment. She made her mouth smile and watched as he removed his horse's bridle so he could graze. "I'll be waiting for you, and may the wind be at your back."

Cain said gruffly, "Be careful while I'm gone, sprite."

Her eyes widened. "Are you worried about Jere?"

"Always. I still wish you'd tell your father or—"

She gave her head an emphatic shake. "Nay. My mind is made up. I can't risk it. Under normal circumstances, Da would never harm a soul, but with Mama gone, we're all he has left. Aimee and I are his weakness."

"You're my weakness, and the danger from Greydon is real. While I'm gone, I don't want you riding in the woods alone or sailing alone. He could waylay you."

"But—"

"I've asked you before to trust me, now I'm asking you again—trust me in this."

Remembering Jeremy's forcing her into the woods and what had happened there, Ayisha nodded. "You're right," she said quietly. "I promise to be careful. I'll not ride or sail without Mac."

Mac. Cain's eyes glittered like ice on a winter lake. The ever-present MacKenzie Fitzgerald was one more thing gnawing at him. He said abruptly, "Why is he jealous of me?"

Ayisha's laughter pealed out. "Mac?"

"Mac." Cain himself was so jealous at that moment that he wanted to carry her to his ship and sail to where no one would ever find them. He muttered, "Is he in love with you?"

"Nay, he's not in love with me." A wonderful warmth was moving through her. She was well used to being loved and guarded and treasured as the child of wealthy, adoring parents—but this was diffeent. Cain's love and fear for her, his cherishing her, was for the woman she had become, the woman who belonged to him. The thought warmed and thrilled her. She said gently, "I've known Mac forever, Cain. He's naught but a brother to me."

"Does he know that?"

"Aye. And he's not jealous of you, it's just that he's—protective of me." She nearly blurted why, but caught herself. Cain would hate her discussing him with another man. She stroked his hand. "And since he is so protective, you really needn't worry about Jeremy's waylaying me. Really. Mac's big—you've seen him. Jere wouldn't dare try anything with him around. I promise, I'll not go off without him."

"It will lessen my worry."

"I don't want you to worry at all!" she protested. "In fact, now I'm the one who's worried about you!"

"Believe me, I take his threat very seriously. No dark alleys on foggy nights for me. At least not if I'm alone."

"Thank goodness." As they neared the stable, she thought of Willi's being plunged back into the dark boredom he had known for so long.

Cain sensed it and took her hand. "You're still concerned about something."

"I'm thinking of Willi. He's going to miss you as much as I will."

Cain grinned. "That's why I thought I'd show you a few things this eve."

Ayisha's mouth fell open. *"Haute école?"*

"Aye."

She nearly uttered an Aimee-like shriek but throttled it and glowed instead. "Do you really think I can learn?"

"If anyone can, you can."

She was a natural. It was a miracle in itself that without any formal training she already had a correct seat, hips pressed slightly forward, her arms precisely where they should be, and the carriage of her head and back wonderful to see. As far as he was concerned, neither she nor Willi needed work on the longe.

"I'm glad you're so confident," she murmured. She was not. Dazed, she followed him inside the stable and heard him tell Griffin to put her saddle on Willi. Still in a daze, she mounted, collected Willi under her, and squeezed his flanks gently with the calves of her legs. As they headed toward the meadow, Cain walked beside them.

"What I'll show you this eve," he said, "is basic and very simple. Willi's used to you, and he'll respond with no problem."

She gave a small nervous laugh. "I know it's ridiculous but I'm scared. Not of Willi but of myself. I want so much to be able to learn for his sake that I feel as stiff and dumb as a post. Damn!"

"It's all right," Cain replied easily. "Don't worry about being tight. Just continue to walk him . . . enjoy him . . . you're going to be fine. Remember, he already knows everything. It's in him. Think of him as an instrument, tuned and ready to be played. All you need to learn are a few elementary aids so you can tell him what you want him to do."

In the meadow, Cain continued walking by their side, talking in a low, soothing, rhythmical voice about the things around them: wildflowers . . . the soft breeze . . . the deep green of the grass and the blue of the sky . . . the fading sun-gleam on Willi's glossy coat. He lay a careful hand on the stallion's flank and then on Ayisha's thigh. "That's good. That's very good. You're relaxing, sprite. You're going to be fine. Just know, remember, you ride like a demon—"

"Not an angel?" she quavered.

"Nay. You ride like a veritable demon from hell and you have a magnificent animal under you. Trust me yet again—you'll know all I know someday." And sooner, he thought, much sooner than it had taken him to learn it. "That's right . . . ease up . . . good . . . that's good, that's very good. You're loosening, and the more you loosen, the more freedom you'll give him."

Hearing the calmness of his voice soothed Ayisha so that she felt her muscles relaxing and warming, felt her fears vanishing. She nodded, smiled down at him, and held out her hand. When he caught and clasped it assuringly, she said, "You're going to be a good teacher."

"You're going to be a good student. All you need is an eagerness to learn." He grinned up at her. "And that you have." He ran a hand over Willi's back, felt its resiliency. She was so very light, so cloud-light, he accepted her weight easily. He stroked the stallion's flank again. "He's accepted your leg. He's relaxed, you're relaxed. Good. Are you ready?"

"Aye." Her heart was pounding, but with excitement, not fear.

"Fine. Now here's the first thing I want you to do . . ."

They worked until late, Cain sometimes walking, sometimes running beside her. Sometimes he stood at a distance, eyes narrowed and noting her mistakes. He would call out corrections to her then or show her, hands-on, how a change in leg or rein pressure or a light shifting of weight in the saddle would give the desired result. Afterwards they gave Willi over to the ministrations of Griffin, and once more they cooled themselves at the pump and drank deeply from the dipper.

As Ayisha dried her face and hands with a towel, she murmured, "What I'd really like is another swim, icy or not, but I'm ready to drop. I had no idea there were so many ways of walking a horse! That was hard work."

Cain smiled at her enthusiasm. "Didn't I tell you?"

"Nay, you did not!" She laughed then, enjoying hugely her sense of accomplishment as well as the bone tiredness that accompanied it. "I feel all limp and giggly, and my legs seem to belong to someone else. I'm not sure I can walk even . . ." As she said it, she was caught up in his arms.

"There's no need for you to walk," he said low. His thoughts were filled with the image of her riding the stallion as the moon rose, her eyes shining and the wind streaming through her hair, lifting it as it lifted Willi's mane and tail. It was a sight he would never forget.

Ayisha sighed in complete contentment and lay her head on his shoulder. "What a lovely way to end a beautiful evening."

"It's not ended yet."

The look in his eyes sent a delicious shiver through her, but there was still much merriment bubbling within her. With a straight face, she said, "You're right. Why don't we go back to the house and see what Seth and Aimee are doing? I'm sure they'll not mind if we join them for cards or—" She felt his arms tighten about her.

"No cards," Cain growled. God's breath, he was burning for her and she talked about cards.

Seeing that she had gone too far, she laughed softly and stroked back his hair. "I'm sorry—I was teasing. In truth I was. I don't want to be with anyone but you. Can we go back to the meadow and just—lie in the grass and watch the moon?"

Lie in the grass and watch the moon ... If he got her in the grass, Cain thought, he damned well would not watch the moon. He would crush her beneath him, run his hands up and down her long smooth legs and arms, bury his face in her softness and his tongue in the sweet, dark cavern of her mouth. And bury himself within her. Ah, God. That was what he craved to do. He had told himself over and over that she was safe with him, but at this moment, he knew he could not trust himself.

A tide of desire was rolling over him, harsh waves of it buffeting him one after another. They had been pounding him all evening as he watched her astride Willi. Until this night, he had never realized how like lovemaking the rhythmic movements of riding were—and to see a beautiful woman performing them, a woman he loved ... He had tried to keep his eyes off her swaying breasts and the sensuous movement of her hips as she posted, her thighs squeezing Willi's barrel, but it was impossible. He had devoured the sight of her, felt his breathing quickening, found himself envying the blasted horse ...

"Cain?" He was silent for so long Ayisha wondered if he had heard her, or if— She asked softly, "Are you angry with me?"

"I'm not angry with you." Carrying her toward the

house, he brushed light kisses over her eyelids, one side of her nose, the faint pucker between her brows.

"Then why aren't we going to the meadow?" It was quiet there, and it smelled of flowers and clover and they could be completely alone. She wanted to stretch out beside him in the deep damp grass and feel his body pressed hard against hers. It was a fever in her. "It's such a beautiful night and the moon is so gorgeous and—"

"If we went to the meadow, Ayisha, I'd want to do more than lie beside you and look at the moon."

Realizing that he wanted to make love to her, she felt a hot pang between her legs. It thrilled her even as it frightened her. She yearned toward it, aye, but she knew she should run from it as if her life depended upon it. It was wicked to make love out of wedlock. And it was stupid. Mama had warned her against it, and Pegeen. No man would buy a cow, they said, if he could get milk for free, and she had seen that it made perfect sense. But for Cain who loved her and who was going to wed her, for Cain she would do anything. She said shyly, "I—might say aye . . ."

Cain shook his head. "But I would say nay."

"Oh." It was as if a lead ball had dropped into her stomach and was rolling about. He didn't want her. Or maybe, oh, horrors, maybe she had misunderstood completely what he meant for them to do in the meadow. Oh, heavens, how embarrassing.

The crestfallen look on her face told Cain exactly what thoughts she was thinking. It amazed him that she still had no awareness of the power she had over him. He said gently, "It's not that I don't want you, Ayisha. I'm nigh perishing for you."

Her face was burning. "Then I don't understand."

He lowered her gently to her feet, cupped her chin in one hand, and traced the winged arch of one mahogany brow with the fingers of his other hand. "I'll not hurt you, sprite, and making love with you now would hurt you. You'd regret it afterwards."

Her relief was as deep as her disappointment. She hoped it did not show. "But—"

"Nay, Ayisha. There will be no lovemaking until after we're wed. Now, about those cards you mentioned earlier,"—he gave her rump a small, affectionate swat—"I've changed my mind. A game of cards sounds like a fine idea."

Chapter 14

A yisha missed Cain, but she was too busy to brood over his absence. Morns and evenings when it was cool, she took Willi to the meadow and practiced the things Cain had taught her. Afternoons she sailed with Mac, visited with friends, or talked and made plans with Aimee for the wedding. When the men had made no objections to a double ceremony, Aimee and Pegeen had plunged into a frenzy of list making and organizing.

Ayisha, too, had been swept into it. She yielded to everything they decided for she saw that it was Aimee's dream coming true—a huge church wedding with several hundred in attendance. She tried to appear bright and interested, but she would have been just as happy, aye, happier, had she and Cain said their vows in a glade in the pine woods with only God looking on. She cared naught about what kind of waistline and neckline and sleeves her gown should have, nor did she care about how her hair was to be dressed or who came to the wedding or what to feed them. What a fuss over things that were of no importance. All that mattered was that Cain would return safely from his journey to Philadelphia and that soon they would be joined forever.

When ten days and then two weeks had come and gone with no sign of him, her concern began to mount. She wondered darkly if he had ever really intended to come back to her. Or had he met someone else on his journey— someone pale and blond and beautiful who did not need to be guarded so carefully from lovemaking? Or had he re-

ceived such a powerful call to go wandering that even his
love for her could not prevent his following it? Maybe he
was on the open sea this instant bound for Africa or
India . . .

But nay, she would not believe such a thing. Cain loved
her. He had said he loved her so deeply he hadn't the
words to describe it, and she had no reason to doubt him.
He would come back to her. He would come back. He
would . . . he would . . . But when his absence stretched
toward three weeks, her heart and her hopes faltered and
images of a more terrible fate filled her mind—the *Sea Eagle* attacked by pirates who slew him . . . Cain pressed
aboard a ship with no hope of escaping . . . or his vessel
sunk by a storm at sea. That was the most likely thing of
all, for two fierce storms had hit the coast since he had
been gone.

She went about sunk in gloom, but she said naught to
anyone of her worries. Everyone was so happy, she could
not bear to drag them down. She fought her fears alone.
Her only peace during that third week came as she rode
Willi or when she and Mac sailed the *Dolphin*. She felt
closer to Cain on the stallion or at sea. And as she rode
Willi in the meadow at dusk on the twentieth day of Cain's
absence, she began to chant over and over, softly and in
rhythm with Willi's four footfalls, Cain . . . Cain . . .
Cain . . . Cain . . . please . . . come . . . back . . . to me.

But she had lost him. She knew it as surely as she knew
that she would never love any man again as she loved him.
It crushed her that she had never told him of the full depth
of her love—that he was part of her as surely as her heart
was, and that only with him did she feel whole. And it
crushed her that she had never lain in the grass in his arms
and made love.

She felt such emptiness she began to weep. Softly, easily the tears stole down her cheeks and were soon a torrent
clogging her nose and throat and blurring her eyes. While
she worked Willi she wept silently, and when she tried to
stop she found she could not. Her beloved was gone, and

she was lost without him. In truth, why shouldn't she weep the rest of the evening . . . the rest of her life?

It was then that she saw him, the man watching her quietly from the far side of the meadow in the fading light. Her eyes were blurred, but there was no doubting who it was as he waved and started toward her. No one else walked as he did, or had such wide shoulders or was so tall.

"Cain? Oh, Cain!" As he broke into a run, she urged Willi to a gallop to reach him, and then she was being lifted down into his arms and his mouth was taking hers hungrily again and again and again. Laughing, weeping, she clung to him and could do naught but murmur his name over and over. He had come home to her. Her life had been given back to her and she could live again.

Cain was touched by the openness and the depth of her emotion. "It's all right, sprite, all's well. I'm here, and there's naught to part us again." He was shaken at actually having her in his arms again. Every night in his dreams he had held her and made love to her and walked and talked and laughed with her. And every night he had been awakened by the same black terrifying nightmare in which he had lost her. He lowered her to her feet.

"Let's lie down . . ."

Ayisha blinked. "In the grass?"

Cain grinned, remembering that when she had suggested it, he'd refused. "In the grass. Just to talk, of course."

She grinned back. "Of course." But her heart went harder.

They tethered Willi and soon were lying close and gazing at the midnight blue canopy of the sky stretching over their heads—like his eyes, she thought, as Cain gathered her within the circle of his arm and tucked her head on his shoulder.

Hearing her contented sigh, he whispered, "I've missed you."

"And I've missed you. What took so long?"

"We ran into a storm on the way and had to put in for repairs."

She caught and held one of his hands tightly. "That was one of my fears—that you'd gone down in a storm. We had two while you were away, and one had terrible winds."

"Probably the same one that snapped a spar and tore two of our sails." He couldn't lie there beside her without sliding his hands over her arms and throat and her face. "When we finally reached Philadelphia, I saw that the yards weren't for us, but I got a lead on three more back in New England, so that's where I've been, Portsmouth, Salem, and Newport."

She was in a daze of contentment feeling his fingertips slowly, sensuously caressing her, listening to his voice, a deep comforting rumble in her ear. She murmured, "Have you decided which you'll buy?"

"Aye. The very first one I looked at here in Boston." He tilted up her face so the light from the heavens, a waxing moon and a million winking stars, touched it. He said huskily, "Maybe we could allow ourselves another kiss or two, what do you think?" When she smiled and lifted parted lips, Cain bent, kissed them, and was astonished by her starving response. He chuckled. "Well now, maybe you did miss me."

"I—thought I'd lost you."

"Because of the storm?"

She hesitated, then murmured finally, "I thought maybe you didn't want to come back to me."

"In God's name, Ayisha . . ." Gently he spanned both her breasts with his big hand and felt her racing heart.

"I know. It sounds silly now, but I thought maybe you'd found someone pale and blond a—and beautiful that—you could make love to—without worrying about her. And then I wondered if maybe your call had returned and called you away from me. And then today I started worrying that you'd been slain by pirates or taken by a press gang, or that the storm sank you and you were lying on the bottom of the sea."

Cain's low laughter caused Willi to prick his ears and turn his head toward them, listening. "God's breath,

Ayisha, this is a thing I hadn't foreseen—your wild imagination. Especially my cavorting with a pale blond when all I could think of day and night, was a maid with hair the color of mahogany—and eyes filled with moon dust."

Ayisha snuggled closer. "You thought of me day and night?"

"Day and night. Have you forgotten I love you and we're going to wed?"

"I haven't forgotten." Her voice was small.

Cain slid his fingers through her hair, felt its cool satin winding about them and caressing them, caught its faint scent of jasmine that made his nostrils flare. She was scorching him, tempting and teasing and tantalizing him, and the little wench didn't even know it. As he fought for control, he ordered himself to talk. He had said they would talk. He said gruffly, "You and Willi looked good. His rhythm was good. You must have worked him regularly."

Ayisha laughed. "I did, but *he's* so good, he makes *me* look good. I'm not even doing all you told me. I couldn't remember it all, but he enjoys working and he's eating well now. Like a horse." She giggled, burrowed happily into his neck, sniffed, kissed the rough flesh she found there and tasted him with the tip of her tongue. As she gently licked the rim of his ear, Cain turned, caught her tongue gently between his teeth, nipped it, and said against her lips, softly but firmly, "Nay, Ayisha, no tongue and no ears. We're going to talk."

"Let's do."

Seeing that her sweet smile was accompanied by an impish gleam in her eyes, Cain shook his head. "Are you bent on seducing me?"

Ayisha blinked. "In truth, I—wouldn't know how . . ." All she knew was that she felt warm and soft and safe and she was tingling all over. And her pulses were throbbing, throbbing everywhere, and her breasts felt strangely full.

"Good," Cain said, but he suppressed a groan. She might think she didn't know how, but just being there, looking as she did, she was seducing him. He felt like a stallion in rut. He made himself ask calmly, "Is everything well with your father, and with Aimee and Seth?"

"Da's fine, and everything's perfect with the two of them." Putting her hand on his chest, she felt the rapid thumping of his heart. She whispered, "Your heart's racing . . ." It was going almost as hard and as fast as her own.

Cain caught her hand, imprisoned it behind her, and heard her breathing quicken. "Never mind my heart. Tell me, has Greydon been around?"

"Nay. I—haven't seen him since that night." Her voice sounded tremulous and she felt weak as a kitten—and all because he was holding her hand behind her. She was completely, deliciously without strength. How silly to feel so, yet how glorious.

"You wouldn't lie?"

"I wouldn't lie."

Gazing at her breasts thrusting against her boy's shirt, Cain saw that her satiny little nipples had peaked and hardened with desire. He yearned to press his lips to them. She was softness and summer and night-blooming blossoms, and the moon's silver light was caught, glittering, in her flame-dark hair. Feeling her warm breath fluttering against his throat and her body melting into his, Cain's muscles knotted painfully with suppressed desire. His control was slipping. He could not keep his hands and his mouth off her. Taking her lips suddenly, he gave her a long hot kiss that left them both breathless. He put her from him then and said thickly, "This wasn't such a good idea." He was hot and hungry and his pulses were pounding, filled to a fullness that was torture.

Ayisha saw that he was miserable, but no more so than she was. She tried to contain her resentment. "I wish you'd treat me like a woman instead of a little girl. Or—or royalty."

Royalty. Hell. Sweat was streaming down his back and beading his brow. He said crisply, "I'm treating you like the maid you are, Ayisha. A maid who has never been in the hands of a starving man."

She stared at him long before asking, "Is it so awful then—lovemaking? Does it hurt a woman that terribly?"

Cain sighed and smoothed her hair. "The first time will hurt, aye, even if a man is careful."

She pushed from her mind the images of mating animals, the whinnies, shrieks, yelps, and hisses. She said firmly, "I don't care. I want to make you happy. It—will make you happy?"

Cain gave a low chuckle. "Happy isn't quite the word I'd use."

"What word then?"

"Paradise. Ecstasy." He continued to smooth her hair, run his fingers through it. "Rapture. Heaven. You'll go there with me someday, I promise you."

Eyes wide, Ayisha asked softly, "You're not just saying that?"

"Never."

She sat up. "I didn't know women could feel that way, too."

"Haven't you liked my kisses and being in my arms?"

"It's wonderful."

Cain whispered, "Then trust me yet again—there's something even more wonderful than being kissed and held waiting for you."

Ayisha sighed and lay back down in his arms. "I can't imagine what. It makes me more eager than ever for us to be wed. Oh, Cain, I wish it could be tomorrow! I don't even want a big church wedding."

"I didn't know." Fear's icy breath touched him. Hell, he was not about to marry her until Ben knew the truth, and for damned sure, he wasn't ready to tell him yet. Not yet. Losing her was too great a danger even though he had vowed, he had promised himself it would all work out and he would have her, no matter what.

"Forget I said that," Ayisha murmured. "About not wanting a big wedding. It would break Aimee's heart if I didn't go through with it."

He felt reprieved. "Have you decided on a date yet? Seth didn't seem to know for sure."

"Next May. May thirtieth."

"May thirtieth?" And this was just the beginning of August. "Ayisha, that's an eternity!"

"I know. But you wouldn't believe all they're finding to do around here, Aimee and Pegeen. It seems the inside of the house needs new paint and new draperies and new furniture. There's to be a huge party here afterwards with all of Boston invited and we daren't let them see how we really live. And the dressmaker who's coming from France to make our gowns and who's also bringing the fabric and lace won't even arrive till the end of April. It's crazy." She looked up at him gloomily. "I might as well be in a nunnery."

He laughed. "Nay, little wench, I'd not allow it." But May thirtieth. He'd be off his head by then.

"There's something that puzzles me," Ayisha murmured.

"What's that?" He was discovering anew the exceptional softness of her skin.

"There must be all sorts of times when a man and woman can't lie together . . ."

"That's so," Cain answered carefully.

"He could have a—a strained back or she could be with child"—her face turned pink—"or be otherwise indisposed."

He said solemnly, "That's so."

"Does that mean they don't make love then?"

"Some do, others don't—at least not in the conventional sense."

She sat up again. "What does that mean? The conventional sense? Do they or don't they?"

His deep laughter filled the quiet meadow. "There are—other ways of being close."

"Tell me."

"They're not exactly the sort of thing an unwed maid should know about, Ayisha."

"We're going to be husband and wife."

"But we're not yet. You're an untouched maid and I won't bring embarrassment or shame down on you."

"In my heart, we're wed."

"And in mine . . ." Cain said softly. The three weeks he had been gone, she had been his, in his mind, heart, and soul, if not in body. There was not a moment when she had not been by his side.

"I've wished,"—she drew a deep breath—"I've wished that instead of wedding in the church we could be wed in the woods with only God looking on . . ."

Cain pulled her back down into his arms. "How about in a meadow under the stars with Willi and the moon looking on? And deer and tree frogs and wildflowers . . ."

She gazed up at the handsome dark face that filled her dreams nightly. "And God," she said.

"I know naught of God, Ayisha."

She smiled. "That's all right. I do. My mother, when she lived, believed, and my father, and Pegeen and Mac and Aimee—all the other ones I love believe. He's there, and He'll hear us if we say our vows."

Cain caught her fingers, kissed them and held her against his heavily beating heart. He might as well begin giving her her every desire, for he meant to make it his life's work. "Then let's do it."

Ayisha blinked. "You mean, say our vows?"

"Aye. Here under the stars." Seeing her astonishment, he said gently, "Would you like that?"

Her breath broke. "Aye. Oh, aye . . ."

"Then we'll do it right now."

Cain got to his feet and drew her up beside him. He took her hands in his, fastened his grave dark eyes on hers, and realized, God Almighty, that he did not know how to talk to God. Not at all. He swallowed and reminded himself angrily that he invoked God's name at least a hundred times a day for reasons that amounted to naught. Now he was calling on Him for something that actually mattered and he'd damned well better do a good job of it. He scowled, and not at all sure what to say or what would come out, drew breath and opened his mouth.

"God, I—claim this woman for my wife. She's more precious to me than any treasure . . . more precious than my own right arm . . . more precious than my life even.

I'll love and cherish and protect her until I close my eyes for the last time. I vow it, God."

Feeling his hands shaking, tears came to Ayisha's eyes, but she did not allow them to fall. She said in a firm, low voice, "Dear God, thank you for this man. I choose him over all others for my husband, to have and to hold and to love a—and to obey until death do us part. Amen."

"Amen," Cain muttered, and wondered what had just happened to him. He had thought to humor her, but something had just touched him so deeply that his heart trembled with the power of it. He ordered himself firmly not to conjure up some holy mystery where there was none. This was a happy occasion, not a godly one. He looked down at her, his child-wife, and marked that her beautiful eyes were glittering with moon and stardust. He smiled down at her. "So, my sea sprite, we're wed."

Ayisha whispered, "Aye. In God's eyes, we're husband and wife." Her own eyes danced. "And now you'll not shame or embarrass me by telling me those things you'd not tell me before. About being close . . ."

Cain grinned and tilted up her chin. "What a little fox you are."

"Aye."

He drew her back down into the grass and took her mouth in a long, sweet, lingering kiss. When it stoked his fires anew, he ran his tongue around the edge of her lips, quickening the breathing of them both. He said huskily, "I'll not mate with you, my little meadow wife, but we are going to be close, I promise you." He felt her shiver as, one by one, he undid the buttons of her shirt and slid it off. Bending his dark head to her breasts, he breathed the scent of jasmine floating up from her warm flesh. "What a beautiful thing you are."

"It's you—you make me feel beautiful." As he touched his tongue to her nipples and drew first one and then the other into his mouth, delight flamed through her. It remained to scorch her as he lay her back in the grass, gently unbuttoned her trews, and slipped them off. She felt pink all over as he trailed kisses from her navel to the dark cloud at the apex of her thighs. She writhed unexpectedly, arching upward under his seeking lips.

"Cain . . ."

"Aye, my goddess?"

"Is the woman the only one without clothes?"

For an answer, Cain pulled his shirt over his head, tugged off his boots, and slowly drew off his trews. In the moon's pale glow his arousal was clearly visible. He said gently, "I didn't want to frighten you."

Ayisha blinked. Once she had compared him to a young stallion in his prime—and indeed he was. He was sleek, gleaming, long limbed, hard muscled, strong boned, and his shaft was as large and strong and straight as the rest of him. She murmured faintly, "You're—very handsome. All of you . . ." Cain's low laughter and the hungry glitter in his eyes sent a thrill rippling over her heated flesh.

"You're sure you're not frightened?"

There was no doubt as to what he meant. She said casually, "I've—seen males before. Just last week Willi—"

Cain forbade himself to laugh, but it rang out. She was adorable—and young and innocent and untouched beyond belief. He lay down and pulled her against him, shaping her soft body against his and sliding his shaft between her thighs. "I fear Willi's out of my league." He heard her own low happy laughter.

"Silly . . ." She was melting like snow against the heat of his hunger and his hard body. He was holding her so tightly, her breasts were crushed and the breath was squeezed out of her. He had said he was starving, and she saw that it was so. She felt a moment's fear, knowing that if he yielded to his hunger, she would be helpless against him—but then he would not harm her. This was Cain. This was her husband.

"Am I hurting you?" Cain asked, hearing the small muffled sounds she was making.

"It would—be nice to breathe . . ."

He loosened his hold and said thickly, "Don't ever let me hurt you." He pressed his mouth to her breasts again, gently. Their fullness and the lush feminine curves of the rest of her body were tempting him beyond endurance. He had meant to prolong this . . . play with her . . . touch and kiss and fondle her . . . teach her . . . but the fire within him was growing more insistent. "I never want to hurt you."

"You're not hurting me. You're making me feel wonderful—shivery and hot and melting all at the same time." In truth, she had never felt so wonderful, so small and soft and desirable. So female.

"You can feel more wonderful still," Cain murmured. For as long as he was able, he would hold back the rising tide so that she could ride the crest with him.

Ayisha shook her head, smiling. "I don't see how I could." She was already reveling in his strength and the way his hands felt on her body and his searching kisses that were covering her everywhere. She gasped as suddenly, unexpectedly, his fingers found a new place to explore and caress and tease.

Hearing her sharp intake of breath, seeing her arch against him, Cain whispered, "Was I right?"

"A—aye . . ." A shivering sigh slipped past her lips. "Oh, Cain . . ." She had never dreamed such a small, hidden part of her could feel so glorious. "I—I can't bear it. It's too wonderful. I—don't know what to do . . ."

Delighting in her delight, Cain whispered, "Do naught, sprite. Just enjoy it." Parting the velvety petals guarding her maidenhood, he briefly, tenderly touched his shaft to them. He heard her small moan, felt the tremor that swept her, and then slid himself harmlessly between her thighs again.

"I—never knew . . ." She was laughing, nigh weeping with the wonder of it as he continued to stroke the newfound place with gentle fingers. "I can—scarce believe the way it feels . . ." It was the sun rising deep within her or maybe it was a bonfire flaming and spreading . . . spreading all through her. "Cain, I'm going to explode—except it's a lovely, shimmery, tingly kind of exploding. It's—like a starburst in heaven. Oh, Cain . . ." She clutched him to her more tightly, felt him moving his shaft rhythmically between her legs, felt it grazing the white-hot heat burning there.

"Hold your legs closer together," Cain rasped suddenly. "Closer . . . closer . . ." His voice broke.

Ayisha obeyed. Compressing him tightly, she saw the harsh transformation of his face, eyes closed, lips drawn back in a grimace, his brow furrowed, head thrown back. Dazed as she was, she knew it was not pain that he was feeling, it was ecstasy. The same fierce shimmering ecstasy that was rushing over her and about to crest. Hearing his ragged breathing, feeling the powerful thrusts that someday would be within her own body brought her excitement boiling to a peak. She felt a rush, a release of creamy wetness between her legs even as Cain's seed was spilled in several powerful thrusts to mingle with it, seed he had spilled to protect her . . .

She pulled his head down to her breasts, cradled his damp body in her arms, felt his manhood still pulsing between her thighs. Melting with tenderness and love and gratitude, she whispered, "I love you, my husband. Thank you for taking me with you."

"That was just the beginning, sprite." Cain gathered her closer. "That was just the beginning."

Chapter 15

Ben reflected that he had not felt this content in a long, long time—not since Ana's illness had come upon her four years ago. Perhaps now he could put some of his sadness away, at least for awhile, and joy in his daughters' joy. His adoring gaze rested on them as they stood on the terrace with their men, chatting, laughing, their beautiful faces and their eyes glowing, lit from within. How very like Ana they were. They reminded him of two lush blossoms from a palace garden in Turkey or Persia, Ayisha sleek in a sari-like gown of saffron and gold with her hair bound back in a glittery net and Aimee in a pale green confection that looked like sea foam. He could not take his eyes off their dazzle, nor could their men. And in truth, the men they had chosen matched them in beauty.

Ben could not remember when he had seen two such splendid physical specimens. They were both tall, strong, wide-shouldered, taut-hipped, wolf-lean men, men fit to protect the jewels they would soon be wedding. Cain Banning, handsome as sin with his dark skin, indigo eyes, and burnished chestnut hair looked for all the world like some roving sea raider, albeit an elegant one in his simply cut white silk shirt and black breeches and boots.

Seth Duncan, on the other hand, reminded him of a much-loved friend he'd once had. The lad was partial to blue cotton shirts and brown breeches and boots, no matter what the occasion, and there was naught of the danger and mystery about him that clung to Cain. His face and smile were beautiful in their openness and gentleness. He was the calm and peace of the English countryside, was Seth.

Aimee had been watching her father for some moments. Now she asked, "What are you thinking, Papa, with that silly little smile on your face?"

Ben grinned. He hadn't even meant to attend this welcome home dinner Ayisha had planned for Cain. He'd had business appointments scheduled. Now he was glad he'd cancelled them. Damned glad. He said, "I was just thinking that this old man hasn't been this happy in years."

"Old man!" Aimee flew to him. "I won't hear it! You're as handsome and distinguished looking as you ever were." She patted his thick silver hair, tied back with a black ribbon, and smoothed his satin waistcoat.

"That's so." Ayisha, too, came over and kissed his cheek. "You're a fine, stalwart example of mature manhood."

Ben chuckled. "Of antiquity, lass. Of antiquity." He finished his champagne whereupon Soames appeared at his elbow to refill it.

"Seth, tell him he's not ancient," Aimee insisted.

"You're not, sir." Seth was mellowed by the beauty of his young bride to be and the imbibing of several tankards of ale. "You're a veritable marvel. You haven't aged in twenty years."

Cain's eyes darted to his friend, saw him flush deeply and blink. He was astonished by Seth's careless remark, but it seemed to have slipped by unnoticed.

"And you, Cain," Aimee persisted. "Don't you think Papa looks good?"

Cain said gravely, "He looks very good." It was the truth. Ben Scott had the high color and big, strong frame of a man of much younger years. Into his thoughts came his last image of his father—skin and bones, frail, eyes dulled, his hair and most of his teeth gone. His father dying in fear for his soul because of what this man had made him do. A wave of resentment hit him that nigh swamped him.

"That's enough talk of me and my good looks," Ben

said, and took an appertif from the tray being passed. "I want to hear about your parents, you lads. I trust they'll be coming for the wedding, and of course you'll tell them they're to stay here at Seacliff with us. In fact, we insist." Seeing Ayisha's quick glance toward Cain, he frowned. "Is there some problem?"

"I've lived with my aunt and uncle for many years," Cain said. "My aunt is no longer able to travel and my uncle won't leave her."

Ben nodded. "I'm sorry to hear it, but I understand." He wished Ayisha had told him. "How about you, Seth?"

"My folks are both gone, sir," Seth said quietly.

Cain knew well what his thoughts were. His eyes said it clearly. But for Ben Scott, his father might be alive this day. Yet had that long-ago tragedy never happened, the two of them never would have met Ayisha and Aimee.

Ben's eyes showed his compassion. "It grieves me to hear this sad news." He did not add that the most important person of all would not be there. If he spoke of Ana, it would bring down the girls' high spirits, and this was an evening for celebration. He said heartily, "In any event, we'll give the four of you a wedding to end all weddings, and you'll have the love and the good wishes of all of Boston, I promise you. We have many good friends in this city."

Cain nodded. "So I've discovered during my stay here. You're highly thought of, sir."

Ben waved it away. "I want to hear about your trip to Philadelphia, son, and about the yard you've bought here in town. Old Timothy Riker never ran it efficiently and didn't know how to deal with his suppliers, but there's no doubt in my mind that you and your uncle made a good buy. Just let me know if there's anything I can do to help."

"I appreciate that."

Cain pondered that when he was with Ben Adair, it was not always easy to think clearly of the crimes he had committed. Ben's choosing piracy over his legitimate business, and abandoning men at sea, men who were friends, was a reality hopelessly interwoven with and diluted by the friendly and compassionate man he saw before him—a man beloved by hundreds, a man who had sired two angels who adored him, and a man whose heart was so tender he took in horses that others would have put to death. The contradiction had puzzled Cain from the first and it puzzled him still.

As they continued to talk, he felt the taut masking of his face and found it harder and harder to meet the older man's probing blue eyes. And of course, Scott—hell, he had to remember not to slip and call him that—was probably wondering why he had not asked for Ayisha's hand formally. It was a thing any father would be pondering. When the thought plagued him throughout the meal and nagged him afterwards as they sipped their liquers on the terrace, Cain knew he could not put it off any longer. It lacked honor, and it was disrespectful to Ayisha. As Seth was spinning an endless yarn about a journey to China, he drew Ben aside.

"Sir, I'm not sure of the customs of this land, but now that my business matters are settled, I'd like to ask you properly for Ayisha's hand. She's told me you approve, of course, but I—want it to be official. May I have her, sir?" He saw the other's eyes brighten in the candle glow.

"The custom's no different here than in the old world," Ben replied, "and I appreciate the courtesy. Nowadays most young folk aren't as much for tradition as they were when I was a young man."

Cain's mouth curved, thinking of those two young rovers of long ago looting the *Safira* and carrying off the Princess Ana. Oh, aye, Ben had been steeped in tradition, all right. He said quietly, "I want you to know that I love your daughter deeply, and she'll never lack for anything that's in my power to give her. I'll take good care of her, sir."

"I know you will, lad. I know you will."

As Ayisha crossed the terrace to join them, love glowing in her eyes, Cain forced a smile to his lips. God knows, all he had said was true. He loved her more than anything else on this earth, and of course he was going to take good care of her. If only he did not break her heart first.

Cain returned to Seacliff regularly in the days that followed—visiting with Ayisha, teaching her the basics of *haute école* and guiding Willi through a progressively complicated series of steps that were already imprinted in the stallion's memory. All the while, one question burned constantly in his mind: How was all of this going to end between the two of them? Was he mad to think it could have a happy conclusion? This was not a fairy tale, after all, this was reality. As he finished the evening's session with Willi, Ayisha asked, "Will I ever be able to do that, do you think—the *passage?*" She pronounced it correctly, in the French way. "You look so beautiful together."

Cain thought tenderly that if he were God Himself, her eyes could not be more worshipful. He smiled down at her. "I've told you, sprite, I'm going to teach you all that I know, and I promise you, you'll ride the *passage* so well, you'll feel as if Willi's floating beneath you."

"Aye, but how many years will it take?" She was walking beside them back to the stable.

Hearing her wistfulness, he reassured her. "We're talking weeks, not years. Don't forget, the hardest part is done. The horse is already trained, and you're—"

She smiled up at him. "—a natural."

"Believe it."

"I'm going to hold you to that, Cain Banning. When can we start? Tomorrow?"

Cain chuckled at her childish eagerness. "Why not?" He dismounted and handed Willi over to a groom who blanketed him and led him off into the dimly lit stable.

When they were alone, Ayisha stood on tiptoe and put her arms around his neck. She whispered, "Thank you, my husband. Thank you, thank you . . ."

Cain pulled her to him, bent, and kissed her lips long and thoroughly. "The teaching of the *passage,*" he said solemnly, "is filled with such difficulty, it may require many such thanks, my lady."

"Then why don't we go back to the house so I can begin in earnest?" She took his hand. "Come on. Seth and
Aimee are at a dinner party and we'll have the terrace to
ourselves. That reminds me, you're probably hungry." Seeing the glint in his eyes, she grinned. "I meant for food,
Cain Banning. How does bread and cold roast beef and
pickles sound?"

He gave her another hug. "Lead me to it."

They ate on the terrace under a waning moon, and as
Ayisha bubbled with excitement about Willi, Cain felt a
sudden regret, an emptiness that he had missed so many
years of her life. He reached across the table and caught
her hand.

"Tell me about yourself."

She frowned and bit into a pickle. "What brought that
on?"

"I know naught about when you were small and when
you were growing up—what you were like, how you
looked and acted. Have you any portraits?" Something was
telling him, urging him to seize as much of her as he could
while he could.

"There are paintings of all of us in the drawing room—I
guess you've not been in there." His unexpected seriousness was subduing her high spirits. "Cain, is something
wrong?"

"Nay, sprite, there's naught wrong." Naught that he
could talk to her about, but his worries weighed on him
heavily. When Ben learned who they were, was her world
going to come crashing down, or would Ben keep his secret hidden from the girls? Cain and Seth were hoping he
would. They were counting on it. He squeezed her hand
and forked into his roast beef. "It's just that I feel cheated
when I think of all the years of your life that I missed. I
want to hear about you from the beginning. Were you born
here at Seacliff?"

"Nay. I was three winters when we moved in. Da had it
built for Mama and it wasn't completed till then."

He nodded. "Go on, I'm listening."

"Well, what kind of things do you want to know?"

"Everything. Start anywhere."

Her eyes danced. "When I was a babe?"

"Absolutely. You must've been an angel."

"Actually, I was horrible and fractious."

He grinned. "It sounds like me."

"I was squawky and demanding and hungry all the time and I threw tantrums. Aimee, on the other hand, sat on a blanket and smiled and loved everyone and ate gently and neatly and on schedule. Da called me his cranky little princess—and he called me Pandora, my middle name. He said Ayisha was too much like a sneeze."

Cain laughed. "It's not like a sneeze. It's a glorious name. And Pandora's quite appropriate, too. It means the 'All-Gifted.' " But unlike that original Pandora whose gift box held all the evils flesh was heir to, this one, this sweet Ayisha Pandora, brought only good to those she knew. He continued to play with her slim, white fingers. "Tell me more."

"Well, let's see, from the time I could walk—" She shook her head. "Nay, you don't want to hear this . . ."

"I want to hear it."

Seeing the intent look on his face, she knew he was serious. "Well, from the moment I started to walk, they tell me I climbed—out of my crib, up steps, up ropes and trees and ladders and cliffs, up the rigging of ships. . . . Mac says I climbed the *Ayisha*'s riggings like a monkey my first time aboard. I was seven."

Cain threw back his head and laughed, picturing it. "The *Ayisha,* eh? I've not seen her in port."

"She's been on the other side of the world on a trading trip these past three months. She'll be back soon. She slid off the docks the same day I was born, so naturally Da had to give her my name."

When they finished their food, Cain led Ayisha to a cushioned settee and nestled her close beside him with his arm around her. "Go on," he whispered.

"I'm not sure what else to say."

"Have you sailed on the *Ayisha?*"

"A hundred times. Up and down the eastern seaboard,

around the tip of Florida, and to Cuba and Bermuda and all of the other islands. As crew, of course."

"Of course." His smile was hidden as he kissed her shoulder. "Who taught you to ride and to sail the *Dolphin?*"

"Da. I wanted to learn and he wanted me to learn. Mac taught me to swim." She snuggled closer to Cain and lay her hand on his chest. "Of course, I tried to make Mama happy, too." She added softly, "She was wonderful, Cain. I wish you could have known her."

"I wish it, too. I want to hear about her whenever you're ready." He'd heard the sudden huskiness in her voice.

"She worried about me terribly when I was off sailing and riding. To make up for it, I tried to learn my school lessons especially well—and my manners. And needlework. Mama's needlework was exquisite."

"I'll bet you sew a beautiful seam," Cain murmured against her neck, touching the tip of his tongue to skin that felt like satin.

"Not I. Aimee. I was always better with a horse than a needle, even when I was little."

"I wish I could have seen you."

Ayisha grinned. "You'd have laughed. I was skinny, and I had freckles and long pigtails that always got caught on things and dragged in mud puddles. Aimee was chubby and cuddly and had nice neat curls and never got dirty. She loved to play with babydolls and take care of sick animals."

Cain chuckled. "She hasn't changed a lot, has she?"

"Nay, except for the babydolls and not being chubby. I'm the one who hasn't changed, more's the pity."

"These"—his hands went to her breasts, closed on them, cupped and squeezed them gently—"don't belong to a skinny girl-child. Nor has your hair been dragged in any mud puddles recently."

Loving his tenderness, Ayisha lay her hands atop his and pressed them to her breasts more closely. "I love you,

my husband," she whispered. "More than there are words
to tell you."

Cain lowered his head and kissed her mouth with exquisite care. "I still haven't found the words to describe
my feelings for you. I'm—not very good at such things."
He'd had women over the years, aye, but never had he
spoken to them of love. Love had never been part of it. He
drew a deep breath, delighting in the fragrance of her and
loving the way her small soft body fit against him. "What
can I say to the one who is my sunrise and my sunset . . .
the first evening star . . . the first violet of spring . . ."

Ayisha gazed up at him, eyes shining, and said faintly,
"You just said it. And how did you know those were some
of my most favorite things? Sunrise . . . sunset . . . the
wishing star . . . the first violet of spring? Finding one is
always like finding treasure."

She was so precious to him at that moment, Cain could
do naught but hold her close, just hold her.

"I've never told you," Ayisha said, almost shy, "but the
first night we met, I had the most vivid feelings about you.
To me, you were excitement and danger and mystery and
power. You were like the open sea under a shining sun,
friendly and welcoming—but with a storm and danger beyond the horizon."

Cain smiled. He was both pleased and embarrassed. "I
fear I'm dull stuff compared to that."

Ayisha shook her head. "You, my beloved, are definitely
not dull stuff, nay. And now I'm tired of talking about me.
I want to hear more about when you were a boy. You've
told me so little."

"What do you want to know?" He was ready to give her
the world.

"When did you grow so tall?"

He frowned, trying to remember. "I was fourteen.
Maybe fifteen."

She smiled, imagining it. He would have been as hard
and strong and brown as a young oak and the maids would
have worshipped him. She ran her fingers lightly along his
jawline and cheeks and felt the familiar exciting roughness

of a day's growth of beard. "Was there—a maid you liked?"

"When a man's at sea, lass, he has a maid in every port." When she sighed, he bent his head to nuzzle her breasts. "I was teasing. I didn't look at women then."

"Now you are teasing."

"Nay. In those days, I feared I was like my father. I wanted no entanglements. I didn't want any woman to suffer on my account as my mother suffered from him."

Ayisha marveled that he could have been so sensitive and caring at such a tender age. Why, he'd been naught but a babe. She said gently, "Your mother had to be a wonderful woman to have raised a son like you."

A son like him.

Cain's worries, briefly forgotten, overtook him. He reached out for his dreams as a drowning man reaches for a rope, dreams of that day when Ayisha would know all, accept all, forgive all, and they would be wed. But that was all they were, dreams. Hell. He could not allow this charade to go on any longer. It had been almost two months now, and this eve he would tell Seth that the damned thing had to end. Before the week was out, it had to end.

"Cain . . ." In the silence, Ayisha heard the muffled sound of the incoming tide and moths beating against the chimneys that covered the candles. Certain that he was thinking of his mother, she asked, "What was her name?"

"Anna."

Anna. And her own mother had been Ana. "What was your father's name?"

"Thomas," Cain replied shortly.

"I guess the coincidence ends there. Was he—"

"Nay, Ayisha, no more."

Stung by his sharpness, Ayisha nearly lashed out, but then she had been pushing, crossing the line in her curiosity. She had seen his retreat when she mentioned his mother and forged on nonetheless. She sighed. "I'm sorry. I know better than that." Hearing talking and laughter, she sat up and straightened her clothing as Aimee and Seth came out onto the terrace.

"So, here you are!" Aimee cried.

"Aye, here we are. How was the party?" She and Cain had been invited, but working Willi was far more important. And she hated the thought of being stuck for hours with folk she did not know and having to talk about things that didn't interest her. And she had feared Jeremy might be there. She was feeling more and more uneasy about his threat to Cain. She asked, "Was it fun?"

"It was boring but the food was grand. They have a new chef from France. Actually, it's a good thing you didn't go. Jeremy was there. He asked about you."

"He was seated right beside her," Seth muttered. "It was damned awkward."

"What did he say?" Cain asked.

Ayisha, sitting beside him, felt his body tense. "It matters little."

"What did he say, Aimee?"

"He wondered if Ayisha still rode and sailed as much— and if you were still riding Willi."

"What did you tell him?"

Ayisha saw that he was angry. Even in the shadows she marked the telltale leaping of a muscle deep in his jaw and saw that his eyes held a dangerous light.

Aimee blinked. "I told him the truth. Shouldn't I have?"

Hell. But then what was done was done. "If it happens again," Cain said, "tell him you know naught." He did not want to alarm Ayisha, but he had a mounting uneasiness about Greydon. In truth, he had nightmares about him. He turned to her. "I'm going to be out of town seeing suppliers from time to time and I'd rather you didn't sail when I'm away."

Ayisha looked at him disbelieving. "Not even with Mac?"

"Not even with Mac. Not at all."

"What do you think Jeremy might do?"

Cain was not about to tell her his nighttime fears—an accident at sea . . . a capsized boat . . . no survivors.

Doubtless he was wrong but never, never would he forget the crazy light in Greydon's eyes the night he'd almost run them down. He shrugged. "He'll probably do naught at all, but I still don't want you at sea."

"Then I'll stay on land."

Aimee said unhappily, "I told him you were affianced. I guess it was a mistake." Her eyes filled. "Oh, dear . . ."

"He's surely heard it already," Ayisha said gently. "It's probably all over town by now. Did he say anything?"

"He asked when the wedding would be and I told him next May. He said naught. He just smiled."

"That sounds very normal, very Jeremy-like. You know him, he smiles at everything." But she was remembering that awful night when he had been so enraged, he'd tried to run them down. He had not been smiling then. He had wanted to kill them both.

Chapter 16

❦❦
~~~~~~~~✧◯◯✧~~~~~~~~

"I know what you're about to say," Seth said through tight lips. They were nearing the city after their evening at Seacliff. "It's time, isn't it."

"Aye. We can't put it off any longer." Cain had been struggling with the thought for hours.

"Man, old Ben's going to skin us alive. Those lasses are his dearest treasure."

"And ours."

"Aye. But we did the right thing to wait, I've nary a doubt of it. If Ben does tell them why we're here—and I doubt he will—Aimee will never turn her back on me now." When Cain made no reply, Seth looked over at him and saw the grim lines of his face reflected in the light of an occasional street lamp. He frowned. "There's naught amiss between you and Ayisha, is there?"

"Nay."

"Then she'll stand by you, too. I know she will."

"I can't predict the future."

Seth's impatience flared. "Man, your pessimism irks the hell out of me. Those lasses love us."

Cain's spirits were so heavy he dared not think of Ayisha just then. Putting her from his thoughts, he said crisply, "We have to tell Ben this week."

"Let's make it the weekend."

"Saturday then."

"Why not Sunday?"

"All right, man, Sunday," Cain said quietly. He saw that Seth was as concerned as he himself was.

* * *

Jeremy Greydon poured himself a third goblet of champagne, stretched out upon his bed, and reread the letter from his man in England yet again. What a treasure it was, and what a boon that it had come so much sooner than expected. He had studied it so thoroughly since its arrival that morn that he knew it word for word, and each time he looked at it, he felt a fresh thrill.

DEAR SIR,

This is to inform you in regards to one Cain Banning of Southampton and London. The subject was adopted by Christopher and Maud Banning of Cockburn Moor at the age of ten after he lost his mother, Mrs. Banning's sister. I found him to be as speckless in character as are his adoptive parents. The subject's natural father will interest you, however. Now deceased, Thomas Gregg was a seafaring man with a reputation of great ill repute. He deserted his wife and child for months at a time and had a mysterious source of wealth which he squandered freely, but he always acquired more. My source believes he engaged in piracy and has heard rumors of the abduction of a mid-eastern princess, the abandonment of men at sea, even murder, but he insists these are naught but rumors.

Thomas Gregg was said to have had a partner in crime called Ben Scott who disappeared mysteriously on one of their voyages in the Sea of Marmara. I will try to ascertain if murder was done and will keep you posted.

Trusting that this is satisfactory, I remain cordially yours, AR.

I might add, Thomas Gregg spent his last months in the home of Cain Banning. It is thought he died a pauper, but my source could not be sure.

Jeremy chuckled, finished off his champagne, poured a fourth glass to overflowing, and rubbed his hands together.

By the gods, it was perfect. The almighty Cain Banning with a criminal, not just a petty thief, for a father. Piracy, abduction, abandonment at sea, murder. It mattered naught that none of it had been proven. In Jeremy's eyes, Thomas Gregg was guilty and he wanted to shout it to the world. But he knew he must not. He must think this through carefully and quickly, and he must plan. His entire future depended upon it.

Ayisha was bewildered by the cloud that seemed to be hanging over Cain. Watching him ride Willi, she pondered that he had first appeared troubled, surly even, Saturday eve when she'd asked about his parents. Now, four days later, his black mood still had not left him. Something was very wrong, but what? Had it to do with the mystery he could not talk about, or did all men have such times when they were not themselves? Seeing Aimee coming toward her through the tall grass and the wildflowers, she smiled and patted the spot beside her.

"Come and sit with me. Did Seth have to leave early?"

"Aye." Aimee lowered herself to the ground and gathered her skirts beneath her.

Ayisha was shocked to see that her eyes were swimming in tears. She took her hand. "Honey, what's wrong?"

For long moments Aimee could not speak. When she did, the tears streamed down her cheeks. She said, small voiced, "I—don't think he loves me anymore."

Ayisha stared at her sister's crumpled face and trembling lips. "Not love you? Aimee, I can't believe that. Did you argue?"

"Nay."

"Did he say or do something to hurt you?"

"N—nay." It was a half hiccough.

Ayisha kept her voice quiet so Cain would not hear. "Then why would you even think such a thing? If ever a man was in love, it's Seth Duncan. You can't tell me he doesn't love you."

"Then why doesn't he look at me or talk to me or kiss me the way he used to? When he left, all he gave me was a stupid little peck on the t—top of my head! He's so polite we might as well be sitting in ch-ch-church . . ."

Ayisha stared at her. "This is amazing. I was just sitting here thinking about Cain and how strangely he's been acting lately."

Aimee's mouth fell open. "Cain?"

"Aye. He's been quiet and moody, he doesn't meet my eyes when we talk . . ." In fact, he could not even meet Seth's eyes when the four of them were together. Maybe what it meant, she thought excitedly, was that Seth had been sharing Cain's mystery and something was about to happen concerning it. Maybe, maybe, please God, the secret would be out in the open soon and Cain would be free of the shadow he'd walked under ever since she had known him.

"What on earth can it mean?" Aimee's outraged gaze followed Cain's stately progress on the gray stallion. She gasped suddenly. "Could it be that they're planning on jilting us?"

Ayisha chortled. "Never."

"How do you know! Oh, Pan, I could just slay them both, the wretches! Except I don't really mean that. I love Seth as much as ever. Oh, dear!" She dabbed her eyes, now flowing again, with a dainty square of linen and lace and stared at her sister's serenity. "Pan, can't you see this is serious? Why aren't you worried?"

"Because I'm sure it's temporary. It's all going to work out. Everything will be fine." He had said it. He'd said all he needed was for her to trust him, and she did. She trusted him . . . she trusted him . . .

"How can you say that when everything's dreadful? What if Seth doesn't come back? What if I never see him again? What if Cain —"

"Aimee!" Ayisha's voice was so crisp, Aimee jumped. "You have not lost Seth, believe me, nor have I lost Cain." She added more gently, "There's something going on just now, some worry they have that will soon be over."

"How do you know? What sort of worry?"

"Cain mentioned it earlier although he couldn't tell me

what it was. He just asked me to trust him that everything would be all right, and I do. So should you."

Aimee's eyes were still wet. "You're sure it involves Seth, too?"

"I'm almost certain."

"Is it serious? But then I guess it would have to be, wouldn't it? Oh, dear." She nibbled her thumbnail and gave a little moan. "I've been so dumb and selfish. I was only thinking about me and my own hurt feelings. I didn't give one single thought to why poor Seth was acting the way he was. Why, he must have been miserable for days, the poor love!" She disentangled herself from her skirts and climbed to her feet. "I'm going to write him a letter. Don't let Cain go without it, please?"

"I won't." As she flew off toward the house, her skirts billowing, Cain and Willi drew near. Ayisha got to her feet. "Are you two through for the evening?"

"Aye. We don't seem to be at our best." Meeting her steady golden gaze, he smiled. "That's not quite right. I'm the one who's not at his best."

"Neither is Seth," Ayisha said as they started toward the stable.

Cain saw Aimee's flying figure nearing the house. "Did I hear her crying?"

"Aye. He left early and she's worried about him." As worried as I've been about you, she wanted to say, but bit her tongue. "He's been very quiet and moody."

Cain gave Willi's neck a reassuring pat. "I hadn't noticed." In truth, he had been so buried in his own concerns, he'd paid little attention to how Seth was looking or acting these days.

"Aimee wants you to take a note back to him."

"Of course."

After Griffin took Willi away, Ayisha lowered her voice. "Is he in this with you, Cain, this thing we can't talk about?"

Cain sighed and put his arm around her as they walked toward the house. "Aye."

"And something's about to happen, isn't it?"

"It's—possible."

She told herself that whatever it was, it was going to have a beautiful ending. It had to. She trusted him to make it so. Life would continue to be as wonderful as it was now. They were in love, they were going to be wed, they were enjoying Willi hugely and Willi was in his glory. Everything was going to be perfect. She leaned her head back against his shoulder and made herself say easily, "Aimee was funny. She was sure she'd been jilted and would never see Seth again. The past few days he's been depressingly chaste."

Cain's laughter was husky. He kissed her breast, kissed her mouth deeply, and said, "I can't be accused of that." Suddenly he saw the fear in her eyes. He frowned. "You're afraid."

"Not really."

He took her face between his hands. "You are. I see it."

"All right," she whispered. "I won't lie. I'm afraid because you are."

He asked quietly, "Why do you think that?"

"I see it. I feel it."

He smoothed back her hair. "It's true I have some concerns."

Suddenly she was trembling. She had no control over it. "Am I going to lose you?"

"Nay, sprite." He could not let her see that losing her was his own biggest worry.

"Oh, Cain, I—couldn't bear it." She threw her arms around his neck and kissed him wildly, his mouth, throat, cheeks, his hands, his hair. "I couldn't live without you . . ."

His voice was low, reassuring. "You'll never have to."

Her smile wavered. "I'm going to hold you to that. And know, Cain Banning, if, for any reason, you should have to leave Boston"—she touched his lips, kissed them, touched them again—"know that I'll be right there beside you. On land or sea, I'll be with you. I vow it."

Cain lifted her into his arms and held her hard against him, just held her with his eyes closed. When he found his voice finally, he said thickly, "Then our vow is a double one, Ayisha, for I'll never let you go. No one and no thing will ever take you away from me."

Jeremy Greydon was unable to sleep. For hours he lay awake with his heart pounding heavily. He could think of naught but Ayisha and of how this news would affect her. Over and over he imagined her falling into his arms and thanking him, aye, thanking him and begging his forgiveness for rebuffing him as she realized she had more than her own selfish desires to consider in a marriage, for marriage meant children—and bad blood would out.

He arose, lit a cigar, and paced his bedchamber like a caged wolf. Imagining her sitting in his bed, soft and white and naked, her eyes burning with desire and her arms held out to him, his manhood throbbed and his breathing quickened. What would it be like to have her, the most luscious wench in Boston? Have her whenever he wanted her, at any hour of the day or night. God's blood, he would never tire of it, of that he was certain . . .

He thrust the delicious image away. This was not the time to think of pleasuring himself with her. He must decide whether to tell her his news on the morrow or wait. But wait for what? Searching his brain again and again for some good reason, he could find none. In fact, the sooner he told her the better, for already many plans were being made for a May wedding in the great castle on the cliff above the sea—plans that might now include himself instead of Banning. It meant most assuredly that he must tell her as soon as possible.

And so it was that when morn came, he set out for Seacliff in his carriage and dressed in his most fashionable attire. He had spent an unconscionable amount of time choosing exactly the right morning wear, and he was now completely satisfied that his appearance would set any maid's heart to flaming. When he found Ayisha having a solitary breakfast on the terrace, his own heart flamed. She was ravishing, all tousled and soft and dewy looking in a satiny wrapper that made her cheeks and lips look pinker than usual. He smiled at her astonishment.

"Good morning, sweeting."

Ayisha put down her teacup with a clatter and got to her feet. "What are you doing here?"

"I have some news that will interest you."

"Nothing you might say could possibly interest me. I want you to leave."

Jeremy sat down at the table with its white linen cloth and its tempting array of breakfast things—a basket heaped with rolls, a dainty crock of butter, an assortment of jellies, a stately silver teapot gleaming in the morning sun. He poured himself a cup of tea, inhaled its fragrance, and took a sip. "Interesting flavor. Ceylon?" He chose a roll and bit into it.

Ayisha could not believe his audacity. "Soames! Come, please!"

Soames appeared magically. "Aye, Miss Adair?" He looked down his thin high-bridged nose at the intruder.

"Show Mr. Greydon out."

"Follow me, please, sir."

Jeremy settled himself more solidly in the wrought iron chair. "Not just yet, Soames. Your mistress and I are not through talking." He caught a glimpse of her nightdress beneath her pink satin wrapper and was tantalized. It was lacy and quite fragile looking, not at all like the boy's garb she usually wore. He added softly, "You would do well to hear me out, Ayisha. This is about Banning."

It was as if a hand had squeezed her heart, but Ayisha kept her face masked. "I know all I need to know about Cain."

His lips curved. "But you can't be certain unless we talk, can you?"

She yearned to slap the smile off his mouth but restrained the impulse. She turned to the butler and said quietly, "You can leave us, Soames."

"I will be close by, Miss."

"Thank you." She returned an icy gaze to Jeremy lounging at the table and sipping his tea. She crossed her arms. "So talk."

"Do sit down and join me." He waved a hand at her plate on which lay a half eaten croissant and a small cluster of grapes. "Finish your breakfast. Don't let me interrupt."

"I'm trying hard to keep my temper, Jere. Say what you have to say and go." She was remembering all over again his brutal handling of her: biting her breasts; kissing her so roughly that her skin was raw; groping, squeezing between her legs; bruising her arms and her throat with his steely fingers . . . She blocked the disgusting image from her mind before she was tempted to flatten him with her mother's teapot. She could not risk damaging it.

Jeremy poured himself a second cup of steaming tea. "I assume Banning has told you his background."

Her eyes flashed angrily. "Get to the point."

"Delighted to. I'm sure he's already told you that Gregg was suspected of piracy, abduction, and abandoning his men at sea,"—he moistened his lips—"but did you know murder may have been committed?" Seeing her beautiful eyes widen and her face grow still, he felt a rush of exhilaration. By the gods, she didn't even know who Gregg was. The bastard had not told her. He smiled. "I speak of Thomas Gregg, of course."

The hand squeezing Ayisha's heart had moved up to her throat and was attempting to cut off her supply of air. Thomas Gregg. Thomas. Cain's father had been Thomas. Was that who Jeremy meant? But surely his father's name would have been Banning.

Jeremy laughed, seeing her confusion and the tightening of her mouth into a thin line. Her lips were far too beautiful to be held so tightly. They were made to be soft and yielding, to open obediently to a man's searching tongue. He had tasted them, tasted deeply the sweet dark mystery of her mouth, and the memory of it had been a torment to him ever since. He was suddenly so hot in his crotch that he got to his feet and stood over her.

"Upon my soul, you don't know about Thomas Gregg?

But you should, fondling. You should. You must ask Banning to tell you about his father."

Ayisha was trying desperately to mask her face, veil her eyes, control her lips, all of those things at which Jeremy was so adept, but she was too shocked to lie. Was this the secret, the mystery that Cain had been hiding from her? "I—know naught of these things," she murmured, knowing the color had left her face.

"Tch, tch." Jeremy shook his golden head and smoothed his beard. "I'm surprised he would keep such an important thing from the woman he intends to wed. It's hardly a fair thing to do."

"If it mattered, he would have told me, but it matters naught. His father is dead."

Jeremy raised his eyebrows. "Matters naught? Come, sweeting." He remembered the delectable vision of her sitting in his bed, hungry eyes, her arms open to him. "Do you actually believe that? And believe that your pater would give his dearest treasure to a man with such a father? Nay, Ayisha, he would not. He will be looking ahead to his grandchildren. Men do, you know. He will not allow the blood of a criminal to mingle with his own—and don't think I'll not tell him this very interesting news because I'm looking forward to it. But all in due time. The moment must be right."

Ayisha felt the blood returning to her face and stinging her cheeks. "My father's not the snob you are, thank God, and Cain is Cain, not his father. He had naught to do with Thomas Gregg. I happen to know he was raised by his aunt and uncle and he rarely saw the man."

"He's a Gregg. He carried Gregg blood in his veins. Everyone knows that bad blood will out."

"That," said Ayisha furiously, "is a load of codswallop!"

"Indeed." He was shocked. He had been about to tell her that his own bloodline was impeccable, but her coarse language and the mutinous look in her eyes and the stubborn set to her jaw suggested to him that he would be wasting his breath.

"I want you to leave," Ayisha said sharply. "Now. And I don't want to hear another word about Gregg blood."

Jeremy breathed hard through his nose. The damned bitch. This was not at all the golden scenario he had envisioned. Why in hell were women so silly? What did she see in Banning that he himself did not have in triple measure? He wanted to shake her, force her to his thinking. "Your father—"

"Soames!" Her every pretense at calm had vanished. Her heart was nigh to leaping out of her throat. When Soames, darling Soames, appeared immediately, she gasped, "Remove this person at once and don't let him in this house again. Tell the others."

"Very well, Miss. Sir?" Soames's chilly gaze, piercing the visitor, asked whether he wished to walk to the front door under his own power or be carried there by the scruff of his neck.

Jeremy glowered at the old relic and was tempted to deck him on the spot. But then he might have retained quite a bit of vigor in his old age and make him look a fool. He growled, "Don't trouble yourself, old fellow. I know the way." He said low for Ayisha's ears alone, "I haven't forgotten what Banning did to me, and he'll pay, lady, I promise you. As for you"—his eyes were pitying—"I see now that you're out of your head over the bastard and aren't accountable for your actions. The devil has you under a spell, but I mean to break it. That's another promise, Ayisha. His hold over you will be broken because you're going to be my wife. Never doubt it. By one means or another, you're going to be mine."

"Soames!"

Jeremy held up a warning hand as Soames reached for him. "Don't touch me, you ugly old fart. I'm leaving." He hurled Ayisha a burning look and left.

Ayisha stared after him. She was numb—and furious. She was furious with Jeremy—why hadn't she asked him where he'd gotten such information? She was furious with Cain for not having told her—didn't he know such a thing mattered naught to her? And she was furious with herself for being frightened. For she was. She was very frightened. Not for herself, never in a million years could Jeremy Greydon persuade her to wed him. Nay, it was Cain she feared for. How could he possibly be on the alert every minute of the day for the traps Jeremy was sure to set for him? And another fear was nagging at her now. What if Jeremy were right about her father? What if this changed completely his feelings toward Cain? She stood, put her hands to her temples, and felt frantic. If only Cain were in town, but he was not. Of all times for him to be visiting suppliers today was the worst. Damn! She yearned to ride to him, warn him of his danger, feel his arms around her, hear his familiar, deep, comforting voice telling her it would be all right, but she had no idea where he was.

Chapter 17

Jeremy Greydon returned to his home on Tremont Street in the foulest of moods, but it was soon dispelled by a second letter that was awaiting him from his man in London. It read:

DEAR SIR:

The very day I sent my last message to you, I learned further about our subject's father from another more reliable source, and am forwarding the information to you posthaste. This new source declares that Thomas Gregg was indeed engaged in piracy as was his partner, Benjamin Scott, and he swears that the other rumors are true also. A fortune was taken from the Turkish vessel, *Safira,* as well as a winsome wench (his words) who might have been the daughter of a maharajah, a sultan, or a mogul. Which, he is not sure. It is safe to assume, however, that her blood was blue and that she was a beauty.

He says murder was indeed done, but Ben Scott was not the victim. Men were abandoned at sea upon Scott's orders, whereupon he fled Thomas Gregg's vessel at Ay Valik and carried the helpless maid off with him. Hoping this is the sort of information you are seeking.

I remain sincerely yours, AR.

Jeremy stood gazing out the window and feeling the warm rush of triumph that was flowing through him. What a find. It was sensational. A man named Ben had stolen a fortune and stolen a woman, a beautiful woman, possibly Turkish or Indian, with royal blood in her veins. And a man named Ben living in this very town and possessed of a vast fortune, had been wed to a beautiful woman he had met in Turkey. God's breath. Ben . . . Could it be? Was it possible that Ben Scott and Ben Adair were one and the same? Was that why the son of Thomas Gregg was here? Had it to do with what had happened so very long ago? He rang for his man and began swiftly to remove his morning attire.

"Have Brooks saddle my mount immediately, Sprigg."

"Right away, sir. Will you be here for the noon meal?"

"Nay, but I'll return for dinner."

"Very good, sir."

Within twenty minutes, Jeremy was nursing a tankard of ale in the smoky shadows of the Yellow Gull. A slight, thin-faced man sat opposite him. Seeing the frown lining his brow, Jeremy asked sharply, "Is there a problem with what I've asked you to do, Hawkins?"

"Not to say a problem," Jim Hawkins answered easily. "It's just that—well, Mr. Adair's not the sort of bloke I usually investigate for you."

Jeremy's hand shot out and closed over his wrist. "I don't pay you to speculate on what you're doing, man, I pay you to do it."

Hawkins hid his resentment at the reprimand. He said easily, "Rest assured, I'll give you complete satisfaction."

"See that you do." Jeremy took a swallow from his tankard. "I want to know what year he came to Boston, where he came from, what vessel he arrived on, and how long it took him to make a name for himself."

Hawkins nodded. "I'll get right on it. It shouldn't be too difficult what with everyone knowing him."

"Be discreet, for God's sake."

Hawkins compressed his lips. "I always am, sir." He finished his ale. "Will that be all?"

He did not like what he was being asked to do, and he damned well did not like Jeremy Greydon. The information he'd collected for him over the years was always just a background check on itinerant seamen who applied for work on the various Greydon ships. But Ben Adair ... Now why on God's green earth would the man want to dig into Ben Adair's business? Nay, he did not like this one bit.

"There's one more thing," Jeremy said low. "I want this done quickly. As quickly as possible. Use as many extra men as you need, and as I said, use discretion."

Hawkins got to his feet. "The job'll be done, sir. Quickly and confidentially." But he would do it alone. He liked Ben Adair. He was a good, decent man and he'd not have any but himself knowing that someone wanted background on him. "Give me three days and I'll give you all there is to know."

"Two days," Jeremy said. "I'll meet you back here on Saturday at the same time."

"I'll be here," Hawkins said crisply. He had already decided it would be the last time. He did not need money so desperately that he had to spy for this bastard to get it.

From the Yellow Gull, Jeremy went to the Red Lion. Banning was out of town, he knew, for he kept a close watch on him, and it was all to the good. It was Duncan he wanted to see. Not finding him in the taproom, he beckoned a barmaid.

"Has Mr. Duncan been about today?"

"Aye, sir. He was in for a bite just a while ago an' then I seen 'im go up t'. 'is room."

Jeremy smiled his white smile and saw her face turn pink. "I want to surprise him. Which room is his?" He pressed a coin into her damp little hand.

"Thank ye, sir. He be number four, second door on th' left. I'm sure he'll be pleased."

"I'm sure he will."

Heart going hard, Jeremy mounted the dark, narrow staircase and stole across the creaking floorboards. Finding room number four, he tapped lightly on the door. Receiving no answer, he tapped again. After long moments, a groggy voice came, "Who is it?"

"Greydon. We must talk."

Awakened out of a sound sleep, Seth sat up, blinked at the door, and tried to clear his head. Greydon? What in the hell did he want? He got to his feet, ran his fingers through his matted hair, and lurched to the door. He flung it open.

Jeremy entered without waiting to be asked and closed the door behind him. "It's imperative that we talk," he said, seating himself in the most comfortable chair in the room.

"Wait a damned minute," Seth growled, now fully awake. "Maybe I don't want to talk. What's this all about?"

"Ayisha. And Banning. Specifically Banning."

Seth scowled down at the other's splendidly carved face. He remembered well how it had looked the night the devil almost ran them down. He moved to the door and opened it. "There's naught you can say about either of them that I want to hear."

"Then you might want to hear about Thomas Gregg." Seeing the slightest narrowing of those gray eyes, Jeremy smiled.

"I know naught of any Thomas Gregg."

"All the more reason then why you should listen to what I have to say."

Seth knew that he was right. Distasteful as it was, he had to know what the bastard had found out. He only hoped his face had not turned white and that his heart would not stop on him. He muttered through stiff lips, "Get on with it then."

"You'll not be sorry. This is quite a tale I have to tell." He leaned forward. "How well do you know Banning?"

"Well enough."

"It surprises me that you're mates. You seem a decent sort." Dull and dumb but decent.

"Cain's one of the finest men I know." Seth's voice and eyes were openly hostile.

Jeremy's mouth curved. "Nay, my friend. There you are wrong."

Seth felt his hackles rise. "I'm not your friend, fella, get that straight."

"Ayisha is." Jeremy fixed a now icy gaze upon him. "And I happen to be protective of my friends. When I first met Banning, I sensed he was predatory and was going to go after her."

"Did you now . . ." God's breath, look who was calling who predatory.

"I did. In fact, I had one of my men in England check his background."

Seth was completely unprepared for the news. Although it left his head spinning, he glowered at Greydon and pointed to the door. "Go before I throw you out."

"Did you know"—Jeremy rose, bristling—"that his father was a pirate by the name of Thomas Gregg? And piracy was the least of his crimes . . ."

Seth bunched his fists and took a threatening step forward. "I don't give a damn about Thomas Gregg. Cain had naught to do with the man for years."

Jeremy moved back. "That's not what I heard."

Seth's big hand caught his coat at the back of his neck. He spun him toward the door. "Out!"

Jeremy struck his arm away. "Get your damned greasy paws off me, you stupid clod." He laughed then. "This is good to know. It would seem you've already heard the tale. Maybe you were part of it—murder done . . . men abandoned at sea . . . a helpless maid carried off to God alone knows what fate . . ." He was given a great shove which landed him in the dim hallway where he crashed heavily against the wall. He gave a roar, turned, and charged, but the door had been slammed in his face. He kicked it as the bolt slid shut. "Bastard! Don't think this is the end. It's barely begun!"

Seth spoke through the door with quiet menace, "I'd consider it libel if you so much as hint to any that Cain Banning was connected to his father in any way . . ." As

Greydon's footsteps faded, he lowered himself to the floor where he sat shaking.

Good God Almighty, of all the unlikely things to happen—to have Cain's personal history dug up and hung out for every eye to see. And by Greydon, of all people. Good God. He climbed to his feet and began pacing, recalling Greydon's words and his own, and wondering, had he protested too much? In truth, he had been in such a state of shock, he was not even sure now what he had said.

Panic hit him. It was a thing he had not felt for a long, long time, not since those days after he'd seen his father slain and his mates slip into the sea one by one to feed the sharks. Now it was back full force, and it was nigh suffocating him. He fought against it, dragging long, deep breaths into his lungs and slamming his fist against his palm again and again, telling himself, Nay! he had no time for such foolishness. Not when Greydon was doubtless on his way to Ben this minute to tell him all. And if he did, that would be the end of it. He would never see Aimee again. God.

He made the decision instantly to go to Seacliff, get his darling, and wed her. Make her his before it was too late. She would give up the idea of a huge wedding, he knew she would, and somehow he would make it up to her. It was the only thing to do. The only thing. His heart pounding so hard he could scarcely breathe, he galloped to the nearest livery, rented a carriage and driver, and gave him the directions to Seacliff. He sat back then and closed his eyes and prayed.

Aimee had just settled herself with her embroidery in a cozy chair in the drawing room when she heard knocking, then Seth's deep voice and Soames telling him where she was. She jumped up as he entered.

"Darling, what a wonderful surprise!" She quickly hid her fancy work behind her. It was the negligee for her wedding night. "I didn't expect you until evening."

"I hope it's all right."

"Of course it's all right. How could you even ask?" She

folded the delicate fabric about her hoop, laid it on her chair, and went into Seth's arms. She said softly, "I wish I could be with you day and night and not wait until next May. Why did I ever choose a time so far away?" She lifted her face for his kiss, and as his mouth closed over hers, she melted against him. She always did. His touch and his command of her left her completely without strength.

"Sweetheart, we have to talk."

"Very well, let's talk."

"Is Ayisha here, or your father?"

"Nay, she's riding with Mac, and Papa's never home at this hour." She grew still seeing his grim face. "Something's wrong . . ."

Seth could not speak. He caught her to him and held her until he had command of his voice. "Aye, something's wrong."

Aimee took his face between her hands and saw that it was drained of color. "You're frightening me! Is it Cain? Has something happened to him?"

He took her hands. "Nay, naught has happened to him. It's that—" He shook his head. Now what? What could he possibly say? He didn't know. He caught her to him again, buried his face in her silky cloud of hair, and felt his heart shaking both their bodies. "My little love . . ."

"Seth, what is it? Is there any way I can help?"

His throat was so tight he could not speak. He muttered finally, "There's only one way . . ."

Aimee said promptly, "Whatever it is, I'll do it. I'll do anything."

"My precious girl, you don't know what it is."

"But I know you," she replied softly. "Is it something to do with Cain's secret?"

"Aye."

"Pan says he's asked her to trust him."

"That's so."

"Then I guess you need for me to trust you, too."

"Aye, if you would." His throat was so constricted his voice was scarcely his own.

All of her life Aimee had been loved and cosseted and protected by everyone—her father and mother, Ayisha and Pegeen, the butler and maids and footmen, the grooms and gardeners and Mac. Everyone. And because she was so adored and babied and guarded, nursing the small injured animals she found was the most important thing in the world to her. It meant she was giving and not merely receiving. She needed to be needed, to heal and comfort and calm the hurt and frightened creatures she found. And now she saw that Seth was one of these. She had never seen a creature more hurt and frightened—not in body, but in spirit. She said firmly, "I trust you. With my whole heart and soul, I trust you."

Seth had never seen her beautiful brown eyes shine so, nor had he ever loved her as he did at that moment. In broad daylight, in the drawing room of Seacliff, she was starry eyed, his darling, in her love and trust of him. He seized the moment before it could vanish.

"Then wed me," he said. "Now. I have a carriage waiting." Hearing her small indrawn breath, he added quickly, "I promise you, my angel, I've committed no crime, nor has Cain. It's—something else entirely. It's the fate that has befallen us."

"Our kismet?"

"Aye. Our kismet."

"Mama said that in all the world, Papa was the one man for her—"

"Did she now?"

"Aye. She said it was her kismet that they met. And I think it's my kismet that Papa brought you home to me. And if you say we must wed now, why then we must wed."

Seth could scarcely believe what he was hearing. "I know you wanted a church wedding, and I wanted you to have it . . ."

She laughed, loving the concern she saw in his gentle gray eyes. "It matters naught. What matters is that you say we must wed now." She stood on tiptoe, brought his face down to hers, and kissed his mouth hungrily. "I'll do anything you say, Seth Duncan. I'll go to the ends of the earth with you if you say I should." Marking that he was in a daze, Aimee knew that it was she who must attend to practical matters. She murmured, "I'll pack a small valise—no one will see it—and I'll leave a note on Pan's pillow. She can tell Papa."

Her trust in him tore Seth's heart. He murmured, deep in guilt, "It kills me to do this to you."

"Papa will be all right. He'll know there's a good reason. He loves you, Seth. I've seen it in his eyes."

At that, Seth gave a muffled groan. If only there were another way, but there was not. He muttered, "Be sure to tell Ayisha you'll come to no harm. I swear it to God."

"She knows it. I needn't say it." Aimee gently extricated herself from his desperate grasp. "I'll pack my things now—and I'll tell Pegeen you're taking me for a ride. Is that all right?"

Seth nodded. It had to be. Before many more minutes had passed, they were in the rented carriage clattering toward the city and his thoughts were flying like dry leaves swept up into a whirlwind. What next? Where would he wed her? Where in God's name did one go? He had no experience with this sort of thing. But when the docks came into sight, he suddenly knew what to do. Any ship's captain could perform the ceremony.

Cain froze. Ayisha was calling to him. He was in a stretch of virgin forest with his supplier choosing the straightest and the tallest of the white pines destined for the first Banning ships when he heard her cry. It came to him as clearly as had his call to wander, and it was as desperate as when Greydon had tried to rape her. He felt his blood run cold.

"Mr. Banning—" The lumberman stared after him as he strode swiftly to his horse and mounted. "Sir, we've hardly even begun . . ."

"It can wait, Mr. Cooper. I'll be back."

He was one hour north of Boston, and his mount was so winded by the time he reached the city, he rented another.

It too was winded and covered with foam when he handed it over to the groom at Seacliff. He asked sharply, "Where's your mistress?"

"I saw 'er headed fer th' beach. T' collect seashells, she said. She took Omar."

"Was she all right?" When the lad looked at him as if he were daft, Cain grabbed a bridle from the wall rack. "Never mind. I'll join her. I'm taking King. No water for that one,"—he indicated his rented mount—"and cool him down. He's a good animal."

Within minutes, he was riding down the steep path to the shore, his heart still thundering in his ears. What in God's name had brought him here in such a panic when everything seemed so blessedly ordinary? Why had he sensed such terrible danger for Ayisha? It made no sense. Emerging from the forest, he saw her wading in the shallows, her back to him. Overjoyed to see her unharmed, he put King in the paddock and strode toward her.

"Ayisha!" The wind caught his voice and carried it out to sea but she heard him and turned. The surprise and gladness on her face lit his heart, and then she was running to meet him, hair flying and eyes glowing.

"Cain! You're here! Oh, Cain!" She had nigh worn out the rug in her bedchamber with her pacing and had come to the beach to pace on the hard-packed sand. She had been so afraid for him, so worried that she could scarcely bear the thought of waiting until tomorrow to see him—and now here he was. It was a miracle. "I'm so glad to see you. I'm so glad!" She went into his arms and returned his kisses again and again and again. Neither of them could get enough of the other.

"You're all right?" Cain asked finally, studying her flushed face and luminous, sun gold eyes.

"I am now."

He held her closer. "And before that?"

"I was afraid for you." She was remembering that he had come riding to her once before when she had been filled with fear, just as he had come now. She said, "You knew again . . ."

"I'll always know. But why were you afraid for me?"

If he had been in town this morn, everything would have been so much simpler. She would have ridden to him on the wind and told him about Jeremy's visit and all that he had said. Now she had had time to think, and she was so confused, so very confused. She said, "It was just a bad feeling I had. I was worried about you and couldn't shake it." If the news about his father was the secret he'd been guarding from her so carefully, it would be awful if he learned she'd heard it before he was ready to tell her. And from the worst possible source. Yet shouldn't he know that Jeremy knew? Help, Lord, help—please . . . But then she didn't have to make a decision this instant, did she? She could just enjoy his being here, safe and sound, and decide later. She clung to him more tightly and buried her face against his chest. "I'm so glad you're here and I love you so much. So very much . . ."

Cain smoothed her hair, pressed his lips to it, and felt relief pulsing through him that no harm had come to her. But the worry that had nagged him for days was as strong as ever: What if Ben did what they feared the most when he learned the truth? What if he hid the maids away so that he and Seth would never find them? He was a powerful and an influential man and it would be a simple thing for him to do. It made Cain wonder and worry for the hundredth time if Ayisha should be told before they gave Ben their news. It was only right that she be prepared for whatever was to come. But he didn't have to decide now. Not now when she was so warm and soft and hungry in his arms.

Chapter 18

Aimee's eyes grew large when she saw that they were in the roughest part of town. Seamen were everywhere and vendors were hawking their wares to them. On either side of the road were ships being loaded and unloaded to the accompaniment of language that fair burned her ears. She asked in a small voice, "Where are we going?"

"I know the captain of a vessel that arrived in port just yesterday," Seth replied. "If we're lucky, he'll be aboard and he can wed us." He stuck his head out the window. "Driver, take us to the *Half Moon* docked straight ahead on the right." He turned to Aimee. "If he's not about, darlin', I'll find us another to perform the ceremony." He was out the door before the carriage had even stopped. "Wait here, driver, and guard my lady well." He sprinted up the gangplank, and within minutes returned with a tall, swarthy older man with dancing dark eyes. "Sweetheart, this is Captain Anderson, an old friend of mine. Con, this is my fiancée, Aimee Adair."

"I'm honored." The dancing eyes moved over Aimee and his big rough hand closed over hers. "I can see why ye didna want t' wait, lad. She's a bonny one."

Seeing Aimee's lips quiver, Seth asked low, "Love, are you absolutely sure you want to go through with this?"

Aimee swallowed. "I'm sure." If it was what Seth wanted, she did, too. Of course she did. It was just that she had been dreaming of a beautiful church wedding for so long . . .

"Well, then, come along, darlin', let's go aboard." He took her arm and they followed Con Anderson up the gangplank and soon were standing in his cabin while he rooted about in his great oaken desk for a Bible.

"Here 'tis." He leafed through the fragile pages and gave Seth a wry grin. "It's been awhile since I've done this, but th' knot'll be well tied, no matter. Now then, lad, d' ye want it drawn out or short an' sweet?"

"Short." Seth gazed down at Aimee anxiously. "If it's all right with you, beloved?"

Aimee drew a deep breath and shivered. She felt her heart thumping. "It is." Her nostrils twitched. The cabin smelled of sweat and brine and stale smoke. And fish.

"Well then, stand on 'er right, lad, an' get th' ring oot."

"The ring? In God's name, I never even thought of a ring!"

Aimee could not suppress a nervous giggle. She held out her right hand to show the small, gold-mounted emerald on her third finger. "Will this do?"

" 'Twill do fine, lass. Gi' it t' yer mon an' tell me ye'r full names, both o' ye."

"Aimee Ana Ayhan Adair," she said obediently.

"Seth Jonathan Richard Darby," said Seth in a hoarse whisper. He squeezed Aimee's hand tightly and his gray eyes holding hers begged her not to stop trusting him now.

Aimee's heart stood still and then began to fly as she stared up at Seth. Darby? His last name was Darby? Why would he have lied about such an important thing as his last name? Why? Dear God, what was she letting herself in for?

Seth put his lips to her ear. "Trust me, Darlin', please . . ."

She nodded. She had to. She could not stop now. In a daze, she heard the captain intoning the familiar words, heard Seth's soft I do, heard herself repeating it, and then they were wed. And if she had made a terrible mistake, why, there was naught to be done about it now. She belonged to Seth, and he belonged to her. They were man and wife until death did them part.

Now Con Anderson studied Aimee with narrowed eyes. "Truly, mon, ye' ha' a rare blossom here. Guard her well, an' rule her wi' a strict hand. It's never good to let a woman taste too much freedom. An' you, Mrs. Darby, be an obedient wife t' ye'r husband an' bring 'im honor. May God go wi' th' both o' ye and bless ye wi' health an' riches an' babes galore."

Seeing that Aimee had turned pale, Seth put his arm about her. He was fuming inwardly as he pressed a remuneration into Con Anderson's hand and muttered, "Thanks. We'll be moving along now." He quickly steered Aimee toward the door. Hell. Why hadn't the old boy just stopped the ceremony instead of bringing up such damned touchy subjects? He doubted Aimee had ever been ruled by anyone in her life, and as for babes, she was naught but a babe herself. Hell and damnation.

"Ye'll likely be headin' for ye'r honeymoon now, an' a grand time it is in a mon's life—this fair young lily bud just waitin' t' be opened—an' ye in th' prime o' ye'r manhood . . ." He sighed as his hungry gaze moved over Aimee. "Enjoy yersel', lad."

Seth was so angry he dared not speak while Aimee, within the circle of his protecting arm, was trembling and stiff as a poker. As he sped her down the gangplank and settled her in the carriage, he thought what a travesty it had been. A veritable farce. His darling wedded, not in her sumptuous French gown and veil, but in a simple cotton dress and with her own ring. Wed in a dim ship's cabin that stank of brine and tobacco, in a ceremony lasting no more than three minutes and attended by only the three of them instead of the multitude she had wanted. And the old boy was hot for her to boot. Hell. He gave a deep sigh and gazed unhappily at his silent young bride as the carriage gave a creak and a jerk and moved forward. Her lips were drawn into a thin pale line.

"I'm sorry. That—wasn't ideal . . ."

"I'm sure what he said was very important." Aimee's voice was tight with fury. "You'll rule me strictly and I'll be a good obedient wife and honor you and doubtless we'll have ten babes. Maybe twenty. Maybe you'll give me some freedom after that." She had never been so mortified in her life. "Let's go back. I want to slay him! Fair young lily bud just waitin' t' be opened indeed! Ugh!"

Seth held back his laughter. She was marvelous. Adorable. And fit to be tied. It tickled him, knowing that if the words had come from his own lips, she would have purred like a kitten. He stuck his head out the window. "Driver, take us back to the *Half Moon*. We have unfinished business with the captain."

Aimee gave a small shriek and called out the other window. "Driver, don't you dare! Keep going wherever we're going." She grinned at Seth then and swatted his arm. "Beast! Where are we going anyway?"

Seth grinned, called once more to the driver, "Continue on to the Red Lion." What he craved, of course, was to sail off with his luscious lily and never return to Boston again. But it was out of the question even if his ship had been in port and Aimee did not fear the sea. The two of them had a lot to talk about and decide. In the meantime, there was something far more interesting to do than talk. He gave Aimee a heavy-lidded look and said huskily, "Come here, Mrs. Darby. It's time I did some of that ruling the old boy mentioned." He pulled her into his arms.

Aimee did not melt. "So it's Darby, is it—or isn't it?" In her outrage, she had forgotten about it. "What is your name, really?" She melted after all when he captured her mouth in a long, sweet, hungry kiss. She sighed, then whispered, "Maybe I'll be obedient some of the time . . ."

"That would be nice." Seth dipped his head to her throat, gently tugged her gown off one shoulder, and kissed its satiny softness. "My name," he murmured, "is Darby. My mother was a Duncan."

Aimee's breath was coming in small, soft pants. "In truth, I—like Darby better. And I'm sure you . . . had a good reason for . . . keeping it from me . . . as you did." At that moment, she did not care what his name was. She sought his mouth hungrily as his hand slid beneath her gown, and when it closed possessively over her breast, her breath caught. "Oh, Seth! My—husband . . ."

Seth had taken her up the backstairs to his room with the full intention of consummating the marriage, but he had fast come to his senses. Even before they removed their clothing, he had learned that the maid knew naught. He had known she was young, aye, but when he saw her total innocence and naiveté, he was hard hit by what his fear of Jeremy Greydon had driven him to do. He had torn a child from her father, possibly shaking the love and trust between the two, and he had turned a day that should have been beautiful into one that was shabby. Not least, if they honeymooned, he would be deserting his mate when Cain needed him the most. He felt sick to his stomach as he wondered what in God's name kind of man he had become. It shamed him to think of the answer.

Aimee lay beside her new husband, her head on his shoulder, and felt him gently stroking her hair and tracing her lips and the curve of her breasts. She murmured, "I'm so sorry—I've disappointed you. I'm so stupid . . ."

She could not believe how stupid. She had been a complete fool, gaping at him, asking him what that strange bulge was beneath his trews. Dear God, asking him what it was! How could she? Why had no one told her what men looked like and what went where and why it went where it went? Why had Pan not told her what happened between married folk and how babes were made? Why? But then she had never asked, and Pan probably thought she knew. Everyone did. Everyone except her. Who on earth was the idiot who had told her that kissing with tongues did it—started babes? Damn. She hated herself. She was stupid, stupid, stupid. Burying her head in Seth's neck, she wept softly.

"There, now, darlin', it's all right. It matters naught if we don't make love now. In fact, it's best that we don't. Just having you here in my arms is heaven. Just being able to look at you . . ." He had to admit that Con Anderson, the old lech, was right. She was a veritable lily bud waiting to be opened and unfolded. All lush and white and plump and fragrant. But he could well bide his time. Getting inside of her was not the main reason he had wed her. He loved her. He ran adoring hands over her skin, marveling at its silkiness and the perfection of her small, rounded breasts and childish hips and the soft down where her thighs met. She could not be more perfect. And she was his. Naught could change that. She was his forever, no matter what Ben Scott did or said, and trusting him as she did, to take her now and frighten and hurt her would be a betrayal. He saw clearly that she had to know about him first. She had to know everything.

Aimee's sobs continued. "You're just s—s—saying that to make me feel better." She was a disaster. Not only for her husband, but for everyone else. What had she done? Papa would die of a broken heart—or of rage. Both, maybe. And Pegeen would feel that she had not guided her well and failed Mama. And Pan would be hurt—but at least she would understand. Or would she? Oh, what on earth had she done?

But she was being stupid again, making a mystery out of it when she knew exactly what she had done and why she had done it. She had run off with Seth Duncan, Seth Darby as it turned out, because he had begged her to. He had looked so pale and frightened and wild-eyed, it seemed a matter of life and death. He had asked her to trust him, and she had. She grew aware suddenly that he was speaking to her and his face had gone pale again. He looked as if someone had died.

"—and so there's naught to do but tell you everything here and now, my angel, and pray you'll not hate me . . ."

Hate him? Hearing such startling words, she put her full attention on him. "I—wasn't listening. My mind was o—on something else. Why would I hate you? Seth, you're scaring me!"

It seemed forever before she could absorb what he was saying—that her father had been a pirate who had robbed a ship, abducted her mother, and ordered his own men to be abandoned at sea. She sat up in bed and stared at him blankly for long moments before she shook her head. "Nay," she said. "It's absolutely not so." Her eyes got wet again. "How can you say such things? How do you know?"

Seth wanted to comfort her but he knew better. Not in the mood she was in. When she began to tremble, he gently draped a sheet over her shoulders to cover her nakedness. He said gently, "I know because I was there. I was a cabin boy aboard his vessel, and my father was his best friend." He saw well that she would not, could not believe anything bad of her father. He understood. It was exactly what he had anticipated. He knew her thoughts were flying.

"Is this what Cain's been hiding from Pan?"

"Aye, lass. His father and yours were partners."

"Partners?" She had never felt so bewildered. "Cain's father was a pirate, too?"

"Aye."

"And yours?"

"Aye. Mine, too." Hoping to soften the shock of it, he added, "You must understand, none of them started out that way. They were businessmen, cargo haulers, but times got hard and they had mouths to feed. Many good men turned to piracy temporarily in those days to make ends meet." He himself had never thought it was a good enough excuse.

Aimee could not drag her eyes from his face. She saw in it the same openness and honesty that had drawn her to him in the beginning. Now it filled her with terror. "I fear you're telling me the truth," she murmured. Or what he thought was the truth. It was her only hope, that this was some terrible misunderstanding which, for some reason, he believed completely.

"Aye, darlin', it's the truth, and we've suffered over it, Cain and I. Once we saw you two maids, we knew we couldn't go through with—" He hesitated, not certain how much to tell her.

"Go through with what?" It was a nightmare, and she

was going to wake up any moment now. Please, God, let it be a nightmare.

"—with what we had intended." Seth could not meet her eyes. "To take Ben Scott back to England for the Crown to prosecute him."

"Ben Scott?"

"It's your papa's real name, lass," he said softly and hated himself. "He changed it when he came to Boston."

"Are you telling me that my name—is Aimee Scott?" She felt completely adrift. No one was who she thought they were—not Seth, not Papa, not even herself or Ayisha.

"Darby's your name now, beloved."

She gave her head a wild shake. "I can't believe this—I just can't! Did you drag Cain's father before the Crown, too? Is that how he died? And your own father?"

"Nay, lass, nay. It's a long story, and someday you'll hear it, I promise, but not right now." He tried to stroke her cheek, but she turned her head.

"He didn't do it! Not Papa. He'd never do such an awful thing!"

Seth looked at her brimming eyes sadly. "He did it, darlin', and no one's sorrier than I am. Now he has to pay reparations."

"To whom?"

"His men died when he ordered them abandoned at sea. They left behind families." He did not mention the sharks as it would serve no purpose, nor did he mention his terrible hunger for revenge and the many years he had been searching for Ben Scott. It did not seem a good time either to mention that her mother was of the royal house of Kemal.

"They—died at sea?" Her voice wavered.

"All of them. I was the lone survivor. A Turkish vessel rescued me."

At that, she sat straighter. It was hideous to think that any man would do such a thing to his fellow men, but she knew now for a fact that it was not her father who was the culprit. Beyond any doubt whatsoever, it was a misunderstanding. She said simply, firmly, "He didn't do it." It was as if a storm had passed and the sun had come out. She crawled out of bed and began calmly to pull on her underthings. "He was your captain, but he's my father. I know him. He's simply not capable of such a thing."

"Darlin' . . ." Realizing that there would be no more playing with her in bed, Seth, too, began to dress.

"Did you see him give the order? Did you hear him?" Aimee asked.

"I saw him loot ship after ship, and I saw your mother carried aboard the *Bluebird* at his orders. He relinquished his share of the booty in exchange for her." And reneged on it. In truth, he had never seen such a change in a man as when Ben had fought Tom Gregg for Ana. His crew were stunned by his savagery.

Aimee's eyes grew distant thinking of it. It was unbelievable, and unbelievably romantic—Mama stolen at sea and Papa giving up everything to have her for himself. She'd had no idea their lives had been so exciting. Why, she'd never even thought of their being young. They were naught but parents, although very wonderful ones. But Mama had been beautiful, and Papa was dashing and— She put it from her mind and held fast to the most important thing. She said imperiously, "You haven't answered my question. Did you hear my father himself give the order to abandon his men?"

Seth frowned. "Not from his own lips."

"Whose then?"

"Cain's father. But Ben gave the orders all right. Tom merely acted on them. Ben had been hit by a spar and was unconscious." It was no surprise to any of them that he'd not shown his face at such a time if he'd wakened.

Aimee donned her simple cotton gown in silence, buttoned it, and sat on the side of the bed to pull on her stockings and slippers. She said quietly but firmly, "I think you'd best hear Papa's side of it."

Seth sighed. "I intend to." Ben would certainly have his side to tell.

"You'll see that he's not guilty, I promise you. And I promise you he'll want to help those poor folk anyway, the ones who lost their men. He'll want to send them money. Let's go to him right now. He'll be in his office."

Seth tugged on his boots and got to his feet. "Not you. I'll go to him. This is between the two of us."

"But—"

"Nay, Aimee. You're going back to Seacliff."

"But—"

"Nay. You know I'll never rule you, sternly or otherwise, but in this instance you'll obey me, for I know what's best. I must see your father alone. I'll come to you later. In fact, it might not be until tomorrow."

"Tomorrow!"

"Hush, lass. Don't argue." He gripped her arm, led her down the back staircase, and settled her in the waiting carriage. He handed the driver several coins. "I'll not be needing you after you take my lady to Seacliff. She'll direct you there. Guard her well, man."

"That I will, sir."

"Seth . . ."

Aimee's anxious brown eyes melted his heart. "Aye, darlin'?"

"Considering everything, maybe you shouldn't tell Papa about us yet. It—might be too much . . ."

Seth nodded gravely. "I think you're right. We'd best save it for another time."

As he rode toward Ben's office, Seth was consumed by dread. He wished to God he and Cain could have confronted the old lion together as they'd planned, but it was not to be. Cain was out of town seeing suppliers, and Ben had to hear the news before Greydon got to him. Maybe it was already too late, but then he'd had to do first what he considered most important. Aimee was his.

Tying his mount to the hitching rail before Ben's building, Seth squared his shoulders and entered the small, dusty waiting room. It was empty, and the door to Ben's office was open. It was always open. Looking in, he saw the older man sitting at his desk leafing through a stack of papers. He knocked.

"Sir. . ." His mouth was so dry, his voice sounded more crow than human. He cleared his throat.

Ben looked up, smiled. "Son! Come in, come in. What brings you by?" He indicated a chair. "Sit down, lad."

"I'll stand."

Marking the strain and pallor on the younger man's face, Ben frowned and got to his feet. "What is it?" His heart felt too big for his chest of a sudden. "Aimee . . .?"

"Aimee's fine. Just fine." He could not meet Ben's worried eyes, but stared at the papers on the desk.

"You're sure? You don't seem yourself, lad."

Seth ordered himself to speak, say what he'd always planned to say . . . hit him broadside with it. He swallowed, drew a long breath, and met the old man's piercing blue eyes. He said gruffly, "I have a message for you from the crew of the *Bluebird,* Ben Scott."

Ben gaped at him, not understanding. "The—*Bluebird?*"

"Aye, the *Bluebird.* I'm Seth Darby, Jonathan's son." He heard the other's sharply indrawn breath, saw the color draining from his face.

Ben was staggered. The *Bluebird.* And this was Jonathan's son? "You're—young Seth?"

"I am," Seth said grimly.

"My God."

Knowing that his legs would not hold him, Ben sank into his chair. He could not tear his eyes from Seth Duncan's face, for now he saw that what he said was so. It was all there—the same wide-spaced gray eyes and sandy hair and generous mouth, the same height and gentle strength and kind face—except that the lad had enough of his mother in him so that Ben did not feel a complete fool for not seeing it sooner. But God Almighty, he saw it now. No wonder it had been so easy to love him. He was Jonathan's seed and Jonathan's blood, Jonathan whom he'd loved like a brother. At the thought, tears gathered in his eyes and ran unchecked down his cheeks. He said hoarsely, "All of these years, I thought you were dead. God has answered my prayers."

Prayers? Seth smiled. He didn't believe it for a minute.

The older man's tears, which had at first horrified him, now left him unmoved. He continued relentlessly, "I was the *Bluebird*'s sole survivor. A Turkish freighter picked me up."

The sole survivor. Ben felt the old familiar leaden cloak weighing him down. It always came when he remembered what had happened that day so long ago. He had suffered cruelly and suffered still, wondering about his men. Now, no matter what the answer, he wanted to know what fate had befallen them. "The others," he muttered, "how did they die?"

"Some were lucky and drowned before the sharks got them."

"Nay . . ."

"What else did you expect?" Seth said sharply, paying no heed to the pain on Ben's gaunt face. "Their message to you, Captain, is to roast in hell for all time. And hear this—it's only because of those two darlin' maids of yours that you're not in chains now and on the high seas. I've been searching for you for twenty years to see justice done, but neither Cain nor I could hurt the maids that way. You'll be getting off easy, just paying retribution to your crews' folk."

"Gladly, lad, gladly. I'd've done it ages ago had I known where they lived." Ben's head was spinning with a hundred different questions, but they could wait. What mattered now was that Seth heard the truth.

Seth's eyes glittered. "Oh, I'm sure you'd've paid—in a pig's eye."

Ben roared, "My men came to me from all over the isles, dammit, you know they did! Scotland, Ireland, England, Man, Wales, Skye, the Hebrides—all over. My God, man, I had no records. They went down with the *Bluebird*! As for the abandonment"—he ran a shaky hand over his eyes—"I've died a thousand deaths knowing I was blamed for that atrocity."

Seth crossed his arms. "So you're saying you're not responsible."

"As God is my witness, I'm not. When I was hit by that

beam, I passed out. When I woke three days and two nights later, Ana told me what had happened. She'd been nursing me and she saw the whole thing through the porthole—Tom Gregg forcing my men into those damned, leaky longboats and saying I'd ordered it. Your father killed . . ." Now sweat rolled down his face. "I dream of it still, what that black-hearted bastard did to my men, and to have laid it at my feet!" He slammed a fist against his desk, got to his feet, and began pacing. "And I couldn't even get revenge. I had to get Ana away from there before his men began raping her. We jumped ship in Ayvalik when they were all in town drinking. Luckily, she'd kept her jewelry hidden in a pouch in her skirts. I sold some to get us to Boston and sold a few more pieces to help set me up in business."

Seth listened quietly, intently, his critical gaze never leaving Ben Scott. The older man was prowling his office as he'd so often prowled the deck of the *Bluebird,* and the sight filled Seth with memories—the deep camaraderie between Ben and his own father, the respect and affection his men had had for him despite his turn to piracy.

Holy Mary, Mother of God, what was he to think? What the old boy said sounded plausible—but then he'd always had a golden tongue. Seth had been prepared for a slick explanation and Ben had had twenty years to prepare it. He said softly, "Tom Gregg was still insisting on his deathbed that you'd ordered him to abandon your men. He still wanted to kill you."

Ben froze in mid-step. "Tom Gregg is dead? You found that bastard dying?"

Seth drew a steadying breath. "Cain told me. He wondered what kind of hold you had on him to make him obey you as he did."

Ben asked hoarsely, "What has Cain to do with that devil incarnate?" But he needed no answer. It was as if lightning had torn through his skull. God, God . . . He had wondered, when he'd first seen Cain Banning, why his eyes seemed so familiar. Now he saw that they were Tom Gregg's eyes. Tom Gregg. Fool that he was, he'd brought the fellow into his home, welcomed him, encouraged Ayisha to see him and, God help him, to wed him. He said thickly, "He's that bastard's son . . ."

"Aye." Not liking the wild look in Ben's eyes, Seth said sharply, "But he's not Tom Gregg. He's Cain Banning. He was adopted by his uncle when he was just a lad and saw naught of his father until the old boy was on his last legs. He took Tom under his own roof out of the kindness of his heart. It wasn't Cain," he added coldly, "who ordered your men abandoned."

Ben sat down heavily. "Nor did I, lad, nor did I, and that's God's own truth."

Seth lowered himself to the visitor's chair before Ben's desk. "Can you prove it?"

Ben loosed a deep sigh. "Ana was my only witness. I doubt even Tom's men knew he lied. If the devils ever wondered why I left behind the loot I supposedly abandoned my men to get, they forgot about it when they got their greedy paws on it." He shrugged. "Nay, you've only my word against the lying tongue of the cruelest bastard ever to sail the seven seas. As I said, I'll gladly give you compensation above and beyond what's required for my poor lads' families, what's left of them. But my girls must know naught of this, do you understand?"

Seth felt relief moving through him, a sweet warm wave of it. It was exactly what he and Cain had both hoped for. That the girls would never know. He said, "I told you, we'll never hurt them. That's a promise."

Ben's eyes glinted. "But know this, Cain Gregg's not to lay his filthy hands on that money."

Seth could not contain a flare of outrage. "His name's Cain Banning, and I'd trust my life with him!"

Ben smiled grimly. "Then you must value it very little, son." All he could think of now when he recalled Cain's dark image was Tom Gregg and the waiting sharks and the bloody water. Sickened, he gritted his teeth, and knew he would never sleep again.

Seth gave a sharp laugh. "That's good, that is, coming from Ben Scott."

"He's not to see Ayisha again."

"Ayisha mightn't agree."

Ben gave his silver head an emphatic shake. "Ayisha will obey her father. You seem not to realize that evil runs in families just as good does. You, I'll give my daughter to for the sake of your father. Now there was a good man . . ." In truth, seeing Seth now and knowing who he was was almost like having Jonathan back again. "But Cain Gregg—"

Seth jumped to his feet. "His name's Banning, and I'll not hear a word against him. You're not fit for him to wipe his feet on!"

Ben slammed his fist on his desk. "He's the son of a monster and I'll not give my firstborn to him. Quibble all you want that he's not like his bloody bastard of a father, but I'll not risk it. I forbid him to see Ayisha again. I forbid it, and you tell him that. Tell him I'll throw him off my land personally if he sets foot on it again, and furthermore—"

Seth's hand shot up in a warning for silence. He put a finger to his lips. He stole across the floor and looked in the waiting room. Empty. He hastened to the outside door, gazed up and down the street and saw naught unusual—two carriages, a man on horseback, two women and a babe, an old man hobbling along with the help of a cane. He returned to Ben's office.

"What is it?" Ben said. "Did you see or hear something?"

"It must have been a noise on the street. No one was about." Even so, they had been fools not to have closed both doors. Seeing suddenly how old and tired Ben looked, Seth said, "We'll talk of this again."

"That we will," Ben muttered. He felt so outraged and betrayed and unforgiving that Seth himself was not safe from his fury just then. "You'd best go now."

"I agree. But before I do"—Seth closed both doors and lowered his voice to a whisper—"I understand well why you won't take my word on Cain. You know naught of him. By the same token, I know naught of you anymore,

Ben Scott. It's been twenty years. You might not be the
bloody bastard I think you are, but I can't risk it. I'm sure
you can see this." When Ben blinked, he knew the barb
had sunk home.

As he rode back toward the Red Lion, Seth was nigh
overcome with worry. Not for himself, nay. By some miracle, he had come out of this mess clean, but Cain—God's
me, Cain was another story. Not only did Ben hate him,
Greydon was bent on destroying him. On the chance that
his friend had finished early with his lumber man and returned to the Riker Yards, Seth turned his mount abruptly
and started there at a gallop. Cain had to know as soon as
possible what was happening.

Chapter 19

◦~⟋⟍⟋⟍~◦

Ayisha took Cain's hand and led him to where the sand was hot and dry and shaded by the cliff. They lowered themselves to it and Cain lay her back in his arms and kissed her with tender hunger. He held and cradled her then, his gratitude for her safety too great for words. Ayisha was content to be held in silence, to see the love in his eyes and feel it in the careful way he held her—as if she were a treasure.

"I love you," she murmured again as he stroked her cheek with the backs of his fingers. "But there's no way I can ever tell you how much—except it's far more than there are stars in the sky and deeper than the deepest ocean."

"That's quite a bit," Cain said gravely.

She laughed, touched his lashes, his hair, his curving lips. "If I were a poet, or could hire a poet, I'd tell you properly."

"No poet's words could compare with your own."

He would never tire of looking at her nor cease to be astonished by her beauty—that long, satiny cape of dark hair, flame streaked and spilling over her breasts; the exotic amber gold of her eyes and the love in them; her mouth so full and ripe and tempting in the sweet ivory innocence of her face. He wondered suddenly, and it was like a dagger in his heart, if this were the last time she would lie in his arms. He thrust the thought away. Nay. He would not think of it now. There was no rush, no need to decide this instant whether to tell her. There was time yet.

There was time. For now he wanted only to feel her body pressed against his, kiss and taste her, hold her, tell her again and again that he loved her.

As Ben's carriage bore him toward Seacliff, he was sick at heart. But his sickness did not replace his fury. It crowned it. He was twice as wretched as he'd been before for now he was brooding over Ayisha. This was going to hit her hard. He had never seen two maids more taken with their men than were Ayisha and Aimee. And what he had told Seth was God's own truth—he could still have Aimee and gladly. But Cain would never, not as long as he himself drew breath, have Ayisha for his own. Never. A man with Tom Gregg's blood running in his veins would bring her naught but heartache. He'd been a veritable lady-killer, Tom Gregg, and he'd left a trail of weeping women and his poisonous spawn all over the globe in his roving.

As for paying retribution, Ben was gladder than glad for the chance to alleviate any suffering he could after all of these years. Somehow he must make Seth see that he was telling the truth. Seth could then tell those many families that it was not he who had abandoned their men so long ago. It was Tom Gregg. In fact—Ben sat straighter at the thought—why didn't he go along and tell them himself? It was only fitting.

He slumped back into his seat again, thinking of the enormity of what had gone on before, thinking that in the twenty winters that had passed, hatreds had burned hotter with each passing year. His own had. Nay, he doubted the wisdom of his seeing those folk. Chances were that he would be slain before ever he could open his mouth. As he mulled it over his carriage came to a stop and a stable lad opened the door.

"G'd afternoon, sir. It's a surprise, seeing ye so early i' th' day."

Ben gave a crisp nod. "Are my daughters about, Griffin?"

"I don't know about Miss Aimee, but Miss Ayisha rode Omar down t' th' beach."

"Is Mac with her?"

"Nay, sir, Mr. Banning's wi' her."

All of the heat in Ben's body seemed to rush into his head and pound there. He rasped, "Bridle Darby for me." Seeing the lad's astonished gaze move over his very proper street wear, he snapped, "Now, Griffin."

"Aye, sir." The boy quickly bridled Darby in his stall and led him out to the master. "Ye'll not be needin' a saddle, I gather?"

"I haven't the time." Grimly, Ben led the gelding to a mounting block, got aboard, and within seconds, was on the path down to the shore. He ordered himself to calm his rage and not make a scene, but God help him, where his girls were concerned he had no ability to reason. And with this man he had every right to be furious. The thought that Cain Banning intended to confront him with the very deed his own black-hearted father had committed was more than Ben could bear. As Tom Gregg had poisoned everyone's mind against him, so was his son continuing the calumny with his damned deathbed tale.

Leaving the narrow trail for the open expanse of beach, Ben gazed about with narrowed eyes. Seeing the two lovers lying in the sand and kissing hungrily, their arms and legs wrapped about each other, he saw red. He gave Darby his heels and sand flew. He shouted, "Damn you, man, unhand her!" He saw the two sit up, startled, and climb hurriedly to their feet. Cain's face turned dark red, Ayisha's showed her bewilderment.

"Da! Wh—what is it? We were—just talking . . . "

Talking? Ben gave her a scathing look which he then directed at Cain Banning. Cain Gregg. How could he have been so blind? The same sinister dark blue eyes under those same bold winging brows; the same width through cheekbones and jaw and cleft by that same arrogant wedge of a nose. It was a handsome face but a devilishly wicked one, and it was the face of Tom Gregg. It had been right there for him to see if he'd ever looked, but he had not. He'd been as bewitched by the man as Ayisha. But no more. Here it ended. He growled, "Go back to the house, lass." He marked that her face had turned white.

Ayisha slid her arm around Cain's waist and stood closer to him. "Nay. I want to know what's going on."

Ben did not answer her. His words were for Cain Gregg alone. He said sharply. "I know everything—who you are and why you're here, and now, by God, I want you to go from here and don't ever come back."

"Da, nay!"

Ben looked at her sternly. "Stay out of this, Ayisha."

"I won't! I can't. Tell me what's happening. Why are you so angry?"

Ben resisted the temptation to turn her over his knee, a thing he had never done in his life. "You need know only that this man has come here under false pretenses. He's stayed not because he gives a damn about you but because he hates me."

Seeing the fright in those beautiful amber eyes, Cain put his arm around Ayisha and spoke low in her ear, "I love you. You know I love you." He was shocked by Ben's sudden appearance and outburst of fury—and he was angered that Seth had gone ahead and talked to him when they had planned to do it together. He didn't understand it.

Ben urged Darby closer and said gruffly, "Step aside, girl. You, Gregg, get on your mount and go—and if you show your face here again, rest assured, I'll kill you."

"Da!"

Eyes molten, Cain put Ayisha behind him. It was too late for regrets that he'd not told her when he had the chance. It meant he had to tell her now. He said, "I'm not leaving. Not until I've told Ayisha what this is about."

Ben's own eyes seemed afire. "So you've kept your scheming from her, have you? I thought as much. Things never would have come to such a pass between you if she'd known your real reason for being here."

"She knew well there were things I couldn't tell her— that I wanted to tell her and promised to tell her when the time was right." He turned to Ayisha. "You know that."

"I know it," she murmured. She slid her hand inside his and leaned her head on his arm.

Ben snorted. "Take it with a grain of salt, lass. Doubtless he'd have handed you a pack of lies." And would have blackmailed him above and beyond the cost of retribution to keep the ugly news from the girls. It was the way his father would have worked it. Tom Gregg would have milked him dry.

Cain kept his tongue still, but he craved to pull the old devil off his horse, sit him forcibly in the sand, and tell him exactly what he thought of him. But he could not. Not with Ayisha looking on. Hell, this was impossible. He needed to talk with them both, but not together. And for certain, Ben was not about to let him talk to Ayisha alone. He said to her quietly, "I want to talk to your father privately, would you mind?" She looked so pale and wide-eyed, so like a small girl in her fright, that Cain took her hand and raised it to his lips. "All will be well," he whispered. "I promise you."

Ben growled. "For a certainty, all will be well once you're gone from my land, and aye, from this city." If he had to ruin Banning Limited to accomplish the feat, so be it. He would buy out all of his suppliers if need be so that he would have no timbers, no canvas, no rope or hardware. He would ruin him.

Ayisha trembled and clung to Cain's hand. She looked from his angry eyes to her father's and back to his. "You're—just going to talk? Naught more? You'll not fight?"

"Nay, sprite. We're just going to talk."

"And you and I can talk later?"

"Aye."

"Ayisha!" Ben's voice was a roar. "You're not to see this man again!" His heart fair turned over at the sad little half smile on her lips. It said she loved him, aye, he was her father, but it also said that she loved Cain Banning more. He was her life now. Ben crossed his arms and simmered silently as she mounted and disappeared into the densely wooded hillside. He then turned to the son of Thomas Gregg.

"You bastard!" His voice shook. "How dare you come here in this guise of complete innocence and friendship and use my daughter as you have?"

"I would never use Ayisha," Cain kept his voice low. "I love her."

"Love?" Ben laughed. "Oh, aye, you love her. I've seen Gregg love in action, spawning bastards all across the seven seas and beyond. Oh, aye. But know this, man, you'll not treat Ayisha as your father treated women. And if you've touched her, by God . . ."

Cain could no longer restrain his own fury. He said sharply, "I've not touched her, nor will I until we wed." Seeing the pulses leap in Ben's temples, he added slowly, emphatically, "Oh, aye, man, I am going to wed her. Know that. And know that I'll never do anything to hurt her—which means you'll never receive the justice you deserve."

"Justice?" Ben gave another shout of laughter that caused Darby to shy and dance beneath him. "By the gods, you should have asked your black-hearted bastard of a father what justice he gave my men when he forced them into those leaky longboats and left them to the sharks! It's him you should have whined to about justice!"

"You don't accept any blame?"

"The only blame I accept is for turning to piracy in the first place and for trusting Tom Gregg to be my partner."

Cain studied him, eyes slitted. "I knew you'd deny it."

"Of course, I deny it!" Ben shouted. "I didn't do it! I wouldn't abandon anyone or anything to the sea, not even the ship's cat, for the love of God. I was hit by a spar and knocked out, and when I wakened three days later, I heard what had happened." He couldn't suppress the angry tears that welled in his eyes. "My girls' mother saw it all through the porthole and told me."

Cain was unmoved by his show of emotion and incensed by his words. "Are you saying my father lied on his deathbed?"

"I'm saying your father could do naught else. After a lifetime of lies, he didn't know how to tell the truth—not even to save his black soul from the hell he deserved."

Cain's flesh crawled. He remembered well the day he had come to that same realization—the day he'd first discovered that the word of his father, the man who was his god, meant little. But lying about small, everyday things, or even big things, was a different matter entirely from lying about the atrocity that had been done. An entire shipload of men abandoned at sea to the sharks. Tom would not have blamed another had he himself done the deed—not as he lay dying. He would not. Cain had to believe that. He had seen his terrible regret, his last agony.

"My father died in terror—" His voice was husky.

"As well he should."

"—because of you." Cain wanted to strangle him, but kept himself reined. "What hold did you have over him to force him to do such a heinous thing for you?"

If Ben had carried a crop, he would have lashed Cain Gregg across the face with it. "God knows his soul was as black as sin before I ever knew him."

"Maybe God knows it, but I don't."

Ben was breathing hard, and his mount was growing agitated. He said sharply, "I see well that blood calls to blood. No one else would defend such a devil. For the last time, Cain Gregg, your father lied through his teeth to you. He knew, I know, and God in his heaven knows I wasn't the one who sinned against my poor lads. I've said all I mean to about it." He turned Darby's head toward the trail. "And I'll tell you one more time, stay away from Ayisha. I meant it when I said I'll kill you—and I'll do it with pleasure." He gave Darby his heels and was gone.

Aimee had been hiding in her bedchamber ever since the rented carriage had returned her to Seacliff early that afternoon. She was so overwrought by all that had happened, she dared not see anyone. She knew that both Ayisha and Pegeen would take one look at her white face and chattering teeth and know immediately that some earth-shaking change had occurred in her life. And it had. She was wed. Irretrievably and forevermore, she was Mrs. Seth Darby. It could not be undone even if he chose to rule her strictly and gave her a hundred babes to bear. She gulped back her tears at the thought and told herself that he would not. He was Seth, the sweetest, gentlest, kindest man she had ever known.

But in truth, it was not Seth who was making her frantic. It was Papa. What if he had killed her darling in a fury when Seth had gone to confess? But nay, she was being ridiculous. More likely they would argue horribly because Papa would have no proof that he'd not committed the terrible deed of which he was accused so long ago. Oh dear oh dear oh dear . . .

She paced, wrung her hands, and flung herself down onto her bed. It was all too dreadful and horribly unfair. It would surely take a miracle to change Seth's mind or Cain's about him. Her tears were about to flow once more when a sound from the next room caused her to lie very still. She sat up, scarcely able to believe her ears. Was that Ayisha weeping? She stole to the wall, pressed her ear to it, and listened carefully. It was! Ayisha was sobbing. But why? Was it Cain? She had said he was acting as strangely as Seth, but she had been so certain it would all work out—but maybe it had not. Forgetting to smooth her tumbled hair and wrinkled skirts, she flew out into the hallway, and tapped softly on Ayisha's door.

"Pan? Honey?"

Long moments passed before Ayisha's voice, clogged with tears, came. "Aye?"

Aimee opened the door a sliver, peeked in, and saw her sister lying on the bed. "May I come in?"

"Aye."

Aimee stared as Ayisha dabbed at her swollen eyes. Never in her life had she seen her weeping. She had seen her wet-eyed, aye, but never weeping. Sitting down on the edge of the bed, she stared, then asked fearfully, "Has—something happened to Cain?"

Ayisha drew a shaky breath. "Aye. Da hates him now.

And Cain hates Da. They're down on the beach talking—unless they've already killed each other. I think they wanted to."

"Oh, Pan!"

"I was afraid to leave them alone, but Da doesn't want me near Cain. He was so furious and growling and red faced, I feared he'd have apoplexy if I didn't do his bidding."

Aimee shivered imagining the scene and what must have caused it. "Do you know what it's about?"

"They didn't say, but it has to be about Cain's father. I think he's"—unable to say it gently, she just said it—"a pirate. . ." To her surprise, Aimee did not shriek or swoon. She nodded.

"I know. Seth told me just today. I guess Cain finally told you."

Ayisha felt as if she were falling into a black pit. Everyone knew, it seemed, but her. She wiped her eyes on her sleeve. "Cain didn't tell me. Jeremy did."

Now Aimee did shriek. "Jeremy! *He* knows that Cain's father and Papa were pirates?"

Ayisha was so stunned she could do naught but gape at her sister. "Our *father* was a pirate?"

Aimee nodded. She began to weep softly.

Ayisha put an arm around her and let her cry. When her tears subsided, she said, "I think you'd best tell me all you know."

Aimee did, and afterwards, the two shared their misery in silence. Ayisha could not have spoken even if she'd had something to say. She was in shock. Her throat felt small and swollen and her head was filled with pounding drums as she mulled over Aimee's terrible news: Da, a pirate like Thomas Gregg and accused of abduction and abandoning men to their deaths at sea. Dear God. No wonder Cain could not tell her his secret. No wonder. She was staring numbly into her black thoughts when Aimee said faintly, "He didn't do it, of course. You do realize that. . ."

"I don't know what to think."

"I guess I don't either." She folded and unfolded her

handkerchief several times before she murmured, "There's more. . ."

"I don't want to hear it!" She was not sure she could bear to hear it.

"Panny, you have to! It's a secret, and I'll explode if I don't tell someone—and you're the only one I can tell."

Ayisha sighed. Another secret. "Go ahead then." It couldn't be any worse than the one she had just heard. Even so, she was filled with dread—which soon turned to astonishment as Aimee began to giggle. Before her eyes, the giggles dissolved into a flurry of tears, and even as they flowed, Aimee began to laugh again, nervous laughter over which she had no control.

Ayisha sat beside her and put an arm around her. "Honey, please, what is it? Tell me." She was growing concerned. She had heard tell of this strange thing, this laughing and crying that came over people, but she had never before witnessed it. Trying to act and speak calmly for Aimee's sake, she said, "Whatever it is, we'll deal with it. I promise. Just tell me. . ."

"I—I daren't!"

"What? You just said you wanted to!"

"I'm afraid to."

"Aimee!"

"Oh, Pan, you're going to hate me! I—I'm wed! Seth and I are wed!"

"Wed!" Relief fell on her like a gentle summer shower.

"Aye. Seth was so afraid he'd lose me when Papa learned the truth, he talked me into it. It was wicked of him, I know—and it was wicked of me to agree, but I couldn't not! He was so sweet, and so scared, and so wonderful and dear . . ."

Now Ayisha, too, was laughing and crying. "Wed . . ."

"You're not angry?"

"I'm thrilled for you—happy for you." Throwing their arms around each other, the two rocked back and forth joyously. "Wed," Ayisha said again and shook her head. "I can't believe it. My baby sister a married woman!" Her eyes shone. "It's weird and it's wonderful, all at the same time." And it was a blessing that softened the other terrible news.

"You don't mind not having a double church wedding?"

"Mind? Aimee, that was for you. I never cared about a church wedding. I guess now Cain and I will do what you did. We'll elope. But we've already exchanged vows. In the meadow."

Aimee looked wistful. "The upper meadow?"

Ayisha smiled. "Aye. In the moonlight, with Willi and the wildflowers and tree frogs to witness us."

It sounded so beautiful and romantic, Aimee could have wept. "We were in a ship's cabin that stank of fish and smoke and the captain had glittery black eyes that slid all over me and he told me to be a good obedient wife and make lots of babies." She shivered. "I can't believe it was just this morn! Which reminds me, Ayisha Adair, why didn't you ever tell me about—things?"

"Things?"

"Wedding night things."

Ayisha stared at her. "You don't know?"

"I know naught. It was hideous. I was and am still the most innocent of innocents . . ."

Ayisha's eyes danced. "Then we must talk. We certainly must talk."

They laughed together then, and it felt good, and for a heartbeat in time they forgot about pirates and the two angry men on the beach and the troubles that lay ahead.

Chapter 20

It was early in the day when Jeremy Greydon cancelled all of his business appointments, summoned his
carriage, and left his office on India Street. After the as-
tounding conversation he had overheard between Ben
Adair and Seth Darby, he was too stunned and elated even
to think about business. Arriving home, he hastened to his
bedchamber and changed into an exceedingly expensive
robe and comfortable slippers. He then descended to his
den on the first floor and rang for his man. Sprigg tapped
on his door within moments and entered.

"Good afternoon, sir, what may I get for you?"

"Fetch me a bottle of champagne, Sprigg, and while
you're down there, bring up a bottle of that Raynaud Burgundy. I'll have it with dinner. And before you leave, give
me a light for my smoke—and I see the fire's on the
peaked side."

"So it is, sir." As he carried a spill to light his employ-
er's pipe and then carefully laid kindling on the dying
flames to encourage a hotter blaze, Sprigg reflected that
his color was high and his eyes were unusually bright. Undoubtedly a woman was involved here. "Will that be all,
sir, before I fetch your champagne?"

"Aye. And when you're in the kitchen, tell Browning I
want something festive for dinner. Beef Wellington will do
nicely."

"Will you be dining alone, sir?"

"Aye. This night is for me." Jeremy stretched out on the
long brocade divan before the fire and drew on his pipe.

"However, before many more days have gone by, a lady will be joining me. Permanently."

Ah. He'd thought as much. "Upon my soul, sir, how gratifying."

"It's damned gratifying, Sprigg." Jeremy laughed, thinking of it. Ayisha in his bed and her father's tainted fortune filling his own coffers. He was not quite sure yet just how to make this new information work for him, but he would, he would. It just needed a bit of mulling over and then he'd have both the maid and the money for his own. He moistened his lips at the incredible thought and found Sprigg gaping at him. Damned fellow reminded him of a suffocated carp. "Go, man, what are you waiting for? I'm dying of thirst."

Following Sprigg's hasty departure, Jeremy went to the French windows, gazed out onto the busy street, and imagined himself living in the regal grandeur and the quiet isolation of Seacliff. That's where he should and would live one day, by heaven, in that incredible castle overlooking the sea. It would be his. In fact, there seemed no limit now to what he might soon call his· all of Ben Adair's businesses and properties, his fleet of ships, the hundreds of acres of pine woods surrounding Seacliff, his dead wife's jewelry, the pirate loot. My God, it was all going to be his, and it would be so simple.

He sank back on the divan, closed his eyes, and saw the plan already laid out to perfection. He would blackmail the old goat, of course—tell him he knew everything, give him all the unsavory details he'd overheard, and assure him he needn't worry a bit about it. He would keep quiet—in return for Ayisha's hand in marriage. And to keep the little witch pliant and obedient, he would seize Cain and sell him into indenture. He'd been considering it from the very first. Of course Ayisha would never know what had become of him. She would know only that he himself was responsible for the devil's disappearance and that Banning's safety, his very life, depended upon her good behavior. It was crude, distasteful even, but he didn't give a damn. It would work. She would do anything to protect the fellow. But wait, wait—Jeremy's pale eyes narrowed—there was something even better coming to mind.

He scowled as Sprigg knocked and entered with a tray holding his champagne and one tall gold-rimmed goblet. He said crisply, "Leave it on the table. I'll pour my own. And light the candles and close those draperies before you go. The traffic is an abomination. I can scarce hear myself think." He needed all his wits about him, for he was onto a marvelous twist with the seizing of Banning. Why make him a victim when he could just as easily make a villain out of him? A villain Ayisha would despise. As for her learning to be obedient and compliant, there were other ways to go about that—many other ways. In the meantime, he had immediately to mail a missive to his man in London and contact Hawkins. There was no sense in spending more money when he already knew more about Ben Adair and Cain Banning than either of them could ever ferret out. He complained to Sprigg, "You've not opened the champagne."

"Sorry, sir." Sprigg popped the cork, carefully wiped the bottle, and then asked, "Will that be all, sir?"

"Aye. Leave me now. I've thinking to do."

"Aye, sir." He closed the door quietly behind him and was glad to be gone. What a devil the fellow was. He felt pity for the lady who would soon be coming to live here, for it meant Greydon intended to wed her. And he had a cruel streak in him, did Jeremy Greydon. It showed clearly whenever he had someone in his power, a servant or a woman or an animal. He wondered if the poor maid knew.

Ayisha had discovered, when she worked Willi, that any excitement or worry she was carrying with her was transferred immediately to him. And so she had learned to empty her mind of both the good and the bad and to give herself over completely to communicating with the stallion when she rode him. Since she had a good seat and the sensitivity to touch and sound that was so important—Cain had assured her of it—all that was left was to learn the "language," the "talking" to Willi through pressure applied to his flanks and back and mouth.

It was never easy, she mused, even when Cain was there to encourage and guide her. This day it was doubly difficult. Two of the three men she loved most in this world wanted to kill each other, and Willi himself was being stupid and ambling all over the place. Not once had she been able to preserve his natural footfall in the running walk she was attempting. In fact, she couldn't even hear his footfalls—and she was contrite when she realized finally that it was her own fault. Her head was too filled with the memory of angry male voices to hear anything else.

Had Cain left by now, she wondered, or were he and Da still on the beach shredding each other to pieces? Whatever the answer, she could not go on with Willi. He felt her anger and fear too deeply. She dismounted, gave him a loving pat, and took him back to the stable. As she handed him over to a groom she saw her father coming toward her. She froze, felt her heart go harder, and hated what was happening to her. She was not used to feeling this way with him.

"Darlin' . . ." Ben put his arm around her. Feeling her stiffen, he was crushed. It was what he'd feared—that his protecting her would cause her to turn from him. "I can't tell you how sorry I am about this, sweetheart."

She said coolly, "But you can tell me what's going on between the two of you." She was not feeling at all friendly.

Ben sighed. "Lass, it's naught but an old feud between his father and me. All of these years it's been buried, and that's the way I want it to stay. Buried."

"If it was between you and his father," she retorted, "why hate Cain?"

"Because he's a Gregg." Ben said sternly. "Believe me, I know from experience, they're the lyingest, thievingest bastards on the face of this earth. They're only out for themselves and all they can squeeze out of a man—or a maid."

Ayisha flared, "Not Cain!"

"Aye, lass. Cain. He's a Gregg through and through. I see it in his looks, and I see well that he's as good a liar as his father was. He's come here under false pretenses, deceived us—"

"Nay!"

"Aye. He's been hanging around here, not because he cares about you or old Willi, but because I have more money than anyone else in Boston." He damned well was not going to tell her the rest of his lying tale.

"He loves me . . ." Ayisha's voice was small.

Ben died inside. Cain Gregg did not love her. Not as she loved him. No Gregg was capable of it. He remembered well Tom's bragging how he, like his father and grandfather before him, had left a long trail of weeping women in his wake. Women he'd "loved" and left. But he could not tell Ayisha that, not with her poor heart already broken. He said gently, "Believe me, lass, I know of what I speak. It's best you forget him. I promise you, there will be others. Come in for dinner now. Pegeen sent me to fetch you. You'll feel better after you eat."

Ayisha trailed after him forlornly. She was thinking of Anna Gregg and her young son waiting and waiting and waiting for the return of their husband and father. She imagined their first joyous sight of him, imagined the hopes they had had that he would stay home, and then imagined his leaving them again. In her mind's eye, he looked just like Cain as he walked away whistling.

As she entered the quiet house and was starting up the stairs, Pegeen called to her, "You've time to wash up, lass. Dinner won't be for a few minutes yet."

"I'm not too hungry now, Peg. I'll come down for something later."

Pegeen drew nearer and lowered her voice. "What's all this about? Your sister said the same thing. Is your poor father to eat alone after coming home early just to be with his girls?"

To be with his girls? Was that what he'd told Peg when

his real reason was to flay Cain and ruin her life forever? She shrugged. "I guess he'll have to."

Keeping her voice down so the servants would not hear, Pegeen said, "What's come over this family? Your father's in a state, and Aimee, and now you . . ."

"I hadn't noticed."

She left Pegeen staring after her, went to her bedchamber, and threw herself down onto her bed. She felt too numb to move, almost too numb to think, except she knew Peg was right. Something had come over their family. Aimee running off to be wed, herself defiant and hateful towards her father for the first time in her life, and Da himself with a secret so terrible she never would have dreamed it possible. Was he never going to tell them about it? And if he didn't, was it because he was guilty? Oh, Da . . .

As she had grieved for her mother, now she mourned him, for it seemed that the man she had known as her father did not exist anymore. Perhaps he had never existed. Frightened and confused, she stared at the flickering of leaves and sunlight on the walls, and into her heart came the words of Cain's love: You are my sunrise, my sunset, the first star of evening, the first violet of spring . . .

Her eyes filled, They were beautiful words, but she wondered if he had really meant them and wondered how she could believe him after all the things her father had said about Gregg men. Cain himself had even said that a man at sea had a maid in every port. Oh, he'd added quickly enough that he was teasing, aye, but now she was not so sure. She watched the leaf shadows dancing, lengthening on her walls, listened to Cain's words over and over until she found the peace she was looking for, and the trust. She had given him her trust and promised to believe in him and believe in him she would.

Cain's fury was under tight control by the time he returned to the city. He would not deck Seth until he heard from his own lips why he'd talked to Ben without him— and the reason had better be a good one. He hadn't expected to find him in their quarters, nor did he. Neither was he in the Red Lion pub nor in any other nearby pub nor on the docks. He wasn't anywhere, so that after several hours of fruitless searching, Cain returned to the Red Lion to quench his thirst and plan his next move. He'd been there only moments when Seth entered and came immediately to his table.

"Man, where in hell have you been?" Seth muttered. He was covered with dust and sweat and was bone tired from his long, hard ride. "I've been looking everywhere for you."

Cain came to a boil instantly. "And I've been looking for you. You have some explaining to do."

Seeing the murderous look on his mate's face, Seth knew the worst had happened. He pulled out a chair, sat down heavily, and motioned the barmaid to bring them both ales. "You've seen Ben?"

"Aye."

"Dammit." He hunched over the table shaking his head. "First off, I rode to the yards hoping you'd returned. When I didn't find you there, I rode on north, but your lumber man said you'd already come and gone and he didn't know where to. Said you just took off like a bat out of hell with no reason given. Man, I tried. I tried hard to warn you about Ben and Greydon."

"Greydon?"

"Greydon." Seth drank long from the tankard when it came, put it down, and wiped his mouth. "All hell's broken loose. He had someone snooping into your life back in England and learned about your father. He came banging on the door this morn before I was awake and asked if I knew the low sort of character I was in cahoots with. I threw him out. Then I started to sweat thinking he'd be on his way to Ben next and there would go the maids, for Ben would hide them away for sure. And so I went out to Seacliff and brought Aimee in to the docks and wed her . . ."

It was not easy, talking to Cain Banning when he said naught, just sat there glaring at him, his face white and his dark eyes crackling like hellfire itself. Seth gave the table a whack with his fist. "All right, so I jumped the gun. I had to. It was first things first. And after we were wed, I told Aimee everything, and she agreed I should go to Ben. I guess I got there before Greydon—he didn't mention him."

Cain drank and wiped his mouth. "I suppose he explained that my father was the sole perpetrator of the crime."

"Aye."

Cain gave a disgusted snort and drank deeply again. "I knew he wouldn't accept any blame."

Seth lowered his eyes and studied the table. He had been remembering all day what he'd not allowed himself to consider fully these past twenty years: that Ben Scott had always been a decent man and a good and just man to work for. Why in hell then had all of them been so quick to take the word of a blackguard like Tom Gregg that it was Ben who had given those orders?

He guessed there were several reasons. Ben had coaxed them into piracy and had gloried in the chase. And it was Ben who'd insisted they take one more ship and had then mopped up the deck with Tom and carried Ana off weeping to his cabin. At the time his ferocity had sent shivers down Seth's spine. Now he had to admit what he'd known all along—that basically Ben was a kind man. A gentle, kind man. But he couldn't admit his doubts to Cain. Not just yet. The lad was having a rough enough time as it was. He put down his tankard. "It was bad, eh?"

Cain shrugged. "No worse than I expected. He hated my father, hates me, and told me to stay away from Ayisha or he'd kill me. It's my Gregg blood. How about you?"

Seth felt two inches tall. "He says I can have Aimee. I swear, man, it's a thing I never expected, and it's all because of his friendship with my father. They were like brothers."

Cain felt no jealousy, only amazement. "How about the money?"

"He's eager to pay—or says he is. Above and beyond."

"Get it before he changes his mind."

"We agreed to talk more about it again." He was tempted to say he doubted Ben would change his mind, that Ben seemed to be grieving still over his lost crew, but he kept silent. Cain was still boiling. He fingered a puddle of ale on the table and said finally, "I defended you, man. I want you to know that."

"Never did I doubt it."

"I told him you weren't Thomas Gregg,"—he related the entire painful conversation—"but it didn't end well. He couldn't believe you are different from your father. I said by the same token I couldn't believe he was innocent . . ."

Cain saw that his friend's gray eyes were troubled. "But you think there's a possibility."

"I didn't say that, man." Seth hid his face in his tankard again and thought what a miserable unholy mess this all was. He asked, "What will you do about Ayisha?"

"I've got to talk to her, but Ben will probably turn the place into a fortress to keep me out." Thinking of her wondering and worrying about him and Willi waiting, his agitation mounted. "I've got to meet her somewhere."

Seth nodded. "That's no problem. I'll arrange it through Aimee. On the other hand, why not just go off and get married like we did?"

"We'll wed, aye, but not just yet. The last thing I want is to make her father resent her because of me. They love each other and I don't want to spoil that for Ayisha."

Seth marveled at the man. Never had he thought so far ahead. He had thought only of himself in his fright, and how best he could keep Aimee for his own, for he could not bear to lose her. He nodded. "You're right. In truth, I'm sorry now I carried Aimee off as I did and deprived her of her church wedding." He could not imagine Cain panicking and doing what he had done. "As for Ayisha, when and where do you want to meet her?"

Cain had been sifting various locations through his head. "Will Ben have her followed, do you think?"

"Would you if she were your daughter?"

"Aye."

"So would I."

Cain's dark eyes glittered with his determination. "Then tell her I'll meet her either at sea or in the woods when she goes riding. Tell her to pick the time and the place and I'll be there."

Seth grinned. "Good. I'll talk to my darlin' the first thing in the morn and we'll get it arranged. And now I'm turning in. You'd best come along. We've had a rough day."

"I haven't the heart for sleep. I'd only keep you awake with my prowling and tossing."

Seth clapped his shoulder. "Suit yourself. I'll see you in the morn."

Ayisha had not eaten nor did she want companionship, not even Aimee's. She wanted only to be alone in her misery. She had tried to read and play solitaire to no avail. Now she could not sleep. She lived over and over the terrible scene between Cain and Da, and it had become so enmeshed with Aimee's awful tale about their father's piracy that she was now twice as confused and unhappy as she'd been before. If only she and Cain could talk. She wanted so much to be with him and hold him and hear it all from his own lips.

But Da had said she was not to see him again, ever. Now she wondered and worried, was he planning something drastic to keep Cain away from the house? Would he hire guards to patrol the grounds and would she be stuck with one every time she left the house? What an awful thought. For certain, she would never see Cain again if he resorted to such strong measures. She sat up suddenly, knowing exactly what she must do. She had to go to Cain now, tonight, while she still could. The very thought of the long ride along the desolate coast road frightened her terribly, and the streets of the city were dangerous for a woman alone even in the daylight, but she had to go. It was the only way.

She climbed out of bed and, her hands shaking, shed her nightdress and quickly pulled on trews, boots, a shirt, and an old hooded jacket of Mac's she used for sailing on blustery days. She crept down the stairs then, and leaving the front door unlocked, stole to the stable in the blessed light of a small, high moon. The clock on the landing had been chiming eleven as she left the house, and when she was finally mounted and on her way, she reckoned it was eleven fifteen. With luck she would arrive at the Red Lion at midnight, and with luck she would pass for a lad with her face dirtied and her long braid of hair tucked out of sight beneath hood and shirt. With luck and with God's help . . .

By the time she reached the Red Lion, Ayisha's spirits were high. The ride had been easy and uneventful, and in the city no man had given a second look to the slim lad on the big Arab gelding. Handing Omar over to a stable lad, she whispered another prayer and entered the pub. It was dim inside and smoke filled. The fire in the great open hearth was smoking, the wall torches were smoking, and the men were smoking. Ayisha coughed, and when she did, every male eye turned toward her. She would have fled then and there except her mission was too important to give up so easily. She stood her ground as the man nearest her came closer and smiled a smile that made her skin crawl.

"Well, well, well, well . . ." He pushed back her hood before she could stop him, drew out her long, gleaming braid from beneath her shirt, and released a long slow breath. His eyes moved over her, slowly, hungrily. "By the gods, a woman all togged out like a lad."

"I'm—looking for someone," Ayisha said, low and firm.

Gripping her hair close to her nape, he thrust his face

close. "Lookin' er no, ye could be arrested, lady. No female's allowed t' dress in a man's garb."

Realizing that the situation was beyond her control, Ayisha cried, "Will someone find Mr. Banning, please? Cain Banning. Please?"

"We know naught o' him, but we do know th' lawman hereabouts. We've but t' step outside an' gi' a shout, an' I promise ye, lassie, ye'll be hauled off t' gaol in a eye blink." He gave her hair a sharp yank, forcing her head back, and ran his big, rough fingers up and down her throat and slid them beneath her shirt to fondle her right breast. He grinned, wet his lips, bent his head to sniff. "Soft an' smooth as silk, by God. I ain't felt nothin' so nice or that smelled so sweet in a long time . . ."

Ayisha screamed for the first time in her life, and then she cried, "Cain, help me! Cain!"

Her captor grinned. "What d' ye say, laddies? Shall we gi' her a chance t' be nice t' us? Just mebbe we'll change our minds about turnin' ye in, little lady. Coax us a bit . . ."

He blinked, seeing a big angry stranger towering over him suddenly and a fist headed into his face. A sickening crunch sent him reeling back against the bar.

"Cain, thank God . . ."

"We're getting out of here right now," Cain growled. "Come on." With his arm around her, he hurried her outside, got her aboard Omar, and mounted behind her.

As they rode into the night, relief sent tears streaming down her cheeks. "I'm so g—glad you were th—th—there. I knew we—had to talk and I couldn't w—wait till t—tomorrow. I'm afraid Da will have the h—house guarded by then."

Cain's arms tightened about her as a new wave of trembling seized her. He said gently, "I think you're right, and I'm glad you came." But what a damned close call it was. He had just turned in and was lying abed staring at the darkness, wishing he had her in his arms, when he heard her scream.

"Where are we g—going?" Her teeth would not stop chattering.

"To my vessel. We can talk there in safety, and then I'll take you back to Seacliff."

Chapter 21

They rode quickly and silently to where the *Sea Eagle* lay berthed at the end of Silver Street. Watchlights glowed on her fore and aft decks, and when they approached her, the guard thrust a torch over the side and peered down at them.

"Halt! Who goes there an' what's yer business here?"

"It's Cain, Dikon. We're coming aboard."

"Aye, cap'n, I didn't expect ye." Dikon quickly raised the gate barring entrance to the vessel. He cast an admiring gaze over Ayisha but expressed no surprise at her unusual clothing. He touched his fingers to his forehead. "Evenin', mistress."

"Good evening."

We need a place to talk," Cain said. With no further explanation, he led Ayisha up the gangplank.

"O' course, sir. C'n I fetch ye anythin' fr'm th' galley?"

When Ayisha shook her head, Cain said, "Thanks, lad, but all we crave is privacy."

"Then privacy ye'll have, cap'n. Watch yer step now, mistress. Likely this is strange turf fer a maid t' tread." As he lit the way to his captain's quarters, he saw that his words had made the lady smile—and what a glorious lady she was despite her odd togs.

As she had stepped aboard, Ayisha's gaze was drawn toward the starboard bow where she had first seen Cain standing and calling down to her. Her beloved. Her beloved protector. How strange, the way things were falling out. She had seen a pirate in his dark dangerous looks and

261

all the while his father had actually been one. And her own father. She shivered as Dikon lighted a lantern for them and then left, closing the door behind him.

Cain pulled Ayisha into his arms, fit her against him, and felt her heart pounding wildly against his chest. Mouth against her hair, he muttered, "My God, sprite, don't ever do that again. You nigh scared the life out of me."

"I'm sorry." She had scared herself. "There's no end to the trouble I cause you, and once, just once, I want it to be the other way around." She managed to grin up at him. "I want to come riding to your rescue. It's only fair."

Cain gave her a long, tender kiss. "You just did. I was dying for this, seeing and holding you." He led her to his bunk, lay down, and drew her close beside him. They lay quietly, their hands moving over each other slowly, sensuously, while the *Sea Eagle* rocked in the ebbing tide and moonlight filtered through the portholes and flickered faintly on one wall. Cain said softly, "Seth was going to take my message to you in the morn to arrange a meeting."

"But here I am, now, and Cain, I want to hear everything from your own lips. Everything there is to know. I can't wait another minute. Da's told me naught except that your father was the world's worst devil and he's convinced you're just like him. I heard from Aimee all that Seth told her."

Seeing how frightened her eyes were, he said gently, "I wish I could have spared you this . . ."

"By waving a wand?" she murmured and smiled up at him.

"Aye." He kissed her nose, her cheek, her lashes, and thought again that there was none other in the world like her. What other maid would have braved the night and the many dangers it held to come to him as she had, dressed as a lad and riding a fiery Arab that would test the mettle of a strong man. On their way to his vessel, he had been trembling with what had nearly happened to her. Thinking of it again, her being at the mercy of a roomful of starving seamen, he was shaken to the core. She deserved only the best in this life, not the misfortune that was coming to her because of him.

"I almost told you when we were on the beach this afternoon—I was torn. Seth and I had planned to talk to Ben on Sunday and I wanted you prepared. I feared he might try to send you away from me when he learned who I was." He added gruffly, "But before I had the chance, he came. Know, sprite, I never intended for you to hear this story from any lips but mine."

She said gently, "Then I'd best tell you, I heard part of it from Jeremy early this morning. The part about your father." She held her breath, expecting an angry explosion but it didn't come.

He said quite calmly, "I'm not surprised. He went to Seth, too, bursting with the news about my defective parentage." He ran his hand up and down her arm, played with her long braid. "I suppose he's even talked to Ben by now."

"I don't know. He said when the time was right he'd tell him. I suppose it hardly matters anymore since Da already knows."

What mattered, Cain thought with murder in his heart, was that the devil doubtless would seek more information, this time about Ben Scott, and that he'd put two and two together. And if he did, his own and Seth's struggle to protect the maids from scandal was all for naught. Greydon would tell everything he knew to the world.

"The other thing he said was—" She hesitated.

"Was what?" He kissed the end of her silky plait.

Jeremy's threat was on her lips, that she was going to be his. She wanted desperately to tell Cain but she didn't dare. His eyes, the look on his face said he would seek him out and slay him on the spot. She caught his hand, held it to her breast.

"I'm waiting. What did he say?" Cain felt the rapid beating of her heart.

She shook her head. "It was naught but foolishness. He ranted on about Gregg blood and how bad blood will out . . ." She stroked his hair and cupped his hand about her breast more firmly. "Know, my husband, naught that he can say or that you or Da can say will ever change the way I feel about you. I trust you and I believe in you. My love for you is forever."

The terrible events of the day had dragged Cain down. He had not forgotten their exchange of vows in the meadow, but he feared she might not want to remember it. Now her words fired his heart. She had called him her husband and said she believed in him and loved him. It gave him the courage to tell her the story that had to be told. He held her more closely and began. Following Seth's example, he did not mention her mother's royal blood nor Jon Darby's murder. Nor did he mention the sharks. He explained very clearly however that his father had followed Ben Scott's orders to abandon his crew at sea, and that all but Seth had perished.

Ayisha's face was white. "Aimee told me, but not in—such detail." She had been in shock upon hearing it the first time. Now, with Cain's arms around her, she wept, and knew the story could not be true. It shamed her that she had doubted her father for even an instant. She shook her head. "I don't believe it."

"I'm sorry, sprite. It happened." It was a torment, seeing her pain and bewilderment.

"Nay. Da wouldn't. He couldn't." Not her gentle father who had taught her and Aimee to respect all life, even a bee on the wing and a spider in its web, for he'd said all creatures had their place and their purpose on this earth. Her tears ended abruptly. She dashed them away with her fingers. "Nay, Cain, there's been a misunderstanding. Da didn't do it."

Cain said gently, "I see well that you can't believe ill of him. I can't believe it of my own father, that he'd tell such a lie on his deathbed."

Ayisha blinked. "Then you think Da had some awful hold over him."

Cain muttered. "Something like that, aye. I'm sorry . . ."

"No wonder you couldn't tell me."

"We'd planned, if we ever found him, to return him to the Crown for punishment."

"What—sort of punishment?"

"He'd be ordered to pay retribution."

"There's more. I hear it in your voice."

"He would've been hanged, Ayisha."

Hanged? Her father? She could see and hear and imagine it so vividly, she trembled. "Nay, Cain . . ."

Cain cradled her, whispered, "You're not to worry. We abandoned the idea the night we saw you two maids." He knew she had not considered the new danger from Greydon nor did he mention it.

"You'll not change your minds and take him back, will you?"

He said sharply, "You need even ask?"

"I'm sorry, this is—all so new, and there's so much to think about."

"I shouldn't have snapped at you. I'm the one who's sorry." He stroked her arms, her hands, kissed each finger tenderly. "God knows, I wanted to tell you a hundred times so it could be over and we could move on, but I was certain you'd hate me and I'd lose you."

"Now you know, Cain Banning," she whispered. "My love is forever."

"Even though I think your father's guilty?"

She said calmly, "He's not, you know. I think your father lied through his teeth to you, and aye, on his deathbed yet. Either that or it's a misunderstanding. Those are the only two possibilities I'll accept. I simply can't believe any other."

His cabin reverberated with Cain's low rich laughter. "You're your father's daughter, by God."

Ayisha looked at him wondering. "You don't mind?"

"I don't mind."

She grinned. "He's not a monster, I promise you."

Cain put one of her small fingertips in his mouth, sucked on it, said softly, "Let's talk about you—I love you, sprite."

"And I love you." She slid her other hand under his

shirt, felt his heated flesh, the broad, smooth muscles of his chest, his big shoulders and ribs, and the hard, flat expanse of his abdomen. Her heart turned over and began to thud. He was so big and strong and beautiful, and at the same time so gentle and loving and caring that her eyes filled. She murmured, "How could I have been so lucky as to find someone like you . . ." He was treasure, and she was not going to let him go. Not ever, no matter what her father said. She whispered, "When can we wed?"

Cain gazed on her hungrily, her hair wine dark in the candlelight, heat gleaming in her tear-sparkled eyes, her hand moving, slow and caressing, over his chest. He cupped her chin, tilted it, kissed her long and tenderly, and then greeted her eager tongue with his. He asked quietly, "When do you want to?"

"Now." The way he was holding her and looking at her was turning her bones to liquid. She could not have stood on her feet just then to save her life—or her soul. She pressed closer to him. "I want us to do what Aimee and Seth did, find a ship's captain and—"

He said abruptly, "Nay, Ayisha." But in truth, the thought tempted him as much as the maid herself did. Why not? Why not wed her, make her his own and to hell with Ben Scott. No matter how the old boy would rage, he could not cut the ties that would bind them in matrimony.

"Surely you know that my father will never change his mind. He's determined to hate you forever, and we'll never wed if he has anything to say about it."

"Even so, I'll not let you rush into this. I don't want you grieving in the light of day for what we did in darkness and without thought."

"I'll not grieve and it's not without thought. It's what I want."

"And it's what I want, but we'll not do it this night." He struggled against her bewitchment of him, her cool fingers teasing over him, her warm breath touching his cheek and neck, her soft breasts, so very soft, pressing against him. He caressed them, gently rolling her small, rosy nipples between thumb and finger, feeling them harden into satiny nubs. He took one in his mouth, sucked on it gently, and heard her small indrawn breath.

"Oh, Cain, I love it—the way that feels. If I . . . touched you there . . . would it feel the same?"

Cain smiled in the shadows. "Not the same—but nice."

"I want to give you more than just nice." Shyly she touched her tongue to his chest, pressed her lips to it and to his nipples. She felt them grow hard. Suddenly, her memories consumed her: his face contorted with passion; his long fingers, so sensitive and careful, doing strange and wonderful things to a part of her she had never felt and never known before; the two of them being transported to paradise. The thought of it produced a deep hot stab of excitement. She whispered, "Can we do now what we did that night in the meadow? And can you show me how to—make you happier than I did then?"

Cain could not hold back a chuckle. "You made me very happy then, little one."

"But I did naught. You did it all. You made me feel like I've never felt before."

Cain said gently, "Surely you saw that it gave me great pleasure, holding you, touching you, looking at you . . ." His voice grew husky. "But to answer your question, aye, I'd like very much to do again what we did in the meadow." He drew off her boots and breeches, and as he quickly removed his own, she sat on the bunk watching him and unbraiding her hair. Cain laughed, seeing the glow in her eyes. "Now what are you thinking, you luscious wench?"

"I'm just realizing what you said—you said we'd not wed this night. Does it mean we'll wed another time soon?"

"Aye. We'll wed soon." There was no longer any reason not to. Ben knew about him, she knew about him and loved him still—but he had reached a second decision. Before they wed, he wanted the old man to have a chance to change his mind.

Ayisha blinked, her eyes wide. "Tomorrow?" She

watched as he unbuttoned his shirt, removed it, and tossed it on the floor.

Cain said softly, "Not tomorrow, sprite, but soon, I promise you. I want you to be absolutely sure about this." He joined her on the bunk.

"I'm sure." Her voice was faint. It made her weak just to look at his hard body and burning eyes.

"So be it then. We'll talk about it afterwards."

"Aye . . ."

His hunger made Cain tremble as he helped unbutton her shirt and drew it down over her shoulders. His breath faltered, seeing her naked. She was so fair, and so very unaware of it, and so trusting of him not to harm her. Nor would he, he promised, as excitement raced throughout his body and he felt the speeding of his heart. He lay her back on the bunk and stretched out on his side, his head cradled on his arm so he could look at her. She gazed back at him, her beautiful golden eyes unblinking, lips parted, her breath coming in shallow pants.

She murmured, "It makes me tremble to look at you."

Cain bent to her lips and touched them with his. "That you exist makes me tremble."

"What a golden tongue you have."

"Only when I'm with you, sprite. Only with you." He spooned her body against him tightly, her back to his chest, captured a breast in each hand, and felt himself swell dangerously. He brushed a kiss over her nape and inhaled the jasmine scenting her long hair. "You're my life, Ayisha . . ."

"And you're mine." Delight was making her dizzy, his kisses soft as moth wings, light as gossamer, fluttering over her temples and shoulders, the sides of her throat, her ears, his warm tongue tasting her everywhere. She turned around to face him then, thinking how once again he was doing all of the pleasuring, and she was doing all of the receiving. She sat up and said huskily, "Lie on your back, my husband."

Cain obeyed. He did not attempt to hide his fierce

arousal. He watched her, amused, as she stared at him in
rapt silence.

"Is it—all right to touch him?"

Him. Cain swallowed a chuckle and replied gravely,
"He would enjoy that very much, aye."

"As much as when you—kiss me here?" She indicated
her nipples, felt her body turn pink with the heat that suddenly scorched her.

"Even more." He watched her consider it, and then
gently, lightly, stroke the blunt head of his staff with her
fingertips. It leapt, and one crystal droplet appeared. She
snatched her hand back and gasped, "I'm sorry. Did I hurt
you?"

He shook his head. Her touch had made flare the bonfire smoldering in his loins. With all of his might he had
been fighting the wild hunger pulsing inside of him, and
he was losing. He caught her hands and said hoarsely, "Sit
astride me . . ."

She obeyed, her breathing so quick and shallow she felt
light-headed. Sitting atop his thighs with his great stiffened rod upthrust before her, nearly touching that secret
part of her that was burning so hotly, she was softening,
weakening, wanting—wanting him to be within her and
herself to be surrounding him, but she knew it would not
happen. He would never couple with her until they were
wed. She asked shyly, "Am I too heavy for you?"

"You weigh naught," Cain breathed. "Stay where you
are . . ." He stroked her smooth thighs, cupped her knees
that were gripping him. "Ah, God, Ayisha." Seeing her,
feeling her warmth and softness atop him, light and
shadow pulsing over the beautiful curves and valleys of
her body, he knew he was going to take her . . . bury himself within her . . . wallow in her. But a wiser part of him
cried nay. It was against all he believed in, and they were
so close to wedding, he could damned well wait another
day for her. But nay, he could not, his hunger shot back
angrily. He had reached his limit. And look at her, grind-
ing her sweet little butt against his thighs, fire in her eyes.
She wanted him. It was time. But when he tried to reach

out for her and roll her under him, his muscles did not respond. Body and mind, he was crying out for her, but his heart, his conscience would not follow.

Ayisha had seen his torment and knew his thoughts. He was as wrenched with hunger as she, but it was as she had suspected. There would be no lovemaking. She saw it in his eyes and the grim set of his jaw. He would not couple with her before they were wed. He was too honorable a man, yet—please God—this time was so very special. She had been drawn to him through the night, and he had saved her from those men, and she had never loved him more than she did at this moment. She touched him again, his swollen manhood, loving it because it was his and because it showed his fierce hunger for her. She put both hands about him, held him tenderly, felt the throbbing and pulsing of his hunger, brushed her lips across the rounded head. Careful not to crush him, she raised herself over his outstretched body to kiss his mouth and graze his chest with the tips of her breasts.

Cain groaned, tantalized beyond endurance by her sweet mouth and warm breath, her hard little nipples trailing lightning in their wake, her cloud of silken scented hair teasing his nostrils and scorching his flesh where it lay coiled upon it. "Ayisha, for God's sake . . ."

"I love you, my husband."

"You little vixen, you just don't realize what you're—doing . . ."

She realized exactly what she was doing. It frightened her a bit, aye, but never had she felt more strongly that making love with Cain Banning was right and good and that it was what they both wanted and needed. Still crouched over him, she lowered her breasts to his face.

Cain moaned as her tongue skimmed his brows, lashes, eyelids, and the full globes of her breasts hung suspended about his hungry mouth. As the faint scent of woman-flesh and jasmine filled his nostrils, he could stand no more. His mouth closed over one breast, and he rolled over, crushing her beneath him. "Do you want me to take you, little wench? Is that what you want?" His lungs were scorched by his hot breath.

"A—aye . . ." A thrill shot through Ayisha, a burning star streaking the heavens as he returned to suckling her deeply, sensuously, one breast and then the other. He sought her mouth again, kissed her almost savagely.

"I've tried to protect you from this."

"I don't want to be protected—not from you . . ." She was nigh weeping with her great love and hunger and the admiration and compassion she felt for him. He was so good and honorable and caring, why did her father refuse to see it? It was tragic that he would not. She cried low, "Please, Cain, I want to belong to you this night. Body and soul. Please, I—need you. I'm on fire . . ."

"As am I," he growled. He was in torment . . . stretched on the rack. Didn't the little wench know the value, the pricelessness of what she was giving him? Her maidenhood, her girlhood and innocence. He told himself angrily that he was being melodramatic. He was not going to rape her and run, for God's sake. They were going to be wed within days. At the thought of it, he put his concerns away and gave her a dark smile. "In truth, every part of me is burning for you, Ayisha, and I'd not have it any other way." He lowered his mouth to her breasts again.

Ayisha closed her eyes and held him as he slowly kissed his way to the soft triangle at the apex of her thighs. The feel of his lips and his hands on her burning flesh was heaven. She did not know how anything could be more wonderful until he separated the petals guarding the bud of her womanhood. It was tightly furled, but as he gazed on it, she felt it opening to him. And when he gently slid a questing finger into the moist, satiny heat of her, she sighed.

In turn, she sought his powerful quivering rod and the taut bulbs beneath which held his seed. She explored them with gentle fingers, testing their textures, teasing, titillating him. She heard his soft groan and knew it for what it was. Intense pleasure.

"Where did you—learn such a thing?" Cain asked hoarsely.

Her laughter was low, throaty. "I have talents of which you know naught." She gave a gasp of delight as his fingers crept into her more deeply. "As do you, my husband . . ."

Cain had felt her body's welcome. She was warm and soft, moist with the dew of her love. Wordlessly, he withdrew his fingers, touched his shaft to her—and cursed himself for still being torn over whether to take her. His hunger was now a fire storm. Sweat streamed down his back and beaded his brow, and his muscles were taut with passion, but none of that mattered—he had to give her one more chance to turn back. He said, his voice a low rasp, "I'll understand if you've changed your mind . . ."

Ayisha was afire where his hands and mouth and his manhood had touched her. She whispered, "I've not changed my mind."

He smiled and cupped her chin. "I'm glad . . ." He parted her then, and gently sought her.

Ayisha's eyes, golden in the light and shadow, grew wide as she felt him easing into her. She tried to see, but could not. "Is that—really you? Not just your fingers?"

"It's me." Cain's breath came in a long shuddering sigh as slowly, delicately, he slid into her silky fire.

She gasped, "It's—so strange . . . I—feel your heartbeat." He was lying within her unmoving, but there was a pulsing, a throbbing within his shaft that tantalized her. Her breathing quickened.

"I'm not hurting you?"

"Nay." She would not have admitted it even if he were, but in truth, he was not. "I feel all hot inside . . . and the heat is spreading . . . it's almost like a tickle . . . only it isn't. Oh, Cain, it's lovely." She sought his kisses on her parted lips and her throat, and wrapped her legs about him. "It's wonderful—and you're wonderful . . ."

Cautiously, Cain slid into her more deeply, withdrew, drove forward a bit further, retreated, returned. Easy, easy. He had not yet broken the fragile veil of her maid-

enhood, and now his breath rasped in his lungs with his
fierce effort to be gentle, to restrain himself. Maybe this
would suffice ... maybe he could keep her intact and not
hurt her. Maybe ... maybe ... He shuddered, knowing
that what he craved was to plunge into her. She was as
glorious within as without. She was flame licking him and
her honied walls held him perfectly, neither impeding him
nor were they too yielding. He breathed, "You're a
miracle ..." He meant it with all his heart.

"So are you." Ayisha threw back her head, laughing, as
the inner warmth spread through her, deepening, intensify-
ing, shimmering, tingling, glowing, mounting in a crest
she could never have imagined and still could not believe.
"Cain ..." Her voice trembled. "I—don't know what's
happening. I'm not sure I—can bear it, it feels s—so
wonderful ..."

"It will get better still, I promise you, sprite, and you'll
bear it just fine." She surprised him then, writhing, arching
against him suddenly so that he was thrust into her, deeply,
unexpectedly—and irrevocably. He felt the tearing of the
veil, heard her cry, and knew it was done. He kissed her,
hoping to kiss away the hurt. A shudder ripped through
him—passion, aye, but sadness, too, that it had been out of
wedlock. But done it was, and his new freedom, and hers,
set him completely afire. His fingers once more sought the
opened bud of her womanhood, and as he moved within
her, he fondled her.

Ayisha had expected the pain, a sharp ripping of some
fragile thing deep inside of her, but it was overwhelmed
and soon forgotten by Cain's hard driving presence within
her. She was consumed by the strength of him, the new
fires he was torching inside of her, and his powerful,
rhythmic thrusting as he claimed her for his own. The
flames were racing through her now, carried by her heated
blood to every part of her—her lips, the sensitive tips of
her breasts, her skin, sleek with sweat, and the mystery between her thighs, that swollen, hot, pulsing secret part of
her of which she knew naught but which was filling her
with such rapture.

The sensations were intense now. She was growing hotter and tighter by the moment, but at the same time it was so heavenly, she wanted to cry out her joy to Cain. But she could not, his men would be sure to hear—and know. Unable to help herself, she arched again and again into his own savage thrusting, felt him thudding into the sensitive wall encasing him, and cried low, "Cain, it's—too glorious. I—I . . ."

He sealed her mouth, took her lower lip gently between his teeth, bit it, bit her tongue, her throat, her shoulder, heard her small moan. "I'm sorry . . . I'm sorry . . . I want to devour you. God, Ayisha . . ."

Just as she was certain she could not bear another moment of rapture, an outpouring from some sweet mysterious wellspring of nectar deep within her was tapped and spurted forth its contents. She closed her eyes, gasped at the sweet pulsing release, and realized only then that Cain's savage thrusting within her was over. She felt only a corresponding gentle pulsing as though his own heart were beating deep within her. For a long time they lay drained and silent in each other's arms. Ayisha murmured finally, "It was all you said it was."

Cain kissed the top of her head. "Nay, sprite. It was more. It was beyond anything I ever imagined. In truth, we belong together."

Ayisha laughed. Never had she felt so completely and utterly content and fulfilled. She whispered, "Didn't I tell you . . .?"

Chapter 22

The next morn, Ayisha's thoughts were so filled with
Cain and their lovemaking that there was no room
left for anything else. She gave thanks at breakfast that she
had risen too late to encounter her father, too early to see
Aimee, and Pegeen was busy elsewhere. As she quickly
ate and walked toward the stable, she relived their lovemaking aboard the *Sea Eagle*. Afterwards, he had not allowed her to journey back to Seacliff alone but had gone
with her. They had first returned to the Red Lion for his
mount and then ridden in silence along the empty coast
road with the tide rolling in and the moon looking down
on them. When they arrived at the house and saw that it
was quiet—she had not been missed—Cain kissed her
good-bye and then remained at a distance while she hurriedly stabled Omar and stole up to her room. She put a
lighted candle in the window then to assure him that she
was safe and all was well.

She smiled thinking of his constant concern for her
well-being and safety. She had never known such a man
before—except for her father and Mac. Despite how they
might feel about each other, they shared a common bond:
Her happiness was their obsession. But in the case of her
father, it had gone awry. He thought that only he knew
what was best for her. She put it from her mind as she entered the stable and Griffin brought Willi to her, groomed
and tacked and ready to ride.

"He's been waitin' f' ye, mistress," Griffin said. "He's
real fond o' ye, he is, an' o' Mr. Banning, too. I think 'e

misses 'im bad an' them fancy things they does t'gether. I hopes 'e comes back soon. They be a marvel together, be'nt they?"

It shook her. "Aye, Griffin. They're a true marvel together." She took Willi's reins and led him out into the sunshine and toward the meadow.

Griffin frowned. "Won't ye be ridin' 'im, mistress?"

"We'll walk a bit first, thanks." She did not dare mount just then. Willi would sense her upset and the morn would be wasted. Nay, she would just wait and walk him awhile. Gazing at the glory everywhere, she marveled that somehow fall was already on its way before she had even enjoyed summer. How had such a thing happened, and where had it gone?

Goldenrod was a blazing carpet of yellow, and sprinkled amongst the spires were asters, tall purple ones, and there was a great dazzling swath of Queen Anne's lace. Locusts hummed, telling of winter's coming, orioles sang, and robins scolded as she and Willi ploughed through the deep meadow grass. Looking off to where the woods began, she saw standing before it the long stretch of wild sunflowers her mother and Aimee had planted. She smiled, remembering the day well, and was glad that something remained to remind her of it. Her peace restored, she kissed Willi's nose, stroked his neck, mounted, and devoted the entire morn to the trotting gait of the *passage* which Cain had tried to explain to her. She waved, seeing Mac's approach.

"How's it going?" he called.

Ayisha shook her head. "I need Cain. There's too much I don't know. I'm trying to learn too much too fast and it doesn't all make sense."

"You both look good to me."

"Watch him and tell me,"—she applied the back and leg aids to Willi—"are his hind legs dragging? I can't see."

Mac shaded his eyes against the sun and watched intently as the two rode about the large circle where the grass had long ago been worn away. He said finally, "They do seem to drag a bit." When she sighed, he added,

"Hell, lass, it doesn't look bad. It's a pretty sight. Nice and showy."

"But it's not what Cain does—it's flashy and not a true *passage*. Willi's not floating." Nor was it his fault. Cain had said the stallion was a finely tuned instrument waiting to be played, and she still did not know how to play him. Maybe now that time would never come—not if she were to go off with Cain and never return to Seacliff. She leaned forward and rubbed his neck and said quietly, "I guess we've done enough for one morn, old boy." She turned him toward the stable.

Mac walked beside them, his hands plunged deep in his pockets. He looked up. "Lass, we need to talk."

His face looked so stern of a sudden that Ayisha touched the reins and Willi stopped. "This instant?"

"Nay. Give him to Griffin and then come up to my rooms. I'll be waiting for you."

"I'll just be a minute."

She had always loved Mac's apartment above the stable. The rooms were large and airy and filled with the good smells of hay and leather and horses. She imagined that when Mac lay on his bed at night he could hear faintly the noises from below, soft nickering, a hoof hitting the stall door, the rattle of halter on water bucket. Comforting sounds. Now she climbed the narrow stairs and found him sitting cross legged on his neatly made bunk. Seeing that his face had not changed expression, she perched at his feet on a rug Peg had braided and met his eyes, half fearful.

"Is one of the horses sick?" She could not imagine what else would make him look so.

"The horses are fine." He was the one who was sick, sick with worry over what was suddenly happening around here. He lowered his voice. "Did you know I have orders from your father to throw Cain off the property if he gets by the men patrolling below?"

So. He had done it. He had actually put a guard on the house. She was glad she was sitting down, for it made her queasy. "I'm not surprised."

"Sweet Jesus, girl, what happened? I thought you were going to wed the fellow."

"I am. Never doubt it."

"Not if your father has anything to say about it, you won't. He doesn't intend to let Cain near you. I have orders to go with you everywhere." Riding and sailing with her were sheer pleasure, aye, but he did not relish the thought of trailing after her while she visited friends or shopped in the city for whatever things females shopped for. He had too much else to do. He said gruffly, "Tell me now, what's this all about?"

She found a piece of straw and played with it as she pondered how much she should tell him. She said finally, "It's an old feud. It turns out that Da and Cain's father were friends and partners once—they hauled cargo. One of their ships went down in a storm and men were lost." She kept her fingers busy with the straw, kept her eyes on it. "Blame was wrongly placed and there were bad feelings. It was all a misunderstanding, but the bitterness is still there."

Mac scowled. "That's it?"

She shrugged. "There's no more to tell."

"Was Cain involved at all?"

"Nay. He was just a lad. But now that Da knows who he is—"

"Why did it take so long? I don't understand."

"Cain took his uncle's name when he was adopted, and Da had never seen him." She hurried on before he thought of more questions. "Anyhow, Da hates him because he's his father's son. He happens to look a bit like his father . . ."

Mac's frown deepened. "That doesn't sound like Ben."

"I know." She bit her lips so they wouldn't quiver. "He sees red where Cain and his father are concerned."

Mac gave a low whistle. "I take it naught's changed between you and Cain?"

"Naught's changed, and if I have to run away to wed him, I will. I love him, Mac."

Mac did not like the sound of it. When this maid said

she would do something, she did it. He muttered, "Now hold on, Ayisha. I'm sure if you just give your father some time, he'll come around." When her eyes swam suddenly and she looked at him in mute helplessness, he gave her a brotherly hug. "Here, now, lass, when did he ever keep you from your heart's desire?"

"Never," she whispered, "but this is different. I'm telling you—Da hates him. And Cain hates Da. Deep, awful hatred. And Da thinks he's doing the absolute best thing for me by keeping us apart. He'll never in this world change his mind about it. He says Cain will ruin my life."

"But you know better . . ."

"Aye." She yearned to pour out and share with him all that she knew. She had always told Mac her troubles, but she could not bear it if he thought the same terrible thoughts about Cain that her father did, and he would. He had no love for Cain, and he was every bit as protective of her as Da was.

Mac patted her shoulder. What a mess this was and him in the middle. There was no maid on this earth he loved more than Ayisha. His strongest instincts were to protect her from danger, keep her happy, and help her in any way he could. Except now he was bound by Ben's orders, and there was no one he respected more. The man was all things to him—father, friend, confidant, mentor. Never had Ben Adair steered him wrong nor said one thing that had not turned out to be so. He loved him as deeply as he did Ayisha, so how could he now side with her against him? Or side with him against her? Sweet Mary and Jesus.

But in all truth, Ben was wrong about Cain. He'd had his eye on the fellow from the very first time he came to Seacliff. It was no secret he'd not liked him, and he'd disliked intensely Cain's mysterious and high-handed treatment of Ayisha earlier in the summer—his saying he couldn't *see* her when he was coming regularly to ride Willi. It had been a strange enough thing so that Mac had lurked about watching him unobserved whenever he came to work the stallion and Ayisha was not about.

His conclusion was that Ayisha was safe with him. Any

fellow who was gentle and careful with animals, large and small, when he didn't know he was being watched was all right in his book. In addition, Cain Banning was as genial and respectful to the lowliest stable lad as he was to the master of the house. Mac saw well why Ayisha liked him. He liked the old boy himself now. And he'd never seen her so happy as when their engagement was announced. He patted her shoulder again.

"I'm sorrier than I can say about all of this, cosset."

Ayisha got to her feet. "It won't come between us." She saw the very real distress in his eyes. "I'll not lie to you, Mac. I'm meeting him on Trilby Isle this afternoon. We thought Da might do just what he did so we planned ahead."

Mac rose, towering over her. "Don't do it."

Ayisha smiled. "Are you going to lock me in the tack room or steal my sails?"

Mac crossed his arms. "I can't let you go."

His face was so doleful, she laughed. "He'll not abduct me, Mac, I promise."

"I can't do it. You know I can't. Ben trusts me."

She caught his hand. "So do I trust you. And I think you trust me."

"I'll always trust you."

"Then trust me now. What Cain and I have is right and good. He's a good man, believe me."

"I swore to your father . . ." He couldn't meet her eyes.

"I'm going, Mac. With or without you."

"For God's sake, Ayisha."

"You always said I had good instincts—"

"Damn it, girl!"

"—and common sense."

Mac held up his hands in surrender. It was not in him to hurt her any more than she'd been hurt already. He would start praying right now that Ben would never find out. He said tersely, "When?"

"I told him I'd be there at two." She saw well it was a thing he did not want to do, but he would. For her, he would.

Mac nodded. "Half past one then."

"I'll be there." She moved toward the stairs, stopped, looked back. Seeing his concern, she returned, stood on tiptoe, and kissed his bearded cheek. "Thanks, Mac. I'll never forget this."

Ayisha spied Cain's craft beached on the eastern side of Trilby Isle, a tiny dense patch of pines riding the blue Atlantic. When the *Dolphin* drew near and dropped sail, she watched him emerge from the woods, raise a hand in greeting, and wade through the boiling shallows to meet them and catch the mooring rope. A fierce wave of love washed over her as she took up an oar and began to paddle. She wanted to fly to him, hold him close, drink his hungry kisses, but not with Mac there. Nay, not in front of Mac.

She contented herself with gazing on him, marveling that while everything about him was stored away in her memory, each time she saw him, it was as thrilling as that first time: his eyes, deeply blue in his dark face; the brief white flash of his smile of greeting; the way the sun burnished his hair and brows and lashes; the way he looked at her, loving her with his eyes . . .

She slid over the *Dolphin*'s side when they reached the shallows and went silently into his arms. As they embraced, she whispered, "Mac had to come. I'm sorry."

"I'm glad. Greydon's out there, and I was worried about you." After helping drag the craft beyond the tide line, he met MacKenzie Fitzgerald's guarded eyes. "I appreciate your bringing her, Mac. Keep a close watch over her."

Mac's narrowed gaze moving over Cain Banning did not reveal his growing approval of him. "That I will, man, never fear."

"Mac—" Ayisha said gently, "would you mind taking a stroll around? Or we can." She knew well the battle he was fighting—his love and deep loyalty for her father pitted against his love and loyalty to her. She was surprised to see his eyes dance suddenly, just for an instant.

"Why don't you two do the strolling," he said casually. "I'd best stay with the boats so you don't go sailing off."

Her heart turned a somersault as she realized he was on their side! He had not said so, but he didn't need to. She knew him, and she saw it now. His feelings toward Cain had changed. She should have known. He would never have gone against her father's wishes had he thought it was the wrong thing to do. Oh, Mac. Darling, darling Mac! She nearly threw her arms around him, but Cain would not have appreciated it. She said easily:

"Good. We'll just walk a bit a—and talk."

"Fine."

"We'll keep in sight, I promise." Her heart was brimming with her love for him and her gratitude.

"Go, lass, just go—and you needn't keep in sight. I'll not be spying on you." Mac lowered himself heavily to the sand and fixed a stony gaze on the sea. God help him. God help them all.

Cain caught Ayisha's hand and drew her toward the pine woods, and when Mac and the sea were out of their sight, he pulled her into his arms. "I've been worried about you . . . dying for you . . ."

"And I for you." She stroked his hair with eager fingers and traced the dear familiar lines of his face and brows, his jaw and throat. How precious he was, more precious than anything else on this earth. "Da did what we feared," she whispered, afraid her voice would carry. "Mac's to go with me everywhere, even into town, and there are men watching the roads to Seacliff and there's a guard on the shore."

"It's all right," Cain murmured. "It's all right." He buried his face in her shining hair and the curve of her neck and shoulder and then took her offered mouth hungrily. For a long time they kissed, starving, and then sank to the piney earth breathless and shaking. They stared at each other, wordless, adoring. Cain fondled her cheek and chin. "Do you still want to wed me?"

"More than ever." She lifted his hands to her breasts, felt him tenderly seeking over them, his hungry lips pressed to them. Her breath broke as delight shimmered through her with memories of the ecstasy they had given each other last night and the thought that it could be theirs again, now. Mac had said he would not spy on them. She sought Cain gently with trembling fingers and found that he was hard with his hunger for her. She murmured, her voice small, "Do we dare?"

Cain covered her hand with his and put it from him. "Nay, little one." He had taken her once out of wedlock. He would not do it again.

Ayisha was so wildly in love, so afire for him she would have done blindly whatever he decided and followed wherever he led. Now she was glad for his wisdom and restraint. It would have been a betrayal of Mac's trust in her to have returned to the boats with her eyes shining and her cheeks all pink. He would have known. She let Cain pull her to her feet.

"Let's walk," he said. He needed to cool off and clear his head.

"I've worn a path to the other shore over the years." She was scarcely aware of the things she loved about this place: the glimmer of sea and sky through the trees, the pungent smell of pine, the murmur of the ocean as it gnawed endlessly on the sandy beaches, the peace and calm. Now all of her awareness was on the man walking beside her. Her beloved. Her hungry gaze stole over him as they trod the soft pine needles on the island floor. She loved him. She loved him and she would die without him. Of that there was no doubt in her heart or her mind. Without him she would have no reason to live. She squeezed his hand tightly and melted when he smiled down at her with his night blue eyes.

Cain grinned. "What are you thinking, sprite, with that look in your eyes?"

"I love you, Cain Banning."

"I'm always glad to hear it." He raised her hand to his lips, kissed it, slid her arm around his waist, and lay his across her shoulders so that they walked as one through the pines.

Ayisha gazed up at him, her head resting against his shoulder. "Can we wed soon?"

"Aye," He had thought of naught else. As they gazed toward the hazy green blur that was Boston, he tightened his arm around her and said quietly, "Ayisha, I think you should tell your father it's our intention."

She looked up at him in disbelief. "Cain, I—I don't dare."

He saw her fear and knew that he had to overcome it. "You must, sprite. Tell him we'll always love each other and we're going to wed, with or without his permission."

She clung to him. "He'll say nay. He'll send me away from you. Cain, please, I want to run away like Aimee did. I can slip away from Mac—he can't possibly watch me every second—and I'm certain Da will forgive me eventually." But if he did not, God forbid, it meant she would be leaving behind everyone and everything she loved—Da himself, Aimee, Mac, and Pegeen, her home, Willi, the other horses. . . . But then she could not be weak in this. If need be, she would make the sacrifice. For Cain, she would do anything. She said firmly, "I want to do it, Cain. Once we're wed, we're wed. Naught can be done about it."

Cain said quietly, "That's so, Ayisha. Once we're wed, it's done. It's exactly why you should give him the chance to change his mind."

She shook her head violently. "He won't! He hates you."

"But he loves you. He needs to see that if he tries to keep us apart, he'll lose you." He wrapped his arms around her, held her. "He's your father, Ayisha. . . ."

And no matter what else Ben Scott had done, Cain thought, he was a loving father. It was a thing he himself had missed, and he wanted never to take that away from Ayisha. More and more, doubts about his own father had been mounting. Tom Gregg had not been a man of honor while he had lived, so why then was Cain so determined that he have honor in death? Why not admit it was possible he had lied and that Ben was telling the truth? But he knew the answer—it was the terror in Tom's dying eyes. The fear of damnation. If he'd truly been alone in committing the deed, Cain brooded, would he have compounded the sin in his maker's eyes by blaming it on another?

"How can you be so generous when he's being so hateful?" Ayisha protested. "It makes me ashamed for him."

"Sprite, listen to me," Cain spoke softly into her ear. "I don't want you to do it for Ben alone—it's for you too. We can run away, aye, and believe me, we will if this fails, but it will cause a wound that might never heal. Everyone will be hurt, and I know you don't want that to happen. Not if it can be avoided."

Ayisha knew he was right. In her mind's eye, she saw Aimee weeping for her, Da pacing the floor, grieving, Peg mourning her as if she were dead, and Mac would hate himself for his part in it. And she thought of Willi—Willi standing in his stall in blackness, waiting, waiting for someone to lead him back into the sunshine and his glory days. She sighed and whispered, "I'll do it."

"Good." Not for one minute did Cain believe Ben Scott would give his daughter to the son of Thomas Gregg. Not for one minute. But he couldn't have lived with himself had they not made this effort. He lifted her hand and kissed her palm and the soft, white inner skin of her wrist. "You'll not regret it."

"I know—but he'll say nay." She knew it as surely as she knew the sun would set that night.

"We'll wed no matter."

She buried her face against his chest. "I wish I weren't so worried about Willi."

"We'll work something out, I promise." He'd no more leave Willi behind than he'd leave Ayisha.

Chapter 23

"**P**an, thank goodness you're here! I've been so worried!" Aimee was descending the staircase as Ayisha came in the front door. "Where have you been?" Without waiting for an answer, she rushed on. "Seth's been here and left already. He'd hoped to give you a message from Cain, but then Cain was already gone when he woke up and never did come back and when I couldn't find you—"

"Griffin knew I went sailing with Mac."

Aimee lay a hand on her heart. "But Griffin wasn't about, and I had such a feeling. I was certain you'd run off a—and gotten wed." Her brown eyes searched her sister's face. "Did you? Did you and Cain wed?"

Ayisha put a finger to her lips and glanced about, but no one was in sight. She said quietly, "Let's walk." She didn't want the servants to overhear, and she especially did not want to upset Peg. She took Aimee's hand and pulled her through the front door and out to the front field where the sheep were grazing.

"Are you wed?" Aimee persisted, her eyes like saucers.

"Nay, pet." How like a child she looked in her speckless gingham dress and her brown hair hanging down her back in smooth, plump curls.

"Seth said men were guarding the roads below."

"They are. It's why Cain and I met this afternoon on Trilby Isle." When Aimee looked at her in bewilderment, Ayisha continued gently, "I saw him last night and we planned it then."

286

"He—came here?"

"I went to see him. I rode to Boston."

"Oh, Ayisha . . ." Aimee sank into the grass whereupon one of the sheep, a pet ewe, trotted over, nosed her and baaed. Aimee stroked its head vaguely and thought of Ayisha riding to Boston. Alone. In the night. It was a thing she herself could never on this earth have done, and she wondered wistfully if Cain Banning knew what manner of woman it was who loved him. Did he know how brave and wonderful and special she was? She whispered, "Was he happy to see you?"

"Very happy." There was no need to speak of that moment in the pub when all of those men were gathered about leering at her and Cain had come to her rescue. "After we—talked for a bit, he brought me home and waited until he knew I was safely in my room. I put a lighted candle in the window."

Aimee sighed thinking of it. It was all so wonderfully romantic. And they had made love, she could tell. She knew her sister. There was a softness, a glow about her. She whispered, "You did more than talk, didn't you?"

Ayisha knew exactly what Aimee was asking and felt herself blushing. "Aye." Never would she have admitted such a thing to anyone else. Seeing another unasked question in Aimee's eyes, she smiled. "It was—like nothing I've ever felt before."

"Did it hurt?"

"Maybe just a little—and only for a little . . ."

Aimee blinked. "How did you know what to do?"

Ayisha laughed and joined in scratching the ewe's soft ears. "Cain knew what to do, and I promise you, Seth will be more than happy to teach you . . ."

"I'm sure he thinks I'm the stupidest thing in the world." She would never recover from yesterday's humiliation.

"He doesn't, believe me. It told him you've not been with any other man and he'll treasure you all the more for it."

"How do you know?"

"Mama told me." Seeing her sister's brown eyes glisten suddenly, she added quickly, "She didn't tell you because you were too young then. I realize that now."

Aimee nodded. "I know—I figured it out. And later she was too sick . . ."

"Aye." Ayisha reached out and patted her flushed cheek. "There's naught to fret about, honey. You have a wonderful, understanding husband."

Time stretched out lazily as they sat thinking their own thoughts, the only sounds the tinkle of sheep bells and the hum of summer insects. Ayisha said finally, "Cain wants me to tell Da that we're going to wed—with or without his permission."

Aimee sat straighter. "Pan, you daren't!"

"That's what I said, that Da would say nay and rage and maybe even try to send me away, but—" She poured it all out, and even though she knew Cain was right, her fears came clawing her again. She got to her feet and put her hands to her temples, not knowing suddenly which way to turn or what to do. "It's impossible!" She felt like weeping, but Aimee looked so forlorn, she laughed instead and threw out her hands. "It's completely impossible."

Aimee was not fooled. She had never seen Ayisha so lost and helpless and frightened—Ayisha who was her own tower of strength and the calm voice of reason and wisdom. These past two terrible years, it was she, no one else, who had held her hand and walked with her through the loss of their mother and the days of grief and loneliness. Now it was Ayisha who needed strength and comfort and mothering. She said carefully, "On second thought, I believe Cain is right. I think you should give Papa a chance to change his mind. Tell him just what you told me—that you two are going to wed, and there's no way short of putting you in a cage and throwing away the key that he's going to stop you. He might surprise you the way he did us. We acted too hastily, Seth and I . . ."

"Oh, Aimee, tell me you don't regret it!"

"I don't, nay. I love him so much I can scarcely bear it! It's that we thought Papa would act a certain way and he didn't. We could have waited, . . ." and had their lovely church wedding after all.

Ayisha said stubbornly, "This is different."

"I know." The two linked hands then and walked slowly, swinging their arms the way they had walked across the field hundreds of times when they were children. "But a miracle can always happen," Aimee continued. "We know this whole thing is a misunderstanding. We know Papa didn't do what they say he did. The truth has to come to light some day."

"And it might not." She didn't want to think about it anymore. Her head was too filled with it and it seemed there was no solution. Gazing up at the sky, she saw that dark clouds were rolling in from the sea and the wind was freshening. "It's going to storm . . ."

"We'd best go back. And Pan, Seth and I want you to know, if you need us, you two, we'll do anything to help. Anything—and that includes helping with Willi. I know you're worried about him, and I am, too. I want him to be happy."

Ayisha squeezed her hand. "I know, and it makes me love you more than I do already. Except I'm not sure how you could help. Seth doesn't know *haute école* riding." Aimee herself loved all horses passionately, but from afar.

"It doesn't matter. What matters is that Papa loves him. He's Jonathan's son and—" She gasped, then covered her mouth. "I'm the stupidest thing."

"Nay, you are not! What you said is the truth. Not for one minute do I begrudge Seth Da's love." But why couldn't Cain, who'd never had a real father, share it? It was so unfair.

"I wish I didn't blurt things so. What I was trying to say was, if worse comes to worst and you leave, Seth will insist that Willi should be with you and Cain. I know Papa will agree. He'd never punish poor Willi intentionally."

"I know he wouldn't." He was an exceedingly loving man, her father. In fact, there was no one in her memory, aside from Jeremy, that he had ever truly disliked—until he had learned that Cain Banning was the son of his worst enemy.

It was storming hard when Ben arrived from the city. He was grateful to be home where it was warm and dry, and he was thankful to learn that both of his daughters were there. Throughout the day, he'd worried that despite the safeguards he had taken, Ayisha would be gone when he got back. But the darling angel had not disappointed him. She was home and she was safe, and in his gratitude he thanked Mary, Jesus, Joseph, and all of the other saints and gods that he could think of. As he hurriedly exchanged his city garb for his old, comfortable clothing, he wondered if it was too good to be true, her still being here. Maybe she was going to try to change his mind . . .

But then he would not borrow trouble. Yesterday had seen the worst of it, and now it was over. Now it was time to get back to normal. But as he left his bedchamber and trod the dim hallway, he wondered what he would say to the lass. Should he apologize for the hurt he'd caused her? Explain more fully why he had done what he'd done? Thank her for allowing him to guide her and guard her as he saw fit? She had always been a good lass, and obedient. Fearless, aye, where danger was concerned, but rarely had she completely disobeyed him. She was respectful of his greater years and experience and wisdom and heeded him without fail. Usually. Except for those damned shipping lanes she loved to cross.

He made his way down the great curving staircase and into the drawing room where Soames had just stirred the fire. Soames straightened, stiffened to the attention he would have accorded royalty.

"Good evening, sir. Your usual?"

"Aye, old friend." Ben sank heavily into the wing chair facing the crackling blaze and stretched out his weary legs to its warmth. He watched as Soames carefully, with proper ritual, opened a bottle of aged La Salle sherry and poured it into the squat cut-glass goblet Ben favored. He then placed it on a small silver salver and presented it to his master. Ben took it, swirled it, inhaled its pungent aroma. "Thanks, Soames. Will my daughters be joining me for dinner, do you know?"

"I have ascertained that the table is set for three, sir."

Ben nodded, satisfied. He touched his lips to the amber nectar and felt his taste buds warm pleasantly. He took a sip, savored it, and said finally, "It's nasty out there."

"Indeed it is." Looking about the drawing room and seeing that everything gleamed and was in place, Soames said, "Will that be all, sir?"

"You might tell my daughters I'm home. I'm sure they didn't expect me this early."

Soames nodded. "I will tell them."

Sitting staring at the fire, Ben's gaze was drawn to the oil above the mantelpiece. Ana. He did not want to think about her now, he had too much else on his mind, but already he was remembering his wedding night and how he and his darling had drunk sherry from one goblet. It was the first time any alcohol had passed her lips, and she had grown charmingly tipsy after just a few sips.

He shook his head. It seemed just last week . . . last night . . . He released a great sigh as he recalled the vision she had been in that gauzy white veil she'd wrapped herself in . . . and how she had entered their bridal bed from the foot, lifting the covers and crawling in after he was already in.

When she was in his arms finally, he'd chuckled softly and asked, "What was that all about, my treasure?"

She had given him a sweet scented kiss and replied shyly, "In my land, Benadair, a wife's place is beneath the soles of her husband's feet. Even in paradise . . ."

Ben had not shown his anger but replied gently, "Not in my land, it isn't, lass. A woman's place is by her husband's side."

He took a heftier swallow and felt the sherry burning all the way down his throat and into his belly. Paradise. He smiled, thinking how frequently the word had come into her conversation when they talked. Living with him had been paradise, the home he had built for her had been paradise, their lovemaking had been paradise . . . And near the end, she had murmured, her voice so faint he'd needed to place his ear to her lips to hear, "I will meet you in paradise, Benadair. Promise you will look for me, beloved . . ." He blinked back his tears, took another scorching mouthful and turned, hearing the soft rustle of his daughters' gowns. Aimee gave him a bright smile.

"Hello, Papa. You're home early."

"Aye—and just in time." He indicated the rain beating against the window and the lightning crashing. He dabbed hastily at his eyes and caught Aimee's hand when she bent to kiss his cheek. "How's my darlin'?" His anxious gaze next went to Ayisha as she came toward him. When she, too, smiled and bent to his cheek with a kiss, his relief was boundless. "Hello, sweetheart."

"Hello, Da."

Ben gazed on them with loving eyes. Every day they grew more like their blessed mother in every way, and Ayisha's tender greeting had just given him the clue as to how to handle this whole damnable thing with Cain Banning. It was over and done with and she was his lass again. She was going to abide by his wishes and forget the man. He would do the same. He smiled up at the two of them.

"So, sit yourself down, lassies, and tell me how your day was." He missed the flicker of disbelief in Ayisha's eyes as his own gaze returned to Ana's portrait. His love reached out to her, touching her, thanking her for giving him such darling girls. He was prouder than proud of them.

Pegeen appeared just then, her worried dark eyes searching over the three of them. "Dinner is served."

Ben got to his feet. "Thank you, Peg. I'm ready for it. Is that roast beef and yorkshire pudding I smell?"

"It is indeed. With fall in the air, it seemed time."

Trailing after her father and Aimee into the candlelit dining chamber, Ayisha wondered resentfully if he were actually going to pretend as if naught had happened . . . as if he had not turned her entire world upside down. She was filled with angry questions, but held them back. Perhaps during dinner he would speak of it. Or afterwards. That was it, doubtless. It was an upsetting enough subject so that he was waiting until after dinner to broach it. With great difficulty, she contained her agitation and tried to enjoy the food.

Toward the end of the meal, Ben's uneasiness returned. Ayisha was far too polite, too quiet, and he recalled with relief that he had some news of interest to her. "I nearly forgot,"—he turned to her—"the *Ayisha*'s back from the Orient. She got into port early this morn and they were still unloading her when I left. She's a veritable treasure trove." As soon as he said, it, he bit his tongue. Hell and damnation.

"Da . . ."

The sound of her voice told him she was angry. His jaws clenched. "Aye?"

Ayisha yearned to rage and weep in an attempt to change his mind about Cain, but her every instinct warned against it. She said quietly, "Why are you acting this way—as though naught has happened?"

Ben held up his hand, a signal for quiet, and then motioned Soames near. He said low, "We'd like privacy, Soames." When the servants had departed, he put down his knife and fork and wiped his mouth carefully with his napkin. "When you came in and smiled at me and gave me a kiss like you always do, I thought—or maybe I wanted to think—that you'd decided I was right, that it was best you never see that man again."

"My feelings haven't changed." She ordered herself to stay calm, breathe slowly, deeply, relax. "In fact, naught has changed. Cain and I love each other and we're going to wed. I want your permission, Da, and your blessing, you know I do, but with or without it, we're going to wed. Know that." When he remained silent, looking at her with stubborn eyes, she continued in the same quiet voice, "Cain has told me everything that happened and Seth has told Aimee. We'd really like to hear your side of it. It's important."

"We don't see why you won't tell us," Aimee added. "We know it was naught but a terrible misunderstanding."

Ben asked in a growl, "What have you been told?"

"That you and Cain's father were partners once," Aimee began, her face going pale, "and that you turned to piracy."

"That's so," Ben said quietly. He did not protest that times had been hard and his men had families to feed. His excuses were no longer good enough. What they had done was wrong.

"Seth said there was a storm and—"

Ben listened closely and carefully to his younger daughter's breathless account of the tale. Eyes wintry now, he said sharply, "That's what Seth told you, did he? That my men were put over the side on my orders and some of them perished?"

Aimee said faintly, "Aye."

Ayisha murmured, "But we know you wouldn't have given such orders."

Ben gave a bitter laugh. "You're right, girl. I didn't give them. Tom Gregg did. And all of my men perished, not just some of them. I lost all of my good lads. All but Seth." It was time they knew. No more kid gloves with these lassies. He said abruptly, "The sharks ate them—and Cain Banning's father slew Seth's father Jonathan. He knifed him and tossed him overboard while he still lived."

Aimee gave a little scream and covered her mouth with her hand. Ayisha's face was white, but Ben went on, relentless with himself and with them. He told them everything, from the beginning to the end, and he did not stop there. He turned to Ayisha.

"You, my darling," he said harshly, "you think you know Cain Banning. Well, let me tell you, you don't. You love him, aye, but what he feels for you is another story. The Gregg men I knew, all of them, were sweet-talking bastards who were handsome as sin and the world's best liars. When Tom wooed a woman, he made her feel as if she was the only female left on this earth and he was the only man. He'd be tender with her and gentle and considerate, oh, aye, you never saw a man more considerate and caring—but it was only a ploy to get what he wanted. And he was relentless. He enjoyed a good, long chase, Tom did."

Seeing her anguish, Ben said more gently, "Darlin', darlin', I'm more sorry than I can say."

"Cain's not like that!"

He shrugged. "Maybe he isn't, but I wouldn't bet on it." His heart ached to be hurting her so, but how could he abandon her to dreams that would soon be nightmares? For sure that was the worse fate of the two. He went on, "His father left more weeping women in the wake of his wanderings than any man alive. Oh, aye, he was a wanderer, was Tom Gregg. All the Greggs were, and doubtless Banning is, too. Tom used to laugh that it was his curse, and then brag how naught and no one could anchor him in one place. He wanted to wander, that one, and his favorite trick was to tell the poor smitten lass that because of his newfound love for her, he'd wander no more. And after she gave herself to him and he'd had his fill of her, he'd move on." Ben shook his head. "Don't let it happen to you, Ayisha. For the love of God, lass, don't let it happen."

Ayisha looked at him blankly, not able to absorb it all. There was too much. The sharks . . . Tom Gregg's betrayal of him . . . the murder of Seth's father—and he'd described Cain so perfectly when he described Cain's father that she knew her life had just ended. She could still see and hear and breathe, aye, but the rest of her was dead. She was a block of wood. A block of ice. And Da—he'd grown so pale and haggard looking and his face was so sweat glistened . . . She was staring, wondering why he looked so when Aimee dropped to her knees beside his chair.

"Papa! What is it? Are you ill?"

"I'm fine, girl, but I'm mad. I'm damned mad about all of this." Never would he let them know how strange he felt of a sudden. It was a thing he had never experienced before, a burning heaviness in his chest. "I—think I'd like a bit of quiet."

Ayisha forced herself to move, to speak, as concern filtered through to her dazed brain. "You're sure you're all right, Da?"

Ben nodded and said gruffly, "Aye. Just hand me the sherry there on the sideboard." Ayisha brought the bottle to the table and poured some into his goblet. He patted her arm. "Know, darlin', I am sorry. I'd have given anything in the world for this day never to have come. Anything." He added low, "And now I just want to sit here a bit. Please tell the others I'd like to be alone." He felt the maids' cool, featherlike kisses brushing his cheeks and then they stole out of the room.

Ben sat in silence, allowing the sherry to seep into his limbs and his brain and dull them pleasantly. He realized eventually that the storm which had been battering them during dinner had finally blown itself back out to sea. Now the sun setting on the far side of the headland had turned the outdoors to gold. He rose, walked unsteadily to one of the casement windows overlooking the front field, and opened both panes. He breathed in the sweet, damp air and thought how good it smelled and how beautiful everything was. The sheep grazing, grass glittering with thousands of crystal water droplets, the plaintive song of a lone oriole breaking the quiet. He smiled, thinking wistfully that his darling would have called it paradise . . .

He stiffened seeing that a tall figure had appeared on the far side of the field. Banning, by God. The devil had somehow slipped past the men patrolling below. He narrowed his eyes and stared harder as the figure paced back and forth as if waiting for someone. He frowned, seeing that it was not Banning. Nay, this fellow was not as tall and he was bearded, and his hair was darker than Banning's. Now who in hell was he? He should know, for it was someone he had seen many times. He recognized well the confident way the man carried himself and his long seaman's stride. Ben's heart turned over as he suddenly identified the stranger. Holy Mary . . .

He watched, thunderstruck, as a maid ran out of the pine woods and into the man's hungry, outstretched arms—a maid slender as a willow wand whose dark hair glinted red in the sun's dying rays. Watching the two kiss, Ben felt his hair standing on end. Dear God, dear God in Heaven, it was Ana—and himself. She was waiting for him, his darling, just as she had said she would. She was waiting in paradise. His breath caught. Was it here then? Was Seacliffe their paradise? God, God . . .

He blinked, rubbed his wet eyes, and when he returned his gaze to the scene, naught was there but the small flock of sheep and the sound of the oriole. Had he imagined it? Had it been naught but the sherry that had gone to his head? Sherry and wishful thinking? But nay, in his heart he knew it had been real. He drew a deep breath as he reflected calmly that he had seen his own wraith. He had heard of such things, and it meant he was going to die before too much longer. He did not know when nor where, he knew only that if Ana were out there waiting for him, he was ready.

Chapter 24

S harks.

Ayisha could not put the terrible image from her head. All night long she thought of those men long ago—how many men?—rowing frantically toward a distant speck of land, looking on in horror at the suddenly bulging seams of their longboats, watching the gray sea pouring in. Men clinging to their overturned crafts, cringing as the first fin appeared, and then another and another, circling, circling endlessly, cautiously, before that first rushing attack. She could imagine the terror and the screams, the water churning and boiling, turning red . . .

She had never seen a shark, but on her many journeys aboard the *Ayisha* she had heard low talk she was not supposed to hear—the crew speaking in hushed voices of mates lost or mutilated, of men keelhauled and how the sharks, smelling, tasting, sensing their blood, had gathered and the frenzy with which they had fed.

She climbed out of bed and paced the floor as the sun began to rise out of the sea. She did not watch it. Her thoughts had turned to Tom Gregg. In her father's description he sounded so much like Cain that it was scaring her nigh to death. Over and over she wondered, had Cain pretended with her as his father had lied to those other poor maids? She could not believe it. She wrung her hands, told herself nay, he loved her, his love and caring for her were genuine. She could tell. But her father's words pounded in her head. He had said bad blood would out. It was a phrase she had heard forever without knowing what it meant. Jeremy had said it.

Jeremy. The thought of him brought new terror. How long before he learned her own father had been Tom Gregg's partner, in crime as well as in business? Remembering how certain he had been that she would wed him, she felt ill. Maybe he already knew and was waiting to pounce. Why on earth hadn't she told Cain? If only she could ride to him this instant, ask him a million questions and pour out her heart to him. But she couldn't slip away unseen anymore, not with her father's guards about. Nay, she had to wait for the rendezvous on the isle this afternoon.

She made a hasty toilette, dressed quickly in fresh riding clothes, and went down to breakfast. She froze, seeing her father on the terrace enjoying the morning and a great bowl of hot porridge. She had thought he'd be gone.

Ben looked up. Seeing the watchfulness in his daughter's eyes, he said quietly, "Good mornin', lass." He had already vowed not to say another word about Cain.

"Good morning." Ayisha gazed in astonishment at his color and bright eyes. She had not seen him look so good or so young in years. "I'm glad you've recovered." It was the truth. She was as angry with him as ever but she certainly wanted him healthy and happy.

Ben shrugged. "There was naught wrong with me. A bit of sherry and some rest cured me as I knew it would." That and his vision of the future that was awaiting him. Ana—and paradise. He smiled then, noting Ayisha's garb. "You're all set to ride, I see." It was good. It would help take her mind off things.

"Aye. I'll be working Willi." If she could calm herself, that is. Otherwise, she and Mac would ride the trails.

"Good, good." He lifted the teapot. "Can I pour you some, sweetheart?"

"Please."

As he filled her cup and his own, Ayisha lightly buttered a biscuit, added a speck of jam, took a small bite, and tried to swallow it. Going to the edge of the terrace, she stared out to sea and thought of the coming meeting between her father and Jeremy. Would it happen today? And what would Da say and do when Jeremy disclosed his triumphant news about Thomas Gregg? Kick him out the door, or tell him he already knew and then kick him out the door.

She took another nibble of the biscuit, choked it down, and wondered, worried why on earth Jeremy had seemed so confident about wedding her. Did he actually expect Da to bow to blackmail—Jeremy's silence about Tom Gregg in exchange for her hand in marriage? Or did Jeremy already know more than he had told her? Did he already know about those long-ago partners in crime? The thought made her heart beat in her throat. Should she tell him, warn him, or was she just imagining the worst of everything in the fragile state she was in? She was startled when he spoke from behind her.

"I'm on my way, darlin'," Ben said. "Don't forget your tea, it's growing cold."

Ayisha turned wide eyes to him. "Da . . ."

"Aye, lass?"

She hesitated, then decided finally that she was making worries where there were none. She shook her head. "Never mind. It's naught."

Ben nodded, relieved she was not about to pester him about Banning again. He said gruffly, "I hope you have a good day, girl." He bent, kissed the top of her head, and wondered what she was thinking. Probably that she would never forgive him . . .

Mac's worried gaze had followed Ayisha all morn. Things were not good with the lass. Her mind had not been on what she was doing so that she'd finally given up on Willi's workout. Hell, she'd been taut as a coiled spring and still was. The ride they had taken afterward over miles of trails had not soothed her either, and now, on her way to meet Cain on Trilby Isle, she was still nervous. He was tempted to probe, but he knew better. If she wanted to talk, she would talk.

As it was, they sailed with a thick silence between
them, the only sounds the slap of the waves on the *Dolphin*'s prow and the wind in her canvas. The isle loomed,
they dropped sail, and as he had before, Cain waded out to
meet them. Mac sensed a heightening of Ayisha's unease.
He fretted over it as he exchanged a friendly nod with
Cain, and when her only greeting to him was a polite
hello, his compassion for the man stirred. He said gruffly,
"I'll wait here with the boats like before."

Cain felt a growing sense of camaraderie with Mac-
Kenzie Fitzgerald, but he was puzzled by the coolness in
Ayisha's eyes. Of the many things he had envisioned for
this meeting, her being remote was not one of them. What
in hell had happened? He did not take her hand as she
moved beside him toward the woods, for he sensed she
would pull away. He asked softly, "Did you tell your father our plans?"

"Aye."

"And?"

"He said nay as I knew he would." She held his eyes
steadily, those thickly lashed eyes that were neither blue
nor black but were like the heavens at midnight. "He also
told me some things I'd not heard before."

Handsome as sin, she thought angrily, just like his father. And he was gentle—just like his father. And he'd
confessed to her that he'd always wanted to wander. It was
his curse. But no more. Oh, nay, not since he'd met her
and fallen in love. Like his father. She wanted to pound
him, but her icy calm held. She lowered her gaze to the
pine needles underfoot and said stiffly, "Why didn't you
tell me there were sharks . . . ?"

Cain saw that she had begun to tremble. He said, "I
didn't want to upset you, nor did Seth want to upset
Aimee."

"Upset me?" She gave a small strangled laugh. "Upset
is hardly the word! I'm furious. I'm enraged and astounded and disappointed in you! Sharks! Really, Cain,
how could you believe so blindly that my father would
ever order his men abandoned in shark-filled water?

You've seen him and gotten to know him. Do you really think he's the kind of man who could do such a thing?"

Cain took a long breath. "In truth, Ayisha, I don't. Not anymore."

Ever since he and Ben had had their confrontation he'd been at war with himself. He had marked well what kind of man Ben Scott was, and from his earliest memories on, he knew what manner of man Thomas Gregg was. He seemed to have changed toward the end—maybe because Cain had wanted so badly for him to change—but in his heart, Cain knew he had not. He knew, finally and irrevocably, that his father had been as much of a liar dying as he was living. No longer did he doubt it.

Ayisha's amber eyes blinked, widened. "What? You mean you don't think Da did it after all?"

"Nay. It's clear my father lied. I tried not to believe it, but I have to."

She went to him, slid her arms around him, and put her head on his chest. She felt his arms go around her. "I'm sorry," she murmured. "I know it's hard for you, but I'm grateful. I'm so grateful."

"And I'm sorry I put you through all of this. I've—"

She lay her fingers over his mouth. "Nay, beloved. It's over now and never will I blame you for defending your father. How could you not defend him, being the man you are? And, Cain, maybe it will make all the difference in the world to Da once he knows you believe him."

"He'll hate me still, sprite," Cain said softly. "That's not going to change."

"Maybe someday it will." She tensed, remembering suddenly the questions she had planned to hurl at him. Thank goodness she hadn't. Oh, thank goodness!

"Aye, maybe someday." Cain hugged her to him more closely and rejoiced in having her in his arms again with no misunderstandings between them. "What matters now is that I have you beside me—and we can wed with a clear conscience." Tilting up her chin to kiss her, he saw her grave face. He frowned. "What's this? Why so quiet?"

"I'm not quiet." She put a smile on her lips. "In fact,

let's talk about where we'll wed. I'm not particular as long as we don't go to Con Anderson. Aimee didn't like him. He leers ..." She looked away, unable to meet his dark eyes.

Cain said low, "Ayisha, what is it?"

"It's naught." She was afraid to tell him.

"It's something. I know you, sprite."

She realized then that she had to tell him. Her father had torn him into little pieces; it was only fair he knew what was said so he could defend himself. She murmured, "It's the other things I'd not heard before—what Da said about your father. I could see him in you and it bothered me."

Cain asked quietly, "What things are those?"

"Just so you know, that was then," she murmured. "I was worried yesterday and earlier today. Not now. Now I'm fine." Except for the look in his eyes.

"What things, Ayisha?"

"It seemed he behaved with maids he w—wanted the way you are with me. All gentle and tender and caring ..."

Cain gritted his teeth. "Would you rather I'd carried you off to a cave then? That can be arranged." When she gave a small wail and buried her face in her hands, he took them away and growled, "Look at me, Ayisha!"

She obeyed. As his blue eyes burned into her, she drew an unsteady breath. "That's not what worried me."

"I'm listening." He told himself he would remain calm. He would not allow his resentment to get the better of him.

Ayisha marked that his sun-darkened skin had blanched and his mouth was pressed into a tight line. A muscle pulsed in his jaw. She swallowed. "Da said that Tom always told a maid he was a born wanderer. He'd promise never to wander again because for the first time in his life he was in l—love and wanted to wed." She drew another shaky breath. "That's—what you said to me. And then they'd make love and when he tired of her, he'd move on to another maid ..."

Cain felt as if a volcano were gathering its white hot

heat and tremendous force within him. By all the gods, it was enough. He'd had all he was going to take of this damned interference from beyond the grave. He put Ayisha from him and gripped her shoulders. "Is that what you think I'll do? Bed you and leave you after promising to wed you?"

She felt her face flaming. "I'm sorry. It—frightened me for a bit. Only a bit." His anger frightened her even more. And when he released her and stormed off, leaving her to stare after him in astonishment, she knew pure panic. She ran after him. "Cain, wait!" He did not. He strode the trail angrily to the northern side of the isle, and she had to run to keep up with him. "Cain, please . . ." He stood stiff and proud, unyielding, arms crossed, scowling out over the sea. She said, "I was wrong to allow Da's words to affect me so. I know I was."

He was incensed that she could doubt him at this late date—and he was hurt. Damned hurt. He said stiffly, "I thought we'd gone beyond this, Ayisha."

"I don't know what came over me." She had never seen him so angry with her. With others, aye. With Jeremy and the man at the Red Lion and with her father, he had been furious, but not with her. Never with her. She murmured again, "I *am* sorry. Can you forgive me?"

"This has naught to do with forgiveness, lady. This has to do with trust."

Lady. A shiver slid up her spine. He was completely and totally disgusted with her. She whispered, "I do trust you, Cain, believe me, I do." He looked so stony and unyielding, she wanted to throw herself at his feet and beg for the old Cain to return. The Cain who was gentle and loving and understanding. The Cain who was her other half.

"Oh, aye, you trust me well when it suits your fancy." Cain's eyes swept her coldly. "But it won't do, Ayisha. I want all of your trust all of the time—or I want naught."

Hearing himself, the sharpness and the finality of what he had said, jolted Cain to his senses. He uttered a silent oath. What in bloody hell was he thinking, giving her that sort of ultimatum? And what was he planning on doing if she said, nay, she could not give him all of her trust? Say good-bye to her and walk away when he couldn't live on this earth without her? To boot, who was he to snarl at her for allowing her father's words to affect her? He who had allowed his father's last words nearly to ruin his life. What had come over him?

Ayisha's heart soared as his fierce love and his hunger for her shone suddenly in those midnight blue eyes of his—and she had seen his terrible fear that he had gone too far. He was angry with her, aye, he had every right to be, and he was disappointed that she had behaved so childishly—but it had all vanished now. He still loved her. He loved her as much as ever. More than ever. She stepped closer and lay her hands on his arms that were still folded stubbornly across his chest.

"You have all of my trust," she said firmly, "and you have it forever, just as you have all of my love forever and whatever else is in my power to give you." She took his face, lowered it to hers, and gently kissed his mouth.

Deep inside, Cain trembled. She had accepted his fury and rejection as her just due when he'd had no right to give it. He was a brute. A monster. He was his father's son. He pulled her into his arms and kissed her mouth long and hungrily.

Ayisha smiled when he released her lips. "Am I forgiven?"

Cain pressed his face into her hair, kissed her shoulder, and inhaled the intoxicating flower scent of her. He muttered, "I'm a fool, and there's naught to forgive."

"You aren't and there is." She spoke quietly although she bubbled inside with hidden laughter, with the sheer joy of having him back again, the Cain she loved so much.

"Nay, sprite, I'm a fool. I was furious with you for doing the same thing I did. I took my father's words to heart. I fully intended to carry Ben Scott back to England to be tried and hanged for a crime he never committed."

"But you didn't." She lay her head on his chest and listened to the heavy thudding of his heart.

"Nay, but only because I was bewitched by the most beautiful maid I had ever seen."

Ayisha felt the familiar sweet fire creeping through her, making her ache even as it tantalized her. She whispered, "When can we wed?"

"Tomorrow," Cain answered against her lips and took them in another kiss. He had nigh lost her several times and it was a risk he would never take again.

"Tomorrow . . ." It was a sigh as his palms glided over Ayisha's shoulders and back, down over her hips and buttocks, back up to her throat, her face. He cradled it, again brushed her mouth with his, gently at first and then more and more greedily. Between kisses Ayisha murmured, "Aimee and I talked . . . and she and Seth . . . mmm-mmmm . . . will help in any . . . Oh, Cain . . . in . . . any way they can . . . They'll even bring Willi . . . to us . . ."

"Good." Cain closed his eyes and basked in the heaven of feeling her pressed against him, of tasting her, inhaling the heady, female fragrance of her, feeling the response of his own body, his mounting need for her carrying him back and forth between pleasure and pain. He drew her down to the sand with him and stretched out beside her, their bodies touching.

"I'm so happy." Wonderingly, Ayisha brushed her fingertips over his dark face, his hair and brows, felt his fire burning through her. She traced his mouth, his ears, his jaw, scarce able to believe that tomorrow he would be hers. It was a miracle she'd feared would never come about. She breathed, "I love you so, Cain Banning."

Her fingers played over his throat and shoulders and tangled deeply in his thick hair as the love hunger grew within her. She was so filled with it, so grateful that this near disaster between them was to have a glorious ending, that she could not contain it within her one small body. She wanted, more than anything, to share her fiercely mounting love with him, to surround him with it. She wrapped her arms and legs about him, pressed herself closer, closer, saw that everything about him revealed his yearning for her—his shaft thrusting hard against her, the gleam of heat in his eyes, the way his hands moved over her, the harshness of his breathing. She reached down and touched gently the swollen mound beneath his trews. It was hard and hot and pulsing, alive beneath her cupped hand.

"Make love to me . . ."

The shy touch of her hand turned Cain's blood to molten fire and sent it searing through his body. Once more, he told himself he must not take her, not until they were wed. But then there was naught to keep them apart now. Not anymore. Everything was right and good and as it should be. She knew all there was to know about him, and by this hour tomorrow, they would be wed. He had given Ben a chance to make peace, and that the old devil had refused was not his concern. He was easy in his heart. He slid his hand beneath her shirt and stroked her breasts, found and teased her hardened nipples. He asked huskily, "You're sure, sprite?"

"I'm sure."

He whispered against her lips, "So am I." He rose and gathered her up easily in his arms, his prize. "But I'm not making love to you here on the beach where every passing ship and seagull can spot us."

Ayisha laughed, imagining it. "There's a cave under a rocky overhang—over there." She pointed, but he had already seen it. As he carried her toward it, holding her close to his heart, she heard her own heart singing. Never had she felt this way before, so free and unafraid and confident that this was the beginning of a whole new life together.

Chapter 25

Later that same afternoon, Jeremy Greydon locked the door of his study, stoked the fire, and sat down at his desk with a quill, an inkpot, and a stack of paper. Two hours later, after completing the letter he'd thought out so carefully, he read through it, and then read it again and again, nodding, chuckling, and rubbing his hands in his satisfaction. It was perfect. A veritable masterpiece. And it was going to destroy Cain Banning. There was no way on this earth the bastard could escape the web being woven around him.

Nightly Banning visited his ship, and tonight as he made his way back to his lodgings, he would be seized on a lonely stretch of dock and thrown into the hold of a Greydon vessel. Afterward, Jeremy himself would slip the damning letter into Ben's postbox and in the morn Ben would find and read it. Jeremy laughed, thinking how the old devil's eyes would bulge when he saw what it said. God's blood, how he wished he could be a fly on the wall to see the sight. It would probably give the old boy apoplexy, but hopefully not before he'd left on Kedrow Island the gold Banning had demanded in exchange for keeping silent about his pirate past.

And what was so fitting and so sweetly ironic—while the Adairs were cursing Banning for his treachery, he would be on the high seas enroute to his new life—the life of an indentured servant on one of the vast plantations in Cuba. Jeremy's blood ran faster at the thought, and at the hope that the devil would be beaten and humiliated daily

as Banning had beaten and humiliated him that day at
Seacliff. Smiling, whistling softly, he locked the letter in a
desk drawer, opened the study door, and shouted:

"Sprigg!"

Sprigg appeared from the gloom at the rear of the
house. "Aye, Sir?"

"My fire's almost out. After you've tended it, fetch me
a bottle of the Suisse Mont Blanc fifty-three. Tell cook I'll
dine in my study at seven."

"Aye, Mr. Greydon." After tending the fire and giving
the cook his master's instructions, Sprigg descended to the
wine cellar, guttering candle in hand. A chill gripped him
as he reflected that the man was up to no good. With that
glittery look in his eyes, he was up to no good . . .

Pegeen Fitzgerald found Ayisha on the terrace gazing at
the sea. What a catastrophe this was, she brooded. Her
fine, young man banished from her life forever and the
child not yet over the death of her blessed mother. Nor
were any of them. It was too sad for words, and she could
not imagine what had happened to cause Ben Adair to do
such a thing. She yearned to know, not just because she
was burning with curiosity, but because she wanted to
help. But then the three of them had been so closemouthed
that that in itself was a mystery. Never before had she
been so shut out of the affairs of this family. She stepped
out onto the terrace.

"I've been looking for you, lass." She stared when
Ayisha turned. Her eyes were bright and clear and her
sweet mouth was turned up in such a lovely smile that it
gave Peg a start. The maid never had been one to show her
hurt and had always licked her wounds in private, but
God's me, to put on this brave front when her heart was
surely breaking nigh broke Peg's own heart. She said
gently, "Your Da won't be here until late and your sister's
not back yet from visiting her friends. There's a cold supper waiting whenever you're hungry."

Ayisha saw well that Peg was grieving for her. She

walked over and put her arms about her. "It's all right, Peg, we're going to work it out, Cain and I."

"I hope so. I've been sick with worry. I just don't understand why or how your father could do such a—" She snapped her mouth shut. Nay. Absolutely not. She absolutely would not beg for information not freely given. Her pride forbade it. "Forget I said that."

Seeing her struggle, Ayisha said, "It's not mine to tell, Peg, or I would. It's between Da and Cain—actually Cain's father. It's something that happened ages ago between the two of them and—"

Pegeen held up her hands. "Not another word. It's not my place to pry."

"It's not prying. You're family, and believe me, Da didn't even want Aimee and me to know." She was tempted to confess that she and Cain were going to wed, and by this time tomorrow they'd be on their way to Providence, but she didn't dare. Like Mac, Pegeen was as loyal to Ben Adair as she was to his daughters, and it would only worry her. Aimee was the only one who would know—and Seth. She smiled and said, "Now promise not to worry anymore. Cain and I have a solution. And guess what—I'm hungry right now. Can we eat together?"

The two shared cold chicken, biscuits, and cheese at the kitchen table and Ayisha watched happily as the sparkle came back into Pegeen's eyes. As they chatted easily about all kinds of things, her thoughts held naught but Cain: the love and tenderness on his face when he looked at her . . . their lovemaking . . . the heat burning in his eyes . . . their flight on the morrow . . . its ramifications. Aye, its ramifications.

She wished that she could somehow slip past Mac tomorrow and not involve him, but it was impossible. The stablehands, too, had their watchful eyes on her, not to mention the guard down on the beach. There was naught left but to use Mac's love for her and his desire for her happiness to get him to help her escape. Or maybe she could stir his sympathy somehow. But she hated the thought of doing either.

She dragged her attention back to the kitchen, to the

ticking clock and Pegeen telling her to take more of the sweet that had been made especially for her. She rose, smiling, and pushed her chair back in place. "It's delicious and I love it, but if I eat another bite I'll not be able to climb aboard Willi." She carried her dishes to the sideboard. "When Aimee gets back, will you please tell her I'm in the meadow?"

"I'll tell her. And lass, however you and your young man work this out, I pray to God that He blesses you and puts the wind at your back."

"Thanks. Thanks so much." She gave her an impulsive kiss. "I love you, Peg."

Ayisha searched for Mac while Griffin saddled Willi and found him in his office working on the books. "Do you have a minute?"

Mac smiled seeing her wide, grave eyes and her hair in a thick braid hanging down her back. She was the young Ayisha this eve, winsome, shy, and about to ask him a favor she did not expect to get. "For you, I'll make a minute, lass. What is it?"

Ayisha could not meet his eyes. She sat on a straight chair and looked at a spot on the wall beside his right shoulder. "Ah, Cain and I were wondering if . . . maybe you would leave us alone tomorrow. On the isle, that is." She added hastily, "It's just that it's so small and we—" She hated lying to him. She really hated it. The words were sticking in her throat.

"—you feel a lack of privacy," Mac offered. He nodded. "I understand."

Ayisha stared at him. "You do?"

"Of course. It's a very small isle." Her pink face and nervous hands told him she was hiding something. The lass was no more capable of deception than a babe.

"You mean you'd actually go off for a bit?"

Mac smiled. "It seems a small enough thing, leaving two lovers alone for a while."

It shattered her. Because of her, he had turned his back on both his conscience and his loyalty to a man who was like a father to him. In return she was planning to betray him. In her eagerness to be with Cain, she was ignoring completely the fate that would await him if she fled while she was under his protection: facing her father with what had happened, losing Da's trust and respect and probably his job. She couldn't do it. She could do no less than tell him the truth and let it be his choice whether or not to help her. She got to her feet.

Mac, too, stood. He tossed down his quill. "I see something's afoot. Should I be worried?"

Ayisha's heart was flying. "I fear it's not a small matter."

Mac sat on the edge of his desk, stretched out his long legs in front of him, and crossed his arms. "Am I to hear it?"

"Aye." She told herself not to dally but to get it over with immediately. She said, "Cain and I hope to wed tomorrow. We need your help, Mac."

Mac studied her face. Her mouth was well controlled, but her breathing was quick and shallow as if she were fleeing even now. He asked easily, "That's why you wanted to be alone with Cain? So you could elude me?"

She gave him an embarrassed grin. "It was a thought, but you know I'd never have gone through with it. I wouldn't do that to you." She yearned to say something, anything to encourage him to help them, but nay, it had to be his decision and his alone. She tightened her lips.

"Nor would I turn my back on you, lass," Mac replied quietly. "I'm for you, you and Cain. I'm sorry I didn't make it clear sooner. I'll help in any way I can."

Ayisha's mouth dropped open. "You mean it?"

He grinned and gave her a quick hug. "I'll do anything you ask, girl, never fear. I like your Cain Banning. There's none other I'd rather see you go to."

"Oh, Mac, I can't believe this! I sort of thought you'd come to like him a bit, but this . . ." She was both weeping and laughing she was so happy and relieved. "This is wonderful, except what will you say to Da?"

"The same thing I'm saying to you. I think he's wrong.

I trust and respect Cain and I haven't any doubt he's the man for you."

"Da will be furious with you . . ."

"Aye."

She had always loved Mac Fitzgerald, but never more than she did at that moment. She caught his strong shoulder and gripped it. "What can I say—except I'm more grateful than you'll ever know."

"For a start, you can tell me what this is all about."

She sighed. "It's a shocker . . ."

"Let's hear it."

Sitting cross legged on the rug and telling him the tale, Ayisha marveled at how little time and breath it took to tell a story that held so much tragedy and had hurt so many lives. "And so Da, when he looks at Cain," she concluded, "sees naught but Tom Gregg—the way he looked and the awful things he did. He's convinced Cain is just like him because he's a Gregg. He says his blood is tainted and that bad blood will out."

Mac gave a snort. "Don't believe that old wives' tale for a minute. It's codswallop. Over and over I've seen colts and fillies that were ten, twenty times the horse their sire or dam was. Don't believe it."

"I don't. Not I!" She was laughing of a sudden. "You're wonderful, Mac, and I only wish Da saw things the way you do."

"He'll come to his senses eventually, I promise you. There was never a fairer man walked this earth than Ben Adair."

"Or MacKenzie Fitzgerald." She rumpled his dark hair as she had so many times. "A thousand thanks, Mac."

"There's none needed." He gave her braid a brotherly tug. "Now get moving. Willi's tacked and ready to go. I heard Griffin calling you five minutes ago."

Ayisha was at peace as she and Willi headed for the meadow in the cool of evening. A flock of bobolinks, feasting on ripening elderberries and wild blackberries, rose as they neared the riding circle, and she smiled, thinking how

beautiful they were, and how amazing and wonderful it was
that everyone was happy for her and Cain and could see
what kind of man he was. And soon, very soon her father
was going to be touched by Mac's common sense. She felt
it in her bones. She rubbed Willi's neck and neatened his
mane.

"What a wonderful night it is, Willi. Do you feel it?"
When he pricked his ears and tossed his handsome head,
she melted with her love for him. "You do feel it, I can
tell. You know this night is special." She lowered her
voice. "And the reason it's special is that tomorrow Cain
and I are going to wed, and you're going to be with us,
wherever we live. It's a promise. You're going to be right
with us, and Cain is going to do wonderful things with
you, old love. He's going to help you soar again . . ."

Taking him from a walk to a trot, she noted instantly
how very relaxed and supple he was and how he responded immediately to the slightest pressure of her legs
and hands. Around and around the ring they rode as a
golden moon rose in the dusky sky and the night insects
began their chirping and humming. She saw that Mac had
walked up from the stable and was watching them from a
distance. Suddenly she sensed a new confidence in Willi.
The movement in his hind legs had improved greatly since
yesterday—his steps were equal with no drag, and he was
lifting his forelegs much higher than in a normal trot and
holding them in suspension longer. A thrill shot through
her as she realized what was happening. He was doing the
passage, a beautiful, effortless, weightless *passage.* Oh,
God, she was floating! They were both floating . . .

Afraid almost to breathe or call out or even wave to
Mac for fear the spell would be broken, she looked over
at him, radiant, eyes glowing. Could he see? Did he understand that at long last she had done everything right and a
miracle was happening? In the fading light, she saw him
smile broadly and clasp his hands over his head in triumph. He knew . . .

Mac's eyes blurred as he watched the maid astride her
great gray stallion on that August eve. She sat unmoving

as a statue on the horse's back, but he knew well it was deceptive. It was Ayisha and Ayisha alone who was communicating to Willi the signals that were propelling him through the elegance of the *passage*—for that was what it was. She had been struggling for days, for hours on end to achieve it, and now here it was. He grinned, gave her a victory signal, and continued to watch happily the magnificent sight. Sweet Jesus, what a lucky day it was when Cain Banning came to this house. He was going to get Ben to recognize the fact or his name was not Mac Fitzgerald. It was a promise.

Seth was ordering an ale and a late supper when Cain entered the Red Lion and spotted him. Seth waved him over. "Sit down, man. Have you eaten yet?"

"Nay. I was hoping I'd find you." Cain sat, gave the barmaid his order, and looked back at his friend, his dark eyes dancing.

Seth grinned. "Man oh man oh man, is it what I think? You and Ayisha are going to tie the knot?"

Cain laughed. "It shows, does it?"

"It's written all over your face, and I'm all for it. Tell me when and where and what I can do to help." The ale was brought just then, and he lifted his tankard high in a salute. "I'm at your service, mate."

Cain touched it with his. "It's appreciated." He took a swallow and lowered his voice, "We're meeting tomorrow on Trilby Isle. I'm not sure how she plans to work it with Mac, but she seems confident. From there we'll sail to the *Sea Eagle* and weigh anchor for Providence. We'll be wed there. I have a friend who's a pastor of a small church in the town."

"Good. That's far better than what I put my own poor lass through. Will she leave a letter for Ben or what?"

"Aye. Aimee will find it and take it to him." Cain scowled into his tankard. "I'm damned if I like it, though. It won't be easy for the maid because Ben's not going to take it well."

"You're not to worry, man. She'll not be alone. I'll be right beside her."

Cain was touched. "You have our thanks."

After studying his mate's grim face, Seth added, "I aim to do more than just stand beside her like a lamppost. It's time Ben knew we're wed—and knows we think he's wrong about you and that we both encouraged you and Ayisha to follow our lead."

Cain gave a soft whistle. "It might not be the wisest course to follow."

"I'll not have it any other way nor will Aimee. It's past time Ben knew."

In silence the two gripped hands, and in silence they ate their meals, each deep in his own thoughts. Afterwards, Cain said, "I'm off. My men have been expecting something like this to happen, and I want to tell them tomorrow's the day."

"Will I see you later?"

"Nay, I'll stay aboard tonight." He grinned. "I suspect they'll break open a keg and we'll do some celebrating. I might as well get my gear now; no sense in coming back for it."

It took but a short time for Cain to gather his belongings and settle his share of the lodging with Seth. He set out on foot then, leaving behind him the rowdy bustle of town as he headed toward where the wharves stretched out endless and silent in the lamp-lit darkness. The solitude suited him. As he left King Street and strode down Long Wharf toward where his vessel was docked, his thoughts were of Ayisha. He smiled, thinking that tomorrow at this time she would be his own wife, his to love and cherish and protect forever. It was such great good fortune he could not always make himself believe it was happening.

Hearing a sound suddenly and seeing movement, his gaze darted to his right. He relaxed. It was only a small lad, a skinny, bedraggled waif he had seen on the docks many times. Wondering for the first time if he had no home of his own, Cain reached into his pocket, found some coins, and approached the boy.

"Son, do me a favor." Cain put the money into the child's grubby hand. "Go and wrap yourself around a good meal."

The boy hesitated and looked at him with suspicious eyes. "What's in it fer ye, mister? What'll ye be wantin' i' return?"

"Naught, son. Only that you go to sleep on a full belly for a change. Run along now. The Red Lion's not far and the grub's good." He had already moved on when the boy called his thanks.

It pleased Cain. The lad seemed a good one, and he reflected briefly that when he returned from Providence, he might take him on as crew. It had been a long while since the *Sea Eagle* had had a cabin boy. It was quickly pushed from his mind as thoughts of Ayisha again overtook him.

He was absorbed in her completely when another faint whisper of sound close behind him, too close, raised the hair on his neck. He spun and drew his knife in one swift motion, but it was too late. Pain exploded inside his head, numbing and blinding him, and then there was naught but blackness.

Aimee entered the front door just as Ayisha was coming from the back of the house. Seeing her flushed face, she whispered, "Pan, you look like a lighted candle!"

Ayisha laughed. "Willi and I did the *passage,* and—" She waited, seeing Pegeen descending the staircase.

"So, Missy, you're home from your visit, are you? Was it a good day? And you, lass, Willi did his steps for you, did he? That's grand." She continued on into the drawing room without waiting for answers.

Aimee's eyes had not left Ayisha. She lowered her voice and said, "You've got far more to talk about than Willi."

Ayisha smiled and put a finger to her lips. "Come upstairs." Together they raced up the curving staircase and down the hall to her bedchamber. Ayisha closed the door behind them, turned and burst out, "We're going to wed tomorrow!"

"Panny!" Aimee clapped a hand over her mouth and her

plump curls quivered with excitement. "It's wonderful! I'm thrilled!" She caught and hugged her sister hard. "I know how much you've both wanted this."

"I wondered if it would ever happen."

"And now it's going to. And you're not to worry about a thing, do you hear? Seth and I want you to go off with light hearts. We've talked about it and decided we'll both break the news to Papa. At the same time, we're going to tell him we're wed and that we encouraged you and Cain."

"I'm speechless." It was a far cry from the note she was going to leave for Aimee to deliver to him.

They sat on Ayisha's bed then talking long and quietly but excitedly until Aimee looked at the clock on the mantelpiece. "My goodness, look at the time—and you have a big day ahead of you. You should be in bed getting your beauty sleep!"

Ayisha yawned. "I guess I am tired. I gave a lot to Willi this eve. We did something we've never done before."

"The *passage?*"

"Aye. I can't explain it but maybe I'll be able to show you some day. Cain's going to be so happy . . ."

"And I'm happy for you, too, and as for tomorrow"— she stood and shook out her shirts—"it's the most perfect thing in the world." She blew Ayisha a kiss from the door. "Sweet dreams now."

"You, too, Aimee, and thanks. For everything."

She donned her nightclothes quickly, stretched out between the cool sheets, and closed her eyes. Despite her excitement, she knew she would sleep well. She was exhausted, and the peaceful mood she had felt in the meadow was still with her. Bed had never felt so good. She was just beginning to feel warm and sleepy when her heart began to pound.

Of a sudden, she was standing on an unfamiliar dock. It was dark, the area was deserted, and she knew she should not be there. She felt danger everywhere. Hearing footsteps, she was ready to flee until she realized the walker was ahead of her, moving away from her. She had barely made out the tall figure of a man when she heard his

hoarse cry and knew he was being set upon. She saw that
there were four or five men and only one of him and they
were beating him! Wanting desperately to help, she tried to
run toward him, tried to call out that she was coming, but
she had no voice, nor would her legs carry her forward.
They seemed weighted with lead. With great effort did she
move—and found herself sitting up in bed, her heart thundering.

She looked about at the familiar, comfortable surround-
ings, shadowy in the light of the banked fire, and told
herself to calm down, she had been dreaming, it was
naught but a dream. But the memory lingered on and on,
filling her with such a feeling of fear that it was a long
time before she finally fell asleep.

Chapter 26

When Cain awakened, his head was throbbing with pain and the memory of how he had acquired it. He had been blackjacked. He'd been walking toward his ship, he'd heard a noise behind him and he had known—dammit, he'd known even as he seized his knife and turned that he was in bad trouble. It had been near midnight as he walked along the deserted wharf toward his vessel, and he should have been filled with caution. Instead he was dreaming of Ayisha. It had cost him dearly, for now he was in the hold of a cargo ship bound for God only knows where. He tried to climb to his feet but an explosion inside of his head sent him reeling back to the damp planking.

"Save yer strength, mate," a gruff voice said from close by. "Ye're dinna goin' nowhere. None o' us are. We've been pressed."

In the feeble light filtering through a grating high over his head, Cain saw the speaker. He sat hunched on a box, a big, raw-boned seaman, and his pale blue eyes showed his rage at the fate that had befallen him. Cain counted four more men, all of them seamen and like the first, all large and muscular. He asked softly, "What vessel is this?"

"We don't know," growled a sandy-haired giant, "but this I do know, whoever owns this damned bucket is a dead man. He walks now, but he's dead."

"We was all blackjacked," muttered a youngster from

320

the British Navy. "I was on me way t' join me mates drinkin' an' now they'll think I jumped ship."

"How long have I been here?" Cain showed no sign of the pain that was nigh blinding him.

"Hours," said an older man with swarthy skin and sharp brown eyes. "Ye were oot cold, same as the rest o' us, when they brought ye aboard. They lowered ye wi' a rope wrapped around yer middle."

"And how long have we been at sea?"

"Since dawn," the first man replied. "Nigh onto two hours."

Cain rested his elbows on his bent knees and sank his aching head in his hands. God's death. Ayisha and Mac would be on their way to Trilby Isle now and she would be all starry eyed and pink cheeked and excited, and he would not be there waiting for her. She would be surprised, aye, but not worried, not until several hours had passed and he still did not come—and then she was going to think he was like his father after all. She would fight the thought, but in the end, she would decide he had deceived her on all counts and given in to his damned wanderlust. He groaned softly in pain and desperation. Moments later, a strong hand grasped his shoulder.

"Get this in ye, man." The dark-eyed man held out a tin cup filled with water. "Ye'll feel better."

Ayisha was disappointed but not concerned when Cain was not waiting to greet her. Mac agreed there were any number of reasons why he might have been delayed. As they walked to the landward side to keep watch, his questions kept her chattering happily and kept her thoughts occupied. They would be wed in Providence and be gone ten days . . . he had a friend there who was a pastor . . . nay, she was not taking anything with her, not even a comb . . . Cain would buy everything she needed when they got there, and they might sail to Nova Scotia—she had never been there . . .

Her eyes scanned the sun-sparkled sea constantly for a speck of canvas, and as time crawled forward and none appeared, her stomach grew smaller and tighter. She said finally, her voice small with fear, "Could something have happened to him, Mac?"

The position of the sun told Mac that approximately one hour had passed and he was concerned. He did not lie to her. "I don't know, lass. It's damned odd he's not come yet."

Ayisha told herself she was being silly. Cain was a grown man who could well take care of himself. He was perfectly safe and any moment now she would see his sail, and then they would be flying through the blue spray toward the *Sea Eagle* and their life together. But reality caught and held her. Something was wrong. She knew it was. Just as Cain seemed always to sense when she was in danger and come to her, so did she sense that he was in danger now. He was in terrible danger.

With the sun shining down on her, she shivered and wondered if the very strange dream she'd had last night had been a warning of some sort. A premonition. The man on the dock . . . his being attacked . . . her trying so desperately to reach him. Eyes still scanning the sea, she began to tremble. "Mac, I'm frightened. Something's wrong, I feel it."

Mac gave her a quick, penetrating look. "I do, too." He caught her hand. "Come on, let's get a move on. This is a waste of time. Let's get back to shore and then I'll head for town to see what I can learn."

"I want to go along! Let's go direct from here."

"You're not thinking, lass. If we aren't back at Sea Cliff in a reasonable time, they'll think we had an accident. It's best we leave from home."

She nodded glumly knowing he was right, and worried, wondered where on earth they would begin to look for Cain. She hadn't a clue. She nearly died of frustration when the wind changed and they had to tack all the way back. At the stable Griffin had a message that frustrated her further. "Ye're t' go straight t' th' house, Miss. Yer father's jist come home an' left word."

"Thanks, Griffin." She dismounted, her body filled with trembling, and murmured to Mac, "I'll find out what this is about and be right back. Wait for me."

"Never fear." He yearned to leave then and there, alone, but he knew better.

At the house, Ayisha was surprised when Soames opened the front door for her. "They're all waiting for you, Miss."

Baffled, she followed him into the drawing room, a large, rectangular chamber with rich-hued rugs from Persia on the polished floorboards and gilt-framed oils mounted on the ivory-colored walls. She held her breath as he closed the double doors behind her, leaving the four of them alone—herself, Aimee, Seth, and her father. When Aimee and Seth gazed at her in astonishment, she realized they were shocked at seeing her. Her father's face was so grim, she wondered fearfully if someone had died. Cain? Oh, God, please, nay—not Cain. Please . . .

"Da, what—is it?"

Ben came forward and wrapped his arms around her. "Darlin', darlin', thank God."

She knew terror. "Is it Cain?" She dreaded to know but she had to. Whatever it was, she had to know.

"Oh, aye. It's Cain, all right."

"He's alive?" Please please please, God. If she never asked for another thing, let this be it. Let him be alive.

Ben growled, "Of course he's alive—"

Ayisha sagged in his arms, her relief and joy so great she could not speak.

"—and every bit as treacherous as I suspected he was." He hugged her hard and planted a fierce kiss on the top of her head. "I just thank God you're here. I thought he might have taken you with him despite what he said." He was shaking like a ship's timbers in a full gale. "The damned gall of the bastard. But then I knew, I knew— he's a Gregg, after all."

Taken her? Despite what he said? Ayisha darted a frantic, questioning look at Aimee and Seth. They shook their heads, as baffled as she. She stepped back from her father's arms and steeled herself. "What's this about? What's happened to Cain?"

Seeing her fright, Ben ordered himself to calm down; he was behaving like an enraged bull. He said, as gently as he was able, "I got a letter this morn. It's what I've feared all this while." He retrieved it from his desk and carried it to his chair by the hearth. "Know, lass"—he looked up at Ayisha sadly—"that if I had the choice, I'd face all the terrors of hell rather than let you hear what this says. But I haven't the choice."

"God's blood, man, read it!" Seth growled.

Ben sat himself down and held the paper close to the candle on the stand. His hand shook so that the letters were a blur. He held it out to Seth. "Would you? My eyes . . ." He covered them with his hand so he could not see Ayisha's stricken face.

Scowling, Seth carried the missive to the window and glanced over it hastily. He snorted. "This is ridiculous. Cain didn't write this."

Ben shot him a look of skepticism. "Who else, pray? Who else would have known such—"

"I can't stand this!" Ayisha cried. "What does it say?"

"I'll read it," Seth said stiffly, "but believe me, Cain didn't write it. This isn't him." He cleared his throat and sped through it rapidly:

Let justice be done you thieving bastard. I want my father's share of the jewelry you took that night you jumped ship with Ana. Put it in a metal cask, wrap it in oilskin, and leave it in the cave on the eastern shore of Kedrow Island before three days have passed. You are being watched. No tricks or traps or the Crown will learn where Ben Scott has been hiding these many years. Tell Ayisha I'm sorry.

Seth looked across the room at her and saw her golden eyes blazing in her white face. Dammit to Hell. What was all of this? And where was Cain? He made an explosive sound. "Cain didn't write this!"

Ben raked his fingers through his hair. "It's no more and no less than I expected. I don't suppose you could talk sense into him."

Seth tossed the letter onto the desk. "Man, I'm telling you, and I'll tell you a hundred times more if I have to, Cain didn't write that anymore than I did. For sure he wouldn't have used block letters. He'd have written it in his own hand and signed his name." His anger was mounting and at the center of it was Jeremy Greydon. He could not think of another blessed soul other than Greydon who hated Cain enough to pull such a bloody, rotten trick on him. And if Greydon had sent the message, it meant he was holding Cain. The thought turned his blood to ice. How could he tell Ayisha?

Aimee went to her husband's side and clung to his arm. "If Seth says Cain didn't do it, Papa, you'd best believe it. Cain would never hurt Ayisha that way."

Listening to the terrible message, Ayisha's faith had faltered, but only for the space of an eyeblink. Even so, it infuriated her to have weakened for even that small amount of time. She had promised Cain she would never doubt him again, nor would she. Not ever again. She said angrily, "They're right. Cain didn't send that letter." She saw suddenly, in a far corner of her mind, the faintest glimmer of what must have happened. It was as though a candle had been lit . . .

"Only three of us knew the story, lass. What else am I to think?"

Ayisha shook her head stubbornly. "He didn't send it, I promise you." She had gone from hopeless bewilderment and fright, from not knowing what to think or where to start looking for the perpetrator of this vile deed, to knowing suddenly, beyond any doubt, who the culprit was. And it frightened her more than ever. It was Jeremy—Jeremy who hated Cain enough to want him dead . . . Jeremy who wanted her for himself . . . Jeremy who had said she was going to be his . . .

He had learned about Tom Gregg, now it was clear he had learned from the same source about her father's partnership with him and its ugly aftermath. That had to be it. He had written that disgusting letter knowing Cain could not defend himself because, oh, God, because he was holding him captive somewhere. Thinking of it, her knees shook. In truth, her entire body was shaking.

"Darlin', darlin'," Ben muttered, "it fair kills me to see you hurting so."

She was hurting, aye, and more frightened than she had ever been in her life. But now she had a direction to take and plans to make. She was ready for battle. She knelt by his chair and took his hand. "Da, listen to me—I know now who wrote that letter. It's someone who hates Cain and has threatened to destroy him. I'm certain of it."

Seth stopped his pacing and looked at her in open admiration. "Greydon," he said softly. "Good lass. It's my own thinking. I was wondering how to tell you."

Aimee's mouth fell open. "My goodness, of course! Jeremy wrote it! But how—"

Ben scowled at the three of them. "This talk is libelous. You're not to say it outside of this house, do you hear? That devil would haul us all into court. And why in the name of all that's holy would you think Greydon was involved in any way?"

"Cain beat him, Papa, when he—" Aimee hesitated and blinked her brown eyes at Ayisha.

Seth added brusquely, "He took liberties with Ayisha and Cain taught the boor some manners."

Ben's face had grown red. "Why wasn't I told of this?"

Ayisha said gently, "Because Cain took care of it then and there and I didn't want to worry you. I was afraid you'd damage Jeremy and end up in jail."

"You're right, I would've." He stroked her soft cheek. "He took liberties, you say? And Cain handled it?"

"Aye. He was furious. But then Jeremy drew a knife, and Cain disarmed him and gave him a terrible thrashing. And then Jeremy threatened to get even with us both."

Ben looked thoughtful. "Thrashed him, eh?"

Ayisha did not allow herself to smile at the wistful look in his eyes. She nodded gravely. "A beautiful thrashing."

Aimee added excitedly, "And Cain made him walk to the bottom of the hill to wait for his horse. But he forgot all about him, and Jeremy trudged back up and got it, the horse, and that was when he tried to run Seth and me down and—"

"What? He tried to run you down?"

"Aye. And he slashed at us with his whip a—and Pan was all black and blue and her shirt was torn a—and everything."

Ben breathed hard. "I'll kill him!"

Ayisha shook her head and lay it against his knee. She said softly, "Nay, Da, I don't want you to kill him. That's exactly why I didn't tell you. But I'm telling you now because I want you to see what kind of man he is and why he'd want revenge against Cain. He's jealous and envious of him, he hates him, and he was humiliated by him." She took his hand again and cupped it in hers. "There's something else you should know—about Jeremy." She saw him gritting his teeth.

"Let's hear it."

"He came to me two mornings ago and said he knew about Tom Gregg. He said you'd never let me wed a man whose father was a criminal—and that *he* would wed me instead."

"The devil he did." His heart thumped harder.

Seth said, "He came to me later the same morn asking if I knew my mate was the son of a murderer and a pirate."

Ben drew a deep breath. "And what did you say?"

"I threw him out. That was when I came to you and confessed. I wanted to tell you who we were before he got to you."

Ayisha held her breath, hoping against hope that Seth would not choose this moment to tell him that he and Aimee were wed. She relaxed when his gray eyes met hers and said nay, lass, not now. Now was not the time.

"He never came," Ben murmured. "I've seen neither hide nor hair of the devil."

Seth said tersely, "I think he came when I was there Thursday—in your office. You'll remember I heard a noise." He saw a flicker of panic in the older man's eyes.

"You said you saw naught unusual—that it must have been a noise in the street."

"That's what I thought, aye, but I fear he was there and overheard us and left before I looked."

"My God . . ."

Ayisha was alarmed when he looked so old and tired of a sudden. "Da! Are you all right?"

Ben patted her hand and wondered if there was no end to the misfortune befalling them. He muttered, "This isn't the best news, lass." How ironic that even if Cain Gregg were as innocent of this blackmail attempt as a newborn lamb, he now had Greydon to contend with. His darlings were in water as deep and dangerous as ever, and all because of his own damned past. To think that he, who loved them beyond all telling, could be the cause of such terrible heartache for them.

Aimee knelt on the floor beside Ayisha. "Papa, I'm worried about you. I think you should lie down."

"I—think you're right, my precious." As he got to his feet, he knew he could not travel as far as his bedchamber. Remembering well that he had seen his own wraith, he wondered if he had reached the end of his days. He moved heavily to the settee. "I'll just stretch out here for a bit."

Ayisha settled several small pillows under his head, and Aimee hurriedly fetched a coverlet. "Papa, would you like for Soames to bring you some tea?"

Ben made a face and felt his heart leaping wildly against his ribs. "No tea. Seth, pour me a tot of rum. In fact, bring me the bottle . . ."

Seth obeyed and watched, relieved, as Ben tossed it down. He had been worried about the old boy there for a minute but he was going to be fine, just fine. He pulled a straight chair close to the settee and sat down. The girls continued to kneel on the floor by their father's side, their anxious hands stroking him.

Seth leaned forward, elbows on his knees. "Sir," he said low, "what do you intend to do about the letter?"

Ben yawned, felt himself relaxing. The rum was moving through his bloodstream and having his feet up made a world of difference. He managed a half smile. "He seems to have me over a barrel, whoever he is."

"As God is my witness, it's not Cain. It's got to be Greydon—which means he's holding Cain." He gripped Ayisha's shoulder and gave her a look of compassion. "I'm sorry, lass. There's no other way he could work it."

Ayisha whispered, "I know." She clenched her jaws so her teeth would not chatter.

Aimee's eyes were teary. "I don't understand. Is he stupid? Didn't he know we'd surely see through such a trick as this?"

Seth said, "I imagine he felt he had to act swiftly—and hope that naught would go wrong."

"Something did," Ayisha said quietly. "He badly underestimated our trust and faith in Cain." Seeing that her father had already drifted off to sleep, she went on, "Mac and I waited an hour for him on the isle. He's concerned."

Seth got to his feet. "Well, I'll not waste another minute. I'm off to town. Try not to fret, lass. I'll get to the bottom of this thing, I promise you. I'll see if Mac wants to join me."

Ayisha said quickly, "Nay, Seth, he's waiting for me. We'll be going in together."

Aimee gaped at her. "What do you mean, you'll be going in together?"

"I can't sit here worrying if I can help look for him."

"Oh, Panny!"

Ayisha took her hand. "It's all right. Naught will happen to me, Mac will see to it. Go on ahead, Seth. We'll be along soon. I want to make absolutely sure Da's feeling better. He frightened me, the way he looked."

"What do you think?" Aimee asked Seth. "Will he be all right? He acted so ill there for a bit."

"He seems fine now." Seth looked at his father-in-law with affection. "We caught the old boy off guard and he was hit hard from all sides." He nodded. "Aye, I'd say he's fine and you shouldn't worry. He's got good color and his breathing's steady." He caught Aimee into his arms and gave her a great hungry kiss. "That'll have to do for now, my little muffin. I'm off." The girls followed him to the front door.

"Do be careful, sweetheart."

Seth loved his young wife with his eyes. "I will, lass, I will. Ayisha, I'll go to the *Sea Eagle* the first thing and enlist Cain's crew to spread out and look for him. I'll ride on to the Banning Yards next and see if anyone there knows anything."

"Thank you." Ayisha was grateful for his generous support. "Cain and I both thank you."

Seth gripped her hand. "Thank me after he's found, lass—and he will be found."

Ayisha nodded. "Aye."

After his departure, the two sisters walked back to the drawing room and stood gazing down at their sleeping father. Ben opened one eye, then the other. He scowled up at them. "You're still here?"

"Are you all right, Papa?"

"I'd be far better if I could sleep in peace without my womenfolk fussing over me and listening to me snore— but aye, I'm all right."

It was true. There for awhile he thought he'd reached the end of his rope, but now he felt good—as good as he'd ever felt, and he was heartened. As much as he yearned to see his darling again, he first wanted the lives of his girls to be in order, and he saw now that he had been too hard on young Gregg. Young Banning. For a fact, he'd not want his daughters judged by the way he'd lived his own life. His course was clear. He was an old dog, but not too old to learn some new tricks.

"Pandora ..."

"Aye, Da?" She smiled, knowing it was a good sign when he called her that. She knelt again, her arm across his chest.

Ben lay his hand on her hair and thought how beautiful it was, how like Ana's, a rich red-brown filled with sun and flame and life itself. He said low, "Young Banning ... you still love him, eh?"

Ayisha's heart went faster, seeing the warmth in his eyes, but she kept her voice easy. "Aye, Da. More than ever, and he still loves me. He's a good man, I promise you."

Ben nodded. "I see it now. I've been stiff and bull-headed and stubborn as an old ass and I was all wrong. You should have him, lass. I should have trusted my first instincts. I liked him, you know. When I first saw him, I thought, now why in hell couldn't my girls bring home someone like this, a real man, instead of that damned hound Greydon?"

Her laughter rang out. "You're making me so happy, Daddy." She lifted his hand to her cheek and held it there.

"It's long overdue, and I'm sorry, girl. I'm sorry."

"It's all right. I understand."

Ben frowned. "Where's Seth?"

"He's on his way to town to look for Cain." She tried to quell the sudden sick feeling in her stomach that dampened her joy. "He's going to have Cain's crew look for him and he'll check the Banning Yards himself."

Ben nodded. "He's a good man, Jonathan's son." He closed his eyes.

"Papa! Are you all right?" Aimee cried.

Ben chuckled. "Aye, kitten, stop your mothering.

Since I'm not needed this minute, I'm going to have another tot and a bit of sleep. Tell Soames if he values his life he'll not let anyone in here 'till noon." He yawned and reached for the rum. "Run along now, both of you."

They obeyed, and after Aimee closed the door behind them she followed Ayisha outside. "Can you believe it, the way he's changed? It's the best news in the world!"

"Aye, but I haven't the time to enjoy it. I must go. Mac will be anxious. I know I am."

"You really meant it then? You're going to look for Cain?"

Ayisha said quietly, "Would you look for Seth?"

Put that way, there was only one answer. Aimee tried to smile. "Aye. A million times aye."

"I thought so. Now promise you'll not worry if we don't come back right away. It may take awhile." When Aimee nodded and twisted her fingers together, Ayisha continued calmly, "It may even take several days."

"Pan!"

"It's so. Just remember, I'll be with Seth and Mac and we'll all be fine—and we'll certainly let you know if we won't be returning today."

"Oh, God . . ."

Ayisha smiled and kissed her cheek. "That's a good start—pray for us."

Seeing Mac coming on his mount and leading hers, she went to meet him, tucking her braid beneath her old blue workshirt as she went. She donned the jacket and the old cap he gave her, pulled the cap well down over her forehead, and smeared some dirt over her face. As she swiftly mounted Omar, she saw that Aimee's mouth had fallen open. She laughed. "How do I look?"

Aimee shook her head. "You're unbelievable . . ."

Ayisha's eyes and mouth lost their laughter. "Nay, not unbelievable, just empty. Empty and lonely. I want Cain back." She raised her arm. "Good-bye . . ."

Aimee cried, "Good-bye. You'll have him back, I know

you will. You'll bring him home safely and we'll have our double wedding after all!" She held back her tears until they were out of sight and the thunder of hoofbeats grew faint and was no more.

Chapter 27

They rode side by side, swiftly and in silence, the intent dark man and his slender companion. Not until they neared the city did Ayisha raise her voice to be heard above the hoofbeats. "I hope you have some idea as to where to start looking. I—can't think, I'm so frightened."

Mac said, "Don't be, we'll find him. How about starting with the Greydon stores?"

She shrugged. "They're as good a place as any." There were five of them scattered about the city, that she recalled. The India Store, Greydon Far East, and three others whose names she could not remember. "We could ask if Jeremy is around—and if any of their merchant ships is about to sail." She shook her head. "Nay, I can't bear thinking he might've been pressed." When Mac remained silent, she added firmly, "Jeremy wouldn't dare. That's a criminal act." But then so was blackmail and abduction.

As they approached Greydon Far East on Water Street, she had convinced herself that Cain was not at sea but was being held in one of the Greydon warehouses or even in Jeremy's home. They simply had to ferret out which warehouse and learn where he lived. She regretted now that she had never been interested enough to ask him.

But the shopkeeper at the Far East offered them naught but icy formality. The sailing information the gentlemen required could be gotten only at the central business office which was closed until Monday morning. Likewise the three warehouses were closed; only the shops were open.

Mr. Jeremy Greydon was rarely there and certainly not on a Saturday. His home address was unavailable.

"The damned stuffy little bastard," Mac muttered as they headed for the Greydon Europa on Crooked Lane.

"And the way he stared at me—" Ayisha knew if she giggled, her laughter would turn to tears. "Do you think he suspected?"

"Nay. He probably thought we were brothers and I should've made you scrub your grimy face before letting you inside his fancy store."

They met with the same frosty reception at the Greydon Europa and the Brasilia. At the India Store near Long Wharf, the clerk, in high dudgeon, said that theirs was the seventh inquiry he'd had about the exact same thing that day. It was a pity some people had naught better to do than pester folk who had to work for their living.

Seeing Ayisha's despair as they left the store, Mac said to her gently, "Now, lass, it's too early to give up. Cain's men are scouting this ground better than we can so let's go on to the Red Lion and some other pubs and sniff around a bit. Someone's sure to know where Greydon lives."

"Aye. Surely someone knows." As they walked toward their tethered horses, she ordered herself to hold on, not to give up hope for an instant. She must keep her faith and courage burning bright, for to do anything less would be to let Cain down.

She had already mounted Omar when a clear, young voice called, "Gents . . ."

Mac turned. It was a young lad, a thin, dirty-faced scamp in ragged clothing, but his bright blue eyes were keen and filled with intelligence. "Aye, lad, what is it?"

"Be ye lookin' fer someone, gents?"

"Aye, son." Mac liked the looks of him and walked over to him. "A man, a good friend of ours, has disappeared, and we're very concerned about him." Noting the narrowing of the boy's sharp eyes, he said, "His vessel's docked on the far end of T Wharf. He may or may not have come this way last night or early this morn. We just don't know. He's a big fellow, a bit taller than I am—"

Ayisha dismounted and joined them. She added, pitching her voice low. "His hair's a bright chestnut color and his eyes are dark blue. And he has a kind face." A kind beautiful face, she wanted to cry.

The boy thought a moment and then replied, "Mebbe I seen him."

Mac smothered his excitement. "Tell us about it."

"It were last eve at dusk so's I don't know much what his colors was—'cepting he wasn't dark-dark. He din't have brown or black hair, that I'd'a seen. An' I don't know if 'is face was kind, but *he* was kind. He was smilin' an' seemed ter like me—an' he were a gent fer sure. An' he were big." He squinted up at Mac. "Bigger'n you an' he was headed down Long Wharf t'ward T Wharf. An' he was happy like. A-whistlin' he was."

Happy, Ayisha thought—and a-whistling. Cain would have been happy. She asked, her heart in her throat, "What do you mean, he was kind?"

"He gi' me coins, he did, an' he din't want naught in return. He told me ter go t' th' Red Lion an' wrap mesel' aroun' a good meal an' sleep on a full belly which I did." He nodded. "He were a kind gent, he were, an' I hope naught bad has happint ter 'im."

All of Mac's senses were alerted. He said carefully, "You seem a good, bright lad, son, and you've helped us a lot. I guess there's not much happening hereabouts that you don't see or know. What's your name?"

"Jack Lace, sir, an' s'true. I knows most o' what goes on around these here docks."

Mac forced himself to go slow, not frighten the lad with his growing elation. He asked easily, "Do you know Mr. Greydon then, the one with the trading stores?"

Jack Lace snorted. "Ol' hoity-toity? Oh, aye, I knows 'im. An' th' stores ain't his, mister. They're 'is ol' man's. He figgers he'll be a ol' man hisself afore th' ol' bugger kicks th' bucket. It makes 'im downright ugly, it does."

Ayisha met Mac's eyes in shared astonishment. She asked, "Do you know where he lives then, young Mr. Greydon?"

"O' course. I c'd take yer right ter 'is doorstep if ye wants, 'ceptin' ye'll nay find 'im there. He's left."

"How do you know?"

"I seen 'im w' me own eyes. Th' *Red Lady* makes a reg'lar run t' Cubee ev'ry month, an' they weighed anchor this morn at sunup."

"To Cuba?"

"Cubee, aye."

Seeing Jack Lace's young face turn thoughtful, Mac asked quickly, "What is it, lad?"

"All these questions about yer friend an' ol' hoity-toity—an' ye said ye were concerned about 'im . . ."

"His name is Cain," Ayisha said. "Cain Banning."

Jack frowned. "Are ye thinkin' he's in danger, this Cain?"

Mac said, "We fear very much that he's met with foul play."

Jack pondered it. "Why would ye think that?"

Ayisha had taken a liking to the boy, and more than that, she sensed strongly now that it was Cain who had befriended him last eve. She sensed, too, that Jack Lace was not telling them everything he might. She continued in her low boyish voice, "It's easy to see you're a warmhearted lad, Jack Lace, so we're going to tell you something we'd not ordinarily tell a stranger." When the boy's eyes widened, she crossed her fingers for luck, looked over each shoulder, and said in a low voice, "We think Mr. Greydon might have harmed Cain. He hates him."

Jack blinked. "Wot? A kindly gent like Cain?"

"It's so," Mac said. "We think he might be holding him somewhere."

"Gor!"

Seeing the boy's genuine distress, Ayisha pushed ahead. "Is there anything more you can remember about last night?"

Mac reached in his pocket as Jack Lace hesitated. He withdrew two silver coins. "We'll gladly pay for your help, son."

The boy gave him a look of contempt. "Put yer money

away, mister. Cain's me friend now an' I wisht I could tell ye what happint ter him but I can't—'ceptin' maybe ye sh'd know ol' hoity-toity sometimes takes more'n cotton an' hardware an' crockery ter Cubee, if yer knows what I mean."

Ayisha stepped closer and tried to fight off the fear settling over her like fog. She said, "I don't think we do. Please tell us what you mean."

Jack Lace scowled and reflected on it. "Like you, it ain't what I normally tells strangers. But then seein' as ye're friends o' Cain . . ." He fidgeted, scratched an itch, stared about to make sure they were alone, and then said in a whisper, "Oncet I seen Greydon's crew carryin' some men aboard, an' I said ter meself, them fellers is knocked out, I said, an' them's bein' pressed. I never knowed fer sure as I din't hang aroun' long enough t' ask. I knowed sure as hell I'd be kilt on th' spot er pressed mesel'. His crew's a nasty bunch o' drunks an' layabouts."

"When was this?" Mac asked.

"Two, three months ago." Jack shivered, remembering. "I was scared t' tell anybody what I seen so I jist kep' me mouth shut. Now I stays far away fr'm the *Red Lady* nights—an' most other times, too." Seeing their solemn faces, he added, still in a whisper, "It wun't s'prise me none, gents, if he carries a cargo o' pressed men each trip t' Cubee. It's what I thought then and what I think now." He shook his head. "Gor. D'ye think they clobbered Cain an' hauled 'im aboard?"

At the thought, Ayisha felt her world falling apart. But at the same time, it made her more fiercely determined to get Cain back. She replied quietly, "I hope they didn't, but we have to assume they did."

"Hell. An' me stuffin' me ugly face at th' Red Lion at th' same time like as not. Gor!"

"You don't know that, lad." Mac gripped the boy's grimy hand and slapped two coins into it. "You've been a tremendous help, and we thank you."

"I don't want yer money, mister!"

"Keep it. It would please Cain." As he and Ayisha

swung into their saddles, he muttered, "Lass, we haven't a moment to lose."

"The *Sea Eagle?*"

"Aye. I doubt anyone's aboard her, but we've got to be sure."

Her tears stung Ayisha's eyes as they galloped toward T Wharf, but she didn't allow them to fall. She was too outraged, too furious to weep. She hissed, "I could slay him! I could absolutely wring his wretched neck!"

Mac growled, "If he's forcing men into indenture or impressment, you'll have to stand in line. I could kill him myself, but we haven't time to dwell on it. We have to decide what to do if no one's on the *Eagle* to sail her. Is Seth's vessel in port?"

"Nay, and the only one of Da's ships that's in town is the *Ayisha,* and she's probably being repaired and refitted." She looked at him wildly. "Why is everything conspiring so against us?" She wanted to shriek at the unfairness of it.

"Hang on, lassie, hang on. It's early days."

His dark eyes were filled with such calm and confidence it gave her heart. She reddened. "I know. I'm sorry. I'm all right." When they arrived at the *Sea Eagle,* she recognized the young seaman who appeared at the rail. She shouted up to him, "We're friends of your captain, Dikon. I came aboard with him the other eve." When he frowned and then stared at her with dawning recognition, she hurried on, "We think we know where Cain is and we need a ship to go after him. How many of your crew are aboard?"

"Gawd, mistress, not enough t' put t' sea. Not near enough—an' I dinna know when the others'll be back. They swore they was goin' to search till they found 'im."

Ayisha nodded. It was what they had expected. She met Mac's eyes. "It's the *Ayisha* then, and if she's not ready to sail, they'll get her ready." She called to Dikon, "When Seth comes back, tell him we've taken the *Ayisha,* we're headed for Cuba, and we're not sure when we'll get back. Ask him to please get the message to my father and say he's not to worry." She gave him a wave as he stood gap-

ing at her and said to Mac, "Come on, she's not far from
here." But as they rode toward Oliver Dock, she was uneasy. "I've just realized—the crew mightn't want to go
along with this."

Mac shot her a look. "That's true. They might argue that
we could force a boarding and not find him—and then
what?"

"He's aboard, I know he is! Jeremy took him. I feel it
in my heart."

Mac said grimly, "It's in my bones that I feel it. Aye,
he's there, all right. The devil has him." And they'd soon
know if they had a ship to go after him for they had
reached their destination.

The *Ayisha*'s crew, seeing the arrival of their vessel's
young namesake, stopped what they were doing, greeted
her, and clustered about her eagerly. But a hush fell as
they marked her white face and saw her go wordlessly into
the open arms of their captain.

Owen Connor took off her grimy boy's cap, tilted her
chin, and said tersely, "Has aught happened to Ben Adair,
girl?" He had watched her grow from child to woman and
never had he seen her look so.

"Nay, Owen. It's my intended."

His reddish brows met over his nose, a grand beak that
dominated his stern face and blue eyes. "So. Ye ha a mon
now. Is he ill then?"

The warmth and deep distress in his eyes and in those
of the crew so touched her that Ayisha could not answer.
Mac spoke for her.

"Not so much ill as disappeared, Owen." He had known
the grizzled old Scotsman longer than he had known Ayisha.
"We think the owner of the *Red Lady* might know something
of the circumstances. Ayisha is very anxious to question him
but it seems he sailed for Cuba at dawn."

"The *Red Lady?* That would be Greydon then."

"Aye, Greydon," Ayisha snapped. She had regained
command of herself and her voice. "Owen, he's pressed
Cain, Cain Banning, we're almost certain of it, and we
need a ship to go after him."

Owen's answer came instantly. "Lass, this vessel is yours, these men are yours—right, men?"—their voices rose in one angry swell of assent—"an' this auld mon is yours. We're all yours to command."

Ayisha felt a telltale tingling behind her eyes but held herself on a tight rein. She stood taller. "You would do that for me, all of you?"

Owen beamed as the air rang with whistles and shouts and a grand chorus of ayes. "There's your answer, lass. She's yer ship, they're yer men. When do we leave?"

She blinked. "She's actually ready to go?"

"All repairs ha been made an' th' breeze is freshenin'."

She met Mac's dancing eyes. "In that case, we leave now. Right now."

"Men," Owen bellowed, "ye hear th' lady. Get a move on!"

"Oh, God, wait—I don't believe this. Our horses! We can't just leave them standing there!"

"It's taken care of," Mac said. "I've sent a message to a friend who owns the Merchant Street Livery. In fact, here he comes now. I'll give him the particulars and be back in a minute."

Watching him go, she thought darling Mac . . . and Owen . . . and this crew . . . and that sweet, grimy little Jack Lace. She pulled in a deep breath and felt the laughter rising within her. After being filled with fear for what seemed like hours, it had vanished completely and the warmth of relief was flowing through her.

In truth, she and Mac had accomplished the impossible with the help of that lad—they had almost certainly pinpointed where Cain was. And because of the love and generosity of these men, another impossible thing was about to happen—she would soon be on her way to him, and they were going to get him back. They were . . . they were. She threw her arms around Owen, gave him a fierce hug, and cried to the crew, already preparing to cast off, "You're wonderful, and I love every single one of you!" Her laughter rang out, and the rich bubbling sound of it

enchanted every man who heard it. "Here's Mac. We can
leave!"

"So be it. Full sails ahead, men!" As the order was
passed, Owen tugged the gleaming plait which had escaped from under Ayisha's faded shirt. "Know, lass,
there's no ship afloat that can outrun us if we've a mind
t' catch it. Let yer mind be at ease."

The number of men imprisoned in the hold of the *Red
Lady* had swelled with each stop she made. Now the five
who had been there when Cain awakened were ordered to
climb a rope ladder that was lowered. Cain went last, and
with each upward step his rage grew. Like his new mates,
he yearned to lay his bare hands on the man in command
and slay him. But when he gained the deck, he saw there
was no hope for them to act on their wishes—not at present.

They were surrounded by crew armed with clubs and
knives, and they were immediately separated and given
work to do. A large mop was thrust into Cain's hands and
a dark-skinned seaman with a jagged scar crossing his face
pointed to a bucket of seawater. "Get busy, boy." The others laughed.

Cain fought the impulse to cut a swath through the bastards with a violent swing of it. He growled, "Who's in
command of this vessel and where are we headed?"

The scarred seaman drew his knife. "No questions, boy.
Swab."

Cain was close to exploding. He wanted to slay not only
the man in charge of this devil ship, he was ready to kill
the entire crew. They were naught but a band of bloody
cutthroats to sail under the flag of a man involved in slavery. But he sensed if he resisted them, they would not hes-
itate to kill or mutilate him, and he had more than himself
to think about now. He had Ayisha to live for. Imagining
her worrying over him, weeping, thinking he had deserted
her sent renewed fury pumping through his veins. Hell and
damnation, to think of it—pressed on the eve of his wedding day. He vented his rage and frustration on the hapless

planking, drawing bucket after bucket from the sea and swabbing it viciously until his arms felt as if they would fall off.

A voice barked suddenly, "You wi' th' swab. Th' master wants t' see ye."

Cain's heart beat harder as he thrust the mop into the bucket, dried his hands on his breeches, and followed the seaman toward the captain's cabin. He warned himself to stay calm. Detached. His life depended on it. He drew a deep breath as the seaman gave two thumps on the heavy door, opened it, and shoved him inside the shadowy cabin.

" 'ere 'e be, sir. Th' one ye wanted t' see." He left, shutting the door behind him.

Cain looked hard at the man who stood gazing out a porthole, his broad, impeccably tailored back to him. As he turned slowly, arms crossed, a sour smile on his handsome face, Cain stared. God's blood.

Jeremy laughed. "Surprise."

The blackhearted bastard. Cain lunged, his reaction beyond his control.

Jeremy's sword hissed out of his scabbard. Touching the point to Cain's heart, he whispered, smiling, "Nay, man, abandon the thought."

It nigh killed Cain, but there was naught else to do but obey. He stood silent, waiting, his arms at his sides and his eyes burning over Jeremy Greydon.

Jeremy nodded. "That's better. Much better. I really don't want to kill you, for then you would never know my plans for you—and for Ayisha." He laughed again, thinking how smoothly everything had gone. Ben would have read the letter hours ago and told Ayisha and by now they both would be so outraged they'd want to slay this devil on sight. He shook his head and his pale eyes gleamed in the cabin's half light. "And such plans they are. Telling them to you will give me far greater pleasure than merely running you through."

Cain said naught. He kept his face masked, told his muscles to relax, his heart to calm itself, and he told himself to think of Ayisha, only Ayisha. His beloved. He gritted his teeth as the point of Greydon's sword pressed into his chest and drew a drop of dark, red blood.

"You see," Jeremy continued softly, "the old man got a nasty letter from you this morn. Oh, aye, from you, be assured of it." He was disappointed when there was not so much as a flicker of fear or confusion in those fathomless eyes. "It seems you want your pater's share of Ana's jewels in exchange for your silence about Ben Scott." His lip curled. "You see, I know all there is to know about the infamous pair." His satisfaction turned to fury when Cain Banning said naught. "You dumb bastard, do you understand what I'm saying? Ben thinks you're blackmailing him. He's ready to kill you by now and doubtless Ayisha is, too. She hates you."

The words nearly brought Cain to his knees but he kept his face and eyes inscrutable. Ben would swallow the tale, aye, but not Ayisha. Never Ayisha. She would believe in him. He said it over and over to make himself believe it. And when he escaped, for he would escape, he'd make his way back to her immediately and set it all straight. He had been making plans ever since he'd awakened. And being on deck would simplify things considerably, especially if they were near land.

"—so you see, your life with her is over. It will be years before you see her again, if ever." Jeremy had reclaimed his good spirits. "The reason, in case you're curious, is that you'll be working on a Cuban sugar plantation." At last. At last a darkening of those masked eyes and a muscle jerking in that granite jaw. He removed the point of his sword from his enemy's chest and raised it to the base of his throat where a pulse pounded. He chuckled. "Oh, aye, man, you're already bought and paid for, you and the others. It will be years before you can buy your freedom. But I pray you, don't worry about Ayisha's welfare. She'll be my wife, and I'll take very good care of her."

His wife. The thought made Cain smile a sour smile. He spoke finally, his voice a rasp, "She'll not wed you. She despises you."

Jeremy was enjoying himself. "That's so. She hates me,

but wed me she will. She has no choice. She'll do it to protect her father. I know too much about Ben Scott, you see." Seeing the murderous light in his prisoner's eyes, Jeremy pressed the point of his sword more firmly against his throat. "Don't move, you devil, not a whisker!" He raised his voice. "Jenkins!" The seaman who had brought Cain appeared instantly. "Take him back where you got him."

"Aye, cap'n." With his dagger between Cain's shoulder blades, Jenkins prodded him back to the foredeck where the bucket and swab awaited him. " 'op to it, boy. There's more when this's done."

Cain did not hear him. His ears were roaring and his head nigh exploding with Greydon's terrible words. Ayisha would be his wife. She had no choice. He knew too much about Ben Scott for her to refuse him. It filled him with such terror for her, and such despair, he could think of naught else. His darling, his beautiful, spirited sprite forced into marriage and into the bed of a man who would bruise her and maul her and—

Cain blocked the horror from his mind and dropped instinctively to his knees. He lifted up a silent cry, a demand to God that if He truly existed, He protect Ayisha until he himself could reach her side. He heard the hiss of the cat before its fiery fingers raked his back.

"Up, ye lazy bastard, up! Ye'll stop when we tell ye t' stop an' not b'fore!"

Cain staggered to his feet and, with great effort, resisted ramming the swab down the devil's throat. He went to the rail, lowered the empty bucket to the sea, and in the distance saw a sight that made his hair stand on end. A ship was flying out of the haze off the larboard bow—a sleek, dark-hulled caravel, golden masts agleam and every sail billowing. As he marveled at her sleek beauty and wondered what she was about, a cry came from the crow's nest: "The *Ayisha* off the larboard bow! She's closin' fast an' just sent up a boardin' flag. She wants t' talk. Fetch th' cap'n, fer godsakes, an' ask 'im what 'e wants us t' do."

Cain's laughter was lost amid the sudden uproar on

deck. The *Ayisha*. What a fantastic, unbelievable thing. Someone—Seth?—had learned somehow what had befallen him and learned—guessed?—where he was and sent the flagship of the Adair line after him under full sail. God Almighty. He yearned to dive into the sea and swim across to her and to safety, but seeing that she bristled suddenly with small cannon, he smiled and stayed where he was. There was no doubt he would be going back to Boston on her.

With narrowed eyes, he watched a lad on the approaching ship climb up swiftly to her crow's nest and fit a glass to his eye. When it pointed at him, Cain smiled and waved. The lad waved back, wildly, and then suddenly, he was not a lad anymore but a maid whose sun-glittered mahogany hair was being whipped by the wind that bore the dove-sleek vessel ever closer. Cain's heart was close to bursting with his love and pride as he realized it was Ayisha herself who had come for him.

Chapter 28

"**H**e's aboard!" Ayisha called down to the others. "He smiled and waved when I pointed the glass at him. He's all right!" She sent her joyful thanks skyward and called down to Owen impatiently, "Hail them! Tell them we want to board her."

"They already know, lass." Owen picked up his speaking-trumpet and spoke into it: *"Red Lady,* we request permission t' board ye. We have business t' discuss."

Ayisha fastened the glass to her eye again and saw Jeremy burst from his cabin and look about in bewilderment at the confusion on deck. After speaking with several of his men, his face reddened and he shook his head in an emphatic denial. Ayisha did not wait to see anymore. She climbed rapidly down the narrow ladder and moved to where Mac and Owen stood talking.

"They're not even slowing down," she cried. "Grapple her before she gets away!"

Owen chuckled. "She's not goin' t' get away, lass. I've told ye—there's not a ship afloat that c'n perform that feat." He called to his men, "Ready th' grapples, lads, an' man th' swivel guns." As the order was repeated throughout the ship, he marked that Ayisha's face had turned pale. "Lass, dinna think I'll fire wi' your Cain aboard. I'll not. Those guns merely tend t' make a man pause and give thought. We've asked, polite, for permission t' board. Now we add a bit o' teeth t' th' request." He gave her a fatherly hug. "All's well, never fear."

Once more he raised the trumpet and his voice filled the

air: *"Red Lady,* gi' us permission t' board, or we board wi' out it."

Mac put a reassuring hand on her shoulder. "We'll get him out of this just fine, but lass, you're not boarding with us. Know that."

Ayisha laughed. She was lighthearted now that she knew that Cain would soon be in her arms. "If you say so."

"I do say so—" As he spoke, the orders were bawled for the grapples to be thrown. "—as does Owen. We'll not risk anything happening to you." He added gruffly, "Give me your promise that you'll stay put." There was a crunching noise as the two vessels met, then ground together.

"I'll not do anything foolish, I promise." Her eyes danced.

"See that you don't." But as he swarmed with the others over the rails, a knife gripped between his teeth and a shortsword tucked into his belt, Mac knew she would cross over. He might as well try to stop the sun from rising.

As they left, Ayisha yearned in the worst way to fly to Cain, but she knew she would be naught but a worry to him and to them all. Desperate to see what was happening, she climbed part way up to the crow's nest and hung there as Owen's men flooded the *Red Lady* amidships. Heart thundering, she watched the boiling melee below and listened to the shouts and screams and curses, the thud of fists and clubs and the clash of metal against metal.

She was unable to distinguish friend from foe, nor could she pinpoint Cain or Mac or Owen. Her fears for them and for the others were about to overwhelm her when suddenly she saw Cain. Backed by Owen, he was fighting, slashing his way across the deck. As she watched, the two lifted a heavy grid from the planking and a torrent of men poured out of the hold. Ayisha realized that, like Cain, they were seamen who had been pressed and imprisoned. Angry and dangerous, they now fought like men possessed beside the men of the *Ayisha* and the crew of the *Red Lady* was quickly subdued.

Jeremy Greydon was ready to kill. And the person he wanted most to destroy was Cain Banning. But nay, that was wrong. First he would slay the silken witch who had caused this entire debacle by teasing and thwarting and defying him from the first moment he had laid eyes on her. Because of her, his entire life was in ruins. Gone were all of his plans for wedding her and taking over her father's extensive empire. Gone. Lost. It sickened him.

He sent a scathing glance over his conquered crew. He had wanted to flee while there was still time, but they had convinced him the *Red Lady* could not outrun Ben Adair's swift armed flagship. And when the *Ayisha's* bloodthirsty hooligans stormed aboard, not a damned one of his men had given him their all. Not a one. The end had come swiftly when someone released the scum in his hold and they'd promptly joined in the fray. And it had all come about because of Ayisha . . .

Cain had eyes only for Ayisha. As she climbed over the rails of the two ships and made her way toward him, her own eyes said she loved him still—as much as ever. Nay, more than ever. He pushed through the throng to meet her, his love and relief for her safety and his gratitude for her becoming a bonfire flaming inside of him.

"Ayisha . . ."

"Cain! Oh, beloved . . ." Ayisha went into his open arms amid the great roar that rose from her crew. And when Cain kissed her fiercely, hungrily, and she returned it in full measure, a second cheer erupted and then a third.

But Cain warned himself that now was not the time to think of love or bed or a lifetime of being together. Not now. This was still a perilous situation. He gave her a final kiss, put her from him, and watched as the formidable captain of the *Ayisha,* his officers flanking him, approached Greydon.

Owen nailed him to the spot with accusing eyes. "I

hope for yere sake, Mr. Greydon," he growled, "th't ye're not aware ye ha' pressed men aboard yer vessel."

Jeremy had watched, seething, as Ayisha, dressed in her disgusting man's garb, had climbed the rails and virtually flown to Banning's arms. And the look she had given him—as if she had just seen heaven itself. The bitch.

"Shall I repeat the question, sir?" Owen's voice boomed across the deck.

Jeremy gritted his teeth. "I am a respected merchant and we are on a peaceful trading voyage. You have boarded us illegally." He had never hated anyone as he hated Ayisha Adair at that moment, and he would have his revenge. Oh, aye. He would not have her in his bed or have her father's fortune or all of the other things he'd been counting on, but he would have his revenge. Boston, aye, the whole world was going to hear what he had kept hidden thus far, and it would destroy her just as surely as it would her father. There was going to be a scandal of international proportions.

"Are ye sayin', sir," Owen persisted, "ye were unaware Mr. Banning and th' others had been brought aboard yere vessel against their wills?"

"He was damned well aware of it," Cain answered. "I just learned from him that I'd been sold into indenture on a Cuban sugar plantation. I'm not sure where the others were bound. There are fourteen of us aboard, all pressed." His angry gaze swept the men about him. "Show yourselves, mates."

As hands shot up, Ayisha said angrily, "And you've done it before, haven't you, Jeremy? We have a witness who saw unconscious men being carried aboard this vessel in darkness."

Jeremy's pulses beat faster as he realized suddenly that he could still turn this disaster to his advantage. The witch was within arm's reach of him, and the dagger which always lay hidden in a fold of his waistcoat had not been found by the fool who had searched him.

"So, sir," Owen's voice was threatening now, "what ha ye t' say for yourself?"

"You'll never get the truth from him," Cain muttered. As he spoke, he caught a swift movement from the corner of his eye. He spun and saw, God Almighty, that Greydon had Ayisha.

Moving with the swiftness of desperation, Jeremy had yanked her roughly into his arms and spooned her against his chest. Pressing the edge of his dagger to her throat, he rasped, "Stand back, all of you!" He smiled, seeing the shock on their faces and how quickly they obeyed. "Very good. And now, gentlemen, I think your plans have just changed. Throw down your weapons, board your own vessel, and head back whence you came if you want this witch to live."

Cain's blood had turned to ice water. Watching Greydon maneuver so that his back was protected against the rail, he said thickly, "Man, don't be a fool. Let her go."

Jeremy gave a sharp bark of laughter. "Oh, aye, you'd like that, wouldn't you? But I think not, Banning. I think I'll keep her close to me. Very close." He tightened his hold on her. "And now, for the last time, get off my vessel, all of you, and take the scum that were in my hold with you. And don't even try to guess where I'm headed because you'll be wrong."

Ayisha whispered, "Jeremy, please—don't do this."

Jeremy paid her no heed. His blazing eyes were locked on Cain Banning. "If you care for this bitch, you'll do as I say. Go. Now. And if I so much as catch a glimpse of your main topgallant within the next two days, she's dead. Believe it." When he saw his enemy's face turn pale, he smiled again, thinly, then ripped open Ayisha's shirt so that the buttons flew and bared one soft, white shoulder. He drew the point of his dagger along the flesh at the base of her throat, watched the thin red line which appeared, felt her trembling. He growled, "Let there be no doubt, Banning—I hate this bitch. If you come after me, I'll kill her—but not before my crew and I make good use of her."

Cain's great fear for her made his knees weak and his mouth dry as dust. There was no doubt in his mind now that the man was far more than merely cruel and childish and vindictive. He was crazy. There was madness in the pitch of his voice and in the roll of his pale eyes. Cain had suspected it after he'd trounced him and Greydon had lashed out at them with the whip and tried to run them down. So how in God's name could he now leave Ayisha behind when the devil had threatened to rape and slay her? The answer was that he could not. But neither did he dare attempt a rescue. Greydon would slay her on the spot.

With the others, he moved in silence toward where the two ships were connected. As the *Ayisha*'s crew climbed reluctantly over the rails, Cain slowed his step, his mind racing, searching wildly for a way out of the nightmare. There had to be a solution, there had to be, but he could not see it. He was as helpless as if he were bound by shackles with Greydon's knife at Ayisha's throat and the hostile eyes of the enemy crew glued upon him.

It was then that Cain saw him—his fellow prisoner from the hold. The sandy-haired giant who had promised that the owner of this ship was a dead man. . . . Cain froze. The fellow was not far from Greydon, and the light burning in his eyes was murderous. Hell, was he going to take his revenge now when it could get Ayisha killed?

As Ayisha watched her friends returning to their ship and saw that Cain was dying a thousand deaths, she knew she had to move, to act, to do something, anything. She was as frightened as ever but she must put it away now, take up the reins again and let her rage take over—rage and disgust and contempt. Who did Jeremy Greydon think he was to dare to do this thing to her? And how dare he steal and sell people into servitude! How dare he try to blackmail, to rob her father of Mama's jewelry and blame it all on Cain? And how dare he actually draw her blood? The wound hurt, but she was damned if she would let him know that, the turnip-headed bugger. Oh, how she despised him!

Growing more incensed by the moment, she yearned to call out to Cain to stay and fight, but if she made a sound, it would be her last. Jeremy would cut her throat. But then he was going to anyway. She had no delusion that he would allow her to live for very long, and she knew well the fate that awaited her before she died. But if she perished now attempting to escape, Jeremy, too, would die, for Cain would slay him. Mac and Owen and the crew would all have a turn at him. She decided what to do that instant.

"Cain!" she called in a ringing voice, her eyes ablaze. "Stay and fight!" Using that one instant of surprise and all of the strength she possessed, Ayisha caught and forced Jeremy's knife hand from her throat. The knife, miracle of miracles, clattered to the deck. Seeing it, the *Ayisha*'s crew returned and the battle resumed.

Jeremy growled. "You damned bitch!"

"You snake-tongued lily-livered bastard!" Ayisha flared. "Your soul to the devil!"

Jeremy's face turned dark red. "You're no lady!" God. Why was she not weak and helpless and frightened, the way any normal female would be in such a desperate situation? But nay, not Ayisha, never Ayisha. And now, because of her, the fighting had resumed and with the coward crew he had, he saw that the battle was lost for the second time. Swept by rage, he said thickly, "No more, Ayisha. I cannot abide any more of this." His fingers sought and closed about her throat, but even as he squeezed, heard her gasping for air, the breath was forced from his own lungs and pain exploded deep inside his head.

Ayisha gasped. The hilt of a small dagger protruded from his temple and blood stained his pale skin and blond hair and was running into his wide, frightened eyes. His breath, as though he breathed liquid, rattled in his lungs.

"Oh, Jere . . ." She had wanted him punished, slain even, aye, but she had not known it would be like this. She had not known. She swayed and felt Cain's arms go around her.

Jeremy sagged against the rail as red swam before his eyes. It was his blood, he thought fleetingly, his life's blood that was flowing out of him. He wondered vaguely if he were dying. Without strength or will, without perception, he dropped to the deck, no longer sure where he was or even who he was. He was aware only of a cool hand, the soft cool hand of a woman touching his face, smoothing back his hair, holding his own hand and stroking it, her gentle voice, low and calm, telling him it was all right, it was all right, he was just going to step into another room now. He looked up at her, tried to curve his mouth into a smile, breathed, "Another—room. Aye . . ."

Kneeling there beside Jeremy's body, Ayisha felt Cain's arms around her still, supporting her. She raised dazed eyes to his. "Cain, he's—gone. Just like that . . ."

"Aye."

Cain did not say that it was all to the good, but God knows, it was. No more would he fear for her safety or fear that she and her family would be blackmailed—or fear the dozens of other worries he conjured up in the night when he thought of Jeremy Greydon. And when an angry voice was raised asking who had done it, who had thrown the dagger that killed the owner of the *Red Lady,* no one answered. Cain wondered if they had all, like himself, seen the sandy-haired seaman throw it and considered it a blessing . . .

As the two ships made their way back to Boston, Cain held Ayisha close and tried to comfort her. They lay on the bunk in Owen Connor's cabin, and she could not stop her trembling. From time to time, he stroked her hair and placed gentle kisses on her lips and fingertips and the tips of her long, wet lashes. All in silence. She was deep in her own thoughts, and his mind was filled with all that had happened: the unanimous decision not to allow the crew of the *Red Lady* to go unpunished . . . the choosing of men to sail her back to Boston . . . Seth and the *Sea Eagle*'s crew searching for him . . . his learning how Ayisha and Mac had discovered what had become of him and how they had come after him. He bent, kissed her shining hair for the hundredth time, and waited for her shock to ease. This had been hard on her, he knew. She had nigh perished of fright for him, she had been seized, a knife used on her—and she had never seen sudden, violent death before.

Ayisha caught Cain's hand suddenly and covered it with kisses. She could not put from her mind the terrible sight of Jeremy's dying. She choked, "That could have been you. He hated you . . ."

"But it wasn't," Cain said gently. "And he could have taken you away from me, but he didn't." He traced her pink mouth with a loving finger. "We're together, and you're safe in my arms."

"—and you're safe in mine. . . ." Ayisha cupped his face and kissed him long and hungrily. "Oh, Cain, I was so afraid for you."

Cain said gravely, "And I was afraid for you." Afraid? God knows, he'd been terrified. And he had prayed for her. Prayed! Never would he forget the spectacular way his prayers had been answered. He chuckled, remembering. "You'll never know what it was like, seeing your caravel coming out of the haze in full sail with all her flags flying—and you up in the crow's nest with the wind whipping your hair. . . ." He shook his head. "Lady, what a sight!"

When she laughed, yawned, and snuggled closer, his relief was enormous. She was recovering, and much sooner than he'd dared hope. He slid his hands over her, sealed her mouth with his hungry kisses, felt her eager response—her tongue greeting his, her own small hands slipping under his shirt, under his trews to seek his taut, bare flesh and send fire coursing through his veins to plunge deep within him. He groaned, a sound of pleasure and relief and happiness and joy. Immense joy. Because she was brave enough and bold enough to have cried out to him and to have caught Greydon off guard, because she was Ayisha, she lived. And because she lived, so did he, for without her his life would have ended.

Ayisha was raining hot kisses across the rough skin of his face and throat, down over his broad chest and the heavy muscles of his shoulders, back up to his mouth. She whispered against his lips huskily, "Cain—please, beloved, now. . . ." She needed desperately to feel him strong and safe within her starving body, needed to prove to herself once and for all that this was not a dream, that he lived and their lives stretched out ahead of them.

Cain needed no coaxing. He craved naught as much as he craved her and he knew immediately that this was not the time for a slow, tantalizing awakening of ecstasy. This would be a joyous overflowing of life and love and their deliverance from darkness into sunlight. Almost immediately he was within her, moving hungrily and powerfully, consuming her with his fire and in return being surrounded and consumed by the heat and intensity of her own passion.

Afterwards as they lay in each other's arms, Ayisha rolled onto her side and studied him in quiet contentment. Feeling her gaze on him, Cain opened his eyes, and smiled. "You look like a kitten with cream."

Ayisha stroked the dark curls on his chest and gave him a mysterious smile. "Something wonderful has happened." In truth, two wonderful things had happened, but she was going to save her news of Willi until later.

Cain's eyes flickered over her. "Let me guess. Owen Connor is waiting to wed us and make an honorable man of me."

Ayisha's laughter rang out. "Why didn't I think of that!"

"That's not it?"

"Nay. This happened while you were gone—but let's do it! Let's wed today just as we planned!"

Cain chuckled. "I like the sound of that."

She gasped when he bent his head to her breasts, took a nipple in his mouth, and sent a silky heat surging through her all over again. It was some moments before she had breath enough to say faintly, "As for my news— it's about Da. The three of us told him about Jeremy and his threats and how you fought him—and Cain, his whole attitude toward you has changed!"

"Has it now?" Cain did not allow his cynicism to show.

"I mean it. You should have seen him. He said he'd been stiff and bullheaded and stubborn as an old ass and he was all wrong. He said I should have you and he should have trusted his first instincts about you because he liked you."

Cain's laughter filled the cabin. "I'll be damned."

A knock sounded on the cabin door followed by Owen Connor's voice, "Ayisha, is all well wi' ye, lassie?"

Ayisha leapt from the bunk and ran to the door. "All's wonderful, Owen. We'll be out in just a few minutes, and Owen—we want you to wed us."

There was a long silence in which they heard only the creak of the ship and the wind in the sails, and then Owen's deep voice, curiously husky, said, "It'll gi' me honor, lass. It'll gi' me great honor t' wed ye an' yere fine mon."

Chapter 29

Owen had read the wedding ceremony in his grave, ringing voice as Mac and the crew looked on in reverent silence. And then Cain had said she was his until death did them part and Owen said they were now man and wife and he could kiss the bride. Ayisha had laughed and cried amid the cheers of her friends, and as the ship sailed past the Brewsters and through the Narrows and eventually into Boston Harbor itself, they were given a jubilant fanfare of pipes and drums. And now, now the two of them were in the carriage and Seacliff lay just ahead in the twilight.

Aimee was the first one out of the house. Her joyous shriek, as they alighted from the carriage and Cain paid the driver, brought everyone running—Soames and Pegeen, the entire household staff, even the stable lads.

"Pan's home!" she cried at the top of her lungs, "and she's found Cain and brought him with her! Oh, my goodness! Oh, Panny! Colette, quick, run and fetch Papa!" She went into Ayisha's arms and embraced and kissed her fiercely. "Oh, honey, I'm so glad you're here, and that you're safe! And you, Cain! Thank goodness you're all right. What a fright you gave us!" She gave him a fierce hug. "Were you on Jeremy's boat as they suspected?"

"Aye," Cain returned his small sister-in-law's exuberant embrace. "He'd pressed fifteen of us."

"The rat!"

"What have you heard from Seth?"

Aimee clutched Ayisha's hand as Pegeen embraced and

kissed her. "He came earlier to tell us that Pan and Mac—" She looked about. "Where is Mac?"

"He's taken our mounts to the stable," Ayisha said. "He wants to make sure they get extra feed tonight."

Aimee filled her lungs. "Anyhow, Seth said you two had gone after Cain on the *Ayisha.*" She shook her head. "He was fit to be tied that he couldn't go after you, too, but his own boat was off somewhere and Papa hadn't any more in port and—"

As she chattered on, Ayisha saw her father coming from the house, his arms open and welcoming. She went into them, kissed him, and said quietly, "Hello, Da. We found him, as you can see."

Ben held his girl for a long, long time. "Never did I doubt you would, lass, and I'm prouder than proud of you. Prouder than proud." Seeing Cain's gaze upon him and the uncertainty in those dark eyes, he held out his hand and saw the worry turn to relief. "Son, welcome home."

Cain clasped his outstretched hand. "Thank you, sir." He said low, "Ayisha has told me . . ."

Ben shook his head. "There's no more to be said— except I'm damned glad you're both back safe and sound and that you're together." It was the main thing. The only thing that mattered. Both of his darlings had men they loved and who loved them, and because of it they could weather any trouble—even the sort Greydon would doubt-less call down on them now.

"Sir . . ."

"Aye, lad?"

Cain said under his breath, "Greydon's dead."

Ben stared at the darkly handsome face looking back at him and felt a shudder pass over him. Young Greydon was dead. Sensing that he himself was not long for this world, he did not like to hear of anyone's passing, especially not one so young. He hoped to God Cain had not been in-volved, nor Ayisha. Pray God, not Ayisha. She would never recover from having killed a man. He asked thickly, "He was—slain?"

"Aye. By one of the men he'd pressed."

He nodded, relieved. "So be it." It solved many problems, and God have mercy on his soul. And on the soul of Thomas Gregg. It was the first time he'd been able to say it, and strangely enough, he meant it.

Pegeen's bright voice broke into his thoughts. "Everyone come inside now, you must all be hungry. Certainly no one in this house has eaten the live long day, and cook has—"

"Wait!" Aimee cried. "I hear a horse! It must be Seth!" She peered into the gathering darkness as a horse and rider materialized. "It is! It's Seth!" As he drew near, she called, "Sweetheart, look! They're all here, Pan and Cain and Mac—he's at the stable—and not one of them was hurt! Isn't it grand?"

Seth dismounted, kissed his wife and Ayisha, and then stood scowling at Cain in the fading light, arms akimbo and breathing hard. "Man oh man oh man, don't ever do that again. Not ever."

Cain grinned and clapped him on the shoulder. "It's not likely." The two embraced roughly, and Seth was seen to wipe his eyes.

Mac arrived then, and after Pegeen had given her son a great hug, Ben caught him close. "Lad, you have my thanks for all of your help and for watching over my girl for me."

Mac laughed. "That's a joke, sir."

"Nay, son, I know you took care of her in your own way. You have a steadying influence." He turned to Pegeen. "And now, Mrs. Fitzgerald, if you'll please tell cook we're ready to have that food we didn't touch all day—and I want you to join us."

Pegeen flushed. "It's a time for family."

Ben put his arm across Mac's broad shoulders. "Who's family if not the Fitzgeralds? Nay, lady, don't say it." He took Pegeen's arm. "You'll eat and sup and celebrate with us. Soames, fetch something festive from the cellar. Fetch a lot."

Not until the meal had ended and they were seated in the drawing room with a fire burning bright and the doors closed was the tale unfolded. It came first from Cain's lips—how his head had been so filled with thoughts of Ayisha that he had not realized his danger until it was too late. Holding her hand tightly, he related all that Greydon had told him. Ayisha and Mac then told of finding young Jack Lace whose story had sent them in hot pursuit of the *Red Lady*.

"I liked that lad on sight," Cain said. "I had it in mind to give him a try as a cabin boy when Ayisha and I got back from our honeymoon." Hearing what he'd just said, he froze until Ben's hearty laughter cracked the silence.

"Come now, son. This old man was young once, and I had a maid as lovely as either of yours—but I was luckier than you two. Her father was too far away to be the damned nuisance I've been." His blue eyes were laughing in the reflected candlelight. "From what I've seen this eve, lads and lassies, I think you'd best wed with all possible haste. Forget the wedding in the spring . . ."

"Oh, Papa, we did! Seth and I were wed three days ago. We really and truly wanted to tell you sooner but . . ."

Ayisha clutched Cain's hand more tightly. "Cain and I were wed on the *Ayisha* on our way home."

Ben's eyes misted. "By Owen?"

"Aye."

"Oh, Panny . . ." Aimee flew to her.

Pegeen was on her feet, tears streaming as she tried to bundle both maids into her arms at once. "My precious lambs, married women. May all the saints preserve the four of you."

Ayisha returned their embraces and looked back at her father anxiously. "It—really seemed the right time and the right place, Da."

Ben had composed himself. He was able to say easily, "It was exactly the right time and the right place. I can confess now, I wasn't looking forward to all of that confounded fuss—that business in the church and having the house torn upside down with cleaning and painting and overrun by hundreds of people. Nay, now, Pegeen, don't look at me so. Truthfully now, isn't this far better? See how happy the lasses are? Why, just look at their angel faces."

He got to his feet, slightly unsteady, and smiled down on them. "I have a little something for you both that I've been saving for this day. I'll fetch it." When he returned, he was carrying a small, wooden chest which he placed on a low table before the settee.

"What is it?" Aimee knelt beside it.

"A wedding present," Ben said quietly. "From your Mama." It was Ana's jewelry, and he was not sure he could look on it without making a spectacle of himself. He had not seen it since that day she had tucked it away for safekeeping for her baby daughters. He watched as Ayisha knelt beside her sister and stroked the carved wood and faded brass hinges with reverent fingers.

Aimee whispered, "Will you open it, Pan?"

Ayisha looked to Cain for the courage that had suddenly vanished. She feared she would weep. This was from their own mother, from her loving hands beyond the grave.

Cain bent to her ear. "Are you all right, sprite?"

Seeing his love and the concern in his dark eyes, feeling his strong hands clasping her shoulders, she said firmly, "Aye."

Returning her gaze to the chest, she twisted the tiny key in its lock, lifted the lid, and blinked at her first sight of the jewels that lay there. Their dazzle—flickering, glittering, leaping in the candle glow—so pained her eyes she had to close them for a moment. When she opened them again, she saw that the colors were of every rich, glowing hue she had ever seen in her life and of some she had not known existed.

Ben said huskily, "They were your mother's, my darlin's. She had them hidden on her when we took the *Safira.* I took a few to buy our passage to Boston and get a business started, but the rest are all there. She never wore them after you little ones arrived. She feared she'd scratch or chip or lose them and she,"—now his voice broke—"she wanted them perfect for you."

Overcome, Aimee wept in Seth's arms. Ayisha yearned

to loose a torrent of her own but knew that if she did, her father would break down. She smiled up at him, a happy smile, and ran her fingers over the incredible dazzle. "I've never seen anything so beautiful."

She began carefully to lift things out of the chest and lay them on the table: bracelets, necklaces, rings, earrings. Some were made with a single type of gem, others were of the most exquisite combinations of emeralds, pearls, rubies, sapphires, and diamonds, all in delicate gold or silver filigree settings. She watched as Cain chose one fragile emerald and seed pearl earring and studied it by candlelight. Wondering at the almost angry look on his face, she murmured, "Isn't it lovely?"

At the sight of the jewels, Cain felt as if Tom Gregg had just reached out from his grave and squeezed his heart. "I—have the mate to this and a matching pendant," he said stiffly. "They were among my father's belongings." These jewels, he thought numbly, this incredible fortune in jewels was what Greydon would have grabbed if his plan had worked. And he would have blamed him . . .

Ayisha caught his hand. "We've let it pass. Won't you let go of it, too? Please?"

"I'll return them to you, of course."

"Cain, half of this is yours."

"Never." His face felt frozen, his mouth, his whole damned body was frozen.

"Half is mine, and what's mine is yours . . ."

"Nay, Ayisha." He could not fathom any of this treasure as belonging to him. He marked that Aimee had dried her eyes and was eagerly helping Ayisha to lay the pieces out, one by one.

"My goodness, look at this sweet little book buried under everything, and what an elegant design on the cover!" Aimee opened it, leafed through several pages, and then looked at her father. "I—think it's Mama's diary. It's dated and it's in a strange language."

Ben took the small, leather-bound book to the hearth and by its light turned the gilt-edged pages tenderly. Seeing the small, neat handwriting that had been so uniquely

Ana's, he sank into his chair. "You're right, lass. It's your mother's diary. The language is Turkish." He thought she had thrown it away, for she had not wanted to remember the terrible scenes she had recorded in it—the murder of Jonathan, the abandonment of his men . . .

Seth cleared his throat. "Sir, I'm familiar with Turkish." When they all turned to stare at him, he said, "It's no secret. I told you I sailed on a Turk freighter for years."

Aimee whispered, "You mean you could read Mama's words to us?"

Ben said abruptly, "Nay, lass! Your mother's diary is a private thing. I doubt it's anything you'd want to hear."

Seeing his quick glance at Cain, Ayisha knew instinctively what had happened. Her mother, witnessing the tragedy, had written it all down in this one small book he held in his hands. Now he was trying to shield Cain from the ugliness on this happiest of days. She, too, wanted to protect him. He had suffered long enough for his father's crimes. "I agree with Da," she said quickly. "A diary is a private thing. I don't want to know what it says."

"I guess I don't either," Aimee murmured, trying on a diamond and emerald ring. "I never thought of it that way."

Cain's dark eyes locked on Ben's. "Has it to do with my father?" When Ben said naught, just stared at him, Cain asked brusquely, "My father and your crew?"

Damn the lad. Ben ran his hands through his hair. "It's all there," he said, tiredly. "My wife said she put it all down, but in truth, son, it's best put behind us now."

Cain's decision was made. He had to know the worst, once and for all. Better that than ever again have cause to doubt this man he was coming to care for and who meant the world to Ayisha. He said, "Sir, I—need to hear it."

Ayisha went to him, the glittering jewels on the table forgotten. "Why?"

Cain saw her concern, but it changed naught. He lowered his voice. "Because I must."

She had such fear of a sudden, she had to voice it. She

whispered, "Because you don't believe it happened the way my father said?"

His face darkened. "God's breath, Ayisha, I thought we were past that. I believe it happened exactly the way he said."

"I'm sorry . . ."

"In fact, it was probably worse than he said. If I'm ever to put the damned thing to rest, I need to know all there is to know." He looked over at Ben, slumped in his chair by the fire. "With your permission?"

Ben said abruptly, "So be it. But it's not for the ears of these lasses."

Ayisha's eyes glinted. She took Cain's hand. "If my husband's going to hear the words of my mother, so am I."

"And if my husband's going to be reading them," said Aimee firmly, "I want to hear them, too."

Mac chuckled.

Pegeen, who had been watching and listening in silence, gave a loud sniff. "You might be married women, but you're still your father's daughters and he knows what's best for you!"

Now Ben laughed and scratched his ear thoughtfully. "Well, now, Peg, at this point in time, I'm not so sure I do." He had botched it pretty well of late, and truth to tell, he was damned glad to be handing over the reins to these tall sons-in-law of his. His eyes lighted lovingly on Jonathan—except he knew the lad was not Jonathan. He knew that. He said to him gently, "I see you've been studying those pages, son. What have you learned?"

Seth met Cain's piercing gaze and looked back down at the diary. "It's hard reading, sir, and I've just skimmed it, of course. Some of the words I don't even know."

"Let's hear it, man. Do your best." Once again Cain assured himself that he was prepared. He'd had weeks to adjust, to remember, to piece together all of the dark, questionable things about his father that he had once excused or ignored. But his heart told him that what he was about to hear was going to crush him—for part of him was still that small, worshipful lad whose laughing, blue-eyed sailor father was his god.

Seth said carefully, "Maybe you should sit down again."

Cain did. He sat down with Ayisha close beside him, her small hands clutching his tightly. For the next hour, there was naught for him but the hiss of fire, the droning of Seth's voice, and the terrible images in his head. So vividly had Ana described the tale that Cain died again and again hearing it. But painful as it was, it was cleansing, purifying to know for a certainty exactly what had happened, and to have no doubts whatsoever about Ben Scott. It was a new beginning for him.

Ayisha watched, smiling, as her husband swiftly stripped off his clothing and crawled into bed beside her. He pulled her naked body against him so tightly that the breath was squeezed out of her, and he kissed her long and hard. She whispered, wondering, "You're my husband—and you're in my house and in my bed. I can scarce believe it. My husband . . ."

Cain continued to hold her close and enjoy the softness of her slender body and the fragrance and silkiness of her skin. He chuckled. "It must be so. Your father's not battering down the door."

Ayisha sought the delectable space between his neck and shoulder, buried her face there, and tasted his salty skin. "I think he's already starting to love you. He sees that you love me and sees how good you are—and how good you are for me."

"Aye." He slid his hands hungrily over the gloss and the satin of her. "I'm very good for you . . ."

"Cain . . ."

"Aye, little temptress?"

"You talked for such a long time with Seth and Da after the diary was read. Is it something I should know?"

His eyes held a mysterious glitter. "It's something you certainly should know, aye."

"Is it—good?"

His mouth tilted. "Only you can be the judge of that."

Ayisha sat up, eyes gold filled in the candle's glow, hair a flame-flecked cape only half concealing her breasts. "Tell me!"

Cain's own gaze, heavy lidded now, swept over her. She was his, this soft young creature with her dew-sweet mouth and creamy skin and her lush, pink-tipped breasts just waiting to be kissed. He brushed away the silky strands of hair covering them, caressed them, and said huskily, "Before or after?"

Ayisha's low laughter bubbled out. "Before or after what?" she teased. When he growled, buried his face between her breasts and then burned a trail of hot kisses to her navel and below, far below, she giggled and covered his mouth with her hands. "I love love love love love you, Cain Banning, but I want to know now. Before . . ."

Cain groaned. "I had to ask." He dragged himself to a sitting position, settled a pillow behind his back, and pulled her close beside him with his arm around her. He then reached for the small, leather-bound book on the bedside table.

Ayisha watched curiously. "It has to do with my mother's diary?"

"Aye." He stroked the butter-smooth cover and traced the small, intricately embossed emblem in its center with a dark finger. When Ayisha, too, ran her fingers over it, he said, "It's the Great Seal of the House of Kemal, Ayisha."

"I don't know what that means. It sounds rather grim and important."

"It was the house of your mother's father."

She blinked her golden eyes at him. "I see. My grandfather . . ."

"Aye, and your father wants you to read this." He took a sheet of foolscap from the bedside table, handed it to her, and brought the candle closer. "Seth translated the first few pages of the diary. Can you read his writing?"

Her breath caught as she saw the first few words. She murmured, "Aye," and began to read in a small voice, "I am the Princess Ana, daughter of Mehmed Kemal, Sultan of Izmir—" She shook her head, her shocked eyes still on the words. "My mother—was a princess?"

"Aye. Go on, sprite."

Heart thumping, she continued reading the words from long ago. "I am aboard the *Safira* on my way to Topkapi Palace in Istanbul. My father has given me to Sultan Abdul Hamid. He has hundreds of wives, but my father says I will eventually become his first wife if I please him well. But what if I do not know how to please him? And it is said that once a woman passes within the walls of his harem, she is lost to the world forever. I am so afraid, and I pray Allah to help me."

Seeing that Ayisha seemed stunned, Cain said gently, "It did have a happy ending, you know. I've got the proof right here." He kissed the side of her neck.

Ayisha was dazed, lost in that strange, far-off world of sultans and harems. "What an awful thing—to be given away. And to a man who already had hundreds of wives. Why, it shouldn't be allowed. I can scarce imagine it. Poor little Mama."

"Read on."

Ayisha returned to Seth's translation eagerly, her eyes flying over his strong, dark handwriting as the candle flame danced and flickered. She read: "I am saved. I will never see Abdul Hamid now. I am free, and I am in love. He is a sea wolf, my beloved, and he and his mates have stolen all of the treasure aboard the *Safira* and they have stolen me, but he alone has stolen my heart. He is tall and so very handsome. He has thick brown hair filled with sunlight and eyes like blue flame and his name is as beautiful as he himself is. It is Benscott. Benscott Benscott Benscott. I cannot get enough of thinking and saying and writing it." Ayisha uttered a small sound, half giggle, half sob, and chewed on a knuckle as she continued. "He is so kind, my Benscott, so kind and gentle and careful of me. He does not yet know it, but I am going to wed him. It is written in my forehead. It is my kismet."

Ayisha's eyes were flowing as Cain returned the foolscap and the candle to the bedside table and put both arms around her. He held her, silently, tenderly.

"What a beautiful story." Warmed by happiness, Ayisha wiped her eyes and basked in it. She was silent for so long that Cain traced her bare shoulder with his finger and bit it gently. He murmured against her neck, "Come back to me, Ayisha."

She sighed. "I was just thinking how amazing it is that everything happened the way it did. By chance. A mere twist of fate." She caught his hand, pressed it to her breasts, spanning them, and whispered, "My mother being on the ship that our fathers looted . . . Da bringing you home on a whim . . . Mac and I just happening on that boy who put us on your trail . . ." She shivered. "Cain, what if we hadn't found you? What then?" She brought his hand to her lips and kissed it savagely, bit his knuckles, and raised her mouth to his.

Cain took it in a deep, questing kiss and replied gruffly, "But you did find me, my princess." It was a sight he would never forget—the *Ayisha* with all her flags flying and all her sails filled and his own Ayisha atop the highest mast searching for him. His need for her was unravelling now, spreading warm and sweet and lazily throughout his body. He relished the thought that tonight there was time aplenty to savor the hot silky softness of her and the wild hunger his hands and kisses would coax from her. From this night forth, time was going to stretch out in one long, endless paradise for the two of them.

Ayisha rose on her elbow and stared at him, her tawny eyes wide. "How could I have forgotten! Cain, I have a surprise for you, too. A wonderful surprise. Shall I tell you before or,"—she felt her face turning pink—"or after?"

Seeing her excitement, Cain reminded himself of the endless nights awaiting them. He said, "I think I have to hear this right now." He watched, wholly enchanted as she knelt beside him, a satin-skinned, golden-eyed Psyche, face flushed, hands steepled and held to her rosy lips.

"It's Willi! That sweet darling angel Willi did the *passage* for me last night! Cain, we floated! Just like you said we would. I felt like I was riding a cloud, and if you don't believe me, ask Mac. He saw the whole thing."

Cain said gravely, "I believe you." He could not keep his caressing hands from the curves and valleys of her body, her chin and throat, her breasts, the luscious white mound of her abdomen, her round firm little bottom.

"I did exactly as you said—strong leg pressure together with the pushing of the back and a—a restraining hand." She was astride him suddenly, hot, hungry, melting, needing him as she had never needed anyone before. She whispered, "Like this . . ."

Cain sucked in his breath as he felt her warm, yielding softness atop him. Gone instantly were his thoughts of savoring her lazily in the days and nights that stretched out without end. They were replaced by a terrible hunger, a wildness that said he wanted her. Now. This instant, this moment. He pulled her down beside him, caging, enfolding her within his long arms and legs. "God, but I love you, Ayisha . . ."

Ayisha saw suddenly and clearly that her meeting this man was no mere whim or twist of fate or chance happening. Nay. She saw what her mother had seen when she first saw Ben Scott. Cain Banning was her kismet. He was her destiny. She whispered, "And I love you, my husband. I love you . . ."

Epilogue

Walking about his land on this mild morn in September, Ben Adair mused how peaceful everything was and how neatly all had fallen into place. Despite his stubborn and mistaken efforts to protect Ayisha, good fortune had touched her nonetheless. Two years had passed and the lass was still crazy in love with Cain Banning, and it was clear he loved her with his whole heart and soul. And the news she had given him this morn crowned their happiness. She was carrying a wee one. Ben smiled thinking of it and thinking of Aimee and Seth and their year-old girl babe, a precious cricket named Kira.

He sighed, drew the warm, sun-filled air of fall into his lungs, and reflected that he had many blessings: the babe coming in the spring, little Kira, his daughters, and their husbands into whose strong hands he had placed their happiness and the running of his businesses. Both men were keen and forward-looking with caution enough to satisfy an old man's natural prudence. And their handling of his girls was naught short of a miracle. To think, Aimee had gone to sea, his shy Aimee.

He chewed on a blade of grass and chuckled, minding how fearfully she had sailed off on a double honeymoon with her sister and come back six weeks later as confident aboard a ship as Ayisha herself. It was all Seth's gentle doing. And Cain's work with Ayisha and Willi was another marvel. Never in his life had he seen such a thing as Ayisha's riding of the old blind stallion—electrifying leaps in the air and such intricate prancing and trotting it fair brought tears to his eyes.

Aye, he had many blessings, he thought again, gazing about him at the sights and sounds of summer's end. Sunflowers ripening, the sun turning fields and meadows to gold, whippoorwills calling from deep within the fragrant pine woods. But one thing was lacking. Ana. If only Ana were here to see it all. He gave his head a brusque shake. Nay. He would not brood on it. Not when she was waiting for him in paradise.

Paradise.

When he thought of it nights as he lay abed, he knew he was a foolish old man filled with delusions. Logic told him the thing was impossible. Such a place did not exist. But in the daytime with the sun warming his old bones and the birds singing, his heart told him it existed just as surely as did this world surrounding him. He would see Ana again, and they would spend eternity together. She would be young and beautiful, the way he always remembered her, and she had promised him that in paradise, a man remained thirty-nine winters forever. He smiled at the thought of his muscles turning hard and full once more and his hair regaining its life and color.

He sat himself down in the tall grass where the sheep had not yet grazed and listened to the many familiar sounds surrounding him. Sea-murmur . . . bluebird-chatter . . . Ayisha talking firmly to Willi in the upper meadow . . . Mac calling to a stable lad . . . the voices of Aimee and Pegeen on the terrace . . . the sweet, high baby noises from Kira . . .

His heart pained him sharply of a sudden as he thought again how Ana would have joyed in the child, a child who was Aimee and Ayisha all over again. He put it away then, the sadness, and got to his feet. He was surprised by the pleasant sense of urgency which was sweeping over him—as if something of great importance were about to happen. Strange. But then doubtless it was naught but the prospect of his taking the *Dolphin* out for an afternoon sail. It was still a luxury for him, having the freedom for such a thing.

Turning, striding toward the stable through the knee-deep grass, he marveled at how strong he felt. Not that he'd felt too bad for an old codger, nay, retirement had been good for him, but by the gods, where had the spring in his legs come from? He felt as if he could run a race—and win. He dug in his heels and was about to test himself when he heard a soft sound from the woods behind him.

Seeing Ayisha coming toward him from among the trees, he frowned, sun in his eyes. What in blazes . . . How could the lass be here when he still heard her talking to Willi up in the meadow? He realized even before she waved, great God Almighty, that it was not Ayisha, it was Ana. His heart soared. Ana. Sweet Jesus, it was his own darling girl, and she was just as he remembered her. And in her wide, admiring gaze, Ben saw that he was young again.

"Benadair!"

"Darlin' . . ." It was a hoarse shout that did not sound as if it belonged to him.

She was running to him then, flying across the field they had trod together so many times in life, her flame-dark hair lifting in the wind, golden eyes alight with love, laughter on her rosy lips. As Ben opened his arms, she went into them, slim and soft and with the faintest scent of roses clinging to her skin. He could not speak. He could only hold and kiss her and rejoice that at last, at long last, he was with her in paradise—and aye, it was here. Their paradise was here.

Dear Reader,

Thank you for your wonderful response to Adam and Alexandra in BELOVED PRETENDER. I hope the time you have just spent with Ayisha and Cain took you into a world that gave you equal pleasure. I loved writing their story and Willi's, and as always, my goal was to make you smile as well as shed a tear or two. I hope I've succeeded.

As my steady readers know, I'm always delighted to hear from you. Send any comments or questions to PO Box 905, Sharon, PA 16146. If you would like a bookmark, please enclose a self-addressed stamped envelope.

Joan Van Nuys

Avon Romances—
the best in exceptional authors and unforgettable novels!

MONTANA ANGEL   **Kathleen Harrington**
77059-8/ $4.50 US/ $5.50 Can

EMBRACE THE WILD DAWN   **Selina MacPherson**
77251-5/ $4.50 US/ $5.50 Can

VIKING'S PRIZE   **Tanya Anne Crosby**
77457-7/ $4.50 US/ $5.50 Can

THE LADY AND THE OUTLAW   **Katherine Compton**
77454-2/ $4.50 US/ $5.50 Can

KENTUCKY BRIDE   **Hannah Howell**
77183-7/ $4.50 US/ $5.50 Can

HIGHLAND JEWEL   **Lois Greiman**
77443-7/ $4.50 US/ $5.50 Can

TENDER IS THE TOUCH   **Ana Leigh**
77350-3/ $4.50 US/ $5.50 Can

PROMISE ME HEAVEN   **Connie Brockway**
77550-6/ $4.50 US/ $5.50 Can

A GENTLE TAMING   **Adrienne Day**
77411-9/ $4.50 US/ $5.50 Can

SCANDALOUS   **Sonia Simone**
77496-8/ $4.50 US/ $5.50 Can